# BADD
# BLOOD

# BADD
# BLOOD

*(Book 3)*

A NOVEL BY
## *ZEE. W*

www.zbookpublishing.com

ZBook Publishing, LLC
P.O. Box 2085
Stone Mountain, GA 30087
www.zbookpublishing.com

Badd Blood
First Edition

ZBook Publishing, LLC

ISBN-13: 9781941689028

# DEDICATION

I dedicate this book to my beautiful sister Buelah Yahmemah Williams; sister number three. You have supported the Badd Wives Series from book one. Your constant excitement and encouragement motivate me every day. I love you more than words can ever describe.

— Zee. W

# BOBBY BADD

"I ain't gon give up on you, girl. I know you know that though," I whisper in Tara's ear then squeeze her frail hand. I kiss her on the forehead and lean up.

"Don't worry. Jayson got a lead on Dalla and Lera. It's going to be any day before she pays for what she did. Then, I'm gon find that nigga and get real medieval on his ass. They gon pay, Tara. I promise I'm going to make them all pay."

I try to let go of her hand, but I can't. So I just keep holding it. Her hand feels so cold and I rub them to make them warm. I know she can feel my touch. My touch is going to bring her back, just like her touch kept me going all these years. Kept me strong. Made me fierce and unbreakable. Just like she is. Even in this state, you can't break her. Nah, not Tara. Tara don't break, and she taught me how not to break. That's why I'm gon stay strong and wait for her to come back to me. I owe it to her and I owe it to our son, Blake. They waited for me all these years. But, I'm here now. I may have showed up late, but I'm here and I will wait forever on her if I have to. I don't give a fuck what nobody say. I ain't giving up on her. I ain't pulling the plug.

Seeing Tara forces me to think about Lera. Then my heart gets burdened by how I treated her. In the heat of the moment, Lera was just as responsible as Ace and Dalla for doing this to Tara. She led them there. I couldn't bring her back to the Ranch, although Mona did it anyway. I thought that Tara was going to wake up, and if she did, I couldn't have her and Lera in the same place. It wouldn't be right. Especially with Blake here. So I did what I did. The last time I seen Lera, she was walking and breathing on her own. She's not in the state Tara is in and I do blame her for that. At least partially. Still, it fucks with me, but I can't allow myself to feel what I'm feeling for her. Not right now. Not while Tara is like this.

It's been four weeks now and there ain't no change yet. About two weeks ago, I saw her blink, but folks around here acting like I ain't got my mind. They don't believe me. They think I will do and say anything to keep Tara alive, but I ain't got to lie to keep my promise to Tara. I'm Bobby mutha-fucking Badd and I don't need nobody's permission to keep Tara alive. My love for Tara runs deeper than this Badd blood line. It always has and it's only now that I'm seeing this. Nobody's had my back like her. None of them know me the way she does. Shit. I been knowing this girl for over 20 years. And to this day, I still ain't met nobody like her. I never will. But that's ok. I don't have to, 'cause Tara's coming back to me. She coming back to us and we gon be a family just like she always wanted. And we gon be away from all this shit I promised to protect her from.

It's funny. All these years, I thought I was protecting Tara, but really, she was protecting me. Mona think she so fucking tough. She a joke when it comes to Tara. But, Tara don't need all that fucking hype and control like Mona. She ain't got to tough talk and be all extra just to prove her point and flex her strength. Tara more humble than that. She subtle with it and never acted as if she had anything to prove to anybody. Tara never cared for the power and privilege that came with the Badd name. That's why she rejected my proposal right before I met Lera. When I proposed to her, I was ready to settle down and have a real family. Someone I can have by my side all the time. I got sick of us hiding and sneaking around as a family, but she told me unless I'm ready to walk away from this Badd life, she ain't gon marry me and contribute to what she thought would eventually bring me down. Hell, she was right. Then, I met Lera and she accepted me for who and what I was. So I wifed her.

When she told me she was pregnant with Blake, I damned near begged her to marry me, that was my first proposal to her, but she refused. She stood her ground. But, I just kept asking her anyway. Almost demanding she marry me but she just ignored me. Then she finally turned to me and said, *"Look, Bobby I mean what I say, and I only say it once. I want nothing to do with this lifestyle and will not have our son be a part of it either."* And, I couldn't do anything but respect that. Her turning down my proposal only caused me to love her more. My respect for her grew to an all-time high that day. And it just kept growing after that. Even after Lera.

The reason why we couldn't be together was real fucked up. Some shit that had nothing to do with either of us affected the way we lived our lives entirely. Back in the day, Tara's father, Taran used to be Papa Badd's right-hand man. Ironically, the same way Jayson is mine. Some shit went down and, somehow, Taran got accused of trying to plot my father's murder. It probably was bullshit, but most shit in our world is. Unfortunately, innocent people die because of it, just like her father, Taran. The night my father had him publicly murdered, Tara was on the Ranch with me. Her mama got addicted to dope, so Tara was raised by her dad. We first met when we were seven years old. We were the same age and were inseparable. At least I was with her. I couldn't stop following her around. I wasn't used to being around other kids my age, especially girls, and when I did interact with other girls my age, they were nothing like Tara. Even as a child Tara was confident, independent, and fearless. Everything I wished to be back then. Back before she showed me how to be the way I am now.

I will never forget the day her father died because it was the day she finally let me tongue kiss her. We were 13. The day we kissed, I felt high and I been chasing that same high all my life with different women, but I never got the same feeling until I kissed Lera. Lera's kiss shocked me. Every time I kissed or fucked another woman, all the suppressed feelings I had for Tara came up but that didn't happen with Lera. It confused me for a while and I tried to fight it but I couldn't. But even with Lera, I never stopped loving Tara. Tara is my soulmate.

The kiss between Tara and I would have lasted longer if I didn't fuck it up by letting my little dick get hard. When Tara felt that bulge against her pelvis, she pushed me off her and slapped the shit out of me. I didn't even feel the sting from the slap. I was too high off her. She ran off and I chased behind her to apologize but we both got stopped in our tracks when we seen her father, Taran tied to a tree with a rusty chain in broad day light.

A group of people surrounded him and they each were holding bricks. They all took turns throwing their bricks at him while my father sat front center and watched, smoking a cigar like he was amused. My father was making a very disturbing example of him by having him publicly stoned. It was a brutal sight to see even for the average person, nevertheless his teenage daughter. My uncle, the main instigator in his death, was dousing him with lighter fluid. They were about to set his body on fire when Tara ran up to him and hit him with a brick of her own. She could have cried and pleaded for her father's life like they would expect a little girl to do but Tara was beyond that. You see, Tara skipped the Princess stage in life and went straight for the Queen crown.

A Princess waits to be saved but a Queen saves herself. She saved herself that night. After she knocked my uncle out, somehow, she ran off the Ranch. I don't know where she went or how she survived but I didn't see her again until I turned 18.

She was bartending at a club one of our affiliates owned. During the five years we were apart, I thought of her every day and reuniting with her felt so natural. Almost like we didn't miss a beat. And once again, we became inseparable. At first, I thought she would blame me for what happened to her father, but she didn't. As a matter of fact, it took a year for us to even talk about it. She said she worried about me every day since she left. Can you believe that? She went through all that and still had enough love in her to worry about me. Right away she tried to pull me away from the Badd life, but I wasn't ready. I couldn't. This life was embedded in my DNA. It's who I was.

She and Jayson had different fathers. Somehow, she ended up with him, his dad, and stepmom. She stayed there a few years before they both ran away and started a life of their own. Jayson's dad kept trying to fuck her and his stepmom wanted to beat her ass for it. Tara wasn't having that. She fought back, and Jayson protected her as long as he could. At 15 she was completely independent. They lived extremely poor and even through all that, she graduated high school and was working the bar scenes to pay her way through college. During the week, she worked at a horse stable, shoveling shit to make extra cash. Tara didn't mind that though. She loved horses just like mama. Mama treated Tara like her daughter. She introduced Tara to horses and got her into riding. That's how she fell in love with them. She had it tough but never complained. That's just who Tara was. Grateful and graceful. She's beautiful and I'm going to love her forever.

It was hard trying to convince Tara she didn't have to work anymore. I tried to give her money, but she wouldn't take. So, I employed Jayson. That was the next best thing. He made enough money to get them out that gutter ass neighborhood into a safer place. I gave him bonus money to buy her a new car, so she didn't have to catch the bus at night. After a while, she would take a little cash here and there from me, but she wouldn't let me do much else.

When she had Blake, I bought her that house out in the country. I knew she wouldn't say no when she saw the four Black Stallion horses I bought her. She finally retired from being overworked and settled for just being Blake's mom. That's when we became an official family.

I cherished every moment we spent together in that house. The laughter, the love, the peace. It was the most normal I felt in my life. Finally, I felt like my own man. Not just a Badd man. I had a family to protect. My own motives. She got pregnant again. We had a little girl, but she died six weeks after she was born. That baby girl was the most beautiful thing I ever laid my eyes on. Tara was resilient through it all but something about her changed. She let fear creep inside of her. She told me once that our little girl died because of all the bad karma surrounding my family. She convinced herself that my family was cursed. She was afraid that I was next.

She started to hover over me and Blake like a protective mama bear. Then she started on me again about leaving the Ranch. She knew I couldn't. Then suddenly, she started to push me away. She said she wanted boundaries but really, she was trying to get me to quit being a Badd. She couldn't understand that I couldn't. At least back then, I thought I couldn't.

She told me we couldn't sleep together anymore but that didn't stop me from coming around. It didn't stop me from kissing her. Nothing could stop me from doing that. It had been years since we shared a bed, but that changed the day I showed up with Lera. Tara was being a little vindictive by sleeping with me. That wasn't her style. Then she started to ask me questions about Lera. She asked me who I loved more. I never answered her because then, I didn't really know. I wanted them both but I felt like I needed Tara.

I think it was something about me faking my death that got to her. She always knew I wasn't dead. She was the first person I told after Dalla gave me the idea, but it still freaked her out. She kissed me the night we got there, and I felt that high feeling again and couldn't reject her. So, I didn't. Making love to her made me forget everything and I needed that. In between her legs was more than a wet pussy, it was a safe and familiar place. I needed to be in that place. It was vital to my survival.

Our relationship was so deep that what we were doing a few doors down from Lera didn't feel wrong. Strangely enough, I always felt like I was cheating on her with, Lera. Before I married Lera, I called her and gave her one last chance to be my wife, but she still refused. When she asked me if I love Lera, I told her yes. And then she asked me why I loved Lera and I couldn't answer her question. But when I think about it, loving Lera was just easy. That's why I loved her. It wasn't dangerous. It wasn't forbidden. It was just plain easy and I needed easy in my life.

I hate that I got Lera caught up in this shit but that still don't change what she did. What she tried to take from me and my son. I loved Lera but my love for her could never match the love I had for Tara. Lera was new love and Tara was old love. New love feels good but old love just feels right; the two couldn't compete. It didn't come close. When I met Lera, I didn't expect the feelings I was having. I didn't have access to Tara like I wanted, and I needed someone to help me blind the feelings I was having about Billy being missing and the speculations around my mother's death. Lera helped me block all that but I should have never married her. I should have just left her at that bar, but there was something about her that I felt I needed. The funny thing is, I never figured out what it was.

Over time, I started to fall in love with her loyalty and it was nice having someone to come home to, but I still loved Tara. Me being the man I am, I'm used to having it all. I just assumed I would keep them both. Have Lera on the side as my wife, as strange as that sounds, and Tara in front of me as the love of my life. The mother to my son. But don't nothing works out that easily. Not even for a Badd. I should have known better but ain't no use in crying over spilled milk. The only thing you can do with spilled milk is wipe it clean. And I plan on doing just that. I'm going to clean up this mess and make right of everyone I did wrong. Lera included but for now, Tara comes first. She needs me more.

Tara's machines are starting to beep. I have to let go of her hand, so I get up and call the nurse, but I don't want to. The sound used to scare me. It used to make me think that she was slipping away but all it means is they need to put more medicine in her I.V. or whatever the fuck the doctor tells them to do. I get up, but I'm still holding her hand. When I hear the door open, I sit back down. The staff here is getting much smarter. I told them before, when they hear the beep, they better come running and they do.

When I turn around, it's not the nurse but Billy. He is standing behind me giving me that sorrowful look he been giving me for weeks. What the fuck does he want? I'm tired of him and his fucking pep talks. Telling me to let her go. Fuck him. Fuck all of them.

"Get the nurse," I yell at him before he says anything. I don't even look at him when I speak. He knows that I mean what I say and does just that. A few minutes later the nurses rush in the room with their apologies. But fuck them. They late. That means that they all fired and I ain't fucking paying them for this week. They got to get the fuck out of here tonight.

"Get security. I want them off the Ranch now," I say to Billy once the nurses finish doing what they supposed to do.

"You sure?" Billy says to me like I stuttered.

"I mean what I say," I tell him, but I didn't even have to say that because he already knows.

When I hear him take a deep breath, then exhale through an exhausted sigh like all the shit I'm doing for Tara is useless, I got a right mind to get up and knock the shit out of him, but I can't let go of Tara's hand. I just can't. It doesn't matter anyway. It won't be long before he's burying that bitch he calls his wife. Dalla just as good as dead.

# BILLY BADD

"Bobby, this the third round of nurses you done fired this week, man. I mean we can't keep firing the folks we hiring to help her if we want her to live. Right?"

I try to talk some sense into my brother, but he is hurting so bad, he not himself. I understand that pain. I've been there. That's why I want to help him get through this, but I can't keep lying to him. Lies done almost destroyed our entire family. I'm tired of the lies. The truth is the only thing that's going to set our family free. And Bobby needs to hear the truth. Tara is dead. She ain't coming back. She's a fucking vegetable being kept alive by this expensive machine we can't keep paying for. Shit, I can't even call her a vegetable because vegetable can breathe on its own.

"What you mean, we?" Bobby replies in a sarcastic tone. He doesn't even look at me when he talks to me. He just keeps his eyes fixed on Tara's limp body.

He angry with me. He angry with the world. I've never seen him like this before. I walk up to him and put my hand on his shoulder and he jumps then yields to my touch like he needs it. "Bobby, we all want Tara to live. She family."

He moves his shoulder, jerking my hand away and scoots up closer to Tara's hospital bed. I try to figure out a different approach, but I can't.

"Any leads on Dalla?" Bobby says and looks me directly in the eye. He gives me an evil stare.

Every time he mentions Dalla, he gives me an intimidating look. It's his way of letting me know that he's going to kill her. I guess he wants to see my reaction, but I don't give him one. I keep a straight face. But what he doesn't know is that I'm not going to let him kill my wife.

"Not, yet," I respond without taking my eyes off him. He stares at me a few seconds longer than necessary then turns back to face Tara.

"How she escape again?" He turns and looks at me again. I keep a straight face.

This is the fifth time he's asked me that. He asks me every time he sees me, and I always tell him the same thing. He asks about Dalla more than he does Ace. Tara's true murderer. But Bobby wants immediate blood and Dalla is the closest he can get to Ace for now.

"I don't know," I respond like I always do.

But I do know how. It was because of me. I fed Mona the lead after I overheard Bobby telling Jayson that once Dalla is in the prison, he was going to kill her. That's not what we agreed on. He has no right to make the call without me. But I'm giving my brother a pass because I know he not thinking straight. I knew this was going to happen. That's why I told Mona to leave after the attack because I figured she was safer on the outside than she would be on the Ranch with Bobby and Brock gunning for her.

I knew Mona would keep them safe. So, I made her feel like I was giving her permission to visits the wives, but I knew she was going to do just what I wanted her to do and free them.

I felt like I could finally breathe once I saw Dalla flying off the Ranch with Lera.

"And you don't know where she can be?" Bobby asked his second round of repeat questions.

"No," I lied.

Dalla had nowhere else to go. The safest place for her was my lake house. No one in my family knew about that house but her. It's where she gave birth to our son. It was going to be a gamble for her to trust that I wouldn't out her. But in the end, I know that she knew I would never do anything to hurt her. I know she's there. I can feel it. Now I can look at my son at night with peace knowing that his mother is safe. At least for now.

"We gon find her man. I promise. She can't run far. But right now, we need to focus on finding Ace Lucky."

"But Dalla is the link to Ace Lucky. Just like Brock been saying all along," Bobby said, disgusted. He hates Dalla more than Brock now. "We find her, we find him. Jayson looking for her now. It won't be long before he finds her." He looks up at me and stares.

I swallow hard. I know Jayson ain't just on a job for Bobby. This is personal for him. Just like Bobby, he believes that Dalla killed his sister. That means he gon do everything he can to find her. I just hope that Dalla is safe. I nod my head at Bobby like everything is cool. I got to play that role for him just to keep the peace between us. "I told him that I want her dead or alive. We ain't got time to fuck around," Bobby added.

My heart starts to race so I turn to walk towards the door. When I place my hand on the knob, Bobby says, "You okay, man? You seem a little spooked."

"I'm good," I respond quickly. "I just got to get back to lil man," I say referring to Billy Jr. "It will be nice for him to meet his uncle. I would love to meet, Blake." I try to change the subject. I want to remind Bobby that we family. Badd blood. But, Bobby don't care.

"Nah, Blake ain't ready to meet nobody, yet," Bobby says then drops his head. He looks back at Tara then takes a deep breath. I know exactly what he's thinking. He's thinking he has to fix this. And what that means to him is killing my wife and keep Tara breathing. "You know Dalla threaten him, right?"

"Nah, man. I don't know nothing about that."

Dalla wouldn't hurt Blake. She was doing what she had to for me and BJ. I understand that now. I wanted to hate her for killing my father, but she did that for us too. Dalla made some fucked up choices, no doubt, but as crazy as the shit sounds they were innocent mistakes. She been dealt bullshit cards her entire life. She watched her mother get murdered. Then she ends up captive with a psycho like Ace Lucky. Who can blame her for fighting her way out the best she could? Through all that, she still has the ability to love. She loves me and she loves our son. She gave birth to him on her own with Brock and Ace hunting for her. Meanwhile, I was doing nothing. Taking a mental vacation. She's a strong woman and I know that she loves me but I'm not so sure I deserve Dalla's love. She's all I think about though.

When I look at my son, I see her. Looking in his eyes is just like looking in her eyes. Through him, I see the innocent parts of Dalla. The part that craves love and protection above anything else. The parts of her that just need to be held and cared for. Something she never had. She could have left and went to Mexico with our son, but she stayed and risked her life because she believed in our family. She fought for us. Now it's my turn to step up and be the man. I'm gon risk it all for them. I ain't scared to admit that I love her now. I lied to myself before. But like I said, I'm done with the lies. When she came to break me out the prison she thought I was trapped in, seeing her again knocked the wind out of me. When she gave me BJ's picture, I knew what I had to do. I had to save them. But, I had to be smart about it.

I know she heard me when I told Mona to leave her, but I didn't mean it. Bobby was holding Tara's bleeding body and he wanted to leave Lera so I had to play the part. Besides, I knew Mona wasn't going to allow it. I just hope after all this is said and done, she can understand the choices I made just like I now understand the choices she made. We gon move pass this. And I'm willing to leave all this bullshit behind and be with her. Fuck this Badd shit. They can have it. The only Badds that concern me are Dalla and BJ. All I want is my family. I'm going to do whatever it takes to keep them safe.

I look back at Bobby. He is kissing Tara's hand now. I understand him. He doing what he got to do for his family as a man but he ain't being wise by threatening mine. I love my brother. Always will but he ain't killing my wife and neither is Jayson. I can't kill Bobby and I won't. But Jayson got to go. I need his ass dead before the end of the week. I just got to figure out how to make that happen.

"We gon get to the bottom of this, man. I promise," I say to Bobby. He doesn't acknowledge me. So, I walk out the door, leaving him with Tara.

I got to warn Dalla. I got to let her know that I got a plan. I got to let her know that I love her and that we gon be alright. Our family is going to survive but in order to do that, I got to get my hands dirty. Just like Dalla did. That means, somebody's got to die. I don't want to kill anyone but what has to be done will be done. My target is going to be easy because she's already dead. I got to pull the plug on Tara without Bobby knowing.

Once Bobby buries Tara, he will come to his senses and remember his real wife Lera and hopefully leave my wife alone.

# LERA BADD

I get this feeling inside me that just wants to go home. I want to go home so bad. Home is where I feel safe. Home is where I feel loved but I don't know where that is anymore. I feel so lost. I have no love. I have no safe place. I gave all that up when I foolishly fell in love with Bobby Badd.

I'm here with Dalla, instead, in this house that looks familiar. I've been here before. But I can't remember much of anything. Only that night when Bobby told them to leave me. I can't believe he said that. He hates me because I killed Tara. I kind of hate myself too now. I hate who I've become. I'm a murderer. A pathetic woman who is so weak that I had to take part in a murder just to feel strong.

After I told Ace to stop, he kept going anyway but I couldn't think about what was happening to me. It didn't hit me until it was all over. Until Bobby told them to leave me. All I could think about when Ace had his hand around my neck, squeezing the life out of me while pushing himself deep inside my most forbidden parts, the parts of me that I thought belonged to Bobby forever, was Tara. I didn't think about how I was being violated. I didn't think about how his penis felt like sharp metal stabbing at my vagina. How his hot breath felt like steam rushing up my nostrils and sliding down my neck. I thought about Tara's bloody body.

I thought about Bobby saying that I was going to pay. I wonder what that meant. Did that mean he was going to kill me? Did that mean he didn't love me? I prayed that she was still alive so that Bobby would forgive me. So that I can have a chance to explain to both of them what happened. I didn't set them up. It wasn't me. I didn't kill Tara. Did I?

Ace was raping me. I was being raped by a mad man and all I thought about was how Bobby felt. Not how much it hurt down there. Not how much I prayed for it to be over. I think I'm crying. I feel water on my cheeks. Yes, I'm crying. Why can't I wipe my tears? Dalla usually wipes them for me. She says "Poor baby" and wipes my tears. Sometimes it's with her bare hands. Sometimes she wipes them with the bottom of her t-shirt and sometimes a soft tissue. I like the touch of her hand better though. Then she starts crying too. I don't like making people cry so I start to cry more. Then I wonder who I'm really crying for? Am I crying for me or am I crying for Bobby and Tara?

Ace wanted to see me cry. When I didn't because I was too deep in thought about Bobby and Tara, he flipped me over and rammed his dick in my ass. I never experienced pain like that before but still, I thought about Tara lying on the carpet bleeding, although I felt myself bleeding from behind. Ace punched my back so many times, I couldn't move. Why was he hurting me? What did I ever do to him? Was he mad because I changed my mind? Was it because of Tara? Maybe I deserved it. When I last saw her, her eyes where half open and half closed. Her mouth was agape, with blood dripping from the corners. I think she's dead. Bobby's going to think I killed her.

"Lera, I need you to eat, ok?" Dalla says and shoves a spoon in my mouth. I spit out the food. You can't eat if you're not hungry. Besides for some reason, I can't remember how to swallow or chew. "Lera, can you hear me?" she asks and then waves her hand in my face. Of course, I can hear her. She's standing right in front of me. I can see her too but she's still waving at me like I'm blind. What's wrong with her? "I need you to talk." She stands up in front of me. "Talk to me. Say something. Say anything."

"I want to go home," I say to her, but she doesn't hear me. She doesn't hear me when I talk anymore.

"Talk to me, Lera." She places both hands on my shoulders and shakes me. "Say something!" She sounds frustrated.

"I want to go home," I scream at her, but she still doesn't hear me. Why can't she hear me?

"I don't have time for this shit," she says to herself and starts to pace back and forth with her hands on her hips. She looks exhausted. Her pupils are red and her eyes look swollen.

She squats down and takes a deep breath then darts back up and places her hands on her head. She looks tired and scared. Her eyes always look red and puffy like she's been crying all night. She must want to go home too. But isn't she already home? This has to be her house because she walks around it like she knows where everything is. Why am I here with her? Why does she care if I eat? Why did she bathe me and wash my hair last night? She was humming a nice song that made me feel calm. Why she do that? Why does she give me pills that make me fall asleep? Why did I wake up last night to her rubbing my head? It did feel good though. Her touch felt warm liked she cared. But why? Bobby doesn't even love me. He doesn't care if I eat. He doesn't care if I'm safe. Why does she?

Dalla's phone rings and she answers it before the second ring. She always does. I hear everything although she thinks I can't. "She's about the same," she says and looks at me. "She won't eat. She's not talking. Staring off into dead space. It's like she's not in there." I hear her say. I wonder if she's talking about Tara. Does this mean Tara is still alive? I hope so. "We're safe but

I don't know for how long. I got a lead on Taffy but it's going to be hard to travel with her." She says. Who is she talking about? Who is she traveling with? She said Taffy's name. I remember Taffy. She hates me too. "I will try my best, but I can't make any promises. I might have to leave her here and go alone. She ain't ready to leave yet. Getting her here was hell. She needs help, Mona." Mona. I know that name too. Who is she again? "We running low on cash too," Dalla continues. "Ok, ok," she says. "Bobby's a real asshole for leaving her like this." Why is she talking about my husband that way? Wait is he really my husband? Did we really get married? I can't remember.

He and Tara are married. She told me. They have a son. They're a real family. Bobby and I were a fake family. Why did he do that to me? When did he stop loving me? He gave Tara everything I dreamed we will have. A beautiful home. A son. Security. Before I took it all away because of jealousy. Maybe if she dies, Bobby will forgive me and remember that he loves me. Wait, did he love me? I need answers. I deserve them. But I can't get answers if no one can hear my voice.

Dalla is finishing up her phone call. She's looking at me and nodding her head. Then she asks about her son. But I think she's talking about Bobby's son. I don't think she has a baby. Although there is a crib in this house. Is this Bobby's house we're in? Is that Blake's crib? It can't be. Blake's not a baby. Is he? I'm so confused.

"I need this to work, Mona. This is my last shot to fix things for me and my son. Are you sure you can pull this off? It's going to be dangerous for me. If Ace is still out there, he's hunting me. And now Bobby and Jayson are too. Plus, Brock. That's too many eyes on me. Too many. I don't think I can do this anymore, Mona. I.." Dalla says and sniffs hard but that doesn't stop her from crying. "I am strong," she says. "I just want my son. I want my life back. I deserve that," she says.

Then I start to think that I deserve the same thing. I deserve to have my life back. But I can't do that if Bobby don't love me. Right? Dalla ends the call and tosses the phone on the bed beside me. She stares at me for a while. I think I'm looking back at her because I can see how her face changes. First, she looks sad, then she looks frustrated. Then she sighs, rolls her eyes, and walks outside and sits on the porch. I can still see her. I can see everything in this house. It's full of glass. She's smoking a cigarette and wiping tears from her eyes.

She's crying because of me. I just know it. First, I kill Tara and now, I'm making Dalla cry. I got to get out of here. Dalla stands up and stretches. She takes one last drag of her cigarette before she tosses it in the yard. She turns around, looks back in the house then across the lake like she's debating something in her mind. I think she doesn't want to come back inside. At least not with me here. But, she decided to come back inside anyway.

"I'm going to take a bath," she says to me carefully. "Do you need anything?" I tell her no, but of course, she doesn't hear me. She sighs and walks to the bathroom. I hear the door shut close and then the water starts to run. She's humming again. Steam from the hot water is sliding under the threshold of the door. Dalla's humming and the steam calms me.

I stare outside. The sun is about to set. I have a direct view to the sky. The orange sun is slowly falling behind a dark gray cloud. It's beautiful. I try to focus on the beauty outside. It makes me feel better. Then, I see someone. He's walking up the porch. This person looks familiar. How do I know him? He stares at me like he wants to kill me. He hates me too. Is it Ace? It has to be Ace. It has to be. I remember now. It's Ace. He's found us.

I start to scream for Dalla to warn her. I need her to protect me. She's stronger than me. I scream for her, but she can't hear me. She's humming too loud. "Dalla," I yell. "Ace is at the door. Ace is at the door." I try to get off the bed, but I fall to the floor instead. I try to crawl towards Dalla but when I see Ace with his hand on the knob, I know it's too late. He's come back for me. For us. It's over.

Dalla must hear me screaming because she turns off the shower and opens the door. "Lera," she calls out. She doesn't know that I'm on the floor trying to crawl. Why can't I walk? When I hear her scream "no wait" to Ace, I stop trying to tell her that he's in the house. She knows that he is here now. Ace points the gun away from me and right at her like killing her was what he really came for. She keeps screaming the same thing to him. **No wait, no wait, no wait**. Over and over again, but Ace doesn't care. He wants more blood.

How did he find us? But that doesn't mean he's not going to kill me, too. I hate to say it, but I kinda want him to. So, I lie on the floor and wait for my turn. I wish I could do something to help Dalla. She's been so nice to me, but my body doesn't work anymore. He pulls the trigger three times and the shots burst through my ear drums just like they did that night. Then, Dalla stops screaming and I start. I'm next.

# TAFFY BADD

I knew this was going to happen. The day I got tied down to a chair in Ace's basement, I knew my baby was going to die. There was no way my child could have survived all that torment. He slipped right out of me. Slid right down my leg just like sperm after a messy fuck. And it didn't even hurt. It was just like he was releasing himself from me. From my life. He wanted no part of it. Ace took away the only chance my child had to survive, and I think he may have killed the husband I betrayed. I pray Brip's ok. I can't bear to lose them both.

I'm back at Mama's place. Tony's here too. He's guarding over me like an angel, but I feel smothered by him. I can't even get up and go to the bathroom without him following me. He's so fucking annoying. I just keep watching the door, hoping that Brip will bust in and carry me back to the Ranch, but it hasn't happened. I fear that it won't because he's dead.

"Here, place this on your stomach," Mama says and hands me a heating pad. "Take these too." She hands me two pills and a glass of water.

"What is this?" I ask.

"I don't damn know!" Mama yells. She's scared and frustrated. This has been too much for her to handle. All of this plus what I told her about Brip killing Keno has burst the bubble she's been comfortably living in all these years. It's starting to take a toll on her. "I look like a damn doctor to you?"

Mama tried to take me to the hospital, but I refused because me checking into the emergency room would be too dangerous, so she's giving me some pill that she got from her dentist. I swallow the pills with water and place the glass on her floor. She snatches it up and wipes underneath it. She not giving me any sympathy. She blames me for all of this. I just take it though. Maybe I went too far with Brip. But what was I supposed to do? I couldn't let him get away with what he did to Keno. I just couldn't. Neither could Tony. Strange enough, he's the only person that understands me. Although he's been annoying the fuck out of me, if it wasn't for him, I would be dead. He saved me because he truly loves me. That's what family is. Not what the Badds portray. That shit is fake. How could they let something like this happen? They can't be as strong as they say they are. Or maybe they just didn't give a fuck about us wives.

I have this recurring nightmare that Ace really throws me in the pool with his gators. They rip away at my flesh and as I'm dying this barbaric death, I see Brip's dead body floating in the pool right next to Malcolm. I wake up screaming every night. Tony runs to my side and shakes me awake. Then Mama comes and wipes the sweat from my forehead with a towel. She's cursing at me to shut up though. She doesn't want the neighbors to hear.

I feel safe being here with Tony, but realistically, I don't know how safe we are here. But we have nowhere else to go. We can't stay long. As soon as I get back on my feet, we all got to go. I know Mama's going to leave kicking and screaming, but I don't care. Ace can find us here easily. I don't have my Badd name to protect me anymore. Shit, I guess I never really had it to protect me. All we have is Tony but he's only one person and I can't let him get hurt. Now, it's time for me to look out for him. But I have to heal first. Both physically and mentally.

Whatever pills Mama gave me is starting to make me feel drowsy. "Scrappy, you ok? You about to take a nap?" Tony kneels down beside me and says. I don't respond, and he gets his response. Then Mama comes rushing in the room holding her iPad like she just won the lottery.

"Taffy, get up," she says and kneels down beside me. She starts to gently slap me against the face. "I need you to look at this." She shoves the iPad in my face. I don't know what I was supposed to be looking at.

"What is it?" I say under my breath.

"Brip's not dead. He can't be!"

"What!" Tony yells and starts pacing angrily around the room. "I'm going to kill that mother fucka"

"Shut up, Tony," Mama screams at him. "Here." She pulls a few dollars out of her bra and hands it to him. "Go to the store and get Taffy her favorite ice cream. That's gon make her feel better."

Tony falls for Mama's bait and snatches the money, eager to do anything that makes me feel better. He rushes out the door, forgetting all about Mama's rant about Brip still being alive. Once he leaves, Mama locks the door behind him and pulls me off the couch. "Damn, girl. Help me out a little bit. You know I got a bad back."

I try to pull my own weight the best I can, but I feel so out of it. Whatever pills she gave me were so strong they make my body feel like wet clay. I can barely stand up on my own. I wrap my arm around Mama and we struggle our way to the bathroom. She bends me over the sink and splashes water over my face like that was going to work. When that doesn't work, she leans me over and sticks her finger so far down my throat that I hurl up the breakfast she made me and the two pills I swallowed. Then, she splashes more water on my face.

She gives me a few minutes to regain myself. "You up?" she asks, excited. I need more time, but I know that doesn't matter to her. Besides, I need to see what she is talking about. Why does she think Brip is alive? What is on her iPad? I nod my head yes and use the walls to anchor myself back up straight. Mama helps me back to the couch.

"Look." She places the iPad back under my nose.

I grab it and squint. "What's this?"

"Brip just made a deposit in my account. It just hit a few minutes ago!" Mama exclaims like she hit the lottery.

"What," I am confused. I grab the iPad for a closer look and she is right. There is a wire transfer of $50,000 to Mama's account. That is more than the monthly allowance we gave her. What does this mean?

I wipe my eyes and stand up too quick because I fall back down on the couch.

"Taffy, he's alive and he forgives you!" Mama is so happy she is almost jumping. "Why else would he do this? He knows you're with me. This is the first deposit he's made into my account since you came and told me that foolishness about him killing... well you know what I'm talking about. He cut me off after that. He cut us both off but look." She grabs the iPad from my hands and stares at it like its gold. "He sent double the amount. It won't be long before he comes to get you girl. You back in!" she jumps up and down then stops to hug me, but I push her off me. I need to process all of this. After all I went through, I now know for a fact that all that glitters isn't gold.

I try to get up again. "I need fresh air," I say, and Mama helps me back up. I stumble my way to her balcony. She follows me. I should have told her that I need privacy too, but Mama doesn't believe in privacy. At least not when it comes to me and Tony.

"You ain't excited?" Mama asks me. She so fucking naïve and money hungry it's disgusting.

Why would Brip be sending me this kind of cash without communicating with me first? I know Brip. This isn't his style. Who's sending the money and why? I start to panic, and I can see that frustrates mama.

"You so ungrateful. It's no wonder Brip left you," she mocks me. I try not to get offended by what she said because I know she just wants everything to go back to normal as quickly as possible.

"Mama I left *him.* Remember?" I snap back, and she slaps me.

"Thanks for reminding me," she yells and storms back inside the house.

I'm thankful for that slap because now I feel more alert. Like I can think better. I take a deep breath and go back in the house to follow her.

"Let me see that iPad again." I hold out my hand and Mama hesitates, but finally gives it to me and rolls her eyes.

"What? You think I'm seeing things? You think I'm lying?"

I ignore Mama and start to look past the $50,000 and closer into the details. That's when I notice that there is a hold on this deposit. Whoever put the money in the account, wants us to go to the bank and sign for it before it's officially released. That's weird. Brip definitely didn't do this. This could be a set up. It could be Ace. Mama sees my facial expression change and snatches the iPad from me.

"You need to call your husband and if he don't answer, you need to catch a plane and go back home to him. He waiting for you. If this ain't proof enough then I don't know what will be."

"Mama, we can't accept that money. It's a setup."

"What the hell are you talking about, girl? Who is setting us up? You been here over a month and ain't nobody been snooping around here trying to kill us. No one has come, Taffy," she says to me like I'm crazy and I start to wonder if she's right and I'm too paranoid. "I ain't never heard of a killer trying to lure someone in with $50,000 when all they got to do is kick in the door and shoot us all. Shit..." She walks to the kitchen and starts to make lemonade. It's what she does when she gets frustrated or nervous.

"I almost died, Mama. You don't want to acknowledge that, but I did. I lost my child and my husband because of it! Don't you understand? He was going to kill me. He had me tied to a chair in his basement. He beat me for days before he tried to kill me. I watched him slice a woman to death and drag Brip's bloody body out the room like he was trash!" I yell to her then I start to cry.

Mama just starts squeezing the lemons even harder. She's trying not to hear me, but she can't help it. She's shaking her head like she wants me to shut up. She tries to slice one of the lemons but cuts her finger instead and yells. When I see that blood and hear her scream, my mind immediately goes back to Ace's basement and I start to panic. I start to scream uncontrollably. Mama runs to me and wraps her arms around me. She's saying something to calm me down, but it's not working. She holds me tighter and I come back to.

When I look back at Mama, she looks terrified. She her hands on my shoulders and tears in her eyes. She is trembling so hard, it looks like she's going to topple over. Finally, I can see that she cares and that she's just as scared as I am. Denial is Mama's way of dealing with stress. I start to feel sorry for her a little, but even with all that, I know she's still going to go to the bank and accept that money. I won't be able stop her.

"Please, Mama. Promise me you will wait a few days before you sign for that money. Please..." I grab her hand and squeeze it. Mama doesn't answer me, but she does give me a half head nod.

She's not going to listen. A few minutes later and someone is banging on the door. We both jump out our skin, then look at each other. I hold my hand up for Mama to wait. I slowly make my way to the door as Mama grabs a frying pan. I tiptoe to the peep hole and its Tony. I turn around and fall back on the door, with a sigh of relief. Mama lowers the frying pan, and I open the door to let him in. I got to get us out of here. It's not safe.

Some kind of way, I manage to fall back to sleep. Then the nightmares start again but this time, I have to wake myself up. When I get up, the house is eerily quiet. I don't see Tony sitting on the couch in front of me, staring me down and I don't hear Mama shuffling around the house, cleaning and complaining about us messing up her condo. Something ain't right.

"Mama… Tony," I call out, but no one responds. I start to walk around the condo but there is no sign of them. That's when I realize they're gone, and I know just where they went. Mama took Tony with her to the bank to sign for that money. Damn, she so fucking stubborn. Is she really that money hungry that she would risk our lives for it? Shit! At least Tony is with her. I pick up the house phone to call her cell, but it goes straight to voicemail. Shit, Mama! The least she could do is make sure her phone is charged. What is she thinking? I try not to panic. I just have to wait for them to come back. I look over at the clock. It's quarter to four. If they not back by five then something is up.

It's 8'O clock and they ain't back yet. I call down to the bank, but I can't get anyone on the phone to confirm that they been there, and I don't have access to Mama's online account, so I can't check to see if she signed for the money or not. The bank closed at 5:00pm. They've been gone for almost four hours. Where the fuck are they? I told her not to go. I begged her but she never fucking listens. They're dead. I know they are. I start to sob uncontrollably. Now, I really have no one. No Mama. No

Keno. No Tony. No baby. No Brip. No Badd. Ace is coming for me next and I can't do anything but wait for him to kill me. Maybe death won't be so bad. Everyone I ever loved is on the other side anyway. At least I won't be alone.

# BRIP BADD

Sixty-seven. No, seventy-five. Shit, I can't fucking remember how many bustas I shot. Ain't no sense in trying either. Most niggas count sheep when they trying to sleep. I'm counting the amount of bodies I put down.

I remember the first one. I didn't even know his fucking name or what he did. It didn't matter to me. All that matter was that Brock needed his ass dead. Brock bought me a custom made Glok. It was black and gold and sexy, just like a woman. That's why I named it, Bo. I couldn't wait to shoot Bo and when I did, it felt like I was fucking. Bo was my first lover. I fucked her before I fucked a real woman. Pulling that trigger felt like finger fucking a bitch. It was orgasmic and I'm still fucking her to this day. That Glok is my soulmate. Bo always got my back and never lets nothing slide. Aside from Mona, she the realest woman I know. Then I met Taffy and in some ways she made me retire Bo. At least I thought about her, differently. I didn't have an urge for her as much.

I was seventeen when I put my first bullet in a man. I fucked Bo and she came hard. So hard that the first nut she bust, put a nigga out on the first shot. Right in-between the eyes; a bull's eye hit. The shot was so clean the hole I put in his head looked pretty. Just like something you seen on TV. Not bad for my first kill. I did it just the way that Brock told me. Quick, steady, and without hesitating. I felt like that was a sign that I was doing exactly what I was called to do on this earth. Inflicting deadly harm on the harmful and deadly.

Afterwards, I felt like the most powerful man on the planet. I felt invisible and I wanted more. That rush ain't never stop. It just intensified every time I pulled the trigger. The average teenager would be excited about getting their first car or fucking their first bitch, but not me. All I wanted for my birthday was my first kill. Or should I say my first *just* kill. That's what Brock called it. Not murder but justice.

I guess that makes me crazy, but I never looked at what I did as murder. All the niggas I let Bo kiss, violated us or fucked with us in some way. What I was doing was no different than what police officers or the military do every day. But after I killed Malcolm, Taffy's bitch ass lover, I felt like a murderer and murder don't feel good. It keeps you up at night. Makes you hear and see things that ain't there.

Brock always told me that Papa Badd would tell him the moment you made a kill personal, was the moment you became a murderer and murderers don't have no peace. Papa Badd was right cause I ain't had no peace since I killed Malcolm. I keep seeing his eyes. They haunt me every night. I blame Taffy for that shit. She caused all of it. I prayed that Taffy wouldn't go back there. I waited for her to come home. Or check in at a hotel or even crash at her mama's house. Anywhere but there. But she went anyway. So, I and Bo had to show up. She fucked him in front of me, so I fucked Bo in front of her and killed his ass.

I ain't never loved anybody like I loved Taffy. Everything about her was orgasmic to me. The way her skin felt. Her natural smell. Her smile. Her wrath. Everything. Taffy was the perfect size, weight, and height for me. She fit into my arms like she belonged there. When I held her at night, my life felt purposeful. Just like God gave Adam, Eve, he gave me Taffy. Then she ate the fucking apple and fucked it up for everybody. Now we all suffering and Malcolm's dead. I still love her though. I can't help it. Before I met her, everybody thought I was a fucking psychopath. Mama used to talk to Papa Badd about getting me help. She thought I had a screw missing. Like I would never be able live a normal life, but I met Taffy and proved them all wrong. She calmed me. Taffy saved me. Then, she killed me.

Vinchi may have shot me but Taffy killed me. No one understands that. I died. I'm fucking dead. But folks walking around here treating me like I'm alive. They need to just let me go cause I ain't good to nobody dead. Mona won't let me go though. She in my face every morning. Just like right now. She is taking good care of me. She sent the nurses off to go tend to Tara cause I don't need them no more now that I have her. She makes me breakfast from scratch every morning and she brings me clean socks.

"Come on, Brip. It's time for our walk. I ain't letting you stay cooped up in this room all day. It ain't healthy," Mona tells me then tugs on my arm for me to get up.

Mona loves me. She told me yesterday and I believe her. Aside from Mama, I think Mona is the only person that ever really loved me. She understands me. Taffy didn't love me. She wanted me dead. The night before Taffy left, she looked at me the same way the niggas I ended looked at me before they died. Like she hated me.

"You think she miss him?" I say to Mona. She don't have to ask who I'm talking about because she already knows. All we talk about is Taffy and Malcolm. Mostly Taffy though. She listens and don't make me feel stupid for having feelings like Brock would. That's how I know she really love me. She don't call me a bitch for crying either. Brock would slap the shit out of me if he knew I was crying over my wife. But if he really loved, Mona why wouldn't he cry over losing her and why the fuck didn't he come when he knew Ace had her? That's real fucked up. Mona talks about Brock a lot too. It pisses me off the way he left her. If anybody deserved more, it's Mona. She's just as much as Badd as us brothers. She was here from day one.

"No, Brip. She don't miss him. Taffy ain't never loved that man. He was too weak for her. She loves you. Every bitch ain't made like me you know. Your brother hurting me but I'm taking it cause I was built that way. Taffy just did whatever she could to stop the pain. Just like you are doing now but she really needs you. She ain't safe out there, Brip."

"She safe," I say and drop my head. I hate thinking about that night and Mona won't tell me everything that happened to her. She said I'm not ready to hear it and I'm not. "Bobby told me she with her brother Tony."

"Yea, Bobby taking care of his but he don't want you taking care of yours. We need to get out there and find her. Bring her home where she belongs."

Mona loves me, but she loves the old Brip. She don't understand that I died that day either. Taffy can't come home if she wanted to because the me that she knew is gone.

"I'm dead," I say to Mona and drop my head. She grabs my chin and raises my face until I am eye level to her.

"Stop with that dead foolishness. You more alive than you ever been. Don't you understand that? You just seeing things differently. You got to use that new sight to change things. We got to get off this Ranch and find Taffy. I can help you."

I ain't never heard Mona talking about getting off this Ranch this much. First Brock, now her. Things really are changing, but I ain't ready to leave yet. She says that Bobby and Billy letting everything fall apart and Brock off somewhere not giving a fuck.

She wants me to stand up and take charge, but I can't. I'm too dead. I can't be this Ranch savior no more than I can be Taffy's savior. I'm not good at saving people. Only killing them.

It's like when I died, Billy rose from the dead. All this time I was missing him, and he was right here. I don't know how I feel about that. When I talked to Mona about it, she told me that you can't trust everybody. I don't know what she meant by that, but I know how it made me feel. It made me feel like my brothers may not have my back the way I have theirs.

"You hear me?" Mona asks. I shrug my shoulders and she gives me a look, so I nod. "Billy and Bobby going to be having a meeting soon. You need to be at that meeting and you need to be fucking alive! Not dead cause that's just how they gon treat you. This Ranch is just as much yours as it is theirs if not more. You do all the fucking dirty work. All the dirt on this Ranch is on your hands. Some may say that means you the rightful owner."

Mona been talking to me about taking a more active role with the Badd business too. She said she can help me learn the ropes. She thinks I can do more than crush skulls. Mona believes in me. I'm just not sure I believe in myself. I fuck things up. I always have but I was able to take that weakness and turn it into a useful talent, crushing skulls. But lately, I don't know where I fit in all of this. I've really lost my way.

She said that getting back into the groove of things will make me feel more alive and once I start living again, I will remember how much I loved Taffy. But I ain't forgot how much I love my wife. I try to, but I can't. I'm going to have to divorce her. I'll start over again and I know that another woman ain't gon come close to Taffy, but I don't want that type of connection again. I can't handle it. It's not safe for me. Taffy was the last woman that would ever be able to kill me on the inside and I can only die once. I got nine lives on the outside. Not the inside.

"I got something else to tell you. I was going to wait until you felt better but this can't wait," Mona says. I don't want to hear what she got to tell me. She seems too excited and I ain't in that mood.

"Brip, this is serious now. I think this is going to revive you."

"What is it, Mona?" The only nigga I know that rose from the dead was Christ and I ain't nothing like him. There ain't no news that can revive me.

"Taffy is still pregnant," Mona says and smiles like that's supposed to mean something to me.

"What the fuck!" I yell back. Mona was right. I do feel revived cause now I want to grab Bo and fuck her. This anger makes me feel alive. Maybe Mona was right. "That baby ain't mine. That's ok though cause as soon as she pushes that little nigga out, I'm killing him."

"Watch yo mouth." Mona slaps me, and I start to feel like I went too far. "Don't be no damn fool. That baby is yours and this is good news. Don't you know that a child brings hope? There ain't nothing like a new life. It changes everything and dammit we need change around here. You gon get your ass together and next week, we going to find Taffy. Understand? Then, I'm gon let her tell you every nasty, hurtful thing that crazy nigga, Ace did to her cause that ain't my story to tell. Then you gon do the right thing by both Taffy and your baby. It's a miracle they still alive. When he had his hand around her throat…"

"Shut the fuck up!" I snap. I punch the wall and Mona jumps. The thought of some nigga hurting Taffy revives me. Now I know that hate is stronger than love cause I hate that motherfucker and his ass is gon die a slow and painful death. I swear he is.

I run out my bedroom in pursuit of the only thing that can give me peace. My soul feels like it's on fire and there is only one thing that can put it out. Mona runs behind me as I charge towards my chest to grab Bo. She screams when she sees the gun like I am going to hurt her, but she should know better than that. I run out the door instead. She doesn't follow me. I need to shoot something. If Ace is still alive, then I can't be dead. At least not anymore. I just need to fuck Bo. Then I can start thinking clear again.

As soon as air hits my face, I hold my Glok in the air and start shooting at the sun. I need the sun to fall because I can see better in the dark than I can in the light. When I shoot my last round, something magical happens. I come back to life. I run back in the house and Mona is looking at me like she's proud of me.

"When is this meeting? Cause I'm going. I'm gon let my brothers know that I ain't waiting on their cue or for their motherfucking permission."

Mona nods at me and smiles. "Don't worry. I'm going to prep you on everything to say."

"We getting off this Ranch cause it's hunting season," I say and cock my gun.

# MONA BADD

I got to get off this Ranch but Brip ain't ready yet. I almost got him where I need him to be, but he got to be more stable for my plan to work. Once I'm off this Ranch, I'm going to make sure the wives are set up then I'm going to start making my moves and shifting all the business in my direction. And, I know just where to start. I got to start with Kong. He's our biggest client and one of my oldest friends. These Badd men have really underestimated me. Don't they know that I can burn all this shit to the ground if I wanted to? Dumb fucks.

Kong and I grew up together as kids in the same fucked up projects; The East Meadows. We literally lived a few doors down from each other. Like most folks in the projects, we got the same story line. A cracked-up mama and a father that either dead or in jail. Kong and I looked out for each other. Together, we ran the East Meadows projects.

Kong ain't to be fucked with. You can take one look at him and know why people call him Kong. God didn't create Kong, he engineered him. First off, he about 6'5 and weighs a solid 300 plus pounds. No part of his body is mushy or soft either. He got a chest that looks like it can break bullets and his hands are the size of lion paws; huge and so thick they can crush a skull with one punch. I've seen him do it before too and on more than one occasion. His fist is like built-in weapons.

Kong skin is blacker than the midnight sky and looks like it's made of leather. The whites of his eyes are more yellow than the sun and the thick gums that almost completely cover his small bite-sized teeth are pinker than pussy. His lips are so thick and wide, they sit right under his nose. He got to have trouble breathing. He literally scares people on the street cause he doesn't look all the way human. I've seen people actually run from him on several occasions. His look alone gives him power but underneath that look is a heart that's probably just as black as his skin. Kong ain't to be fucked with and people know it. But, he ain't never scared me.

Before I got recruited by Papa Badd, Kong and I looked out for The East Meadows. We fed the hungry. Took care of the kids and brought in revenue to keep the place floating cause the government surely didn't give a fuck about us. The only reason why Kong allowed Papa Badd and his crew to come to our projects was because of me. I trusted Papa Badd. Kong and I could only do so much, but I knew the Badds could take us further than we expected, and they did. He was pissed when I decided to leave and move to the Ranch and even more pissed when I married Brock considering he's been in love with me since I was 12. We fucked a few times. Kong's dick was the size of a baby python. I was the only woman that could take that shit without squirming and he liked that but Kong just didn't do it for me. I needed more out of a man and I didn't know what that more was until I met Brock. To this day, Brock and Kong don't get along.

Kong and I had too much history for me to cut ties with him completely, so I put him onto the Badds. Now he is our biggest client. He makes up about a good 60% of our revenue just off his connections alone. Brock hates that. It makes him feel like we tied to Kong, but Kong is tied to us. If we Badds are the universe, Kong is the planet. Yeah, one really can't exist without the other, but the universe can swallow up the planet in one gulp. Kong brings us new business partners every year. He's expanding our brand. I always remind Brock of that when he starts talking about cutting his contract.

Kong supplies all the major drug dealers. He got a fucking monopoly on the dope game. With us backing him, no one challenges him either. Not rivals or the law. Kong got free rein to do what he wants outside of the Ranch. I took Kong's power and put that shit on steroids because now, he's untouchable. But what makes him even more powerful than being the only chain drug supplier in the south, is the exclusive contract he has with the Ranch's crematory. If anybody needs to get rid of a body, they reach out to Kong and then Kong reaches out to us. That makes Kong god on the streets. I know how much Kong likes being god so, in turn, he's dependent on us. Kong makes more money and connections burning bodies on the Ranch than he does in the drug game alone.

It took a lot of convincing for me to get Brock to agree to this, but in the end he saw it my way. Since we started this exclusive contract, our clientele has shot through the roof and we got less dirt on our hands. It was a lot of work processing bodies for so many different people. Our labor hours are down, and our inventory went up. That's a fucking win and it all came from a woman that dropped out of 6th grade. Now we got clients in Alabama, Tennessee, Florida, New Orleans; all over the south, and they all paying taxes and renting our facilities because of our connection with Kong. The money doesn't lie so Brock had to push his pride aside and let it happen.

In the business we in, people like to feel special. Like some of the power we got belongs to them. So when we built the Casino, I had Billy design a special suite just for Kong. Brock was pissed. He don't like when Kong is on the Ranch. He says he walks around like he owns the place but that's just how Kong walks anyway. He ain't dumb and he don't want this Ranch. His Ranch is the East Meadows projects. It's where he lives to this day. He took an entire building and made it into his castle. People worship him there. On the Ranch, he's just an upscale guest. Not a King. Besides, Kong don't visit the Ranch that often. He stays here about two weeks out the year, during New Years. He calls it his vacation. Other than that, he's only in and out for business deals and events.

Brock don't like the power that Kong has on the streets. Next to us, Kong is the final say and he got more face time with the people so in a sense they seem more loyal to him but they ain't crazy. It's just like church. People love and worship their pastor until they see God for themselves, then the pastor ain't nothing but a man. That's just how Kong's relationship with the people is. He's the pastor, spreading *our* word but we god; the creators of the word. I told Brock that people's loyalty to Kong can't keep up with a name that goes back three generations. Unless I start manipulating Kong's privilege and that won't be hard to do. It looks like that's what going to have to happen in order for me to take the Ranch.

It's like I ain't got no power here anymore. Thinking that forces me to wonder if I ever had power at all. If I knew it was going to turn out like this, I would have stayed and invested more into The East Meadows projects. I overheard one of the guards talking about a meeting that Bobby and Billy are having. Usually all the meetings take place at the big house, but I don't know where they are having this meeting. When I asked the guard for details, he just walked past me like I didn't exist. Wait till Brip get back on his feet for good. He gon put an end to all this disrespect.

Brip is the only person that stills listens to me. Thank God for that because I need him. Brip still respects me. He listens to every word I say. He always been loyal to me that way. I've been looking out for Brip for a long time now. Bobby and Billy ain't been up here to check on him. They too focused on they own drama. That works out better for me though. Brip is my seat at the table and my way off this Ranch. If my plan is going to work. I got to get out here, but they won't let me leave. That's gon change when I drive out here with, Brip. Who the fuck is going to challenge him? Not they bitch asses.

What the fuck are they meeting about anyway? Neither one of them know how shit run on this Ranch. Billy been MIA for a year and Bobby ain't spent more than three nights here in years. How the fuck they gon run this place? I need to be at that meeting. I'm not letting years of my hard work go down the drain. Besides, if I plan to take this place, I need to be in the know. Especially if that meeting got something do with my son. They been keeping Vinchi from me. But I'm going to see Vinchi today and I ain't letting them stop me this time.

They already sent away me and Brock's kids that came from the breeders. They completely closed down shop. Got that whole area we attached to the house blocked off. Who's next? Me and my kids? Vinchi? I can't believe this shit is going down like this and Brock ain't here to stop it. He really don't give a fuck.

I just keep waiting for him to come home. I'm such a damn fool. Even after all this, a part of me still believes in him. I believe in him more than I believe in my own eyes. My eyes tell the truth. I don't see Brock here. No sign of him. Not a note, not a phone call, nothing. But my heart keeps bullshitting me. My heart says that he gon come back, apologize to me, and set things straight. He gon give me back the crown I deserve to wear around here. The crown that Billy and Bobby snatched off my head. But not Brip. To him, I always will be the Queen. Hell, King even.

This my second attempt at trying to find the prison Brock had me and Billy in. The first time I went I was blindfolded. The second time they didn't bother but there was so much going on after that debacle with Ace that I was too distracted to pay attention. I always end up getting stopped by security anyway. Just like now.

"Mrs. Badd, this is a restricted area. I'm going to have to ask you to turn around," the guard says to me like he always does.

"Get me to Zone 6," I ignore him like I always do.

"There is no Zone 6, mam," he lies. "Beyond this point is restricted."

It's sad that these guards know more about this Ranch than I do. As much work as I put in around here, no part of this land should be restricted to me. All of it is just as much mine as it's theirs. All this time, Brock been hiding shit from me. There are two things in this world that turn my stomach. The first one is betrayal and the second one is disloyalty and Brock done both to me.

"I'll be back tomorrow," I say to the guard. He looks at me and shakes his head like he wants me to give up, but I won't. Tomorrow, I'm going to have the energy to fight him. Today, I don't. So, he lucky.

Why the fuck they keeping my own child away from me anyway? Got him locked up like he's an enemy of the Ranch. It ain't his fault he did what he did. Brock sent him there. He was on official Badd business when he went to see Ace. Now they treating him like he committed treason because he shot Brip and supposedly partnered with Ace but that was all Brock's doing. They can't keep my son locked up in there forever. It's been weeks already. I know he wonder where I am. Why I ain't got him out yet. He probably thinks I failed him just like Brock did but I'm gon find him and let him know that ain't true. I will never turn my back on family. I ain't a bitch like his dad.

I hope that Vinchi is okay. I need to talk to him. I want to understand why he shot Brip. Brip don't care though. He forgives him. That situation with Ace has been traumatic for all of us. As his mother, I got to make sure he is getting proper help. The last thing I want for my oldest son is for him to turn out like Brip. I love Brip, but they fucked that boy up. I don't trust Billy and Bobby with my son either. They don't love him because they too selfish. They both walking around here with their own agendas. They don't give a fuck about this family or this Ranch. They never have. Look how they are treating their own wives.

I never in a million years thought that Dalla Badd would be one of my most trusted accomplices but she is. All these years, Brock had me hating her because she intimidated him. He pushes away everyone who intimidates him. Look what he did to Billy. Dalla is going to help me take this Ranch. I know she can do it. That girl can move around better than a ghost. When this all over, I'm going to makes sure that all the wives are taken care of and that monster Ace pays for his crimes against us. I'm going to do everything I can on my end to help while she's on the outside. But first things first, I got to get off this Ranch, so I can get to Kong.

It's about time for me to check on Brip. When I last saw him, he was heading to the gun range. I got to start prepping him for the meeting. I need him to do and say exactly what I tell him to. I turn the cart around and start heading in the direction of the gun range and I see a security car speeding my way. What the fuck is going on? I hope Brip is okay. I pray he didn't shoot one of the guards. I pull over to the side of the road to make way for them but instead of zooming pass me, they pull up behind me.

I step out the cart and turn to face the guards. They rushing out the car and at me like I'm an escaped prisoner.

"What the fuck y'all want?" I ain't in the mood today.

"We been ordered to take you in, Mrs. Badd," they say and pull out their cuffs before they reach for me.

"By who?" I say and step back, ready to fight. They see my stance and know that taking me is not going to be easy.

"Mr. Badd, Mam," one of the guard responds and starts confirming to someone on his two way that they've located me.

"Which Mr. Badd?" I say, wondering if they talking about Brock but they don't respond. They just reach for me.

I duck and swing. I get a few good hits in and then they get violent. One of them pulls out their pepper spray and sprays at my face like they trying to kill a roach. The shit feels like tiny shards of glass that's been soaking in acid. It hurt so bad, I fall to my knees and give in. What in the hell did I do to deserve this? And why the fuck they taking me to the prison? I hope they put me in with Vinchi but I got a feeling I'm going to Brock's dungeon. This is fucked up. They will pay for this. All of them. I swear it!

# DALLA BADD

I'm a dumb bitch. A dumb bitch that can protect my ass way better than I can my heart. I convinced myself that Billy still loved me.

Lera and I been at his secret lake house all that time and no one has come for us. Billy knew that this was the only place I had to go. This hideout kept me safe over the past year. He knew that if I ran, this is where I would be. But he sent Jayson here for us. There is no other way Jayson could find us unless Billy told him where to look. Nobody knows about this place but me and Billy. Jayson didn't come to take me back to the Ranch either. He came to kill me. That can only mean one thing. Billy doesn't love me.

I didn't waste any time leaving. It's probably just a matter of time before they realize Jayson is missing and send someone else for us. Thank God Mona came through in time with that money she wired to Taffy's mother from Brip's account. That will help us but it's still not enough. We don't have anywhere to go and Lera is in desperate need of a stable environment. I had to give her something to sedate her while I drove up to Vegas with her knocked out in the backseat and Jayson in the trunk of the car.

I know it's fucked up but I was thinking about leaving her before Jayson barged in shooting at us. Then she saved my life. Jayson looked at me with pure raw hate his eyes. He wasn't just on a job. This was a personal matter. After I found out who Tara was, I later learned that she and Jayson were brother and sister. So now, I got another mutha-fucka that wants me dead. His emotions had the best of him so much that he shot four rounds directly at me but missed me every time. Just when he was about to shoot the fifth, Lera jumped up from underneath the bed where she was smart enough to hide and hit him with Billy's steel bat. Although she knocked him, she kept hitting him across the back. As she hit him, she screamed Ace's name. I didn't correct her. I let her believe that Jayson was Ace and that she killed him although Jayson was still breathing when I tied him up with a chain against the boat dock. I think that helped her because now she's talking again but she still fucked up in the head.

I put Jayson's body in the boat and threw him in the trunk of the car with us. I couldn't kill him. I didn't have the heart to. Besides, too much blood has been spilled already. I can't take seeing any more blood on my hands. I couldn't leave him at the lake house either. When he comes too, he would just escape and continue to hunt us. I don't know what I'm going to do with him yet, but maybe he will come in handy. When Mona calls me, she will know what to do.

Being around Lera reminds me of how strong I am because I survived Ace. I feel sorry for her. The brutality that she endured for a night was what I suffered night after night for years. I could have snapped like her but I didn't. I stayed strong. It's that same strength coupled with the strength of seeing my son again that's keeping me going but I'm tired as fuck. I'm tired of people trying to kill me. I'm tired of hiding and running. And I'm tired of not being trusted by the people I love the most.

Taffy won't speak to me. When she saw me walk through the door with her mom and brother, she lunged at me. Tony had to restrain her to keep from punching me. I took the hits she gave me. She, like everyone else, blames me for all this mess but hopefully, it won't be much longer before I'm gone and everyone can rest easy.

I was expecting Taffy to be at that bank but it was her mother instead. If it wasn't for Tony being there with her, I would have never known. I waited there for them for three hours before they walked through the door. Once they had the money, I stuck a gun in her back and told Tony to calm down and trust me. He followed my orders because that was what he was used to doing. He's the only person that still trusts me. It took me hours to convince Taffy's mother that I wasn't going to hurt her or Taffy but that bitch is stubborn as hell. If Tony had good sense, he would have been able to get us back to her condo but he couldn't remember the way back. He tried to tell his mother that she could trust me but she wasn't buying it. When she seen how Lera was starting to freak out, that softened her heart a little so she took a chance. Now, I'm trying to convince both Taffy and her mom that we have to leave. We're not safe here.

"I ain't leaving my home and I'm not giving up the money my son-in-law sent for me," Taffy's mother complained.

I tried to explain to Taffy why Mona sent the money. Taffy seemed a little disappointed that it didn't come from Brip, but she got over it because she was just happy to know that he was alive. I understood where she was coming from but all of us wives are in the same predicament. We've been fucked over big time by our husbands.

"Taffy, I know you don't trust me," I said to her softly, but I was getting impatient, "but you have to listen to me. It's not safe here. Mona is trying to help us. Brip, Billy, Bobby, and Brock don't give a fuck about us. And I promise you, Ace is out there. He knows we're alone. At any moment he can make his move on us."

At the mention of Ace's name, Taffy's entire body shakes. Then Lera starts to freak out.

"I killed him. You said I killed him. I remember it. I killed him!" she screams and starts to pull at her hair. Taffy's mom grabs her and tries to calm her down but Lera knocks her down and runs towards the door. Taffy looks at me and I look back at her and shake my head. When she first saw Lera, she tried to attack her too but Lera just curled up in a ball and took her punches. That's when Taffy stopped hitting her and came to her senses.

"Tony, grab her," I say and he jumps in front of the door and holds her in his arms until she stops screaming. "Take her to the back room and give her this," I pull out the last two pills I stole from the clinic and hand them to Taffy's mom.

"What is this?" she looks down at the pills and back at me like I'm trying to poison her.

"Trust me, it's going to keep her calm," I say, and she looks at Taffy and gives her mother a "it's ok" nod.

"Come with me, baby," she says and walks down the hall with her arm draped around Lera. "Poor baby. It's going to be ok." She continues to nurture Lera. It's just what she needs.

Tony follows behind them. For some reason, he's fixated on helping Lera. I don't know if he remembers who she is, but he looks at her like he feels sorry for her. Maybe he can relate.

"Tony," I say. He turns and faces me right away and waits for my order. "Go and check on the situation we have in the trunk," I say to him, referring to Jayson.

"Roger that," he says and flies out the front door.

Now I'm alone with Taffy. She starts to cry. I want to wrap my arm around her, but I'm afraid that she's going to attack me again. So, I just sit on the couch beside her. I don't' say anything.

"How long has she been like this?" Taffy says and sniffs up tears.

"Since that night. She's getting a little better though. She just starting talking again but she's going to need help."

"Does Bobby know this?"

"Yes, they all know. They were going to leave us at Ace's house that night but Mona stepped in and made them take us. Only after a few days in the clinic, Bobby wanted Lera off the Ranch."

"But, I don't understand. Bobby loves Lera. He couldn't have been faking that. I was at their wedding party. I spent time with them. He loves her."

Taffy says like she's trying to convince herself more than me.

"Yea, just like Billy loves me, right?" I try to remind her that we are both alone, just like Lera.

"That's different. You betrayed the family," she says and gets up from the couch. She starts to pace back and forth.

"How did I do that, Taffy?" I challenge the rumor, but she has no answers. She shrugs her shoulders. "I don't have time to tell you the story and I don't have time to convince you that you need to trust me, but you do. They sent Jayson to kill us both. It's only a matter of time before they send someone here. We have to leave."

"Where are we going to go?"

I don't know how to respond to her question because I honestly don't know. Mona is supposed to be setting us somewhere safe, but I don't know where that is yet and when I tried to call her to confirm I located Taffy, the phone went straight to voicemail.

"We are going to have to take this day by day until Mona calls again. She'll know what to do."

"I can't believe this is happening. Brip didn't even ask about me?"

"I gave up everything for Billy and my son and I have nothing now," I say then lost myself in Taffy's mother's marble floors like they hold the solution to all my problems.

"Son?" Taffy doesn't know.

"It's a lot you don't know, Taffy. I've been running for my life and trying to protect Billy and my son, and it was all in vain. Billy took him and kicked me off the Ranch. You got to start thinking about yourself now. That means giving up on Brip. I know that's hard but they don't give a fuck about us. Brock even dropped Mona."

I know that would get her attention. Brock and Mona are one. Together, they are the true power behind the Badd name.

"No fucking way!" Taffy says like she is about to panic. That news makes everything real for her.

"I think after everything that happened, they're regrouping and we ain't nowhere in that picture. Mona promised she's going to get us our fair share. What we deserve but we all have to play our parts."

"What's my part?" Taffy says quickly.

"You not going to like it," I tell her, and she gives me a nervous look. She sits back down beside me and takes a deep breath. "I'm sorry about your baby, Taffy. Your mother told me what happened." Taffy lowers her chin and shakes off the pain by nodding her head. "Mona needs you to make Brip think you're still in danger" I say and look at her carefully. "She's going to tell him that someone kidnapped you and is holding you for ransom."

Taffy jumps up. "No, that's fucked up. I can't hurt him like that. I won't. He's been through too much."

"Him?" I say to her like I'm confused. "What about you? None of this shit is your fault, Taffy. Please don't let them make you think that." I get up and place my hand on her shoulder, and, at first, she jumps, but then quickly yields to the comfort of my touch. She's starting to trust me again.

49

"That's not going to work. Brip doesn't care about the baby I lost. He doesn't think it's his," Taffy reveals. I don't understand what she means, and I don't have time to dig into the back story.

"Well, you're going to have to convince him. It's the only way we can get him on our side." I stare at her gravely. "You're a big part of Mona's plan. It's a few other things Mona's going to need you to do and I need you to be up for it all. It's the only way it's going to work."

Taffy sighs again and then leans over like she's trying to catch her breath. She darts back up and raises her head to the ceiling. Then she looks at me. "Did he try to look for me? Did he even ask about me?"

I look at her and shake my head no like I really know the truth. I have to lie to her. Otherwise, she will not agree to be a part of the plan. That lie hurts her. She looks like she's about to break but after a few deep breaths she regains her strength. Now, she's looking angry. Vengeful even. This is where I need her to be. "Don't worry though. He has Mona's trust. If anybody can talk some sense in him, it's her."

"Why aren't they looking for Ace? Why aren't they trying to make him pay for what he done to us." Taffy is pissed now.

"I can't answer that. Our lives aren't in their hands anymore. We have to look out for ourselves now. If anybody going to make Ace pay, it's going to be us. And don't worry, Mona has a plan for that too. Trust us Taffy. We are going to get everything we deserve and then some."

Taffy sighs and starts to cry. "I can't believe this is happening. I just want everything to go back to the way it was. I just wish everything was normal again, Dalla."

"Taffy, it was never normal," I say and rub her back. She lays her head against my shoulder and starts to sob. "That's enough," I turn her to face me. "No more tears. We got to get our heads in the games and we got to get the fuck out of here."

"Okay," she says and sniffs hard.

"What about your mama? She has to give up the money and she needs to leave too."

"I'll handle, Mama. Don't worry."

"Ok, we'll lay low here a few days or until Mona calls, but no one leaves the house. Tony can keep watch for us."

"What's going to happen when this is all over?" Taffy asks.

"We take the money and go back to being our old selves. The women we were before we became Badd Wives," I say to her. It's all I had for her.

"But, I don't know who that woman is anymore," Taffy replies like she is afraid.

I am afraid too.

"None of us does, but we all gon find out real soon. I just pray that the women we were before are better than the women that we had to become." I place my hand on Taffy shoulder and we share a brief stare before Tony burst through the front door, startling us both. We jump back, ready to defend ourselves.

"Shit, Tony. What the fuck is your problem?" Taffy yells at her brother.

"Dalla we got a problem," Tony says and comes towards me. "He's gone. That nigga is gone!" he says referring to Jayson.

"Shit!" I sigh. "We got to find him quick!"

Tony runs out the door and Taffy starts to pace back and forth nervous. I didn't tell her about Jayson.

"Who is he talking about?" she asks, but I ignore her question. "Lock the doors. Don't open it for anybody." I run out the door behind Tony. If we don't find Jayson, we're fucked.

# BILLY BADD

Tara is looking right at me. Fuck! That makes pulling her plug a lot harder than I planned but I still got to do it.

I walk over to her and wave my hand in her face. She's still not responsive. She blinks a bit, but I can tell she ain't in there. I don't know why or how her eyes are open, but this has to happen now. The more false hope Bobby has about Tara living, the more propelled he's going to be to kill my wife. With Tara dead, at least he can start to mourn her. Her death will slow things down enough for me to find Dalla before Jayson or Ace does and get the fuck out this country.

I already know where we going to: Spain. Maybe Barcelona or Madrid. Somewhere far away where we can start over. Where our son can have a chance at a normal life. So can Dalla. I already started setting shit up too. Fake ID's, passports; the whole works. I just got to play the game for now but when I leave this Ranch it won't be empty handed. Brock told the family before that Dalla and I stole from the family safe. Well now, I'm going to turn that fiction into fact. I'm going to take all I can. I need enough money to set my family up for life. Enough money where I ain't never going to have to come back. I just got to figure out how to get into the safe.

It took a lot for me to convince Bobby that he needed to integrate Mona. I overheard him telling one of the guards that he hadn't heard from Jayson. He sent people out to go and find him. That meant that Dalla is still alive, but I don't know for how long. Bobby ain't gon let up, unless Tara dies. At least that's how I see it. He kept questioning me about how they escaped, and I diverted him Mona's way. I heard he got her in Brock's dungeon now, questioning her about everything she knows. When Brock finds that out, he ain't gon like it, but Bobby don't give a fuck about nothing right now but revenge. Just like I don't give a fuck about nothing but getting the fuck out.

I look at all the machines Tara is hooked too, and I realize that I don't know what the fuck I'm doing. Which one is keeping her alive? Maybe all of them but how in the fuck do I disconnect them? Tara blinks again. She staring up at the ceiling. Fuck! Can I really do this? I need to man up. This girl is already dead. She just fucking stuck in this body. I'm really freeing her. Right? Nah, I'm freeing myself. My family. I snatch the first wire I see, and the machine starts to beep like crazy. Did I do it? Her eyes are still open, and that suction machine is still moving. One of the nurses rush in the room and I jump back.

"I think I tripped over something," I say quickly. The nurse gives me a strange look and I can't even look her in the eye.

"It's ok. It was just her I.V." she says to me.

"Her eyes are open. Does that mean anything?" I ask.

"Yea it could but it may not mean what Mr. Badd thinks," she says to me like she is trying to hint something to me. "I tried to call Mr. Badd but his phone is going straight to voicemail."

You can't get cell services in Brock's dungeon. Bobby doesn't know that, but I do. When he had me in there the night Dalla killed our father, I tried to call her, but my phone wouldn't work.

"She's hooked up to a lot of shit," I say to the nurse looking over all the wires. She nods. She doesn't know where I'm getting at. "So, which one is keeping her alive. I would hate to trip over the wrong one." I kind of laugh because the nurse is giving me a strange look like she knows what I'm thinking.

"Just stay away from the ventilator and she should be fine," she says and writes something on pad before she heads towards the door.

She didn't tell me which machine the ventilator was. When the door closes, I realize that I didn't think this through enough. If I pulled another cord, she would know what I was up to. I ain't going to be able to do this myself and I don't think I can kill her with my own hands. I take one last look at Tara and walk out her room. The nurse watches me as I walk down the hall. I can feel her staring at my back until I walk out the door.

I don't even get out the door good enough before I'm bombarded by Brip. He looks pissed off but that's better than the hopeless way he's been looking these past few weeks.

"Where's Mona?"

"She's with Bobby," is all I tell him.

"Bobby? Why?"

"He had to ask her about a few things. Why? What's up?"

"I need to be at this meeting y'all having. That's what's up!" Brip says defensively.

"Who told you about a meeting?" I ask, confused.

Brock called a meeting. I'm just waiting on him to get back to me with a date and time. He's going to dial-in and join us though a telephone conference, but I haven't heard back from him yet. I only told Bobby about the meeting because Brip really ain't in the condition to be making decisions. Brock wants him to take it easy and recover before he puts him back on the street. He's been through a lot. We all have.

"That don't fucking matter," Brip says and spits at my feet. He sniffs and leans back on one leg, waiting for me to challenge him. He's looking for a fight but I'm not the enemy.

"Calm down, lil brother," I say and try to place my hand on his shoulder, but he pulls away from me. "What's going on man? You want to talk?"

"To you?" he laughs sarcastically, then shakes his head no. "Hell, no!"

Brip's pissed at me for not being here all this time. I can understand him feeling like I abandoned him but it's complicated. It always is.

"I respect that," I say and hold my hands up in a surrendering motion. "But if you ever need to talk, you know I'm here man."

"Yeah, you here for now." He chuckles and turns to walk away but stops. "Where Bobby got Mona?"

I hesitate before I answer, and he notices. He starts to walk towards me aggressively.

"I think he may got her in Brock's dungeon," I reveal. If I can't distract Bobby with Tara's death right now, I'll distract him with Brip's wrath. I don't know what type of hold Mona got on Brip, but it ain't good for any of us. She's up to something but I'm too preoccupied with my own shit to give a fuck.

"What the fuck!" Brip screams and punches into thin air. "She ain't no prisoner. She's done more for this place than all y'all niggas. Brock included!"

That statement alone sounded more like Mona than it did Brip. Now, it's confirmed that she's brainwashing him. But for what? Shit, as long as it doesn't fuck up my plan to find my wife then I don't' give a damn.

"That's what you think?" Is all I say to him. He doesn't respond. He just shakes his head at me before jumping in his car to speed off and rescue Mona.

As I watch Brip speed down the road like a maniac, my cell phone rings. Every time my phone rings, my heart skips a beat. Even though Dalla doesn't have my number, I know that she's resourceful enough to find it if she wanted to. I always hope it's her calling me to tell me she's ok, but it never is. It's just Brock calling to give his orders over the phone. It's been two weeks since I heard from him. He's calling less and less, and he still hasn't told us anything about where he is. He just says he is handling business. He still got the Ranch on lock down. All business is frozen. There is no one allowed on the Ranch but us and security. Following the chain of command, I just do what I'm told. I need him to trust me. Or at least trust me enough to give me the code to the safe. Once I get that, my work here is done.

"Yeah," I answer.

"We need to have that meeting now. Get with Bobby and I'm going to call y'all back in 30 minutes," he says.

He sounds like he's in a rush. He's out of breath when he talks. When I talked to him a week ago, he was adamant about us not killing Ace. He said that Ace has letters that mama wrote before she died that he needs to talk to us about. He says it's important and that we all need to hear what he has to say. He letting that nigga get in his head just like I did but I don't say nothing.

"Brip knows about the meeting. He wants to be there."

"I told you to keep Brip out of this shit!" He screams and breathes even harder. If I didn't know any better it sounds like he's been running.

"It ain't me. It's your wife. She's been talking in his ear."

"Mona," Brock says like he knows just what his wife is capable of. "Keep her away from Brip and make sure she doesn't leave the Ranch. Understand?" he pauses. "Mona been through enough. I don't want her involved in none of this shit."

"How am I going to do that? She ain't no prisoner, man. You need to handle your own wife," I tell him. I got my own situation to take care of. I don't have time to handle his wife who ain't keen on being handled by anyone but him.

"You need to fall in line and do what I tell you. Lock her up if you have to, but she's not to leave the Ranch. I'll figure out what to do with her later."

"You need to call her man. If she hears from you, maybe she'll come down a bit. Stop all the plotting she's doing."

"Plotting? What you think she's plotting?"

"Mona ain't about to sit back and knit while Bobby and I run this Ranch. You know that. She's going make sure she stays on top and without you, she gon want to protect her interest. Besides, she's pissed that we got Vinchi in Zone 6."

"Let her see Vinchi, but the visit has to be supervised. I want all eyes on her at all times." Brock takes another deep breath like he's just finished running a marathon.

"Where the fuck are you, man?" Brock went silent for a while. The silence gives me an eerie feeling. "Brock?" I say making sure he is still on the line. "Hello?"

"I'm ok," is all he says, but something is telling me otherwise. His voice sounds different. Every time he calls, he sounds weird.

"You sure?" I ask and he's silent again. "Brock? Brock?" I repeat. I hear shuffling in the background. I can't make out the sound.

"I'm going to fix all of this. I promise. I'm going to make shit right," he says and goes silent again. "Wait for my call. 30 minutes," he says in a huff. "Just make sure you.." He tries to say something but he stops and yells instead. Then I hear a loud bang. It sounds like a popping noise but it wasn't a gun.

"Brock? Hey, Brock what the fuck is going on?" Brock doesn't respond. I just hear more shuffling before the phone hangs up.

The night he left, Brock told me and Bobby that that he was going to meet us at Ace's places, but he never showed up. I didn't understand why he didn't ride with us but at the time, all I could think about was saving my son and Dalla. He called later that night after it was all over to check on us. He didn't say where he was. Just that he was handling business and that we needed to lay low and wait for his cue before we opened the Ranch back up for business. Now I know that Ace was fucking with his head, talking about the letter mama wrote before she died.

I pick up the phone and try to call back. Someone picks it up but doesn't say anything. "Hello? Brock? You okay, man?" I can hear the person breathing on the other end of the phone. They say nothing. I call Brock's name a few more times and the phone just hangs up. When I try to call back, it doesn't ring.

# BOBBY BADD

"I know you had something to do with it. Why did you let her go?" I say to Mona. She's staring back at me like she wants to smack me in the face. She actually did hit me. She suckered me in the jaw when I forced her in this room. That's why I had to handcuff her to Brocks interrogation chair. Now, she ain't talking at all. Maybe I went too far but I got a feeling she knows where Dalla is.

The last time I heard from Jayson, he told me he had eyes on Dalla. That was two days ago. Now, I can't get him on the phone. That's not like him. Something's up. I told him that I wanted Dalla dead or alive but she must have gotten to him first. If I don't hear from Jayson soon, I may have to leave this place and kill her myself.

I look back at Mona. She's giving me the evil eye. When I talk to her, I'm sure that I don't yell. I keep my deposition calm. I don't want her to think that she's a hostage although she is handcuffed. I take Brock's wooden chair and drag it across the concrete floor closer to Mona. The quicker we can get out of this place, the better. It's cold and wet down here and cobwebs are attaching themselves to both of us. I pull one off her face. When my hand moves towards her face, she flinches a little. I'm not here to hurt Mona. I just want answers. I take a seat in front of her and stare back at her.

Billy thinks I'm dumb. He should know better than anybody that I'm not no dumb nigga. He still got feelings for his conniving wife. Billy always been soft. That's why his ass been in Zone 6 all this time, taking a mental vacation while I was out risking my life trying to find him. I could have been with Tara and my son. If he wasn't my brother, I would off his ass too just for wasting my fucking time. I blame him too but he blood so there ain't much I can do with him. Killing Dalla will be revenge enough for me. She's responsible for what happened to Tara. Hell, she's responsible for what happened to all of us that night. She got to pay, whether he likes it or not. I said I was going to kill her, and I mean what I say. I won't rest until she's dead. If I had my choice, I'd like to think I would kill Ace first but that's neither here nor there because Brock has strict orders for us to keep him alive for whatever fucking reason. So Dalla's blood is the only blood I have a taste for right now.

"The sooner you answer my questions, the quicker we can get out of here, Mona. Where is she?"

"Uncuff me," Mona says calmly to me, but I can see the fear in her eyes.

"I will uncuff you," is all I say to her before I lean back in my chair. I place my right leg over my left knee and wait for her patiently.

"Fuck you?" Mona says back to me. "When Brock hears about this shit, you finished."

I know Brock wouldn't approve of this but he ain't here. As a man, I got to do what I feel is right. So here we are.

"I'm gon let Brock know myself what I done because it's the right thing to do. He will understand. Dalla tried to bring this family down and you hiding her. He ain't gon like that either."

"Where is Brock?" Mona asks me. Now she has a desperate look on her face.

I remain quiet.

"Y'all don't think it's strange that he ain't here. What if he hurt?"

"Brock is fine, Mona," I say to her confidently.

"You don't know that," she shot back.

"I do. I talked to him a few weeks ago and everything is fine. He's putting things in order."

"You talked to him?" Mona seems shocked. I don't respond to her question. I just stare at her.

"Mona, we here to discuss Dalla," I remind her why she's here.

"Ace brought this family down. Not Dalla. He also fucked your wife. She walking around without good sense and all you concerned about is Tara. That's fucked up."

Just at the mention of Lera's name, I start to squirm in my seat. I hate when she brings up Lera. I know it's fucked up but I can't think about her right now. It will distract me from Tara. I already let that happen once. I can't do it again. I know I seem like a hypocrite focusing on Dalla although Lera was the one that led her to our house, but I know she didn't mean it. Besides, she suffered enough.

Lately, I been thinking about Lera a lot more. It started it in my dreams. I keep having dreams that she ends up dead on the streets. When I'm not dreaming about that, I'm dreaming about lying with her on the beach like we used to do. Lera helped take my mind off so much but she ain't Tara. She wasn't there from day one like Tara. She don't have my child like Tara but she does have my heart; just like Tara but I'm too consumed with Tara to even consider my feelings for Lera or her wellbeing right know. I know it's fucked up but it is what it is. I never was taught how to be 100 percent loyal to two people. I do know that when Mona mentions Ace fucking her, I get this crushing feeling in my gut and it makes me angry but I redirect that anger and put it on Dalla. I know she ain't the culprit like Ace but she's the closest thing I can grab for right now. Trust me, Ace is going to pay but Dalla is the one I can reach out and touch right now. She's a quick fix to curb this rage I have inside of me. I need her dead. I promised Tara and I never broke a promise to her. Then, I can concentrate on Ace and sorting through the buried feelings I have for Lera.

"Ace gon get what's coming to him. Trust," I say to her.

"So you ain't never love, Lera?" she asks me and I'm forced to think about her question. I wish she would stop fucking mentioning Lera. We here to talk about Dalla. It wasn't too long ago that she was right where I am. Concentered on finding Dalla but something's changed. That's how I know she's hiding something.

"If all that shit was fake just to hide Tara and your son from us then you a punk. You weak as fuck!" Mona shakes her head at me and the shame falls on me just as heavy as my burden about Tara's life. I can't take the heat so I jump up from my seat and turn my back to her. But that doesn't stop her from talking. "You brought that innocent girl into all this shit just to distract us from what you really had going on. Now look at her. She probably dead already. The way you threw her out on the street, she ain't got a chance to survive. You think Dalla a murderer! So the fuck are you! And you murder your own at that. That's fucked up. That ain't the Badd way."

She's flipping this thing around on me. She starting to make me feel even more guilty about how I fucked up.

"You had everybody fooled. That poor girl actually thought you loved her."

"I did love Lera!" I blurt out and shock myself. This was a truth I've been hiding from myself but I had a choice to make and I chose Tara. She's the only mother Blake will ever have. "You don't know what the fuck you talking about," I say while walking towards her. I'm defending myself and totally losing my cool at the same time. "Tara needs me. Our son needs her. Lera wasn't innocent in this either, Mona. She had to go. She had to." Before I can finish my sentence, I hear someone crashing through the door. It's Brip.

He's charging towards me like I'm the enemy. I don't jump. Brip knows I don't budge for no one. He doesn't either. He jumps up and hooks his arm around my neck and throws me in a head lock. I body slam him to the floor and we roll around wrestling in mud puddles like two dogs. What the fuck is his problem? The last time Brip and I had a physical altercation I was 12 years old and he set my favorite remote control car on fire.

"What the fuck is wrong with you man?" I manage to take control of Brip. I'm holding him down with my knee pressed deep in his chest. Trying to tame him is like trying to tame a rabid pit bull. Brip is wild and out of control.

"You the one with the problem. Let her go! Let her the fuck go!" He screams. He's talking about Mona.

I jump off of him and he jumps up and runs towards Mona who is smiling at me with her eyes. What kind of fucking spell does she have on Brip?

"This is official Badd business, Brip. What the fuck are you doing?"

"Mona is Badd business. Y'all ain't about to be treating her like she's a fucking prisoner. You got her chained to this fucking chair like a dog. What the fuck is wrong with you?" He charges towards me again but Mona stops him.

"Calm down, Brip. Just uncuff me," she says to him calmly. She's always so calm.

He turns to me and holds out his hand. "Give me the fucking keys, nigga." I just throw him the keys. I don't feel like fighting with him. He ain't in his right mind. He never is. Mona and I give each other evil stares until she's free. She rubs her wrists like I had them cuffed too tight. Brip sees this and shoots me another vicious look. He holds her hands in his and carefully looks over her wrist like he's checking to make sure nothing is broken.

"You ok? Are you hurt?" Mona shakes her head no. "I'm sorry, Mona. Billy told me you were down here. I didn't know about this shit. I would have come sooner."

Billy is the one that encouraged me to question Mona. Now, he sicks Brip on me. He's definitely up to something. Mona places her hands on Brip's shoulder letting him know that she doesn't blame him. He leads Mona to the door but gives me an evil stare before they leave.

"Stay the fuck away from her." Brip points as he warns me. "Both y'all niggas," he says referring to Billy I assume. "Any crime against Mona is a crime against me. Believe that," Brip warns.

"I hear you," I say to try and keep the peace. Now that it's all said and done, I think that maybe I have gone too far. I'm man enough to admit that, but I ain't crying over spilled milk.

"And we both gon be at the meeting!" he adds. How did Brip know about the meeting? I give Mona another look. She's playing Brip like a fucking chime. "Yeah, you didn't think I knew, huh? Y'all trying to shut me out but that shit ain't happening." He gives me an evil stare and gently leads Mona out the door.

I ain't trying to fight with my brother. I'm just trying to make things right with Tara. I don't' understand why they can't get that. They can't feel what I'm feeling. What the fuck am I supposed to do? Sit here and do nothing. Brock don't want us hunting Ace right now and we can't work or leave the Ranch until he says so. I can't sit here and watch Tara waste away and do nothing. I can't be a father to my son either because when he asks about his mama, I don't know what to tell him. I can't wake her up. I can't get to Ace but this.. I can do. It all makes me feel less helpless. Feeling helpless ain't a good feeling. I ain't cut out for that shit.

I take a deep breath and try and regroup before I leave. I try my best to shake off the thoughts of Lera that Mona forced in my head. I need fresh air. That's the only thing that's going to help me. I walk down the long hallways and past the empty cells towards the stairs. I see the light peeking out from the door and for some reason, I start to feel calm. Like maybe everything is going to work out. Tara is going to survive and Lera is going to be ok. I start walking towards the light at the end of this imaginary tunnel and step outside. As soon as the sun hits my face, I take another deep breath. When I exhale, I feel drained. I'm tired. So tired that I can't sleep. I'm hungry too. Once Tara wakes up, everything is going back to normal.

On my way to my car, I run into Billy. He gives me that I'm sorry look and that tells me that he already knew Brip was on a fucking rampage when he sent him my way.

"Look, man," he says and holds up his hands like he's surrendering to me, "I had to tell him. He.."

"Don't worry about it," I say quickly. I don't feel like chatting with him.

Billy looks shocked that I'm not trying to fight him. I already had my fight for the day. I just need to get back to Tara now. I start walking towards my car and Billy follows behind me.

"Did she know anything?"

"Yeah, but she ain't saying." I turn to him and watch him hard. I want to see his reaction. You can never tell with this nigga. He's a fucking poker pro. I ain't never going to be able to read what he's thinking on his face so I just got to pick sense from nonsense.

"Look, man we gon figure all of this out. I promise." Billy places his hand on my shoulder and his touch comforts me. Its feels supportive. It feels like the hand of my big brother. I almost believe him. "I'm really sorry about Tara man. I hope you know that. I can't imagine what you going through."

For some reason I get pissed when he mentions Tara's name and move away from his touch. Maybe because I don't believe that he gives a fuck about Tara. "You will though," I say back to him and try to walk away. I know it was harsh, but it's how I feel.

"Bobby," Billy says to my back. I turn around to face him.

"I'm asking you to let it go," he says calm and hopeful.

"You mean, let Dalla go?"

"Yes," he says and looks me straight in the eyes.

"Why would I do that?" I say and chuckle.

"Cause she's the mother of my son, man. The nephew you haven't even met yet."

"Oh, yeah?" I say sarcastic. "Why should I put the mother of your son above the mother of mine?" Billy doesn't respond. He can't. "Huh?" I ask him again. He doesn't have a response for me. "You know where she is, don't you?"

"No, I don't," he responds so quick that I believe him.

"If you did, would you tell me?" I ask him and he doesn't respond. I get my answer. "Typical," I say and try to walk away again.

"Wait. You ain't going about this right, man."

"Man fuck the right way. Fuck the wrong way too. In my mind, there's only one way to make this right," I gesture by pulling my trigger finger.

Billy looks at me like he wants to say something but he doesn't. I open the door to my car and he stops me again.

"I know you got shit to do," he says carefully, "But Brock called. He's going to be calling any minute now for a meeting. He wants us both there," he says like he knows I'm going to visit Tara. "He talking about those letters again, man. I think we need to hear him out."

"Where we meeting?" I say to him calmly. I haven't seen Tara all day, but I need to know what's going on. Maybe Brock got leads on Ace. Maybe he knows something about Dalla too. I got a lot to talk to him about. I need clearance to leave the Ranch too.

"Let's meet in the conference room at the Casino."

"You might as well send Brip the location. He knows about the meeting. He's bringing Mona." I say to him and get in the car.

"Mona?" he repeats back. "Man, Mona can't be there. Neither can Brip. Brock don't want that."

I shrug and close my door. Billy runs to the passenger side of my car and opens the door.

"Can I get a lift?" he asks, although he's already inside, tugging at the seat belt. He's trying to call a truce. I don't respond but I don't put him out my car either.

We head straight to the Casino. To keep the peace, Billy text Brip the location.

# MONA BADD

All this time, I've been half stepping on doing the shit I was supposed to do because I was holding on to the possibility that Brock was being held captive somewhere but that shit ain't true. He out here somewhere making moves and calling meetings. Fuck him! I heard just what I needed to hear from Bobby. Now it's time to make my move. The first thing I need to do is get the code to the Ranch's safe. It's where most of the cash is. The cash we don't keep in banks. Brock is supposed to be the only one that has it but I know for a fact that he gave it to one of his brothers. I got to figure out which one. Once I get that code, I can do what I need to do.

Brip just got a text from Billy saying that the meeting is going to be held at the Casino. We driving there now. Apparently Brock is calling in to host the meeting through the phone. I can't wait to talk to him. It's gon take all I have to keep my fucking cool. Where the fuck is he?

"You make sure you hold your own at this meeting, Brip. You got a right to ask questions and demand answers," I tell him. He just shakes his head at me. Brip is doing better but he still not his self all the way. He stays deep in thought and keeps this tortured look on his face. I think he angry at the world right now. That ain't good for nobody. But I'm gon use that anger to my advantage like I've been doing.

Brock must not remember admitting to me that he killed his mother. Or is that the reason he hiding like a little bitch? He knows I can destroy his ass with this news and he got the nerve to be fucking with me this way. I'm gon blow his shit up. The brothers deserve to know that their mother was murdered at the hand of their fucked up brother. Other than me being a real ass bitch, I don't have no proof. I wonder if they would even believe me. A year ago, Billy would have but he over all that now. Him thinking he ain't a real Badd is proof enough. I just got to be careful with this information. If I say too much, I'm likely to fuck up my own chances of taking this Ranch.

If Brock is making phone calls that can only mean one thing, the brothers know where he is. I got a feeling he right here on this Ranch. Just like Billy was all this time. The only person willing to tell me anything is Brip. He trusts me.

"Why you think Brock don't want you at this meeting?" I ask him.

He doesn't respond right away. He looks like he doesn't even think about the question I ask him. He just shrugs his shoulders like he don't know or care. "Did you know he's been in contact with Billy?"

"I don't know shit, Mona." Brip responds like he's frustrated. He turns into the Casino. "All I can think about is killing that nigga, Ace. That's it." He says to me like he trying to tell me something else. Like he can't help me the way I need him to. I don't bother him anymore. I don't want to tick him off. He's my way into this meeting. I will get the truth out of him later.

Brip jumps out the car and opens my door. I walk out and security is already standing at the door. I'd like to see them try and stop me with Brip by my side. Brip takes my arm and leads me towards the Casino like he's my bodyguard. The guards don't intervene when they see me. They open the door and we walk right in and head straight to the conference room.

The Casino feels so dead. Hell, this whole Ranch feels dead. It's weird. It's like a ghost town. Brock knows that I would've never let him shut down business for so long. We probably done already lost several millions in these few weeks. It's a shame and it makes us look weak and unreliable to our clients. They still paying taxes but we ain't providing no kind of services. This shit has to stop.

I walk into the conference room and Billy and Bobby are already there. Bobby sitting down looking like he feel too guilty to look me in the eye. Billy gives me a weird look like he knows what I'm trying to do. I just ignore them both. It's Mr. Badd that I need to address. Brip pulls out a chair at the head of the table for me to sit at. Bobby and Billy look at each other like they are confirming what they already discussed and I sit down. Brip sits next to me.

"Brip, we just waiting on Brock to call. It should be any minute now," Billy says without looking at me. Fuck his weak ass.

Brip nods his head and stares down at the table like he's being haunted by his thoughts. Bobby looks like he's lost in anger and Billy seems confused like all of this shit is one big algebra test that he didn't study for. These motherfuckers are who Brock left in charge of this Ranch? I can't believe this shit.

A few minutes go by and Billy's phone doesn't ring. No one says anything to anyone. So, I speak up. Someone has to.

"When is he calling?" I ask Billy.

"I don't know," he answers my question but looks at Brip.

"Well, it ain't like Mr. Badd to be late. You sure he didn't already call and y'all just fucking with us." I stir the pot.

Brip shoots his head up and looks at both his brothers.

"He hasn't called yet, Mona," Bobby says to me.

"Well we can start without him," I say, then motion for one of the guards. Hesitantly, they come. "Bring me one of the notebooks and a pen from the shelf in the back room." The guard does just what I ask.

Billy and Bobby start looking at each other again like they need to stop me but they don't. They ain't got the balls to.

"We need to wait on Brock," Billy says to Bobby. Bobby doesn't respond. He's looking like he just wants to get this meeting over with and if that means me putting it in order, he doesn't care.

"If Brock calls, then I'll update him," I say to Billy.

"Brock don't want you here. He gave me strict orders to keep you out of the meetings. You only here because of Brip, Mona. It's best you just sit and listen in."

"Fuck that!" I say. "If Brock don't want me here, then he needs to say that to me."

"I agree," Brip says.

The guard comes back with my notepad and pen and I get in gear.

"There are three things we need to discuss. First, we need to be planning to find that walking dead man, Ace."

"I agree!" Brip yells and punches the table.

"Then we need to open this Ranch back up for business before we lose it all. Then, y'all need to deal with y'all wives the proper way." On that note, they all look guiltily at each other. Their wives is the last thing they want to talk about. "It's been weeks since Ace attacked us. We fools if we believe that no one on the outside knows that. Especially now that we closed to business. We losing money like a motherfucker and it's making us look weak. Like we can't handle an attack. We ain't been seen on the streets or heard from since the attack. Keeping quiet like this is only going to lead to two things. One, someone is going to strike us and two, we gon go broke."

"I don't agree with that, Mona," Billy says. "Ain't nobody crazy enough to strike us."

"You really gon say that dumb shit after what Ace did to our women?" Brip says to Billy and he backs down. "I agree with Mona. Brock got us locked up on this Ranch like we scared of something. We need to go out and show our faces."

"You right, Brip" I say to him. I'm proud that he's speaking up and that he's agreeing with me. Bobby is just listening. He's in a dark place right now but he the most level headed of all the brothers. If I make sense to him, he going to agree with me. "People ain't gon sit around for much longer. They gon try to take advantage first by not paying their taxes and who gon be there to stop them if we stuck here? Plus Kong ain't a patient man. We fucking up his business by shutting down the crematory. Ain't nobody called him to say anything. That's not how we do business. If Kong walks, we screwed. Period."

I let what I say soak in. I can tell by the look on their faces that they all considering what I'm saying.

"We need to let Brip and his crew get an army out there searching for Ace. When we find Ace, we need to make his ass pay. It needs to be public and it needs to be brutal as fuck. So brutal that it gives folks chills. That will keep them from trying to fuck with us. We need to use him as an example."

"Hell, yeah!" Brip jumps up. He's coming back to life now.

"Then, we need to get your wives off the streets. People know they faces and they know they alone. If they think we weak, they gon be weak enough to try one of them and that can only hurt us worst."

"What do you suggest we do about them?" Bobby asks without making eye contact with me.

"Let me set them up. I can get them new identities, give them cash, and a house in another state. But they can't be here no more."

"How we gon get the cash?" Brip says quickly. "Brock is the only one that has the code to the safe."

Brip said just what I needed him to say. I can't just ask them for the code. Then they will know something is up but Brip can. My conversation went exactly where I needed it to go.

"That's true Mona," Billy says. "Without that code all this shit you talking about is pointless. We need money to open up the Ranch. Brock froze the main accounts. We can't do business with nothing."

Two out of three claim they don't have the code and I believe them. Brock don't trust Billy and Brip ain't responsible enough. That can only mean one thing, Bobby has the code. We all look at Bobby who ain't saying nothing. That's confirmation enough for me.

"Dalla ain't getting shit," Bobby says. "She don't deserve it. I agree that Lera and Taffy need to be set up."

I am shocked that he mentioned Lera. Maybe he's coming to his senses.

"That ain't your call, man," Billy says to his brother. "Just like killing her ain't your call either. That's something we all need to discuss."

I feel an argument brewing so I stop it before it starts. "Let's stay focused," I say. I know for a fact that agreeing to a fair settlement for the wives ain't gon be easily done if I leave it all up to them. That's why I'm gon set them up the way I see fit. But, I can't do that until I take control of this place.

"Billy, you right. If nobody here has the code, then all of this shit is pointless," I say and look at Bobby. So do Brip and Billy. "We need money to operate and without that code, not only do we risk losing it all, your wives risk being attacked and Ace continues to walk. We fucked," I say and look at Brip. I need him to react. I need him to put the pressure on Bobby.

"Fuck being fucked. Bobby do you have the code or not?" Brip says and stares straight at Bobby.

"We need to wait for Brock to call," Bobby says. He still doesn't answer the question. "We can't be out of order right now. We don't know anything about what he's doing on the outside. If we move too quick, we may fuck up the plan he already has in place."

"If that's the case, I got to leave the Ranch. I need to meet with Kong in person. Let him know personally that we need everybody to be patient," I say. This gives me the perfect reason to leave the Ranch.

Billy gives me a strange look. "If you try to leave, the guards gon take you and lock you down. They have strict orders from Brock. That goes for all of us," Billy says then eyes each of his brothers. He stares longer at Brip.

"Fuck that! Let them try. I'm gon shoot them all like dogs. One by one they gon fall," Brip starts to rage. "Brock don't give a fuck about this Ranch. Today makes that more obvious. He ain't called yet. He left us here to deal with this shit and that's what we need to do until he gets back. I'm leaving tonight to find that nigga with or without Brocks permission," Brip says.

"Brip, calm down," I say. "We gon have to make a few exceptions until Brock calls. I got to meet with Kong. If I don't, he gon react. I know him better than all of you. We can't sit silent anymore. We need a face to face." I try to get them to see it my way.

Bobby shoots me a look that says 'see what you caused.' Now I see why Brock didn't want Brip at the meeting. I know that he will shoot them all. I don't need that. I just need the code. I'm going to have to calm Brip down later. Bobby phone starts to vibrate. My heart stops. It's Brock. I know it is. We all stare at Bobby as he stares down at his phone. He doesn't answer at first. Why is he hesitating? Is it Brock? He looks so spooked. He answers the phone and then jumps up.

"Is it Brock?" Brip asks. "Put him on speaker," he demands.

Bobby goes to a corner to talk in private.

"What the fuck is going on?" Brip yells.

Bobby turns to us and says, "I got to go."

"What? Hell no! This meeting is still in progress," Brip says. "Was that Brock?'

"No, it's Tara's nurse. She's awake," he says and flies out the door.

We all sit and stare at each other stunned. Everybody except Billy.

"I got to go too. My son will be up soon," Billy says quickly.

I wonder why he's in such a hurry to leave all of a sudden.

"When will you talk to Brock again?" I ask him.

"I don't know Mona. He calls me. It's always from a restricted number." He tells me and gets up to walk out the room but stops like he has to get something off his chest before he leaves. "It's weird that he didn't call," Billy says and then looks at me. I can tell he's concerned.

"What you mean, Billy?" Now I'm concerned, although Brock don't deserve it.

"He sounded a little weird the last time I talked to him. Right before he called this meeting."

"Weird how?" I say. My heart is pounding.

"I don't know. Just weird," he says. "If he don't call by tomorrow. You may need to go meet with Kong but you got to take Brip with you. I will smooth things over with the guards," he says and looks at me like he has no choice but to trust my judgment right now. "Oh, and Brock gave you clearance to see Vinchi. I will let the guards know," he says before he leaves.

Finally, I get to see my son. I would be thankful but I shouldn't be thankful for something that I'm entitled to. I'm afraid at how he's doing though. Whatever Vinchi needs, I'm going to make sure he gets it. I hope Brock don't expect me to be grateful to him for this. Just thinking about Brock makes my stomach hurt. I get a strange feeling that Brock may be in trouble but I let my anger fight it off. This meeting went just the way I needed it to go. But something may be up with Brock.

* * *

Brip is driving me back to the Big House. He's pissed off. He ain't stopped talking about the harm he gon inflict on the guards if they touch him or me. I don't even try to calm him down. It don't make sense.

"Brock is doing us all wrong. I expected more from him," he complains. "Treating us like we fucking prisoners."

"Do you believe what Billy said?" I ask him and he gets silent. "Maybe something is up with him. How if Ace got him?"

"Ace ain't fucking with Brock. He may have been able to fuck with Billy but not Brock," Brip responds. He's making sense.

"I think Brock is on the Ranch," I say to Brip.

"He ain't on **this** Ranch," he answers too quick and too confident. He knows something.

I start to wonder why he lay emphasis on the word "this." Could he be at another location?

"You right. He probably working out of the other Ranch," I say, just get a reaction out of Brip. "He's ok."

"You know about the other Ranch too?" Brip asks me rhetorically. So Brock's location is confirmed. "Yea, Brock is cool, but he needs to let us know what the fuck he's doing. He can't just hideout there like a hermit not letting us know what's what."

"Maybe we should stop by and see him before we visit with Kong," I say.

Brip starts looking confused. "I ain't never been there. I didn't know that you had either. The location is so secure that Brock and Papa Badd is the only two that knows about it. I guess

Brock did trust you a lot. He was right too, Mona. I got faith in you. I know you gon get things back to normal with us," He says as he pulls up the circular driveway of the Big House.

"I promise I will," I say and try not to sound too shocked about what he revealed to me. "I got your back, Brip. I'm gon make all of this right for all of us," I say before I get out the car.

\* \* \*

As soon as I get settled, I call Dalla. She answers on the first ring. I need her to find out all she can about this second Ranch. I know about the mini Ranches, but never knew a second Ranch exists. This don't sound like the same thing. The mini ranches are just a further extension of the facilities that we offer on the Badd Ranch; just for convenience and we don't have more than three of them. At least that I know of. What Brip is talking about sounds different. It sounds like a second headquarters.

"Mona, what's going on? We've been waiting on you to call. Is everything ok? Is my son ok?" Dalla says all in one breath.

"Everything is ok. Your son is fine. So is Billy."

I let her know just in case she was wondering. "I just got held up. They watching me like a hawk but things are starting to turn around. Did you get to Taffy yet?" I need Taffy on board with this plan. It's important. If this works, I'm gon have the code to the safe by the end of the month.

"Yes, but it wasn't easy. Bobby sent Jayson to kill me. He came at me shooting. No warning," she says surprisingly calm.

"What?" I try to act like I didn't know Jayson was after her. I swear this bitch got nine lives. "Where is he now?"

"He's with us. We were at Taffy's mom place in Vegas but I knew we wasn't safe there so I'm back at my other spot a little outside of Atlanta," Dalla said. She never did tell me where that other spot is. "Jayson already tried to escape once. I don't know what to do with him. I can't kill him, Mona."

"You don't have to. We can use him. Just keep him on lock down," I tell her. "You get the money?"

"Yes," she says in a thank you voice. "But we had to use half of it to send Taffy mom off somewhere safe. She's with one of my contacts at the Dominican Republic. We gon need more."

"Don't worry. I'm gon get you all some aid and shelter. I got a meeting this week with someone that may be able to help us. I trust him. Just lay low and wait for my call but in the meantime, I need you to get some information for me."

"What is it?" She asks without hesitating. Dalla got way more heart than all the Badd men put together.

"A second Ranch. I think it's where Brock may be. You still got those maps you said you found at Billy's place?"

"I can get to them but it ain't gon be easy."

"Good," I say relieved. "Find out what you can and be careful."

"I always am," she says and we hang up.

My next call is to Kong. Kong is more of a face to face person than a phone person. I leave him a message first – 911. It's our emergency code. I haven't used it since I became a Badd. I know he's going to call me back right away. He can help me get the wives set up and provide protection. Then, I can schedule a time to meet with him to propose the deal I'm gon offer him and let him know that I'm taking the Ranch. I just got to figure out what to do with Brip. He can't hear the conversation I'm going to have. I got an idea to keep him busy while I'm with Kong.

While I'm waiting on Kong to call me back. I start setting my plan in motion. Now that Dalla got Taffy on her side, it's game time. It's time to put my plan in action. Kong can help with this too and now that Dalla got Jayson, this shit is going to be even more perfect than I planned.

In less than 60 days, I will have this Ranch. Brock can stay where the fuck he's at. But in the meantime, I'm going to see my son. I'm going to assure him that we gon be ok and that he gon get everything he deserves. When death retires me from running this empire that I helped build, I'm gon hand it over to him on a gold platter. I'm gon let Vinchi know that I'm getting his throne ready for him and that I need him to be ready to receive it. He got to get his head right.

# LERA BADD

The vibrating of these clippers feels so good against my head. As my hair detaches from my scalp and falls to the floor, I start to feel free. Tony said that the first step to recovery is giving up something. So, I gave up my hair; I cut my locs.

People say that your hair holds memories and can be a store place for negative emotions. I don't want to remember Ace. I don't want to remember Tara bleeding and I don't want to remember that Bobby doesn't love me. I glide the clippers from the front of my head to the back one last time. Now that I'm completely bald, I can process my thoughts in a healthier way. I feel like a new person. And that's exactly what I need to be right now; new. Because the old me wouldn't have survived. I was dying.

I stare back at my new self in the mirror and start to talk. Tony says that reprogramming my mind will help clear it. I stare back at myself and say, "I did not kill Tara. I will not be a victim to Ace. I will not let Bobby be blamed for what happened. I am strong." I say that about four times. I start believing by the third and the fourth time, it feels locked in. Now, I'm going to meet Tony for meditation.

Tony's been helping me with my recovery. He is an unexpected miracle. I told him that he saved me, and he told me that he didn't save me but gave me the tools to save myself. He thinks I'm stronger than what I am. He believes in my strength so much that I can't help but to believe in it myself. I feel bad for the way I used to judge him. I used to think he was beneath me. That he was a nut case but now I understand him. I don't think I've ever met anyone as strong as Tony. Despite all the obstacles against him, he survived. He says survival after tragedy is a daily thing. I can relate to that.

After he told me what happened to him, I got inspired. He took a bullet to the head and survived. Now, he's struggling to remember but he's getting stronger every day. He hasn't given up on himself. He meditates to help him remember things. He told me that I can use meditation to help me forget things. Tony says that meditation can help me reroute negative emotions and put them into something positive. I want to focus on getting stronger and getting even. I have decided that I want to kill Ace for what he did to me.

About a week ago, I thought I had killed Ace but it was just Jayson; and he's not dead. But if anybody deserved an ass beating it was him. Protecting myself and Dalla by attacking Jayson gave me some of my strength back. I wonder what's going to happen when I kill Ace. Maybe I will turn into superwoman.

Taffy is so blessed to have a real family. She gave them up to be a Badd. I wonder if she regrets that. I would. Especially if I had a brother like Tony. He loves her so much that he would take a bullet for her. Her mother is feisty but nurturing. Her motherly touch helped bring me back to life. We had to send her overseas for safety. I miss her. Before she left, she gave me the warmest hug and kiss I've felt in a long time.

I walk out to the back patio and Tony is already sitting on the ground on top of a pillow with his legs crossed Indian style.

He has a pillow out for me. When he sees my hair, he jumps up and stares at me like he's looking at a Queen. He doesn't say anything, but he doesn't have to. His look says it all. He smiles at me and nods then gently grabs my hand and assists me as I lower myself onto the pillow. He's staring at me. It feels like Tony looks at me from the inside out. His stare can be so intense, but I never shy away from it. I look directly into his eyes and I feel stronger. I also start to feel something else. I'm not sure what it is but it feels like butterflies but on a whole other level.

Now that I understand him more and I'm not writing him off as a nut case, I notice things about him that I didn't before. His eyes are so beautiful. Looking at them gives me this intense feeling. Long eyelashes feather the tips of his deep set dark brown eyes. His lips are perfectly full and round. They stick out of his mouth like they're begging to be kissed. His peanut butter brown complexion is smooth like butter. His shiny bald head shows off its perfect round shape and although he doesn't wear cologne, his body has a natural sweet scent to it. Plus, his body is ripped from the neck down. I'm sure he has zero percent body fat. His militant-like discipline shows in his posture and how he moves. Every step is precise and confident. He's fearless and has a nice swag about himself. He's just a little slow but he can't help that.

"You ready to start?" He asks and is shaking his head at me like he's answering a question I asked him. Tony is facing me. He holds out his hands for me to grab. I nod my head and grab his hands. His hands feel rough. It feels like he rubs them against sandpaper, yet his touch is so soft. So soft that I feel it on the inside. "Close," he pauses, "your," he pauses again, "eyes," he finishes his sentence. I do what he says. "Just work with what you see and don't fear it. Conquer it," he says in a strong voice like a teacher coaching their student before a tournament. Then he goes silent.

The first person I see is Bobby. He's walking away from me and I start to feel sad. Then I see Tara. Her blood is coming out her mouth and pouring from her stomach. I get scared. Then Ace appears. He slaps me down. He's holding me down by the back of my neck. I can't move. He snatches off my pants and I open my eyes. It's too much. When my eyes are open, I see Tony staring back at me. He nods at me, encouraging me to continue and I close my eyes again and try to refocus.

Now when I see Bobby, I confront him. I tell him how he wronged me. I tell him that I didn't deserve what he did to me. I tell him that he caused all of this including Tara's death. Then I tell him that I don't need him anymore. I tell him that every day my love for him fades into a distant memory. I tell him I don't need him to protect me. I don't need his necklace or his name. I tell him that I'm strong on my own. Stronger than Tara. Stronger than him.

When I see Tara, I try to help her but when I can't, I just tell her that I'm sorry. I tell her she's to blame for what happened too. I tell her that she taunted me. That she knew how much I loved Bobby and disrespected our relationship by fucking him right under my nose. I tell her that I don't wish death on her, but she has to take part in what she done as well.

Then I see Ace and I say nothing. I just act. When he tries to pin me down, I fight. I fight and fight until I see him coughing up blood. Blood is coming from his stomach and I'm holding the knife over his dead body. I feel powerful and stronger than I ever felt before. When I open my eyes, Tony is smiling at me.

"I can feel," he pauses for a while like he's trying to remember what he was about to say, "I can feel." He closes his eyes, takes a deep breath and reopens them. "I can feel your energy in my hands," he says quickly like he was trying to get it all out before he forgets. "I'm feeding off of it. It's causing me to remember," he pauses again, "more," he adds.

"What are you remembering?" I ask.

"A kiss," he says immediately. "I'm remembering what my body feels like inside when I kiss a bea..uti...ful," he stutters, "woman," he forces the words out his mouth like they were stuck in his head. Then stares deep at me.

I move in closer to him and he does as well. I stretch out my neck and our lips finally meet. I close my eyes as we kiss. I want to feel every second of it. His kiss feels like an escape. It also feels like a weapon to help aid me in the war I'm battling in my mind. Then, it just feels soft and sexy. He places both hands on my shoulders then starts to softly rub against my back. He massages my neck. I feel so connected to him in the moment of our kiss that I feel like I know what he must be feeling. Unsure but focused. Disregarded but still determined. Hurt but strong.

He pulls away from me first. I don't want him to, but I guess we have to breath. It is the longest kiss I ever shared with a man.

"Tank...tha..." he starts to stutter. He swallows hard and I smile softly at him. He takes a deep breath and continues, "thank you," he says to me like I did him a favor. He still has my face cupped in his large hands. I press my cheeks against the palm of his hands and rub against him.

"You don't have to thank me for this, Tony. This is what we both deserved. It's what we needed," I say to him. I want to kiss him again but I'm not sure if the kiss is a part of his therapy or something he desires. It is both for me.

"Tony," Dalla opens the sliding door and calls out.

I wonder if she saw us. I really don't care if she did. Tony lets go of my face like it's hot and jumps up at the sound of her voice. He follows her command like a police dog. He really trusts her.

"We got to hit the road," she says to him.

"10-4," he says back to her and rushes towards the door then stops like he's forgetting something. And he was. He forgot me. He turns and walks back towards me. He leans down and grabs my hand, carefully guiding me to my feet. He nods at me again. "I'll be back. Keep practicing. You got to keep practicing," he says to me in one breath.

"I will," I say and squeeze his hand. I want to hug him. I don't want him to leave, but I have to be strong on my own. "Where are you taking him?" I ask Dalla.

She looks at me like I have no claims to Tony. "We got work to do," is all she says.

"I want to go too," I blurt out.

"No," she answers quickly like her voice is the voice of authority. "It's too dangerous. You stay here with Taffy and you two are not to leave."

"I can help," I tell her. I feel like she's judging me because of before.

"You will get your chance to help but not like this," she says and walks back in the house. Tony doesn't follow her. At least not right away.

He looks at me and smiles before winking. Then he gestures a muscle with his right arm. His bicep looks like it's about to pop out. His vein wraps around his entire arm like python. I nod at him and he winks at me. "Keep practicing. Keep practicing," he repeats until he closes the sliding door. Even when he gets inside, he's still chanting it.

I sit back down and close my eyes. I do just what he says, and I continue to practice meditation. I'm going to get my chance and I'm not waiting on Dalla or anyone else to give it to me. I'm taking it. If I'm going to kill Ace, I have to practice and the first person I'm going to practice on is Jayson.

I have to kill him. If I can kill him, then I know that it won't be hard to kill another person. Jayson is going to be my first target and Ace my second. I'm not ready to accept who my second target has to be, but I have to do what needs to be done in order to get stronger. Bobby has to die too. If someone wants you dead, killing them first may help you sleep better at night.

\* \* \*

Dalla left Taffy in charge. I guess that means she's supposed to be keeping an eye on Jayson and keeping us safe. Like I really need her protection. I'm going to prove to Dalla that I can take care of my damn self. At least better than Taffy. Taffy is out on the front porch crying. She's been sobbing for the last twenty minutes. How is she supposed to protect me in that state? I saw her throwing up earlier. I don't have to guess what she's so sick about. It's Brip. She doesn't want to accept that it's over.

Jayson is tied to a chair in the kitchen with some sort of wire Tony bought. His hands and feet are bound so tight he looks like a mummy. Tony assured Dalla that he won't be able to escape this time and he's right. The only thing Jayson can move on his body is his eyes when he blinks. He has duct tape across his mouth. Dalla carefully takes it out when she's about to spoon feed him. He never eats. He spits out the food ever time and threatens her. He drinks the water she gives him though. I don't know why she's being so fucking nice to the man that wants us dead.

I peek out the window at Taffy. She's still bent over in a depression. So, I walk over to Jayson and rip the tape off his mouth. He flinches. I know it hurts. Inflicting pain on him makes me feel good; powerful even. He looks up at me and gives me an evil stare.

"New hairdo?" He chuckles sarcastically. "You think that's going to get you Bobby back?" He laughs again. Dalla put the tape on his mouth to keep him from taunting us. Mostly me. Every time Jayson saw me, he had something harsh to say to me. I can take it now though.

I kneel down on one leg in front of him and smile at him. I laugh at the remarks he thinks are hurting me. They only make me feel more powerful. I have the gun that Dalla left for Taffy in the waist of my pants. She left it on the coffee table before she went outside to take a cry break.

"I think it's really smart of you to style yourself before your funeral. That new do will go perfect with your coffin," Jayson hissed. I moved in closer to him to show him that his words didn't affect me. "Did you enjoy getting fucked by Ace?" he paused and gave me a serious look. At that moment, I was ready to blow his brains out. I reached for my gun but stopped myself. I used my meditation tactics to balance my emotions.

"About just as much as your sister enjoyed getting gutted by him," I chuckled back at him. He became so enraged that he started to squirm around his chair. His eyes bulged with rage. "Speaking of coffins," I pull out the gun and place the barrel against his neck, "I think it's time you meet that ugly fucking bitch, Tara. She was pathetic. I see why Bobby didn't take her out in public."

"He had me on his arm as his acceptable public display and her to fuck in private. I'm sure he only fucked her when it was super dark. That's all she was to him. You two gon get matching coffins or what?" I say and stick the gun in his mouth. Jayson stops moving. He can see in my eyes that I'm serious. This makes me feel powerful. I like the control I have. His life is in my hands and the feeling is godlike. "What?" I say to him and stick the gun deeper into his mouth, "you not hungry? Not ready to swallow these bullets?" I want this so bad, I'm shaking. "Tara is waiting for you on the other side, you know. You don't want to reunite with her?"

My breathing has increased. I'm staring back at him between two slits in my eyes. My cruel words are healing me. Speaking them makes me feel less like a victim. "The bitch looked like a fucking monkey. Just like you. Y'all mamma must have been one ugly bitch. Your matching caskets should be banana yellow," I say and wrap my finger around the trigger.

Jayson tries to say something, but I have the gun pushed too deep in his mouth. Saliva is dripping from the sides of his mouth and attaching itself to the gun. Some of it is running down my hand.

"Say good night, Jayson," I say and prepare to pull the trigger. I keep my eyes fixed on his. I don't want to miss a beat. I want to see his body jump when I pull the trigger. I want to see his brain shoot across the kitchen and splatter onto the cabinets. I want to see his neck go limp. I want to see it all. A tear is falling from Jayson's eyes. He knows it's over.

But just when I'm about to pull the trigger, I hear Taffy scream my name. I take my finger off the trigger but I keep the gun in his mouth. I don't turn around to face Taffy. I don't want her to witness this. It's not for her to see but she's here now.

"Go back outside, Taffy," I say to her.

"Don't, Lera! Please..."

I turn around and face her. I give her an evil stare. Why in the fuck does she want to protect Jayson?

"What you and this nigga best friends now?" I say to her. She's startled at the look in my eyes. She's staring at the new me.

"No. Fuck him. But Mona wants him alive. It's going to help us. Let's stick to the plan," she says and slowly walks up to me with her hands up in the air like I'm going to shoot her next. "Just give me the gun. Let's stick to the plan. Otherwise we all going to be screwed," she says.

I take a deep breath. I look at her and then back at Jayson. Tears are staining his cheeks. I give it a considerate thought and for no reason at all other than Taffy is behind me, I decide not to shoot him. At least not today. Taffy's been through a lot. This will be too much for her to witness.

I yank the gun out of his mouth and he starts to cough and spit up mucus. I immediately cover his mouth with tape but not before I spit in his face and hit him with the back of the gun. The skin on his temple pops and blood starts to stream down the sides of his face. I hand Taffy the gun without looking at her.

"Your days are numbered, asshole. I hope you're saying your prayers at night."

# DALLA BADD

"There are about four guards from what I can see," Tony calls and tells me. "All armed. Camera's surrounding the building too. Let me know when you want me to make the move."

"Can you get around the cameras?" I ask him.

"I can do what I can," he responds.

"Move forward," I give him the go ahead.

I'm about three blocks from the condo I once shared with Billy. Being on this street brings back so many memories. All the restaurants we use to eat at and the shopping is conjuring up feelings I'm desperately trying to bury. So much has happened since then. Being here is hard. But I have to get those maps and a bunch of other documents that can help Mona. I pray that they are still where he left them. They were in a shoe box in his closet the last time I checked. If it's still there, I know just where to find them.

I thought that Billy sent Jayson to us, but I got a feeling that he didn't. When I interrogated Jayson about how he found us, he evaded my questions but always mentioned Bobby, not Billy. Tony being the half-witted geniuses that he is, searched my car and found a tracking device. Jayson tracked us here. He wasn't told anything by Billy. Tony also found Jayson's car hidden in the woods. It had a tracking device on it too, but he was able to dismantle it. Lucky for us, the signal was too weak for Ranch to trace our location. I took a gamble with everybody lives returning to the lake house, but it was the safest place for us to be. Now that we have Jayson in our custody, I don't have to worry about anyone else finding us. At least for now.

I pray Mona's plan works. I don't see why it wouldn't. It's brilliant. As soon as she gives me the go ahead, we are going to fake Taffy's kidnapping and set up a ransom. This is going to get her the code to the safe. Taffy is the only person this will work for. Bobby has shown that he doesn't give a fuck about Lera and Billy has shown that same sentiment towards me but Brip definitely will open the safe for Taffy. I know he really loves her. I just hope she's game. I'm ready for all of this to end. Once Mona has the code to the safe, she can give us our cut and send us on our way. Then I can regroup and work with her about getting me my son. But then again, nothing has ever worked out that easily for me.

I'm not sure how I feel about Billy not ratting us out. In a way, I kind of wish he had. It would make forgetting him easy. Billy is all I thought about for the past two years. Letting him go is not easy but I have to do it. Leaving him is the only chance I have to survive but I'm still in love with him. His love makes me weak and in my world being weak gets you killed.

My phone is vibrating. I barely let it ring before I answer it. I know it's Tony.

"I've cleared the area," he says and I know just what he means.

"I'm on my way back up," I tell him before hanging up the phone.

I start to walk quickly back up the street towards the condo. Tony cleared the place quicker than I thought. Thank God that Billy owned the entire building. That creates fewer casualties for Tony. I'm not sure if I would have made it this far without him. He really is an amazing person and just like us wives, he's been affected by Ace. Tony was working with Ace the entire time and never knew he was the one that got Keno killed. He didn't remember Ace at all but Ace remembered him. Tony is the type of person that you don't forget. Ace manipulated him into thinking that the Badds were his enemy and in a way they were but not as big of an enemy as he was. He doesn't remember much about that night after leaving with Taffy. He just says he did something wrong. That he caused Taffy to get hurt.

He and Lera are getting close. I'm not sure if Lera knows what she's doing but he seems to be helping her. I hope she's not thinking of getting too serious with him. That will only cause more heartache. I saw them kissing. When I asked Tony about it, he had to think hard to remember kissing her. He can only focus on one thing at a time. He won't remember Lera again until he sees her. He's helping me now because I told him that we are on a mission to make the people that hurt Taffy pay. Later, I'm going to tell him who that person is but I don't think he will remember Ace unless I show him a picture.

When I get to the front of the building, I look around for cameras. I don't see any but Tony said they were there and I believe him. Tony's better at this kind of stuff than he is at anything else. I throw my hoodie over my head and put on my shades before rushing in towards the back door where Tony is waiting for me. He has his foot on the chest of one the guards. When I look over his shoulder, I see a few more men tied up and squirming. I don't know how he does it but I'm grateful.

"Get in and get out. I'll keep watch," he says to me. It's funny how he can be so wise and so ignorant at the same time. Poor Tony. I often wonder if he will ever lead a normal life.

I rush past Tony and as soon as I step inside, the familiar smell of the house hits me like a ton of bricks. Nothing has changed. Everything is just how we left it. When I walk past my dining room table, I can almost hear Billy and me laughing. When I pass the couch, I remember straddling his lap and fucking him. Living here with him was the most normal my life has ever been for me. I take a deep breath in an attempt to shake off the memories as I rush up the stairs.

Things look different upstairs. I step into our loft bedroom and instantly stop and then take a few steps back to listen. My heart starts to race at what I'm seeing. Everything is out of place. It looks like a tornado hit the bedroom. The mattress is flipped over. The dresser drawers have been completely pulled off the hinges and the tops cleared. A lamp is broken on the floor. Someone has been here, for all I know they may still be here. What where they looking for? Maybe they want the same thing that I want. I immediately start to worry that whoever was here before me, took what I came here for. They have the maps.

I look towards the closet. The door is half open and the light is still on. With Tony being within ear shot, I slowly start to make my way to the closet. If something pops off, I will fight my way out of the situation like I always do then scream for backup. I carefully make my move trying to remain as quiet as possible. Occasionally, the floor boards make a slight creaking noise as I step against them. I stop for a while then start to increase my pace. When I get to the door, I stop and listen for a moment. I don't hear anything, so I push the door open.

I'm relieved that everything is the same. Whoever destroyed the bedroom didn't bother coming in the closet or something spooked them, and they ran off. I start to get a weird feeling. Something is up. I don't have time to soak in that feeling. Whoever was here first, may be coming back. So, I get to work. I flip on the light and start pulling down shoe boxes to try and find where I last saw the maps. I remember poking tiny holes in the shoe box so I could identify it again. About the fifth box in, I hit the jackpot. I open the box and see a bunch of folded papers inside. I grab them quickly before looking over my shoulder and leaping off the floor.

* * *

It didn't take us long to find this place. Tony was able to piece together the pieces and read these maps like a pro. Mona was right. There is a second Ranch and it's not the mini Ranches that the Badds own publicly. This place is different. Much more discreet and way smaller. It can't be more than 10 acres and is not developed like the Badd Ranch. A large house sits in the middle of the land and is surrounded by trees and over grown weeds. The house is beautiful though. It looks like more of a mall than n house; it's huge. Even bigger than the big house on the Ranch. It's all white with huge windows that are covered with shutters. If it wasn't for Brock's Hummer outside, I would have thought the house was vacant. Although the house is beautiful, there is a creepiness that looms around it.

Thankfully, the map showed us a backway in. There was no way we were getting past the gate that surrounds the front entrance of the property. This place is strange. It has no guards or cameras that we can see. Whatever happens here, Brock wants no record of it.

"Are we going in?" Tony asks. He is glued to his binoculars but doesn't see any movement.

"No," I say and start to snap photos of Brock's Hummer. Going in would be suicide for both of us with Brock inside. "Let's just watch from afar and see if anything happens," I tell Tony.

"10-4," he replies.

I try to take as many pictures as I can but aside from Brock's signature Hummer parked outside, there is nothing to see. Nothing is moving. What is Brock doing in there? The house seems so quiet. Maybe it seems empty because the shutters are covering the windows but who wants to live in a dark house? I guess we are talking about Brock though.

"I think we should keep moving. Let's walk around towards the back. There ain't nothing happening in the front," Tony says. He's right.

I follow behind him. We walk through a ton of weeds and bushes to get behind the house. Vines wrap around my legs and I get stuck. I pull myself out only to step into a ditch. I can't free myself, so Tony pulls me out the rubbish of weeds and mulch. Branches and dry leaves slap me in the face as I try my best to keep up with Tony who seems unaffected by this jungle. He was about four paces ahead of me when my foot gets stuck again. When I look up at him for assistance, he is waving me in his direction and motioning for me to keep silent. Anxious to see what he is talking about, I yank my foot out the weeds so hard that I fall over in a pile of leaves and dirt. I jump back up and try my best to quietly walk towards Tony who is aggressively waving me in his direction and holding the gun that's securely placed in his waist belt. Does he have eyes on Brock? When I get to him, he points towards the back of the house and hands me his binoculars.

I push my eyes against them and see a foggy image. It's a person sitting on the back patio from the basement level of house. It has to be Brock. I hand Tony my camera and gesture for him to snap photos before I adjust the binoculars and zoom in closer to the image. Once the reflection of the image is crystal clear, my body goes numb. I don't even notice that I have dropped the binoculars out my hand until Tony picks them up and hands them back to me. This doesn't make any sense. My breathing increases and I feel like I'm having an asthma attack. I ball up my fist really tight and try to regain control. Tony is whispering something to me while he's snapping shots, but I can't hear him.

The image is stuck in my head. I convince myself that I'm seeing things, so I take a deep breath and then take another look.

Unfortunately, the image doesn't change. It's still Ace Lucky.

# BILLY BADD

I carefully stick a spoon into BJ's mouth, but he spits it out and starts wailing again. He won't stop crying. I've tried everything. I've changed him. I tried rocking him to sleep but nothing works. He misses Dalla. I know it. I miss her too.

I lift him out of his chair and try to hold him in my arms but he's fighting me. He's squirming around and kicking his little legs. My boy's a fighter. Just like his mama. I pat him on the back and pace around the room. It's all I know to do but he ain't having it. BJ's pissed. I put him in the crib I made for him and he grabs one of the wooden rails and pulls himself up. He's trying to escape. So, I lift him back up and throw him over my hip. Now he's screaming in my ear. He doesn't want me to hold him and he doesn't want me to put him down. I kiss him on the cheek and that pisses him off even more. So, I just let him scream.

Every time I look down at his big brown eyes, I see her face. He even smells the sweet way I remember her hair smelling. I sniff him every time he's in my arms. I try to sing him a song, but I don't have Dalla's voice. I remember her humming. She would hum to herself for hours and the mellow tune coming from her voice sounded like the soft sounds of a flute. It was beautiful and serene. I never told her how much her humming calmed me down. It reminded me of Mama. Mama's singing would put me to sleep. I know if Dalla was here, she would just hum to BJ and he would calm down. I can't replace her. I can't let Bobby kill her either. I have to protect her.

Bobby's got all the power right now. He has the code to the safe and a hit on my wife. I don't even have enough cash to get to the next town but the safe has all I need to put me and Dalla in early retirement. I wish I could just tell my brothers that I want out. I wish it was set up where I can sell them my shares in the Ranch but Papa Badd designed it so that we were forever bond to it. There is no way out unless I escape. This Badd way of life is worse than a blood religion.

No one has seen or heard from Bobby since he fled to the clinic. Now that Tara's eyes are open, it can only fuel his charge against Dalla. He's really going to want her dead now. If I know my brother like I think I do, the first thing he wants to tell Tara when she wakes up is that he made her pay. That's why I can't let her wake up.

I don't know what that nurse told Bobby but when I tried to visit both him and Tara in the clinic, security wouldn't let me in the room. They said they had strict orders from Bobby to guard the door and not let anyone through unless he gives them clearance. I figure she told him that I was there when her eyes opened, now he's probably wondering why I didn't say anything. That only makes Bobby trust me less. I hate that I'm losing my brother after reconnecting after being separated for so long. I love Bobby. We used to be close but this Tara and Dalla thing is going to change our relationship forever. It's sad. I want him to meet my son and I want to meet his but that ain't happening no time soon.

All I know is that his son's name is Blake and he's about 12 years old. Bobby's got him locked up like he ain't safe on the

Ranch. He don't even let him out for air. That's fucked up. Does he really think we will hurt him? The Ranch is the safest place for him to be right now. He got some retired school teacher living in the house giving him lessons and keeping him entertained. I'm not sure how much he's told him about his mother but if I know Bobby, he ain't tell the boy nothing. He needs to know about what's happening with his mother. That way, when Tara dies it won't be such a shock to him.

I told myself that if I pull Tara's plug, it won't be murder but me freeing her. Her body is still alive, but her brain is dead. Bobby just needs to let her go. Then we all can unite and focus on finding Ace and making him pay. But, I don't see that happening either. I hate to admit it, but Mona made a lot of good points at the meeting. People ain't dumb. The Ranch is closed, our wives have been cast out, and the rumors about the attack probably are spreading like wildfire. If we don't do something, we will lose it all. Honestly, I don't care though. I just need a few millions and then me, my wife, and my son are gone.

Mona think we all stupid. Bobby and Brip too distracted to see it but I know she's up to something. If I trusted her enough, I could help her get what she wants. This Ranch. She's already managed to put herself back in control. That's fine by me. It gives me more time to focus on BJ. I got a feeling that she's still in contact with Dalla. She's been barging in my house every day, helping out with BJ. At first, I resisted her help but then I just gave in. I need her. She can get him quiet. I don't know shit about babies. I just know that I love my son.

I just can't help but to wonder why she has the sudden interest in him. I know that she takes Badd blood seriously, but she's been giving BJ more attention than normal. She's checking on him and reporting back to Dalla. She has to be. At least I hope she is.

Mona is planning to meet with one of our biggest clients, Kong. She's going to reassure him that everything is ok and that we are just reorganizing our business. I got a feeling she's going to make more than one trip. She probably going to meet up with Dalla. That's why I put the tracking device in her car. A little tip I learned from Bobby. That's how Jayson was able to find Dalla. At least that's what I'm guessing.

I know Dalla went back to my lake house. It's where she's been hiding all these years. It's where she gave birth to BJ. No one knows about that place but me. If Jayson found her there, he had to be tracking her. Hopefully, Mona leads me right to my wife. My brothers are forgetting that I helped design this entire place. I know ways off this Ranch that does not require me driving out the front gate. I can come and go as I please without anyone knowing. It's what I'm going to have to do to find Dalla.

BJ is getting exhausted from all the crying he's doing. His voice is cracking and he's squirming less. He's slowing down. I guess that means he's getting sleepy. Thank God. I start rocking him even more intensely hoping it will hypnotize him to sleep. It's hard to think when he's throwing his tantrums. My son's only been on this earth a minute and he's already been through so much. Maybe that's why he is screaming so much. He's traumatized. As soon as Dalla had him, he was ripped from her arms then stolen by a maniac. I kiss my son softly, hoping that my kiss alone will erase all his bad memories.

When I look up, Mona is standing in front of me.

"That ain't gon stop him from crying," she says and walks towards us. "Give me the boy," she says and holds out her hand. I hesitate but she grabs him out of my arms already. Right away, BJ starts to calm down. That makes me wonder if BJ just doesn't want to be around me. Maybe he blames me for all this. He wouldn't be wrong.

"He been crying all morning. He won't eat nothing either," I say to Mona before falling down on to the couch exhausted.

Mona places her hand on BJ's forehead and then his neck. She's checking to see if he has a temperature. I don't know why I didn't think of that. I watch her every move and take mental notes. I have to be taught how to take care of my son.

"He's a little warm," she reveals. Then she looks in his mouth. "It's probably that new tooth coming in that's bothering him. Go get me some ice," she says and I do what she says. I return with an ice cube and Mona starts to rub it around BJ's mouth and instantly the crying stops. "Yea, that's it," she says and cradles BJ in her breast. I sigh, relieved "I'll have the nurse bring something up for him," she says to me.

"Thanks, Mona," I say genuinely. Moments like these make me realize that Mona isn't so bad.

"You ain't got to thank me. I always take care of Badd blood. You know that," she says. She looks at me for a while then asks, "Did he call you back, yet?" She's talking about Brock.

"No," I answer quickly. Mona looks disappointed although she's trying to hide it. Her eyes instantly drop, and she stares down at BJ like he has all her attention. But I know she's worried about Brock. I would be too if I wasn't putting my own family first.

"My meeting with Kong is all set up," she says. She still doesn't make eye contact with me. "I can smooth things over with him for a while, but we still gon need to open back up shop. Bobby is going to have to trust us with that code," she says.

"Well, he ain't gon trust me that's for sure and Brip ain't an option," I say to her and she gives me a strange look like she wants to tell me something but then changed her mind.

"The only way Bobby is going to give up the code is if it's guaranteed to save Tara's life and you and I both know that girl ain't waking up at least not on this side of the universe," she says and moves BJ from one arm to the next. The ice is starting to melt in his mouth.

"We got to figure something out then," I say to her and then head to the kitchen to get more ice. I want what I said to her to sink. I want her to think she can use me as an ally because just like her, I got my own plans for that safe.

I return and hand her the ice. She takes it and places it in BJ's mouth. He's starting to fall asleep in her arms now. She's silent. She's thinking about what I said.

"Brip can get us that code," she says.

"Brip?" Now I'm confused. Brip is the last person Bobby will trust with the code.

She hands me BJ. He's knocked out now. "Put him in his crib," she says, and I take him and lower him in the crib I have for him in the living room. Mona sits down on my couch and looks at me.

"I may have a plan that can save this Ranch. At least until Mr. Badd gets back," she tells me. I look at her and nod for her to keep going. "Can I trust you?" Mona asks like she's taking a gamble with me.

I don't reply right away. I just stare back at her. "As long as your plan doesn't get anybody hurt, yeah you can trust me."

"Enough people been hurt. This is purely for the sake of the Ranch. Bobby ain't in his right mind and that doesn't make him fit to control the Ranch."

"Who do you think is fit enough to take control?" I ask already knowing her response. She replies, knowing that I know she's going to respond.

"Me," she says, "At least until Mr. Badd gets back," she quickly adds again. But I don't buy that. Brock really fucked up with Mona. She doesn't need him to run this place. She never has.

"How do you know he's coming back?" I ask her.

"What you mean?" She snaps like it's the first time she's ever considered that. "Of course, he's coming back and I want to be sure the Ranch is still standing when he does."

"What's the plan?" I get back to the point.

"One of my informants got eyes on Taffy. They keeping her safe," she says but avoids eye contact with me.

"Informant?" I say to her. She's talking about Dalla. I know she is. "Who's this informant?"

"Somebody I can trust. They from the East Meadows projects," she says, still avoiding eye contact with me. I know she's lying. "We can fake a ransom," she says and looks up at me to study my reaction but I don't have one. At least not one that I'm willing to show. "They gon take pictures of Taffy all tied up and make it seem like someone got her on the streets. They won't release her until they get two million dollars. When Brip finds this out, Bobby is going to be forced to open the safe."

"That still doesn't give us the code. He can unlock the safe get the money and then relock it."

Mona gives me a strange look. She's leaving something out of her plan.

"Not if we distract him long enough to take him to Zone 6. That way, he won't have time to close the doors," she gives me a serious look. "We'll only leave him there until we regain control of this place. Then we let him out," she tries to make holding Bobby hostage sound like a formality and not a kidnapping but she's on to something.

If Bobby is in prison, then he ain't out trying to kill Dalla. With the safe unlocked, I can take my money and flee. Mona's plan is perfect, and I have the perfect thing to distract Bobby. Tara's death.

"What's your plan to distract him?" I ask her.

"I ain't thought that far into it, yet," she admits.

"I got a plan," I say and look her directly in the eyes.

"What is it?" she says.

As soon as I open my mouth to speak about it, her phone beeps three times. She's getting a text message. She looks down at the phone and jumps up.

"What the fuck!" she yells.

She is scrolling through her phone. Someone is sending her pictures. She only stops scrolling when the phone rings.

"Get Bobby and Brip. We need to meet at the Big House now!" She's so upset she's shaking. "I'm calling an emergency meeting. Set the alarms. The Ranch needs to go on immediate lock down," she says and runs out the door before answering her phone.

"What the fuck is going on?" I yell, but she doesn't stop to respond.

# MONA BADD

"We got eyes on Ace," I say to Brip and Billy. They the only two that showed up to the big house for the meeting.

Brip jumps up and pulls his gun out the waist of his pants like Ace is hiding under the table. I don't know why he has to walk around the Ranch armed 24x7. I think he's just itching to shoot a guard.

"Well what the fuck we sittin here fo, let's go!" Brip says, waving his gun in the air.

"Man put that fucking gun up! My son in this room," Billy challenges him. Brip looks at BJ and backs down. Billy turns and looks at me. "Are you sure it's him?"

I printed the photos of Ace that Dalla text me. I pulled them out my folder and placed them on the center of the table. "This is definitely him. Looks like he's trying to heal from the attack."

"Who's the informant?" Billy gives me a serious look.

"What the fuck does that matter?" Brip interjects. "Let's go kill this nigga." Brip punches the table and snarls at Ace's picture.

"We got to make sure this ain't a setup, Brip," Billy says and then looks at me.

"Fuck that." Brip pushes back in his seat and pouts. "Mona, do you have an address?"

"Yes," I say and nod my head. "I say it's worth checking out. We need to leave now," I add.

Bobby walks into the room and we all look up at him. He don't give a fuck that he late. He doesn't even apologize. He got a look on his face like we inconveniencing him.

"Man where the fuck you been?" Brip jumps up. Bobby ignores his little brother. "Mona found Ace," Brip says quickly. "We going to get him today," Brip says like everything is already confirmed.

Bobby doesn't respond. He pulls the pictures towards him and takes a seat.

"How did you get these?" he asks me.

"Man, y'all trippin right now. Y'all worried about the wrong fuckin thing. It don't fuckin matter, Bobby. She found him."

"Brips, right."

To my surprise, Billy agrees with Brip. Just a few seconds ago, he was asking the same question. "We got Tara's killer. That's all that matters," he adds.

Bobby shoots Billy an evil stare. He looks like he wants to slap the shit out of Billy. "Tara ain't dead," Bobby spits out. "You should know that more than anybody," Bobby says to Billy. The two stare each other down for a while. Then I break it up.

"Look, we need to make a move quick. Ace seems like that type a nigga that don't stay in one place too long," I say to them.

I don't tell them that Ace was at the other Ranch. I don't tell them that Brock's Hummer was there either. Until I figure out how Brock is involved with this, the less I tell them the better. But I'm confused myself. Could Brock be protecting Ace? I can't accept that. If that's true, Brock ain't just betray this Ranch but me and his kids. My other fear is that Ace is holding Brock hostage but by the looks of the photos, Ace is in no condition to be holding anyone hostage. He got a cast on his leg. He looks like he's recovering; somebody is helping him. Why the fuck is Brock keeping him safe? I got to get down there. Brock is the only person that can answer these questions for me. I don't know what they gon do when they find Brock there with Ace. I'm sure Brock will have a reasonable explanation for all this.

"Brip, get your crew together. No more than five men. We don't want to cause a big scene if this whole thing falls through," Bobby says like my information is fake news. "Billy and I will stay here and keep the Ranch on lockdown," Bobby says like he's Brock. He may have the code to the safe but he don't call no fucking shots around here.

"I'm going too," I say.

"No," Bobby says and gets up to leave like his word is final.

"She needs to be there. She can stay in the car while Brip raids the place but it's her informant that got us this info. They ain't fucking with nobody else but her. This may be our last chance to get Ace," Billy comes to my defense. He gives me a look and just like that our partnership is confirmed. "Besides, she's got an important meeting with Kong scheduled. She needs to make that meeting too. If Ace is still there, we will bring him in and take it from there."

Bobby stops at the door like he's considering what Billy is saying. Then he turns back around and faces us. "All right but Brip think strategic and not emotional," Bobby gives Brip a stern look. Brip nods at him even though we all know Brip will never be able to do what Bobby asked him. "Don't kill him. I want him alive," he says before he leaves.

"I'll try my best," Brip says. He so anxious his pupils are dilating.

Ace is going to learn just how bad he fucked up.

\* \* \*

Thank God Billy was able to get me off this Ranch and with my own driver. That way, Brip don't have to hear the conversation I'm going to have with Kong. We about 30 minutes from our location. Brip is driving like a bat out of hell. He got his whole crew with him. He actually hit a car from behind and kept going. When the car tried to chase him down for a tag number, he had one of his men point their Uzi at them. That stopped them in their tracks. You can't get more reckless than Brip Badd.

I have to admit that I'm nervous. I got a feeling we gon find more than Ace in that house. Who the fuck nurses their enemy? The man that tried to kill their wife and brainwashed his son. I guess the same man that will have gall to kill his own mother. I wonder what Brock is going to say when he sees me. When he finds out that I'm the one that found him. I don't really give a fuck. There ain't nothing he can say to me that makes any of this alright. Brock don't deserve to be the head of the Badd Ranch. This shit right here is beyond treason and I'm going to get his brothers to see that. Especially when they find out how Mama Badd really died. They may try to kick us all off the Ranch but if my plan with Kong works out, then they gon be the only niggas leaving.

While Brip is still hype, I got to put Taffy's ransom plan in motion. Catching Ace may unsettle him too much and I'm relying on his rage to push Bobby to unlock that safe. When Brip finds out that someone has "kidnapped" Taffy, hell ain't gon have no fury like his rage. I hate that Brock put me in this situation where I have to turn on my own, but I got to look out for me and mine.

I got a feeling that Billy want out of this shit anyway. That makes my moves even easier. He's one less Badd I have to worry about when it comes time for me to put them off the Ranch. I can't tell him that I'm working with Dalla though. He going to try and find her, and I can't have that, yet. If Dalla finds out that Billy's still in love with her, which he is, she's dumb enough to drop everything she's doing for me and run off with him. I still need her. She's too valuable for me to cut ties with right now. I can't take the Badd Ranch without her. Honestly, it would be nice to keep her on the payroll. She's too resourceful.

"We will be pulling up in just a minute, Mrs. Badd," my driver tells me. We are tailing as close behind Brip as we can.

I look out the window and notice that much like the Ranch, it's out in the middle of nowhere. Some small hick town with dirt roads pastures full of yellow bladed grass. We take a sharp turn and the car starts to crush gravels. We stop behind Brip. There's a gate but it doesn't have the signature Badd emblem on it. Brip jumps at the car and places both hands on the gate like he really can yank it open. He motions for my driver to back up and he does just that then he hops in the car, backs up a bit and speeds toward the gate. I close my eyes and hear a large popping sound, Brip is already inside. We follow behind him. So much for being discreet.

We pull up a long narrow drive way. It curves like a half moon and is surrounded by weeds that are taller than me. This place is not kept. I start to see the roof of the house as we continue to make our way up the hill. I know we are in the right place when I see the clay colored shingles on the roof that looks the same as the pics Dalla sent me. Brip is speeding so fast that a huge dirt cloud fogs in front of us, blocking our view. I wish he would be a little more discreet. Ace is in no condition to run but I don't want him to spook Brock. Brock is liable to shoot us all.

We stop in front of a house the size of a mini mall. The house is nice, but it looks out of place with the jungle that's surrounding it. The first thing that I notice is that Brock's Hummer is gone. I look down at the picture and then at the spot where it was last parked. I can still see the tire marks pressed in the dirt. Maybe he put the car in the garage. It's definitely enough room for it. I set my sights on what looks like a five-car garage. My eyes lead up and I see the blinds bend down. Someone is inside. They know we are here. I bet it's Ace.

Brip doesn't waste any time. He and the men jump out the car and start shooting up the house. "Brip." I jump out the car, duck, and yell, but he can't hear me. I jump back in the car and take cover. I cover my ears and stick my head in between my legs. Glass is shattering everywhere. I can hear it breaking against the concrete. When the gun fire stops, I pop my head up and Brip shoots at the door enough to kick it open. He's already inside. I open the door to follow behind them, but my driver jumps out the car and grabs me.

"Mr. Badd gave me strict orders to keep you out the house until the subject has been apprehended," he says. I don't fight him. He's right. Brip is going so crazy; I'm likely to catch one of his bullets. I just pray he doesn't mistake Brock for Ace and end up shooting him.

We take cover in the car for all of 15 minutes when the gun fire finally stops.

"I'm going in," I tell my driver and he doesn't stop me. When I get inside, the first thing I notice is that the house smells like fresh paint. I walk further inside and see the mess Brip made of the place. Bullets blasted through the walls, causing large holes. Chandeliers and ceiling fans are hanging on by a string waiting to crash on to the marble floors, but the house looks like it's under construction anyway. Some rooms are finished, and some are not. There is no sign of Ace or Brock either. Someone is here though. I saw them from the window.

"Brip," I call out, but he doesn't respond. I see one of his men clearing a room and I grab him. "Where's Brip?"

"He went upstairs," he responds.

"Go check the basement," I tell him and he follows my orders.

I look up the staircase. I don't see anything, so I start to explore the house. The inside is fancy. I can't imagine Brock decorating this place. He don't give a shit about decorating a house. When I make my way to the dining room, I get confused. A beautiful long table dressed with plate settings and goblets adorn the table. This house is lived in. This is not what I expected. I expected a work station and a blow-up mattress. That's more of Brock style.

When I get to the kitchen, it's fully loaded. I open the fridge and food is inside. He's been feeding this nigga? By the looks of it, Ace has been eating good. Then I notice something odd. Food for a toddler. The top shelf is full of those little kid-sized lunches you get pre- packaged. I know Ace got hurt during the attack but is he so fucked that he on baby food now? I close the fridge and move on.

I walk back towards the foyer. Brip is coming down the stairs holding his gun. He looks disappointed.

"You didn't find him?" I ask.

"Man, ain't nobody here," he says disappointed.

"No, somebody is upstairs. You ain't look good enough. I saw the blinds move above the garage."

"Above the garage. Shit!" He cocks his gun and takes off. "That ain't upstairs. Where the fuck is the garage?"

I don't know. This house is too big for me to guess. "It's got to be to the left of the foyer. That's where it's located outside." Brip runs in the direction that I point him in. We open a door and I was right. A long narrow hallway leads us to the garage and the in-law suite that's on top of it. Brip runs up the stairs but I flick on the light. I have to see Brock's Hummer but to my surprise, the garage is empty. Nothing is in it but a kid's tricycle and a discarded box to what looks like a toddler bed. Now, I'm really confused. I begin to wonder if we are at the right house.

Just as I go to meet Brip upstairs, I hear a woman screaming. Who the fuck is that?" Brip comes downstairs, holding a woman by her hair. Following behind her is a little boy a little older than

BJ. When I get a closer look, I realize that I know who this bitch is. She's one of the breeders I put off the Ranch for claiming Brock was in love with her. What the fuck was she doing here? As soon as I ask myself that question, I realize I already know the answer. This is her and Brock's home. When she sees me, she freaks out, but I don't want her to blow my cover. I act like I don't know her. Brip don't need to know this is the second Ranch.

"Where the fuck is that nigga?" Brip yells, holding her in one hand and his gun in the other but she just keeps screaming.

"Please don't hurt my son. Please don't hurt my baby."

"Answer the question bitch or you dead," Brip says.

"Brip, cuff her and put her in the car. Take them back to the Ranch for questioning. We ain't gon get nothing out of her, here," I say.

"You sure? She could be hiding that nigga." Brip looks at me.

"He's not here. I promise. It's just me and my son now," she says, and I start to wonder if she's talking about Brock or Ace.

"Get her in the car and go check out the basement," I tell Brip, just so I can get a moment to explode on the inside.

He follows my orders and leaves me to collect myself. Brock isn't here. Neither is Ace. That's why his Hummer is gone. If he returns, he'll know by the looks of his house and his missing whore and child that Brip's been here. Brock being here with Ace was one thing, but him having a whole other life behind my back is a whole other story. My entire life with him has been a fucking lie. The pain of it all is starting to burn my eyes, but I take it. I'll be damned if I cry. I take a few deep breaths and redirect my emotions into anger. Fuck Brock and his new partner Ace. I sniff up my negative emotions like I have a hoover vac built into my spirit. By the time I exhale, they gone. At least for now.

I walk back down the hall towards the foyer when I start to hear a lot of commotion. What the fuck is going on now?

"Mona," Brip runs to me, meeting me midway in the hallway, "you got to get to the basement. You won't believe this shit." I increase my steps. I pray that Ace is down there with his head blown off his neck but that's just wishful thinking.

Brip rushes down the wide staircase leading to the basement. I still feel sick after seeing Brock's mistress. My legs don't feel stable, so I grab on to the banister and carefully take my time. Brip is long gone before I take the last few steps that lead into the basement.

"Mona," Brip calls out. He's rushing me. When I step into the basement, it's one huge room with a hallway that branches off into smaller rooms. The floor is carpeted. If it wasn't for sun light shining in through the patio door, it would have been completely dark. When I see a wheelchair, I know this is where Ace had been hiding out. There is no sign of Brock though.

I walk over to Brip who is standing outside a huge metal door. There is a digital keypad attached to the door. The door is eerily similar to the door we installed for our safe at the Ranch. If I'm not mistaken, this is exactly what that is. It's a safe but it's not locked. The door is wide open. Brip is standing half in the door and half out. He's waving me in and shaking his head in disbelief.

When I step inside, I stop instantly. I'm shocked. The safe is not just a safe but a surveillance room. Every entry point and the facilities at the Ranch is being monitored live. We even see Bobby sitting at Tara's bedside at the clinic. What the fuck was Brock thinking exposing us like this? Aside from the occasional stack of rolled up bills sporadically placed on the floor, the safe has been completely emptied. Ace must have emptied the safe in a hurry.

"This nigga been watching our every move. Can you believe this shit?!" Brip is pissed. He still has no idea that this is the second Ranch and I don't plan to tell him. "He must have seen us leave the Ranch and put two and two together. He knew we were coming for him," Brip said. That made sense but it's not Ace that knew, it's Brock.

So many things are going through my mind that I can't pull together one single thought. Brip is looking at me for instructions and answers but I'm too speechless. So I look down at the floor and start to count the money rolls when my eyes land in the corner at a man with his back against the wall and his hands up. He's trembling. Blood is gushing from his lip and head. Brip's put a good whooping on him. Now they got their guns on him.

"Who the fuck is that?" I point.

"I don't fucking know," Brip says. Like this mystery is beyond solving. "We found him in here. The nigga won't speak, either" Brip says and kicks at the man who tumbles over to his sides and curls up into a ball like a baby. He's babbling like a baby too. Brip kicks him again. "You been spying on us, nigga? Huh?" Brip starts to get violent but I stop him.

"Cuff him. Take him back to the Ranch. We will get him to talk," I say and Brip's men pull him up and pin him against the wall. The man continues to babble like he got a speech impediment or something.

"Mrs. Badd, I don't think you gon be able to get this nigga to talk," one of Brip's men say before prying the man's mouth open with his finger, "somebody cut this nigga's tongue out."

Even Brip gasp at the sight of the man's empty mouth. "What the fuck!" Brip and I both say in unison. We both look at each other. We're speechless.

# TAFFY BADD

This can't be real. It can't be. Or maybe it's a sign that everything is going to be okay. That Brip will forgive me and our lives will go back to normal. Or maybe it's a curse. Either way, I don't understand how it's real.

I flush the toilet and roll up the pregnancy test in a piece of tissue then hide it in the trash can. It's the third test I took this week. I convinced Dalla to let me go on a store run with Tony and picked up four different brands of the test; I needed to be sure. I've had enough miscarriages to know when I'm losing a baby. That's what I assumed was happening when a gush of blood fell out my body and into mama's toilet but lately my body hasn't felt the same. Or maybe it has. I'm having the symptoms that I been having when pregnant: fatigue, nausea, and extreme exhaustion. The first week, I wrote it off as stress but when my period never returned, I couldn't deny it. I had to address this. So, I took the test. All three of them and they all came back positive.

At first, I told myself I was imagining the symptoms because I just wanted everything to go back to normal but I'm still pregnant. I'm going to take the last pregnancy test tomorrow just to confirm. But I already know. I'll just give myself until tomorrow to be in denial but then I'm going to have to deal with what this means for me. And Dalla and Mona's plan. This gives me even more reason not to go through with it.

Brip and I have hurt each other enough. Even if we don't end up together, I can't betray him the way they're asking me to. I plan on keeping this pregnancy a secret. I don't trust any of these women. Everyone has their own agenda. Even Lera. Dalla thinks she's doing ok now that she's talking but she's not back to normal or the way I remembered her to be. She's someone else and it's sad but I don't think she'll ever be the same again. When I saw her in the kitchen with Jayson, I knew it took everything in her not to shoot him. She has so much anger in her that hurting people is the only way to stop the pain. When I look in her eyes, it's like someone else is staring back at me. I feel sorry for her but we all got screwed over. I would have never in a million years thought it would have ended like this for any of us but here we are.

I feel strong enough to survive without Brip. That's just who I am but I also feel weak enough to stop everything just for another chance with him. Including this plan. Dalla ask me every day if I'm ready because she knows I'm not. I never officially confirmed that I would do it. The chances of Brip forgiving me will go from zero to negative zero if I betray his entire family by faking my own ransom. I broke his heart, his nephew shot him, and his enemy tried to kill him. How much more can a person take?

I'd rather we all sit down and discuss this amicably. Why do we have to steal? Why the lies? Why the betrayal? Haven't we all been through enough? Now that I'm pregnant, I have my family to think about. I don't even consider Malcolm as the father anymore. When Brip shot Malcolm, my feelings for him died with him. Thoughts of him are gone. I should have never gone back there. I really played myself allowing him to set me up like that. But I was hurt. When you hurt, you do stupid shit. But not this time. I ain't fucking doing what they're asking me. I'll leave before they make me do it. I'll take my chances out on the street. The thought of this makes me gag. I turn on the sink and my body tries to throw up but my stomach is too empty. Nothing comes out but saliva and yellowish stomach acid.

"You okay?" I hear Lera ask from behind the bathroom door. I guess she hears me in here, spitting up.

"I'm fine. I just need some privacy," I say to her with annoyance. I need my own space. This house is too small for all of us.

"Ok, but we have talk. I'll give you a minute," she says before she leaves.

I don't know what the fuck Lera wants to talk with me about but I'm not in the mood to talk. I've been avoiding Dalla and now I have to deal with her crazy ass. I take a deep breath and splash cold water on my face before I exit the bathroom. I want to appear normal as possible. I don't trust what Dalla or Lera will do once they find out that I'm still pregnant. Lera will kill for revenge and Dalla will kill for money. That makes both of them dangerous bitches.

I step out the bathroom and see Dalla sitting on that makeshift couch in the so called living room. The only room this house has is the bathroom. The rest of it is one big open space. No walls to lend any privacy. Jayson is asleep in the chair they keep him tied to. He's eating now. I guess Lera putting a gun in his mouth woke up his appetite. Dalla looks directly at me like she's been waiting for me to come out the bathroom, but I ignore her. I turn around and see Lera on the back porch with Tony. She and Tony have been getting chummy with each other. Lera acts like a school girl around him and Tony actually blushes when he sees her. I didn't know that was possible.

"You got a minute?" Dalla asks and gets up.

"No, Lera wants to talk with me," I tell her.

"About what?" She seems concerned. I shrug my shoulders. "Jayson told me what happened," she says, but she's really trying to ask why I didn't tell her.

"So," I turn to her, "he deserved it."

"Yeah, but he's a part of our plan. Our plan will sound more believable if we throw Jayson in the mix. Had Lera killed him, we would be set back. This plan is happening Taffy," she says to me like she's confirming it instead of informing me. "I hope you're ready."

"Why is all this banking on me?" I ask. "Lera's here. You hear. Hell, they'll pay anything to get you on the Ranch. Bobby will even pay to get Jayson back. So, why me?"

"We're both doing what Mona thinks is best?"

"When did you start eating Mona's ass?"

"Hey, I don't eat ass," Dalla snaps. "Mona is the only person that can fix this shit we're in and I trust her. Without her we are fucked," Dalla folds her arms defensively around her chest. "I know you're still in love with Brip. I still love Billy but loving on a person who doesn't love you back is like watering a dead plant. It's a waste of your emotions."

"Brip loves me," I say to her and she rolls her eyes like I'm delusional but she doesn't know shit.

"Well why isn't he here?" I can't answer her question. "How are you going to survive? How are you going to take care of your mother and brother? You going to become an actress?" she says condescendingly, "a gas station clerk? Maybe you all can move in the projects, get on welfare, and sign Tony up for disability."

"Fuck you," I snap. She has struck a nerve. Everything she's mentioned is my worst nightmare. I have no way to take care of myself or mama or Tony. I'm worse than I was before I met Brip. Mama and I were struggling and I'm not as young as I used to be. I have no ambitions, no skill, and no will to try anything new. Mama's getting old and Tony isn't getting any better. They're both going to need my support. I think about what Keno would want me to do in this situation. I know that he would want me to put family first but that's hard because I consider Brip to be family too.

"I'm not trying to be a bitch, Taffy," Dalla says to me. Her voice is softer. "I'm trying to get you to wake up and see the light." She stares back at me. She's giving her words time to sink in but I don't need any time. I know she's right. I just don't want to go about it the way her and Mona want. I don't want to betray Brip.

Dalla sits back down on the couch and stares at me with her legs crossed. When she's finished staring at me, she uncrosses her legs, picks up a notebook, and flips it open. She starts writing something. I wonder if she's plotting out her and Mona's plan for me. I don't stay long enough to ask. I walk toward the patio to meet Lera, but I can feel her staring at my back. When I pass the kitchen, Jayson is sipping on bottled water. Dalla loosened up the grips on his hands so he can have more movement and removed the tape from his mouth. That really pissed Lera off. Now, she's even more motivated to kill Jayson. I hope that's not what she wants to talk to me about.

I see Tony training Lera to fight from the sliding glass door. He is showing her the same moves he showed me over 20 years ago. I watch them before I step outside. Lera is starting to act just as crazy as Tony. Maybe they are a perfect match. Tony's teaching her how to punch and kick. He's taking it serious and so is she. When Lera tries to punch him, he blocks her hit and she falls to the ground. Tony bends over quickly and scoops her up with one pull then analyzes her entire body for any signs of injury. Lera tries to assure him she's ok. She blushes at him before she wraps her arms around his neck to hug him. She kisses him on the forehead and then the lips and Tony looks like he's about to faint with excitement. Then he switches gears and continues to train her like the kiss never happened.

I hate to break up their little romantic karate session, but after I speak with Lera, I plan to go out to the front porch with a blanket and fall asleep on the hammock. It's the most peaceful place in this tiny house. And the only place I can get some privacy. I don't want to be disturbed.

At the sound of the door sliding open, they both immediately stop. Lera gets in a fighting stance and turns towards me. When she sees it's just me, she relaxes and straightens up her posture. She looks up at Tony for approval and he nods his head and smiles at her like a job well done.

"What's up?" I say to Lera through a heavy sigh.

Lera looks over my shoulder for Dalla. She whispers for me to close the door and motions for me to follow her and Tony further into the yard. What the fuck are they up to? I don't have time for this shit. But, I follow them anyway. They walk down the stairs that leads out to the woods a few feet away from the house. When we stop, Lera looks at me like she has something important to tell me. But first, she inquires about Dalla and Jayson.

"Are they still up?" she asks, looking over my shoulder. I just lie and shake my head no to avoid Lera's pre-rant. Lera takes a deep breath and places her hands on her hip. She paces around a bit before she exhales. Tony gives her a supportive rub on the back. "Tony and I are leaving tonight, and we want you to come with us," she says carefully. She keeps her eyes fixed on me and rubs the top of her head. Her hair is starting to grow back and the cut actually shapes her face nicely. It brings out her feminine features. Her beautiful deep-set brown eyes pop but the hair cut does nothing for the crazy look behind her eyes.

"What?" Is all I can bring myself to say. I'm too exhausted to talk Lera out of this crazy idea. I hate that she has Tony involved in it. "I'm not going anywhere, Lera. You know it's not safe out there for you. Once we get the money, you can go wherever you want and do whatever you want," I feed her the same rhetoric Dalla fed to me a few minutes ago.

"Fuck the money. I want blood," Lera snarls. "Who's supposed to be protecting me here? Dalla?" she mocks, then sucks her teeth. "You really think if it came down to it, she'd protect you?" Lera stares hard at me. She has her arms defensively folded against her chest. She takes two slow steps toward me. I take one step back because I don't trust the crazy bitch. "Maybe you waiting on Brip to arrive on his black horse and save you," she chuckles. She's mocking me now. "If that's the case, you keep waiting because he doesn't love you or that baby, Taffy," she says casually. I gasp at her revelation and then quickly look up at Tony. How did she know about the baby? I can't let Dalla find out.

"Lera, I lost the baby. You don't remember...I..."

Lera cuts me off. "I'm not stupid." She taps on her temple with her index finger. "You're still pregnant. Brip would rather you and that baby die. That means he ain't never going to show up for you like you think he is. Brip is no longer your husband, he's just a fantasy" she says to me like I'm dumb and shakes her head then steps back.

This bitch just pissed me off. I don't give a fuck how screwed her mind is right now. She don't come at me like that. She don't know shit about me and Brip's relationship. Unlike her and Bobby, our relationship was real.

"Look," I step towards her waving my finger but Lera stands her ground, "just because your marriage to Bobby was fake doesn't mean mine was with Brip. Brip wasn't perfect but when he said those vows to me, he meant it. He's nothing like Bobby. Bobby was in love with another woman way before he ever considered being with you, they have a family and..."

Before I can finish my last sentence, Lera hauls off and slaps the shit out of me. I am stunned. When I look back at her, she has her fist balled up and ready to swing. I look at Tony and he is staring at the moon, unfazed by what is happening between us. I have two choices. Knock this bitch out cold, just like I know I could or just walk away and leave her to her sad pathetic self. I thought about it hard. The more my face stung from her slap, the more I wanted to retaliate, but I had to think about my child. My babies been through enough and honestly, I feel sorry for Lera. Bobby broke her heart and Ace turned it black. That makes her a sad but scary case. I look at her, still rubbing the sides of my face and give her my best fuck you bitch look before I walk away.

"Wait," she cries out desperately. I stop for a few seconds. "I'm sorry," she says like she's about to break down and cry. She's the most fragile, defensive woman I know. "I'm asking you to come because I actually care about you. Tony needs you too."

"I'm staying because of Tony and my mother. And this baby," I admit to her. "After everything we been through, we need a stable home environment and that money Mona and Dalla are working on getting us is going to provide that," I say more to myself than her. "If you want to go, then we can't stop you but you're not taking my brother with you," I say in a strict tone. "Sorry, Lera."

"But I don't have any family. I don't have anyone. You have it all," her voice cracked.

"After you get the money, you can have it all too. Just be patient, Lera. You going to get what you deserve and you're going to get your revenge," I say to her.

Tears are streaming down her eyes. Tony sees her crying and wraps his arm around her shoulders and kisses her on top of her head. He doesn't even know why she's crying.

"You're right. I will get my revenge. Every Badd is going to pay," she says and gives me an evil stare before walking further into the woods. Tony follows behind her like a puppy.

Is she threatening Brip now? I shake off another added fear of someone hurting Brip and walk back in the house. Lera is the last person that I should be concerned about hurting Brip. She'll do more damage to herself than she ever can do to him.

*  *  *

"Wake up," I feel someone shaking me. I think I'm still dreaming. About four hours into the best sleep I've had since we got here, someone is waking me up. I open my eye and pray it's not Lera. It's not. It's Dalla.

"What?" I groan. "What's going on?"

"Lera is gone! And she took Jayson, Tony, and both our guns with her," Dalla says in one breath.

"Fuck!" I sigh and stumble to my feet.

# MONA BADD

The East Meadows Projects is always going to be home to me. These are my people. Before I swore my oath to the Badds, they had my complete loyalty. They still do but just in a different way.

I opened the door and let them get a peek inside of this Badd life. That's why Kong is able to run the place like he does. These projects look a lot better than I remembered them looking. He's keeping everything up just like he promised to do. All the roofs got new shingles. The streets are freshly paved. The laundromat got new washer and dryers and the kids got a playground that's better than Disney Land. Kong keeps his word. That's why I trust him so much.

I'm sitting in the waiting area of his building now. He took one of the buildings and busted through all the walls, making it his own castle. Apparently, a lot has changed since I left. One thing is that my sister Nicchi is to these projects what I am to the Ranch. She and Kong supposed to be fucking now and she is confusing that shit for a relationship. That don't surprise me though. Nicchi stay confused. Fucking Kong is the closest she can get to being on my level and the bitch still got mountain to climb before she can meet me eye to eye.

I almost didn't get this meeting because of her. Everything goes through Nicchi now. A few years ago, I used to be able to reach Kong direct. Now that her ass is blocking, I got to wait at least 48 hours before I hear anything back. If she wasn't my sister, her ass would be fucked up already. All I got to do is say the word and Kong will be done with her ass but I don't. These projects and Kong is all Nicchi got going for herself. Without it, she another welfare bitch from 6B.

"Nicchi, how much longer you gon make me wait? I got business to get back to on the Ranch. I ain't got time for all this shit. You know we don't wait," I tell Nicchi to let her know I'm done playing her ego game. I got business to tend to after this.

Kong ain't gon like it but I ain't gon be able to stay as long as I planned. Kong hates when people change plans on him. When we set up our meeting, he put it on his calendar for an hour. Kong is anal as fuck and usually I don't buy into his little games but I got to come humble today. That's one reason I ain't slap the shit out of Nicchi yet.

"Who is we?" Nicchi smacked her lips and raised her brow at me.

Now, she looking down at them nine-inch acrylic nails of her. She got them painted bright orange. She's chewing gum with her mouth open revealing her gold fronts. She's eating off most of her lipstick and the black eyeliner she used to line her red lips. I guess she's supposed to be dressed to impress cause she got them fat ass thighs stuffed inside a pencil skirt. If the bitch was going for a corporate look, she could have at least put on a button-down shirt, but instead she is wearing white halter top and her body is in no condition to be doing that. Jelly rolls are doing a 360 around her entire body, encircling her like a literal spare tire but you can't tell this bitch she don't look fly.

"Nicchi, you my sister but don't forget who you talking to. You hear me?" I warn her and she sucks her teeth and rolls her eyes at me.

"I'm just trying to look out for you, sister," she says condescendingly.

Nicchi has always been a smart ass but she ain't never got out of line and disrespected like she is doing now.

"When the fuck I ever need you to look out for me?" I stand up. I think I know where she getting at.

"The streets talk, Mona. All ain't good in paradise so don't come over here tripping and slanging orders like you run shit. The East Meadows projects ain't a part of yo Ranch. Some say y'all voice ain't got the same bass it used to have. That lion starting to roar like a pussy," she pauses for emphasis, "cat," she adds then snickers and walks away. "Gon on back to see Kong but don't go over time. He got another important meeting after you," she says to me with her back turned.

I got a right mind to jump and snatch that bitch back. I watch her fat ass wobbling down the hallway like she something. Her fucking ass looks like garbage full of boiling hot water that toppled over. I keep my composure though. What I feared has come to pass if Nicchi is bold enough to talk shit. People know about the attack. We getting weak and it ain't even been a full two months yet. I got to play it cool for Kong though. He knows me better than anybody and if he sees any sign of worry on my face, then the ball is going to be in his court. And I like to be on top. If he remembers how we used to fuck, he'd know that.

I try to suppress my anger by squeezing and releasing my hands into fist. It helps a little but not nearly enough. If Nicchi feeling bold enough to talk shit right to my face, what the fuck is everybody else thinking? How much does one bitch have to take? First, I find out about Brock's live in house whore, then I learn that he may be in cahoots with Ace Lucky. Did he really give Ace full access to surveillance of the Ranch? And why did he clear the safe? What the fuck is he planning? I got to get back to the Ranch to question that whore before she blows Brock's entire cover. I don't want the brothers to know that the house Ace was at belongs to the Ranch. They likely to throw me out on the street for that shit.

I don't know what to think about Brock anymore. I'm dead in the middle of fuck you and I love you with him. But, every day, I'm leaning more to the fuck you side. I start to pace around the room. When I sit still for too long, thoughts of Brock and Ace and this entire disaster starts to possess me and I ain't able to think right. I need my right mind when I talk to Kong. I hear children laughing and focus on that sound; it helps take my mind off things.

I walk over to the window and look down at children playing on the playground we donated to them. I like that Kong got they playground literally in his backyard. The kids can play knowing that ain't nobody gon fuck with them. I watch them swinging off the monkey bars and sliding down that custom made seven-foot sliding board. They are having a ball. They are having such a good time that don't even know they mama's on crack and they daddies in prison and that they dirt poor. When most of them get of age, they come work for Kong. They got it made and all that shit is because of the name Nicchi trying to disrespect. I'll woman up and let that shit slide today though. But, today and today only.

Just as I'm about to walk away from the window, I notice two of me and Brock's boys from the breeders. The breeding quarters was my idea. I did it as a way to prove that I was open-minded and devoted to the Badd life. It was my sacrifice. Allowing Brock to sleep with all those women wasn't easy, but I trusted him and I trusted my plan. I took all that pain and swallowed that shit whole. It made me stronger than ever. I thought that more Badds was what we needed to stay strong. I hope I'm not wrong.

It's so shameful. I know that Brock shut down the breeding quarters and sent our children back to their birth moms, but it's still hard seeing them here. I loved those kids just like they were my own. When I'm screening breeders, I disclose that there may be a rare chance that the kids may have to return. I'm sure they happy. It gives them more street creds to walk around claiming Badd blood plus they get a nice check every month too. This makes us look like fools. Now, I'm pissed off again. That's why Nicchi being so fucking bold. I walk away from the window. It's time that I meet with Kong. It's now or never.

*  *  *

Kong is sitting down on a custom made lazy boy that's the size of three chairs with his legs spread open. He got a huge plate of ox tails and red beans and rice in between them. He is eating with his hands. Even the rice. When he looks up at me, he smiles but really it looks like he's growling. That's just how that nigga smile looks; like a Pit Bull's growl. All gums and little bit size teeth.

"Mona," he says my name. He talks like he gargling but his voice is just as deep as the ocean. Words flow out of his mouth like waves crashing against rocks. He starts to lick his large sausage-like fingers and snaps them for Nicchi to grab the plate. He leans up three times at a fail attempt to lift his weight from the low sitting chair. The fourth time is the charm. Now, he's standing up and is even bigger than he was the last time I saw him. His body is blocking the sun light. All of a sudden the room gets dim as he walks toward me with his arms stretched out and lips perched for a kiss.

Nicchi is really getting pissed now. I hug him and he plants a greasy kiss on the side of my cheek.

"We need to talk in private," I dictate, looking directly at Nicchi.

"You the boss," he says through a smile. "Get the fuck out," he says to Nicchi and she does just what he says but gives me the evil eye on her way out.

Kong walks less than two feet back to his chair and is already out of breath. When he plops down in it, it feels like the floor underneath us is going to cave in.

"You look troubled, Mona," he says.

"Well then you ain't looking at me right," I reply and stare. I don't want him to see me sweat. I don't know how much he knows about Ace's attack on us but by the way he's acting, he knows enough.

"Nothing's changed," he says, then looks at me with admiration. "You still ain't to be fucked with."

"Now why would that ever change?" I ask but don't leave any time for him to reply. "I got a proposition for you."

"Straight to business, huh?" he says and places his hands on his stomach. "Well, I can't consider what you offering until you open the Ranch back up for business. I need my crematory back. I got about 40 bodies that need to burn before they rot. They can only stay in my freezer for so long," he starts to complain.

"I came here to tell you in person that the Ranch is opening back up for business. And to personally apologize for the delay. We just had some issues we had to work through," I give him a sincere look, but he smiles at me like I'm bullshitting him.

"Issues?" he repeats. "That's putting it lightly," he says through another chuckle. "You guys came real close to being took. That makes my clients nervous and it makes me look fucking weak. You know I don't like that, Mona," Kong shakes his head in disagreement.

"I ain't never known you to be one to gossip," I sternly reply. "You know as well as I do that niggas gon try you every day but only the strongest survive. Am I not facing you right now?"

"What about Brock?" he says quickly, but I can't respond right away. I hesitate.

"What about him?" I repeat, and he laughs again. Does he know something I don't know?

"What's the proposition?" he asks me like I'm humoring him.

I don't respond right away. I just look him dead in the eyes. Then I pick up my purse and prepare to leave. I play it real tough just to remind him that it would be helpful to have him but I really don't need him.

"Fuck it," I say and swing my purse over my shoulder. "When you ready to respect and honor what I have to offer you, I may give you a second chance. Everything you got right now is because of us Kong," I say to him and his nostrils start to flare. He hates when I remind him that his ass wouldn't be shit without the Badds. "And just as quick as the Badds giveth, the Badds can take it away. You worrying about some dead ass nigga trying us? Shit, even Satan tempted Christ twice but he died and rose again cause he's immortal. And you know us Badds are like Christ. Don't ever forget that shit, nigga!" I stare back at him. He's feeling unsettled in his chair. He starting to squirm around a bit. "A wise man says it's foolish to turn your back on your religion cuz come judgment day, there will be no mercy," I warn him and walk out the door.

"Mona wait," Kong yells my name before I even get a foot out the door. I can hear the fear in his voice. Good. I wait few seconds before I turn around just to remind him who the fuck I am. "Damn, I'm just trying to see if you still got it. That's all," he says and opens his arms like I'm supposed to come and hug him. "Whatever you got for me, I'm game, but I'm gon need that crematory back up and running," he says. Now he's almost begging. He's tough, but there are hundred niggas that will give their first born for the exclusive contract we have with him. Without the crematory, Kong can't play the reaper and that's what keeps him feared and relevant.

I turn and stare Kong down before I speak. I make sure to give his ass my best don't fuck with me look and he gets it. "I'll call you," I tell him. "You've already wasted enough of my time," I say.

"Mona...please..wait," he yells.

Now, I got that nigga right where I want him. Begging. I turn around slowly.

"You don't ask why, you just ask when and where," I tell him before I go on. He nods. I have his full attention. "I need an army. No less than 25 of your best men. I want them young. All between the ages of 18-25 and ready to lay down they life for me and only me. When I ask them mutha-fuckas to jump, you already know how I want them to reply." Kong nods. He gets where I'm coming from. "Then, I want you to put the word out on the street that any nigga who can deliver me Ace Lucky, dead or alive, will have a seat at my table." Kong's eyes widen with curiosity. I'm confirming the rumors for him.

"That ain't gon be easy. He got his own network you know," Kong informs me.

"Fuck his network and fuck the easy route. You got plenty of hungry niggas out here that are ambitious enough to do anything to eat at our table. Just put the word out," I stare back at Kong and he looks uncomfortable. I can't read it. Kong ain't never uncomfortable and I know he ain't threatened by Ace Lucky. Or is he?

"You right," he agrees with me.

"Also, I need you to ask around and see if anybody knows who this nigga is," I put my phone under his nose and flash a picture of the tongueless man we found at the second Ranch. I got to know who he is and he ain't the talkative type to tell me.

Kong stares down hard at the photo without blinking. For a split second, I get the feeling he already knows this dude.

"Send me the pic. I'll do what I can," he says and pushes back in his seat. He's looking directly at me. It's like he purposely trying not to avoid eye contact with me. "Where you say you find him at again?"

"I didn't say," I repeat quickly and walk towards him. He's still staring at me.

"Anything else?" He asks with eyes fixed on me. I don't respond at first. Something feels strange. Or, maybe I'm just paranoid. Kong raises his hands at me as if to say "is that it?"

"Naw, one more thing," I say. I'm hesitating now but I got to gamble right now. Kong waits for me to speak. "I need a house. A nice spot. An in-ground pool. A 24-hour chef and housekeeper. Plus I need it to be guarded around the clock. Nobody goes in or leaves without permission."

"I got something like that in Gwinnet. Real discreet and luxurious. It's fit for a Queen."

"Perfect, text me the address. I may need this house for a few months."

"Cool," he says to me.

"Cool?" I repeat to him more like a question. Then, looked intently at him.

When I realize that I have Kong right where I want him, I stop feeling paranoid.

I turn to walk out the door.

"Ain't you forgetting something?" When I hear the floor boards squeaking and the room dims, I know Kong is standing up. I turn back around and he is towering over me like mountain to a tree. "What's in it for me?" he says and waves his hands in the air.

"If you do everything I ask, I'm going to give you an exclusive contract to a mini Ranch. I'll have the crematory moved there plus put a house and two other facilities of your choice on your land to start you off. I'll do all of this shit for you at the same price we are renting the crematory to you at." I step back and let what I say sink in but I don't have to. Kong is looking at me like it's Christmas morning and I'm fucking Santa Claus. He's happy as fuck but trying his best to hide it.

He starts laughing but really it sounds like he's having an asthma attack. "I got you Mona. You know I'm good for it," he says and gives me a confident look.

"I'll be in touch," I say, "and I ain't got to tell you that everything we discussed today is private, right?"

Kong nods and beats against his chest with his fist. He's giving me his word. Between him and my new partnership with Billy, I know I'm going to be able to pull this shit off.

# BOBBY BADD

I've been in Brock's dungeon for hours with Mona, Billy, and Brip trying to think of creative ways to get information from the man they found at Ace's spot. I hand him a notepad and a pen.

"Look at his hands," Mona says to me and I stare at what she's pointing out. Not only does this dude's tongue keep him from talking but he's missing his thumbs, so he can't communicate with us through writing.

"Ace really did damage control with him. He went through a lot of measures to keep him silent," Billy says and sweeps his hands over his head.

"Mona, show him the photo of Ace," I say. Mona pulls her phone out of her bra and pulls up the photo. She holds the phone under the man's nose. He looks down at it and start to nod his head. "You know this man?" He's nodding his head yes aggressively then start gesturing a punch with his hands. He starts to go a little crazy. "You work for Ace?" I ask, but he just keeps on fighting the air and moaning. He trying to tell us something.

"Fuck that!" Brip yells. He pulls out his gun and places it against the dude's head. "Maybe I'll fucking blow his brains out and we get the answers from the left over pieces on the floor."

The man starts to moan and squirm. He's so afraid, he pisses his pants. Fuck! Now along with mold, I got to be trapped down here and smell his fucking piss. I don't have time for this shit. I got to get back to Tara. She's making progress. She needs me by her side but if I leave now, I know I won't hear the end of it.

"Maybe this dude is just a victim of Ace and not a partner," I try to reason with Mona and my brothers.

"Nah," Brip says and jumps over the stream of piss on the floor that's flowing into a tiny puddle. "This nigga knows a lot. There's got to be a way he communicates. How else did Ace talk to him?"

"Well, we ain't going to get shit out of him today," I say and step back, letting them know that I'm about to leave.

"You gone?" Brip says and gives me an irritated look.

"This is pointless," I say to all of them. "Until we can figure out how to communicate with him, what the fuck are we doing? We need to regroup and meet up in the morning."

"This shit ain't pointless." Brip points his finger at me like it's his gun. "Me and Mona was at that house. We know what we saw. This nigga was in the room with money and the surveillance of the Ranch. This nigga," Brip turns around to look at the helpless man who is now trembling, "and Ace had eyes on both y'all and you say the shit is pointless."

I stare back at Billy and Mona waiting for an intervention. Mona jumps in and Brip backs down a little.

"No, Brip. What he's saying is we got to figure out another way to find out who he is," Mona gives me a "you owe me" look and I gather my stuff so I can get the fuck out here.

"What about his bitch?" Brip says to me. "Let's get her down here."

"She ain't ready yet either," Mona says quickly. "She too busy crying over her child. Y'all need to let me handle her. The last thing she need right now is to feel threatened by three men."

"I agree," Billy says quickly and Mona shoots him a quick glance that she didn't think I noticed. What the fuck these two got going on?

"Ok."

"No, fuck that bitch," Brip interjects. "If she sleeping with the enemy, she is the fucking enemy," he yells and his voice echoes. "I'm gon have a little conversation with her." Brip cocks his gun.

Mona looks up at me. She's right. She don't need us plus Brip intimidating her. We won't get nothing that way.

"No, Brip. We gon let Mona take the lead on this one," I intervene and he sucks his teeth and shakes his head.

"So, we just continue to sit here and do fucking nothing?" Brip starts to pout.

"We ain't doing nothing, Brip. We doing what we can," Mona says. "You got security posted at his spot and I got an extra 25 men coming in to cover the Ranch." Mona slips that info in casually and then looks up at me like I didn't hear her.

"Who made that call?" I ask her.

"I did," she says. "If this nigga got eyes on this Ranch, we need more protection. We don't know what the fuck he gon do. Another attack will bury us right now. Some of this shit already done hit the streets. I visited Kong. Folks are talking."

"Shit!" Brip punches at the air, "he got these niggas out here thinking we punks."

After all this, I have to admit that Mona's right. We do look weak but I'm not sure about opening the Ranch back up for business right now. I'm still hoping that Brock calls. I don't know what the fuck he's up to, but I don't want to make a move that fucks up whatever he got planned. I'm gon sit on this shit a little while longer. Mainly because I got my family to think about. I need to keep Brip busy though. Otherwise, he gon fuck us all up.

"Brip, get a small crew out to do some damage control," I say to him and his eyes beam with excitement.

"Damage control?" Billy asks, but he already knows what I'm talking about. "If that's how we gon do it, Brip you got to be organized and not random."

"Billy's right," I say to Brip and Billy looks at me like he's wondering if that means I'm fucking with him again.

He's right about Brip. But he's wrong about me. Tara's nurse told me that Billy was there when she opened her eyes. It's weird that he didn't share that news with me right away. It makes me feel like he's disappointed about how far Tara's coming along. That's why I cut him and the rest of them off from seeing her. It's fucked up that I can't trust my own family but that's just where I'm at right now.

I give Brip a serious look. "This ain't no killing spree. People just need to be reminded about the power in our name."

"Death is power," Brip says. "This is my shit. I know exactly what to do," he says and rushes out the door.

Me, Billy, and Mona all look at each other like we hoping we didn't make a mistake. When Brip leaves, so does the energy of the chaos. I don't know about them, but I feel like I can think clearer.

I look at Mona. "Who did you say your informant was again?" I don't remember her saying the person's name. I'm thinking if this person was connected enough to tell us about Ace's whereabouts, then maybe they know more.

"Just somebody from The East Meadows projects," she quickly replies and looks away from me. I hope Mona knows that I'm catching all of her weird vibes.

"Yea, but who? What's the person's name?"

Mona hesitates like I'm catching her off guard. She starts to look around the room like she's searching for a name to pull out of thin air.

"Whoever it is, we should keep them anonymous. They will tell us more that way," Billy comes to her defense and Mona gives that nigga "thank you" eyes. That's when I decide not to trust them. "When Brip get done ripping through them streets, it's gon be hard for anyone to want to talk to us. They gon be too scared. Let's not start interrogating the person that's giving us good information."

"Hm," was all I say and when they lock eyes briefly, I already know that they both know what that means. I walk out the room. I'm gon find out what they up too. But first I got to check in on Tara and Blake. They have my full attention right now.

* * *

Tara is trying to squeeze my hand. Her fingers are slightly tapping against mine. She's working so hard to come back to us. I look at her and smile. Her stare is blank but I know she's in there. I know her better than these doctors do. They told me she would never regain consciousness then she opened her eyes. Then they said she wouldn't ever regain her mobility. Now, she's trying to squeeze my hand. So, I guess it's safe to say fuck they diagnosis. Tara's a fighter. They underestimate how strong she is.

"We need to do more," I say to the doctor who is examining her. "I want to amp up the therapy."

The doctor raises his eyebrows at me and puts his pen light in his jacket pocket. He's giving me that "you don't know shit" look and I'm giving him that "I dare you to say it" **look.**

"We need to take our time with this. Recovery is something you don't want to rush," he says to me in a very careful voice.

"I got a son that needs his mother," I say back to him.

"I understand that Mr. Badd but all of these developments are new for Mrs. Badd," he says to me and I get disappointed that I never married Tara. I wonder if it's too late now. Then a thought of Lera pops in my head. I instantly shake off the thought and put my focus back on Tara.

"Nah, they new to you," I say. "You didn't think none of this would happen, but I knew she would come around just like I know that with aggressive therapy she gon be back on her feet."

The doctor sighs heavily and looks at me like he's trying to choose his words before he addresses me.

"Mr. Badd, even when Tara does come back around, she's not going to ever be the same again. She may never walk again. She may need a feeding tube and colonoscopy bag for the rest of her life. Yes, she will be able to blink at you and squeeze your hand but that may be it...she's not.."

"You don't know shit." I jump up. As soon as my feet hit the floor, I regain my composure. The doctor jumps back like he's dodging an imaginary punch I threw at him. "Fix her," I say to him, more like a warning than the desperate plea for help that it really is.

I lean down and kiss Tara on the forehead. I whisper in her ear that I will be back in a few hours. I got to check on my son.

\* \* \*

When Blake ain't studying, all he does is plays video games. I don't let him leave the backyard. I installed a basketball court to keep him busy. I try to shoot hoops with him as often as I can, but work and Tara really has been keeping me from him. I'm trying to keep his life as structured as Tara had but I'm failing. Tara was, I mean is, a great mom. I don't think I can raise Blake without her.

Blake hates being here. He asks about Tara every day and I always lie to him, but I got to tell him the truth today. Then, we got to get on a plane. I'm sending him back to Tara's mom. If Mona and Brip are right about Ace having footage of the Ranch, he don't need to be here. It's not as safe as I thought it was. Besides, he needs to be somewhere that feels normal and that ain't here. But before he goes, I got to let him see his mama. I've been avoiding this shit but he deserves to know what's going on. He ain't four years old no more. In a few years, he gon be a man and I got to start treating him like one.

"What's up little man," I say to Blake and playfully throw a pillow at him. He barely looks up at me and when he does, his eyes look too burdened for a person his age.

Blake is sitting on the couch playing video games. I hired a retired school teacher to help with him. She teaches him during the day and I tell her to let him do whatever he wants in the afternoon. I thought the extra freedom will take his mind off things, but it hasn't. He ain't used to doing whatever he wants. Blake respects the order that Tara enforces. Although I told him he can play video games as long as he wants, he still just sticks to the two hours his mother gave him. He actually times himself when he's playing. That's how much respect he has for Tara.

"Oh, hey dad," Blake says in a low voice. He sighs and throws his Xbox controller to the side and gets up to give me a hug. I squeeze him as tight as I can and then kiss him on the forehead.

Blake looks at his phone and then turns off the Xbox. I guess his time is up. He looks up at me like he wants to ask me something but then gives up. He doesn't say anything. This breaks my heart. I know he wants to ask me about his mama but he don't trust my information. I can't have my son not trusting me.

"You good," I say and playfully punch him on the shoulder.

Blake shrugs. "I want to go home," he says.

"I know you do," I say and squeeze his shoulders, "you will soon. Everything is.." I stop myself. I don't want to lie to my son. Blake looks up at me and wonders why I haven't finished the same "everything is going to be ok" speech that I've been giving him. "Sit down, son," I say.

He sits back down on the couch.

I sit beside him and clear my throat. "I'm taking you back to grandma's tonight," I say.

He shrugs his shoulders again. His response is emotionless. "When do I get to go home? Is Mom back yet?"

I get silent. I can't tell him, but I have to.

"No," I say to him. "Mom's here," I force myself to say. Blake jumps up and gives his first genuine smile in weeks. This hurts me but at least I got to see a real smile from him. "Where is she?" He looks over my shoulder at the door. "Is she coming in?" he says and starts running towards the door.

"Blake," I call for him, but he doesn't stop. He's too excited. "Blake," I say again. I get up to follow him. He swings open the door and doesn't see Tara then turns around at me disappointed like I lied to him. "Go sit back down on the couch. We got to talk." I give him a serious look and right away, he starts to cry.

He tries to cover his tears with his hands. He always tries to act so tough around me. I never make him feel like he can't cry. I remember my dad beat the shit out of me for crying when I got stung by a bee. I was only 10. He said men didn't cry. When Mama tried to pull him off of me, he started to beat the shit out of her too. After that day, seeing my mom get hurt because of my tears, I decided that I would never cry again. And I haven't. But, Blake can cry all he wants. I ain't the man my father was. I try hard every day not to be. I remove his hands from his face and let him know that it's ok to cry.

"She's dead, isn't she?"

"No," I quickly say. "She's alive, but she's sick."

"Well, when is she going to get better?"

"Soon," I say. "I'm gon take you to see her before we leave."

He sniffs up his tears. "Really?" he says and wipes his eyes. "I can see Mom?"

I nod at him. "But don't get scared, ok?"

He nods.

* * *

Blake is staring back at Tara like she's possessed. He looks at her hard like he's trying to see the resemblance of his mother but can't find it. Then he looks up at me and gives me a weird look.

"Mom," he says and shakes her. Tara just blinks at him. "Mom," he says again like he trying to wake her up. "Mom," he says and his voice cracks. He's fighting off tears.

"She can hear you, son. She just can't talk to you," I say and rub his back.

Blake starts analyzing all the machines that Tara is hooked up to. He touches the tub under her nose then looks up at me confused.

"This doesn't look like Mom," he says to me. "This isn't Mom," he says like he's refusing to believe his own eyes.

I understand him, but we don't have time to bullshit ourselves.

"It's Mom. She's sick, but she's getting better."

"Why she looking at me as if she can't talk?" Blake says and starts to back away from the bed like he's getting afraid.

"I told you she was sick," I say softly.

"How did she get sick? What happened to her? Does Uncle Jayson know?" he says in one breath.

His Uncle Jayson is a whole other issue I've been avoiding. I still haven't heard back from him. That can only mean one thing; he's dead. I just haven't taken the time to accept that yet. I can't lose everybody. I just can't. Then another flash of Lera jumps in my mind. It's too much. I keep my focus on Blake.

"A bad accident," is all I say.

"A car accident?" Blake continues to question me. I try not to get frustrated. I don't respond. "Dad, Mom is dead," he says to me like he's informing me about something I'm not aware of. When he says that, I snap.

I grab his arms and shake him. "You gon give up on your own mama, boy? That ain't what a man do. Understand?" Blake shakes his head no at me. Now he's trying to hit me.

"No, Dad! You told me the last person a man should ever lie to is himself," I stop shaking him and step back. What he says catches me off guard.

"And Mom's dead!" He yells and wipes tears from his eyes.

I look back at Tara. She's motionless. She ain't trying to get off that bed to stop what's going on. She just blinking and looking into dead space. I flip him around to face her. "Yo, Mama ain't dead," I say, "look at her? That's what dead looks like to you?"

"Yes," Blake says and breaks away from my grip and tries to run towards the door. I grab him, and he starts punching me. I let him. I pull him into a hug and he's screaming for me to get off of him.

"I want to go live with Grandma," he says, "right now," he demands. "Mom's dead...she's dead. She's dead," he keeps repeating. The more he says it, the tighter I squeeze him.

I look back at Tara again. She still ain't moving. Then all of sudden it hits me. Maybe she is dead.

# BILLY BADD

I'm outside this nice spot located a few miles from the city. The house can pass for one of my designs; it's dope. But, I'm not in the market for a house. Just my family. I'm about three houses down, parked on the other side of the street, just waiting. Someone is out front cutting the lawn and another person is pressure washing the sidings. Whoever owns this house is serious about the up-keep.

I've been staring at the long driveway that leads to the front door for two and a half hours now but there is still no sign of Dalla. I know she's here though. I tracked Mona here twice. With all this talk about Ace being spotted, I'm starting to get nervous. He wants my wife dead. I got to protect her for BJ. And for me.

Leaving the Ranch wasn't easy with Bobby gone. For all Mona and Brip know, I'm at the Casino playing poker with myself. What none of them know is that I'm the only one that knows the alternative way in and out. I designed it. It's easy, but there is an alternative route that don't require the security check at the front gate. That's the way me and BJ plan to leave here for good but I got to find Dalla first. Then we out.

I just can't believe that Brock would tell Ace about the second Ranch. Either Brock is in trouble or he's partnered with Ace. We all know that the second location is only supposed to be used as a safe house. Only one of us at a time would know the exact location. At one time, it was our father, now it's Brock. And apparently Ace Lucky.

Someone is backing out the driveway now. I lean up to take a closer look at the car backing out of the three-car garage, but the windows of the black Escalade are tinted too dark. The only dudes I know that drive cars with window tinted that dark are shooters. They surrounding the whole house. If I want to get inside, I'm going to have to get creative. I leave to follow the Escalade.

Bobby must be nervous too. He took his son Blake straight to the airport. He said he would be back, but I got a feeling Blake ain't returning to the Ranch. I was shocked that he left Tara. My love for my brother keeps me from reacting to how he's feeling about my wife. Losing the mother of his child and the woman he loves hits close to home for me. Bobby is acting that way because he hurt. Bobby has always been on the operations side of the business. The less he knows about niggas getting killed. the better because he ain't no murderer. Him talking about killing Dalla ain't nothing but his anger but I can't trust him right now. I think he's angry enough to pull that shit off but what he don't know is that none of that will make him feel better or bring Tara back to the way she was.

If all goes as planned, Bobby will be free from Tara cause right now; he's in bondage to her lifeless body. That's why he ain't thinking straight. Mona said that we needed to distract Bobby if he does decide to open the safe for Brip and when I told her my idea about helping Tara die, she orchestrated a plan that I think will work. According to her, what I was suggesting wasn't murder, but more like an assisted suicide. She said that we weren't killing

Tara but just helping her die peacefully. She convinced me and herself that this is what Tara wanted. She made it sound better. That made me feel less guilt over what had to be done.

Mona got it all set up with the nurse. When Bobby opens the safe, she gon send her a text and then the nurse is going to inject Tara with enough poison to really allow her to rest in peace. Then the nurse will text Bobby to let him know that Tara passed. If I know my brother like I think I do, he's going to go running. He gon leave us with the money.

I told Mona that I want to be paid off. She didn't question me. She just agreed to it. Mona will do anything to keep me out her way. She wants all us Badd men gone. Once we get into the safe, Dalla and I should be set for life.

Mona's plan is going down tonight. That's why I have to contact Dalla. I got to give her heads up that we leaving. I got to set up a spot for us to meet. I know she's not going to trust me. I gave her no reason to trust me, but I know she still loves me. I'm gambling on her love and I never place a bet that I think I'll lose.

Mona knows that I know she wants this Ranch and she also knows that I want Dalla. That I want my family. She keeps telling me that she ain't heard from Dalla since she fled the Ranch but I know its bull. That's ok though. Mona was the one that got Dalla and the other wives set up in a safe house. She's been keeping her safe. For that, I owe her.

I'm still following behind this Escalade. The driver is driving like he ain't trying to get pulled over. I try to be discreet. I'm driving a beat up Honda that I stole from a gas station. It don't get more discreet than this fucking piece of shit of a car. It smells like motor oil and Fritos. There's a hole in the floor on the passenger side. The engine chokes when it starts and cuts off every time I put my foot on the brake.

I let them get about a half a mile ahead of me before I catch up. When I do, they pull into a grocery store. I follow behind them and park at the first spot I see and watch. They trying to find better parking. When they can't, they settle for a handicap space. No one gets out the car yet. The front window rolls down a bit and I see cigarette smoke escaping from the crack.

When I see the brake lights flash on, I get ready to put the car in reverse. They pull out the parking lot and drive right past me. I watch them from my rearview mirror and wait a few seconds before I start to trail behind them again. I got to see who's driving this car. That way I'll know what I'm up against the next time I come out here. I follow them a few miles down the road into a Super Walmart. Why the sudden change of plans? For a second, I thought that maybe they spotted me but once they parked, a few seconds later both the back doors swing open and out steps Dalla and Taffy.

When I see Dalla, my heart stops. So, does everything around me. The sounds of cars and people chattering just goes mute. She has her hair pushed back tight and she's wearing an oversized t-shirt with the sleeves cut off and some tight jeans that has holes in the knee. She's really pulling of this whole shabby sexy look. I can tell by the way she's walking, that she's tired. She places her hand on Taffy's back and says something to her. Taffy stops walking and turns like she's about to get back in the car and Dalla continues to whisper in her ear. Whatever she saying to her, she's convincing Taffy because they continue to walk towards the entrance.

Dalla is casing the parking lot. She's paranoid. And she's stressed. Tension is pushing her shoulders up and making her fidgety. Her hands go from being swept across her face to place on her hips in a matter of minutes. In this moment, just seeing her makes me want to say "fuck Mona's plan and fuck the money." I want to jump out this car, grab her, and rescue her from all this shit, but I can't. It's not time.

When Dalla tries to grab Taffy's hand, Taffy pulls away from her. Taffy looks upset and reluctant but she's still walking beside Dalla. Two men get out the driver and passenger sides of the car and follow behind Dalla and Taffy. They supposed to be looking out for them, but they already fucking up. One of them is glued to his cell phone and the other is ass watching. Good thing my wife is the type of chick that can handle her own. She looks out for herself.

I keep watching. The guy that's ass watching turns to look at another dude wearing a black NY hat and some fresh J's. He's walking aggressively towards them. The ass watcher stops the other guy that's looking at his cell phone and points at the dude in the NY hat. They both stop walking and stare at him. The dude with the cell phone lifts his shirt and quickly flashes his gun at the dude wearing the NY hat, stopping him in his tracks. NY hat raises his chin bucks like he's challenging them but backs off before turning to walk back in the store. The guy with the cell phone points in his direction and hands his partner the gun. His partner takes the gun, nods and runs after the guy in the NY hat. The other guy starts fiddling with his cell phone again. He's making a phone call. Something is going down and Dalla is still inside.

# DALLA BADD

"Slow down, Taffy," I yell from behind her. I can't get too close to her now that we are in the store. It will fuck up the plan. Taffy doesn't listen to me. She's been pissed off at me since Tony left. She wants to find him, but we don't have no time. Lera leaving cuts her out of the deal but Tony will come back. He always does.

Mona set us up in a nice house. Besides security and in-house staff, Taffy and I have the house to ourselves. She even has her own suite and bath. I thought that would make her feel better, but it doesn't. I just hope she goes through with the rest of the plan. I got a feeling she may be a flight risk just like Lera. That's why I'm keeping a close eye on her. Mona has someone out looking for Lera. I don't know why. Lera is proving herself to be more of a liability to us every day.

I'm actually relieved that she is gone because I couldn't trust her but I hate that she took Tony and Jayson with her. I needed Tony and if she hadn't already killed Jayson, he probably gon kill her. If Tony let's him. We are so close to the end of the road. I don't have time to turn and look back. I have to keep moving forward. I just need to get through these last few parts and then it will finally be over.

"Taffy," I say again. This time she stops and turns around.

"Stop calling my fucking name for everybody to hear," she yells at me. "If you don't like how I'm doing things then do this grimy shit yourself!"

"Keep walking," I say before I stop and pretend to be looking at the clothing. "Don't bring any attention to me and stay in the camera zone. This shit will be over soon. Ok?"

"Fuck you!" she says and turns to keep walking. She's still walking too fast but this time I don't follow her. I don't want to trigger her anger.

My eyes lead to the baby isle. I walk over and rub my hands across the little bibs and baby shoes. I start to think about BJ. He's getting bigger every day. I wonder how Billy is handling him. Mona told me that he was teething. I've missed so many of his moments. Moments that I will never get back. Thinking about BJ makes me sad. It makes me think of Billy too, so I stop. I leave the baby section and search for a restroom sign. I need to splash some water on my face. I'll be glad when this shit over. Then I can retire somewhere and never hear the words "I want you dead again." I'll be safe. We'll be safe.

When I asked Mona about Ace, she just said that they were handling it. Who is they? Billy? And she never said they caught him. When I asked her why he was at their second Ranch, she couldn't answer my question. That makes me wonder if Ace got his hands-on Brock and is mind fucking him the same way he did Billy. Ace looked comfortable there. He didn't look like he was running for his life or scared that one of the Badds was going to find him. That means he's ok and if he's ok then it's only a matter of time before he's back at it again. That's why I pray Taffy doesn't fuck this shit up. Something is up and Mona's not going to tell me what's going on and I don't need her to anymore. I leave Ace and Brock's possible collusion to her. I just want out of this whole thing before it gets deadly. I don't have the strength to fight for my life anymore. I'm too tired.

When I see the signs for the restroom, I rush towards it. I have to get back to Taffy before she screws this thing up or runs off. I'm a few feet away from the bathroom when I feel someone rushing from behind me. Before I can turn around, they grab me from behind and place their hand over my mouth and nose, muting my screams and cutting off my air. I try to kick and wiggle my way to freedom, but the grip is too tight. Ace found me. It's over. He quickly carries me towards the bathroom. He kicks open the door and carries me to the handicap stall. No one is in the bathroom to witness and help. I try to sneak a peek of the person in the mirror but he's too quick. He moves past the mirror with lightning speed. Everything is happening so fast. They open the door and push me inside before quickly letting me go. When I turn around, ready to fight, I see Billy. I'm so shocked, I almost pass out, but Billy holds me up. Not even two seconds go by before we are kissing. I don't know if he kissed me first or I kissed him first. In the moment, it doesn't matter.

I pull away from him to catch my breath and wrap my mind around what's happening. I'm so tired, I could be hallucinating. It could be Ace kissing me. I stare up at Billy, holding his face.

"It's me," he says softly. He places warm lips me on my forehead and I pull him into another kiss.

I don't want him to let me go. How is he here? Why is here? Did Mona send him? When I realize that Billy can answer these questions for me, I pull away from him. I look at him and then I get angry. So angry that I slap him. He doesn't flinch. So, I slap him harder. Then, I go wild punching and fighting him. He takes the hits for a while like he knows he deserves it then he grabs my hands, spins me around and pushes me back into his chest. He's holding me tight but gentle.

"I'm sorry. I'm so sorry," he says to me. "Just calm down. Please."

I stop fighting him and break free from his grip. I wrap my arms around him and kiss him again. As I'm kissing him, I start crying. I'm confused and dazed. Billy's presence has me in a trance and I almost forget where I am. And what's happening. I almost forget about Taffy and the plan.

"Why are you here? You left me." I ask in one breath.

"I had to. I didn't want to. Trust me." He strokes the side of my face.

"I don't trust you," I let Billy know immediately.

"I understand that," he says and keeps stroking my face. He's looking over me like he's analyzing my body for damages. "Are you ok?" he asks.

"No," I say. "I'm exhausted. I'm alone. I'm scared..."

Billy pulls me into his chest and wraps his arms around me. His touch is so comforting but I know it won't last.

"Listen," he cups my face with his hands, "we getting out of here. Me, you, and BJ."

"BJ," I say under my breath, remembering my son. *Our family*.

"I know you been working with Mona. She don't know that, and we need to keep it that way. When you get that money, we leaving." I nod my head agreeing with him. "I got somebody working on our passports. We going to Spain." Billy looks down at me and smiles. "We leaving all this shit behind and we ain't never looking back, you hear me?"

I nod. "How if it doesn't work? Lera ran off and Taffy doesn't want to do this shit. It may not work, Billy."

"It's going to work one way or the other," he says. I don't know what he means by that, but I take it all as hope. "I just need you to trust me, baby."

He called me baby. He's begging for my trust. This feels like a dream. Billy loves me. He wants our family just as bad as I do.

"I don't know who to trust anymore," I say to him honestly. "How if this is a setup?" I say and immediately search his face for clues. Loving Billy is effortless but trusting him is a challenge. "Ace was at one of y'all spots. Are you still working with him?" I ask. I had to ask. I needed to see his reaction.

Billy seemed disappointed by my questions. "I will never hurt you. If I knew that nigga was there, he would be dead already," Billy lifted my chin so that I was eye to eye with him, "you hear me?" I nod. "Do you hear me?" he asked again, sternly. He wants to hear my voice.

"Yes," I respond. Pushing the words out of my throat so fast my voice cracks. Our eyes lock and we lean in to kiss. At that moment I realize just how in sync Billy and I are. Billy pushes his tongue inside my mouth and hits all the corners of my inner jaw like he's trying to clean up all the mess that developing inside of me. I let him clean house, falling back against the wall. His touch melts me.

This kiss is more intense than the others. It is passionate. He knows I forgave him, and I know he loves me. There is no more questions, so we shut up and allowed our bodies to speak for us. Billy rubbed his hand down my back before moving them inside my shirt. He massages my breast and I press my body against his. He unzips my jeans and I pull them off before he lifts me and pins me against the wall. As soon as I open my legs, Billy is inside of me like his penis is made of a magnet and my insides metal. I hold on to his neck and squeeze my legs around his back as he passionately pushes himself inside of me. He makes love to me like we aren't in a Walmart bathroom, but on a beach in Spain. His body feels even better than I remember. Better even. He kisses my neck and then my lips.

We can't take our eyes off each other. Finally being together after all that lost time is mesmerizing. I miss his smell. I miss feeling his hot breath against my neck and moaning softly in his ear. I lick against his earlobe. It is his sweet spot. He pumps harder and goes deeper inside of me. I feel him everywhere all at once. I rub the top of his head, feeling whatever parts of him my arms could reach. His pumps increase, and his breathing gets heavier, I feel him even more. He swells bigger inside of me, pushing his way closer towards my spot. My insides tighten and wrap around his dick, squeezing him into ecstasy. He grabs my legs and tilts them so that my spot is bullseye to his dick and I squeeze him even more. Then he ignites the bomb that has been ticking in-between my legs since the first day I saw him. I explode with him still inside of me and then he explodes inside of me and goes limp. He can't hold my weight anymore. I slid down the bathroom wall as he kisses me until I am done exploding.

We look at each other. We are so overwhelmed with passion that we can barely keep our eyelids open. We smile at each other at the same time. Billy leans in and whispers "I love you," in my ear and a single tear escapes from my eye and runs down my cheek. He doesn't need me to say it back. He wipes the tear and softly presses his lips on to the side of my face and holds them there before leaning up.

"It's almost over," he says to me and zips up his pants.

"And then we can finally begin?" I ask him and he nods.

"Take my phone. I'm going to get another one. It's how we can keep in contact." He hands me the phone and I pull up my pants and put it in my back pocket.

"I got to go," I say quickly, getting my head back in the game.

He looks at me like he doesn't want me to leave. "I know," he says. "Watch your back. Those niggas got some kind of beef going on with some other nigga. Some dude in a red hat."

"Taffy!" I yelled. "They here for Taffy. It's part of the plan. I got to go," I say and try to rush out the door, but he pulls me back into one last kiss. "I love you," I say to him.

He nods and winks at me. I don't want to leave. But I have to. Like Billy said, it's almost over. I unlock the bathroom door.

"Wait," he says and pulls out a gun. "Never go anywhere without this," he adds.

"I don't know how to shoot," I say to him.

"Just aim and pull the trigger. Then boom," Billy says with a hand gesture.

I take the gun and stuff it in the waist of my jeans. I look at Billy one last time, giving him an "I love you" with my eyes. Then I leave.

* * *

I'm spying on Taffy from a distance. I don't want her to know that I'm watching. She's causing a scene, but I know that none of the shit is fake. She wants out but it's too late. After seeing Billy, it's all or nothing for me. We too close to turn back. In the middle of watching Taffy, the phone Billy gave me rings. I look down and the number is listed as unknown. I know it's him; it has to be. He's calling me already. I answer before the first ring ends.

"Hello?" I say, anxious to hear his voice again. In a way, I'm hoping he says fuck everything and let's leave now but that's not practical for either of us. The person on the other end doesn't say anything. "Billy?" I say again.

"Is this Dalla?" The first thing I notice is that it's not Billy's voice that's addressing me. I don't say anything. I just listen. My heart is pounding so hard against my chest, I feel like the person on the other end of the phone can hear it. "Dalla, this is Brock. Please put Billy on the phone."

"Brock?" His name flies out of my mouth like vomit.

I'm shocked. I wonder if Mona knows that Billy and Brock are still talking. Should I tell her? I can't because then she will know that I've been in contact with Billy too. I appreciate everything Mona has done but my loyalty is solely for Billy and BJ. My family.

"Billy's not here," I say quickly. I just want this call to end. I debate just hanging up the phone.

"Dalla, listen to me please," he says in a desperate voice. My heart starts to beat again. Something is telling me to take him seriously, but I don't want to. Brock is trouble, but I can't let Brock fuck up me and Billy's escape plan. Not this time. But I never heard Brock sound so desperate and helpless. "We're all in trouble," he says quickly. He sounds like he's out of breath. "I need you to tell Billy to get..." he stops talking and yells then quickly clears his throat and composes himself. "Tell him to protect the safe. Don't open the safe. Don't..." It sounds like someone hit him. Then something falls. Someone else picks up the phone. I can hear them breathing. The person doesn't speak and neither do I. I know the sound of that breath. The chill my soul gets from it tells me who's on the other end of the phone. It's Ace.

Brock is still trying to say something to me in the background, but I can't make out what he's saying? At least not at first. Then I hear him yell, "don't open the safe!"

I end the call immediately and start to panic. Why is he mentioning the safe? What does he know? I debate if I should tell Mona or even Billy about this call. We need that money. All of us. This could just be a setup. After all, Ace looked real comfortable at his second Ranch. If I say something, it will change everything. It will no longer be about me and Billy but their family; the Badds. They have taken too much of our lives from us already. I just need to get this money and leave. Whatever happens with Brock, Mona can handle it. But that safe has to open. We are too close to stop everything. I shake off the phone call like I shake off every other vile thing I've had to do. I'm not saying shit. This plan is going down tonight.

# TAFFY BADD

This is so fucked up, but it's too late now. I'm doing it. Some nigga in a loud ass red hat grabbed me from behind and placed a gun to my head. He made a scene just like Mona and Dalla wanted. Everybody in the store is screaming and grabbing their children. Even the employees ran. No one tried to help me. It's a good thing then that this shit is fake and I don't really need the help because everyone ran.

The other dude filmed the whole thing on his phone. I made sure I was in front of the cameras just like Dalla told me before she ran off. I guess she got chicken shit at the last minute. I thought she would be somewhere I could make eye contact with in the moments leading up to this, but the bitch is nowhere to be found. That's typical of her. As soon as the shit hit the fan, she goes running.

I'm uncomfortable with this in more than one way. It's too soon for this shit. Although I know we planned this, somewhere in the back of my mind, I keep thinking that the guy behind me is Ace and he taking me back to his pool with his gators. That helps makes this whole thing look real. I fight. I have to remind myself that this is made up but my fight is still real.

"Chill out," the guy whispers loudly in my ear. "You ain't got to do all that. We good." But I ignore him. I keep fighting. I'm crying too. What is Brip going to think when he sees this? He's going to be so upset. Then when he finds out this whole thing is fake, he's really going to be done with me. My love for Brip is worth more than money. I don't want to do this shit anymore.

"Let me go!" I say to the guy, but he thinks I'm faking it. He keeps walking me towards the exit door. "I said let me the fuck go!"

"Shut up, bitch," he says back to me. I can't tell if that is fake or real. I keep fighting him.

"Let me go. Let me go!" I scream. "Help!" I yell. "Somebody help me," I scream.

"What the fuck are you doing?" he says. He starts to walk faster. He tightens his grip around my chest.

I look up and I see Dalla. She's looking at me like she knows I want out, but she doesn't tell the guy to let me go. She just runs to the car and jumps in.

"Don't put me in this fucking truck. I'm not going!" I say to the guy. I elbow him in the stomach and he forcefully pushes me to the ground. I fall, and he yanks me back up and pushes me towards his truck. Someone, Dalla I assume, opens the back door and he throws me in.

"I'm done!" I say to Dalla. I try to open the door, but the child lock is on. "Let me out of this fucking car, Dalla."

"No," is all she says.

"Fuck you!" I scream and try to swing at her, but she grabs my hand.

"Tie her up," Dalla demands. "I'm sorry, Taffy, but you're not fucking this up for me. We're too close."

Dalla looks at me, but looks away when the guy starts tying my hands together.

"I can't believe you," I say to her. "I can't believe you're doing this shit to me again," I sob.

Dalla turns her head and looks out the window. She can't watch the men tie me up. I see her wiping tears. This bitch is grimy as fuck. I should have never got involved with her. I should have just left with Lera and Tony. Lera's smarter than me. Dalla don't give a fuck about nobody but herself.

"Dalla, please. Don't put me and Brip through this again."

"It will be over soon," Dalla says. "It will all be over soon," she repeats. She still can't look at me.

One of the men tries to blindfold me. I immediately have a flash back of Ace. So I start to fight as hard as I can. I kick him and he flies back towards the windshield. "Fuck," he yells. He jumps up and comes for me with his fist but Dalla stops him. She pulls out a gun.

"If you fucking touch her, I'm gon blow your brains out!"

"Chill out. Chill out," the driver says. "We cool. Your girl is tripping though," he says and looks at me through the rear-view mirror. "We got to blindfold her, right?"

"Not now," Dalla says and looks at me like she's got my back.

Where in the fuck did she get a gun? I know she didn't have it before we left. At least I don't think she did. Dalla looks at me and places her hand on my knee. "I'm sorry," she says. "It will all be over soon," she repeats. I don't know if she's talking to me or herself.

\* \* \*

When we get back to the house, I'm forced to finish the last piece of their plan. They got me all tied up and pushed in a corner. Tape is around my mouth. My hands are tied to my back and a gun is against my head. They take photos of me at different angles and then confer amongst each other about which one is the best to send. The guy that I kicked don't think they look real enough. I untie the loose knot and free my hands and then remove the tape from my mouth and sit up comfortably.

"She just sitting there too calm," he says. Dalla grabs the phone from him and looks at the photo.

"I see what you mean," she says.

"We need to do something. Slap her or something," he says and looks down at me like he's wanting payback for the way I handled him in the truck. That's not going to happen.

"You touch and I'm going to fuck you up," I say to him quickly.

"Me too," Dalla says and draws her gun.

"Damn, ya'll some bad bitches," he says, and me and Dalla look at each other.

The men assisting with this don't know who we are. Mona doesn't want this to get out beyond her control.

"Taffy," Dalla says my name and sighs like she's exhausted. She knows that I'm going to be difficult. "You think you can make this look a little more real?"

"What do you want me to do?" I say. I just want to get this over with, so I can go to my room and plan my way out of this mess.

"I don't know. Look a little more scared or something. You have a fucking gun to your head for god sakes!"

I take a deep breath and lean back in my corner. "Tie my hands back up," I yell to one of the men. They do what I say. I close my eyes. "Get the gun," I say before they tape my mouth shut. I start to think about Ace and shortly after that, the anguish shows on my face. I must be doing a better job because the guys are raving about the pictures now.

"Now she looking like she scared for her life," one of them says. "Ya'll trying to fool some dope boy or something?" one of them asks.

"Mind your fucking business and get the fuck out," Dalla says and snatches the phone from his hand.

She motions for security and they escort the men out the room. I untie myself again. Dalla tries to help me up but I use the wall instead of her hand.

"Where did you get that gun?" I ask her.

"I found it here," she says too quickly. I look at her. She's up to something.

"Just lying around?" I ask her.

She nods. "You did good, Taffy." She changes the subject. "I'm sending these to Mona now. It won't be long before we have our money," she says trying to cheer me up.

"Whatever," I say and walk out the room. She follows behind me.

"Have you thought about where you going to go?" she asks me.

"Why the fuck do you care?" I turn to her and ask.

She gives me a weird look then says, "I'm so sorry, Taffy."

Dalla apologizing sets off an alarm inside of me and I step back, defensive.

"What?" I ask, but before I can finish my question, security is grabbing me.

"Lock her in the room. Make sure she doesn't leave," Dalla tells them.

"You bitch!" I yell to her. "When Brip finds out what you did, he's going to fucking kill you. You and Mona both."

"He's not going to find out," Dalla says confidently. "I'm not going to let you fuck this up for me," she says back to me. "I'm sorry, Taffy, but I can't let you leave this house. Not until we get the money. Afterwards, you can tell Brip everything. But, be careful when you do. I don't think that's going to be enough to get him back."

"You don't know shit!" I say to her.

"Maybe not. Maybe so," she says and turns her back to me. "I want three guards at her door at all times. Don't underestimate her, she small but she can fight her way out of anything."

"Yes, ma'am," they say and escort me to my room.

I got to figure out how to get out of here. I have to warn Brip about what Dalla and Mona are doing. Even if he doesn't take me back, he doesn't deserve the pain they are about to inflict on him. I won't let them hurt him. I just won't!

# MONA BADD

"You want me to bring your son, back?" I say to this whore. She gives me a desperate head nod and extends her hands like she's reaching for her son but he ain't here. I got one of the nannies looking after him. "Then tell me the fucking truth!" I say to her.

This is the third time I am questioning the bitch but she won't say a word. She just as useless as the man without a tongue and thumbs. We still can't get him to talk but he responds to pictures. They been throwing Ace's picture in his face and every time they do, he starts to go crazy. He jumps up and starts acting out. I think he's trying to show us what happen. He's waving his fist in the air. He's trying to gesture something with his fingers. I say it's a gun but Bobby says it could be anything. Then he starts punching and kicking at the air. The others don't know this but when I showed him Brock's photo, he does the same thing. I think Brock and Ace had a fight but that still doesn't explain why Ace was at the second Ranch.

We took all the security cameras down and rewired the system but that don't mean Ace ain't get what he needed already. Whenever Ace is feeling up to it, he can ambush us at any time and I'm the only one who seems to care. I tried to call Kong to see if he had any updates and to thank him for sending my army but he ain't answering. That's kind of weird. I wonder if Nicchi got into his head. I'm not sure anybody can get into Kong's head though. He ain't built like that. Maybe he pissed at me cause I let Brip loose in his projects and he out there putting niggas down to show folks our weight ain't dropped none. If Kong just answers the phone, I can explain why Brip's been in the East Meadows projects.

Brip came back home with blood all over his t-shirt and sneakers. His knuckles are swollen, and the barrel of his gun is empty. I know what that means. That was supposed to be a onetime thing but Brip keep going out terrorizing people. I guess fear does feed our power but that don't make it right. He out of order and I ain't got time to deal with it.

"Look, I don't want you here no more than you want to be here. I already put you out once and I had no plans on bringing you back, but you know something."

"I told you, I don't know anything. I just want my son," She sobs.

"Is that Mr. Badd's son?" I ask her.

She hesitates, then shakes her head no. "How many times do I have to tell you no?" she says.

"If I do a DNA on him and it comes back that that child belongs to my husband, you will never see him again unless you tell me the truth. As a matter of fact, I'll sell the little mutha-fucka to the highest bidder. You know how much Badd blood goes for on the streets?"

I try to intimidate her. I hate she pushing me to this little. Even though I know this bitch is lying, she's still a mother. Threatening a woman's child is low but sometimes you got to do some low shit in order to get to high places. Fuck it. I need answers.

"Please don't hurt my son," she starts to sob again.

"Done that crying shit! I don 't need your tears. I need answers," I jump up and say to her face. I'm nose to nose with her. "Don't make me do something I don't want to do," I threaten her.

"Ok," she says in a faint voice. I can tell she's exhausted by the way she's holding her head. Her voice is cracking too. She's been in the dungeon tied to a chair. She hasn't eaten since she got here.

"Say what you got to say?" I pull my chair in closer to her. My ears are ready to listen but my heart ain't ready to hear the shit she about to reveal.

"I was sent here," she revealed, then dropped her head and flinched like I was about to hit her. Not yet.

"By who?" I say and pull her head up by her weave.

"My fiancé," she says. "He sent me here to get close to Brock. Applying to be a breeder was my only way in. I couldn't get anything out of Brock and I was tired of fucking him so I lied to you just so I can get off the Ranch. My fiancé got pissed when I got back and I hadn't seen him since until a few months ago. He was in trouble. He said he needed my help so he had someone pick me up in one of ya'll Hummers and brought me to the house you found me at," she swallowed and looked up at me, shaking. She's scared.

"Your fiancé?" I question her knowing exactly who she's talking about. "Ace Lucky?" I ask and she nods. "Answer me!" I yell. I need to hear her say it. "Yes! Ace Lucky is my fiancé."

"Was Brock at the house with him?"

I knew about the mole Dalla had at my breeding quarters but thought that there could be another one never crossed my mind. It was too farfetched. I mean what the fuck are the chances of that happening?

"I didn't see Brock, but I know the Hummer the person was driving belonged to you all. Everyone knows the signature Badd Hummers," she says.

"Who was driving the Hummer?"

"I don't know! Please, bring me my son."

I lean down and slap the shit out of her. Slapping her was easier than slapping myself for making such a foolish mistake by opening the breeding quarters to outsiders. Now look.

"Who was it?!" I yell.

"He didn't talk much and some of his fingers were missing! That's all I know, I swear!"

Now we getting somewhere. So the man without a tongue was Ace's driver. But how in the fuck they get Brock's Hummer?

"Where did Ace go? When did he leave?"

"He didn't tell me. He stayed in the basement most of the time with his driver. He wouldn't let me down there. Usually, I would help him back up at night because somebody shot him in the leg or thigh or something but the night before you, I went down there and he was gone."

"Who does the boy belong to?"

She looks up at me and burst into tears. "I'm sorry. I didn't know.." That tells me everything. Her son belongs to Brock. I don't know why, but I feel like I have been stabbed in the chest. I allowed Brock to impregnate several women, but for some reason this hurts. Maybe it had always hurt and I'm just now feeling it. Or maybe I'm hurting because I've been so angry thinking that Brock betrayed us and I've been wrong this entire time. Brock didn't betray us. He got side swiped by Ace. He has him somehow. I just know it.

"Do you know how to contact Ace?"

"No," she answers immediately. "He only contacts me. Always," she says. I believe her. "Can I please see my son now? Please let us go. I promise I'll stay away from Ace and all of this."

"That ain't your son. That boy was conceived on Badd property by Badd blood. He belongs to us now and you ain't going nowhere for a long time," I say to her and turn to leave. She lets out a gut-wrenching scream but I'm not fazed by it. The bitch fucked up when she tried to fuck us over. She don't deserve Badd blood.

Everything is in place. Dalla sent me the photos and Taffy's fake abduction made the local news just as planned. The camera shows an innocent woman being picked up and dragged out the store. You can't really see her face so that makes it perfect. The general public will never be able to link it back to us so we won't look weak. Plus, my connect got the real tape from Walmart. I'm gon play that back for Bobby when he starts to speculate that maybe it ain't Taffy we seeing. Everything is working out perfect. My army literally answers my every command and I even got Vinchi out the prison but all of a sudden, I'm thinking that maybe I'm not doing the right thing.

It was one thing when I thought that Brock betrayed us and that he was fucking that bitch behind my back but now this just feels wrong. Here I am planning to break into the safe and take this Ranch .And I'm promising Kong a stake in it all. All while Brock is out there somewhere, needing me. I can't do this shit. I just can't. I got to put all my efforts into finding my husband. But on the other hand, how does Ace know so much? You don't just stumble upon the second Ranch and steal a Badd Hummer. Brock has a panic button installed in all the Badd Hummers. If something is wrong, he would have warned us. Plus he's been in contact with Billy and Bobby.

I don't know what to believe. Tonight is the only night to do this shit. Everything is setup that way. The news story is only airing once and afterwards, the video and pictures Dalla sent me of Taffy's capture will go away forever. I don't know what the fuck to do! I've never been in a situation where I couldn't make a decision. If I make the wrong move, I could lose it all, including Brock. But I'm a woman of my word. The wives need my support. I'm all they have right now and believe it or not, that means something to me. If I don't make a move, I risk the chance of getting phased out and everything I sacrificed all these years goes to shit. Either way it goes, it's a gamble.

I gotta flip a coin and then act fast. Damn you Brock for putting me in this situation.

# BROCK BADD

"You haven't given up the code to the safe yet."

The woman says calmly, but gives me an evil stare. She wants the code to the safe and I want the letters. She's pretending to be patient but I can tell by her dipped brow and clutched fist that she's frustrated. I'm not giving her the code to the safe. I'll die first and she ain't giving up the letters that hold the answers to all my family's secrets.

"I thought you'd do anything to protect your family?" She asks and waits for my response. I don't respond. Who is she to be questioning me about my family?

I need to make it out of here alive so I can protect my family. I have to stay alive for them. But it ain't looking good right now. Protecting them ain't easy from where I'm sitting. I'm stuck. I can't make moves when I'm stuck. I got to get flexible. Somehow, I got to make a move or it's all gon be over.

I'll do anything for the Badd name. It's part of the reason why I'm here now. Stuck. In danger. And over my fucking head. But it's all in the name of Badd. I've proven that I'll kill for it. Now I have to prove that I'll die for it. My word is all I have. Without my word, I'm nothing; even after death. But my life won't be in vain and neither will my mother's. I'm going to make this thing right for all of us. In my world, you're either a Badd or you're nothing at all. I chose to be a Badd. It's just too bad that my mother didn't choose that for me. If she had, she'd still be alive.

I waited until she fell asleep before I made my move. Every night, my mother took a sleeping pill at approximately 9pm. By 10pm, she was out cold. 10:05 was the time I chose to make my move. I tiptoed towards her room. At this point, she and my father slept in separate rooms on separate sides of the house. I planted my ear to the door and when I didn't hear anything, I turned the knob and crept in. I charged towards her bed without hesitating. I had to get it over with before I changed my mind. Mama's entire body was covered in blanket. It was how she slept. I was glad I didn't have to see her face.

I still see her limp body every time I close my eyes. Even when I close them to blink. I can still see the face print in the pillow I used to suffocate her. She didn't struggle. She didn't fight. My mother took her death like she'd been waiting on it. You'd think that would have made killing her easy, but it didn't. Maybe if she fought me off, I would have come to my senses and ran. She didn't fight. So I kept the pillow on top of the blanket that covered her face.

I timed myself. I researched that 10 minutes was enough time to squeeze the life out of her. Ten minutes felt like ten years. I never knew I could cry until I saw my own tears dropping on the pillow. Killing her was premeditated but it wasn't an easy decision. It was either her life or mine and she'd proven time and time again that she'd lost her will to live. So, I chose my life. My Badd life.

When she told me that I wasn't my father's son, I felt like I didn't know myself anymore. I felt like a stranger inside of my body. All I ever known was Badd. I was proud to be a Badd. Proud to be my father's son. Although I feared him up until the day he died. When I was younger, I used to mimic everything he did. His walk. His talk. His ruthlessness. I wanted it all. When I finally mastered his everything, my mother tells me that I don't belong to him and that she can't keep the secret anymore. So it had to be done.

I couldn't let it get out. I know my father. He would have thrown me and my family off the Ranch. Maybe even had us killed to protect the Badd image. I would have lost everything. An entire legacy would have fallen in-between my fingers. I was my father's second in command. The prince to his empire. I couldn't hand that over to my brothers. For one, they didn't deserve it the way I did. And two, without the Badd name, I'm nothing. Badd blood is what keeps me thriving. I need to be a part of that name just as much as I need air in my lungs.

I was groomed to sit on the Badd throne from the moment my mother pushed me out. Billy, Bobby, and Brip got to shoot the breeze. They got to go out and play and have somewhat of a normal life while I was my father's apprentice. I had no childhood. My father used to say a boy in my position will not benefit from silly childhood memories. The memories would only weaken me he would say. I had no room to be soft. When mother tried to oppose, he hit her. She always tried to protect me until the day I stopped her. I didn't stop her because I didn't want her protection; I stopped her because I wanted her to be safe.

I killed my mother in the name of all things, Badd. If I hadn't, then we wouldn't be where we are now as an organization. I promised myself that my mother would be the last Badd I killed. That's why Billy is still alive. One thing I believe in more than my name is justice. Doing what's right washes blood off my hands but sometimes, things flip and the only way to do what's right is to get my hands bloody. Soon, my hands will be dripping with blood but I have to get out of here first.

She walks closer towards me and tries to kiss me, but I pull away. She's been trying to kiss me since I got here. She even grabs my dick. She is disappointed when it don't get hard for her. She gets upset and slaps me but what she doesn't know is that I like the pain from her slaps. The sting from her violence grounds me. I feel centered. More focused.

This woman is abusive. She's full of anger and rage. I don't mind her physical violence. But what she doesn't know is that her violent ways motivate me.

"I've always hated her," she says to me. She's talking about my mother. "She had everything handed to her. That made her think she was better than me. So much better that she decided to take what's mine," the woman grimaced at the memory. She clutches her fist before raising it in the air, ready to strike me but she doesn't hit me. She chuckles and pats me on the head. "But I didn't worry because I knew that one day she would get just what she deserved. Thanks, for that," she whispers in my ear and takes a few steps back to look at me.

She knows I killed my mother, but she'll never understand why. None of them will. She thinks that I killed my mother because I hated her, but I loved her like a second skin. My father used to tell me that every man will come to a point where they will be faced with the choice to make the ultimate sacrifice. He said that only brave men seize the moment. I made the cut; I was brave enough to make the sacrifice to kill her but now, I'm not sure I did the right thing. And the woman standing in front of me has the answer to that question. But she won't give me any answers until she gets the code to the safe.

My mother was beautiful. She was everything the woman standing in front of me is not. When she walked, her body moved like a bag blowing in the wind. It swayed from side to side effortlessly. Like she was flying instead of walking. She was angel-like. Soft and elegant. Her touch was healing. And her hugs gave people life. The energy her body gave off felt like warmth from a fireplace, comforting you from the inside out.

Everyone took her outer beauty for weakness, but people who did that weren't looking at her hard enough. My mother was strong and fierce. Like me, she made sacrifices too. Her biggest sacrifice was staying married to our father. Living out her days as a prisoner to a life that was given to her; not one she chose. But she took it with stride.

I'll never forgive myself for killing my mother if it was a mistake. First, my mother told me the truth and then Ace confirmed it. Ace's confirmation made me feel like what I did wasn't a mistake but now a new discovery has changed everything. I just need answers.

Men in my position can't afford to make mistakes. I have to learn the truth before it all ends. Before it's too late. I don't want to believe that I did the wrong thing. That would make her killing unjust. That would make me a murderer. Actually, what I did would be worse than murder. It would be genocide. Dad used to say, the last person a man should ever lie to is himself.

I spent a lot of time with Billy when he was at the prison. We reconnected with each other as brothers. Spending so much one on one time together connected us. I kept encouraging him to return to society. Our society. But he wasn't ready. He felt too guilty for all the confusion he caused. I never told Billy the truth.

He finally believes that our mother killed herself. We talked a lot about mom and her sadness. I gained his trust then betrayed him with my lies. There is only one way to make this thing right. Only one way he will forgive me for the atrocities I caused him. I have to find the truth and then come clean to everybody.

Spending time with Billy is where I also learned that I may have made a mistake. Ace may have been playing both of us. Billy didn't know it, but I had the nurse draw his blood. He thought it was a common checkup but it really was genetic testing. I needed to see the results on paper. Feeling the truth on the inside didn't burn enough. I had to physically see it. When the results came back, I was expecting it to reveal that I was his half-brother, but it showed that we were full blooded brothers. That's when the mistake hit me like a ton of bricks. So, I reached out to Ace. He was the only one that had the answers I needed. So does his mother. I'm looking up at her. She wants me to beg her for the truth, but I don't beg.

According to Ace, the truth is in a stash of letters that my mother wrote to Carlo Lucky. Ace claims the truth will shock me. He said it will shake our whole world but he ain't giving up the letters unless I give up the code to the safe. It's why I'm still here.

"You want answers, don't you?" She looks at me and smiles.

"The letters," I say to her. "He told me you have them," I say.

Ace ambushed me and I ended up at his mother's house. Everywhere else he tried to take me, I was able to escape. There was always a guard that let me go because they respect and fear my power. I've been running around trying to make things right but somehow I got caught. All of the hidden secrets about my family has taken a toll on me. It's making me weak. It's forcing my guard down but I got to stay strong. Otherwise I'm going to end up dead.

Ace is working with someone. Whoever it is, they got good eyes on me. They been watching my every move. They can hide real good in plain sight. They are the visibly invisible. Someone is watching me. Ace hauled me to three different places before he finally put me in a place where he knows I can't escape from. At least that's what he thinks. I got to get back to the Ranch because my family needs me. They don't know what's coming. They think the attack is over, but it's only the beginning. This is all my fault. I'm man enough to admit that. Now I have to be man enough to fix it. I should have just killed that nigga when I had the chance, but he has something that I need more than anything right now.

Ace knows the truth about my family. He has the other side of the story. All the rumors we were forbidden to speak of may be true. And, Ace and his mother have the full story. Our full story. He knows shit that I don't know. Shit that I need to know. Including who my father is. He lured Billy into his web with our mother's autopsy report. I thought I destroyed it but he had it. I moved past that and got Billy back on my side. Aside from Ace and Dalla, only I know the truth. But, now, he has me trapped with all the talks of letters written between my mother and his father. He says the letters reveal everything. I read one from my mother. I know her handwriting and how she speaks. The letters are real, but it didn't give me all the information I need. It was only the beginning. The only one Ace's mother allowed me to read. She knows that I believe her now. She knows how much I need answers but what she doesn't know is that I'm not desperate. The Ranch and the safety of my family comes before anything. That's my duty to the Badd family. To put them first.

Ace says he has over fifty letters detailing all the dirt on our family and who we really are. I had to know so I made him believe that I was giving him what he wanted. I made him believe that I loved him like a brother and that I would hand over my family, including my own son just to prove my loyalty to him but that's not what I was doing. What went down wasn't a part of my plan. It was a mistake.

I've been operating under lies for so long that shit started to break me down way before Ace attacked our wives. My wife noticed me breaking, but she still didn't understand what she was seeing in me. She didn't know what was going on inside of me. Me being weak is unfathomable to her. To her, I'm stronger than steel. I'm unbreakable. Me telling her that I killed my mother was me attempting to show her my weak side. It was my cry for help, but she couldn't hear me. That's why I started fucking around with one of the breeders. It's part of the reason why I'm in this situation. I trusted a woman that wasn't my wife.

I don't know what it was about Goldie. Really, it could have been any one of them. She was just the one I chose to listen to me. Mona was always planning, organizing, and thinking one step ahead. I respected her for that, but with all I had on my mind, I just needed to live in the moment for once. Goldie helped me do that. I put her in the second Ranch and made her feel special. In turn, she made me forget my mistakes. She made me forget so much that I didn't realize the mistake I was making with her. Like every whore, she got comfortable with the life I provided for her and my son and wanted me to leave my wife. I never spend more than a few days there with her but after all this shit happened, I had no choice but to be at the second Ranch, and she got confused thinking I was there to play house. She was never allowed in the basement. She knew the rules and usually followed them, but one day she came down in her night gown and saw me going into the safe.

I was so distracted with Ace and everything going on that I didn't challenge her on how much she saw. I just reacted. I slapped her down and cursed at her. I called her dumb and ungrateful. She ran back upstairs crying. On her way, I'm sure she noticed Ace. A few days later, his men were at my door. He got to her. I should have never left them in the house alone but like I said, I forgot that she isn't Mona. So here I am.

I love Mona more than anyone. I love her more than our children. I love her more than my skin. If I wasn't trained to think otherwise, I would even say that I loved her more than the Badd name. But, I never told her that I loved her. Ever. I wish I had. But I showed my love for her daily and that was enough. She looks and carries herself nothing like my mother, but in a lot of ways, she reminds me of her. Her strength is the same. Mona just shows her strength more on the outside than my mother did. They handled things differently. That's what attracted me to her. Aside from my mother, I know that I will never meet another woman as strong and loyal as Mona, again. Right now, she's thinking that I've betrayed her, that I've turned my back on my family. I have to get out of here to prove her wrong. She doesn't trust me anymore and as a result of the mistrust, she's retaliating against us. I can't blame her and I can't protect her from the trouble she's in. Not right now. I'm so thankful that I never gave her the code to the safe. If I had, it would all be over and I would be dead.

By now, Mona knows about the second Ranch and Goldie. Billy is the only other person that knows the exact location of the second Ranch. I don't think he told Mona. It had to be Dalla who helped her find it. When I left the second Ranch, I went to Billy's condo to do damage control. I know that's where Billy keeps his maps; his hiding spots hadn't changed since we were little. I tore Billy's room apart looking for them but before I could get into his shoe boxes, Dalla showed up. If Goldie was smart, she would lie to Mona, but that bitch is dumb and vindictive like most bitches who are born to fuck and suck. That means Mona knows everything and that will only fuel her fire to make a move against us; against me.

Looking at Ace's mother, I understand why he turned out so fucked up. She doesn't have me chained to a wall like a common thief. I'm being treated pretty well for a captive. That's a mistake on her part. Ace had me delivered to her all tied up but she went over his command and had his muscle untie me; she would do anything to defy him. I still have my track phone hidden in my pants. I spent the last few minutes I had calling Billy to warn him about everything but Dalla picks up instead. Dalla has been a thorn in my side since she lied to me about Billy killing our father. I made a mistake not killing her that day. She fucked everything up then and she's fucking everything up now. She won't tell him because she has her own plans. She always does.

Ace's mother is looking in the mirror. She's adjusting her hair or weave or wig or whatever the fuck that is hanging off her head. She's wearing a pink night gown. It matches her hair. Every look she gives me is seductive and evil.

"You look just like him, you know that?" she says and moves closer to me. She's smiling at me like she's remembering something. I just wonder who she is saying I look like. My father or her husband.

"Do you have the letters or not?"

"Yes," she says and smiles. "All of them. Every last one of those filthy, disgusting love letters they wrote to each other. The truth is all there," she says to me. Then spits at my face and wipes the corner of her mouth. "Disgusting," she says and slaps me so hard, her wig slides down. She readjusts it and fixes the bra to her night gown. Then sashays towards the door like she's the Queen of England. "I'm burning them tonight," she tells me and smiles. She puts her hand on the knob to leave.

"I can pay you," I say quickly and she stops. She loves money more than life. That makes her weak.

"Pay with what? My son is taking you for all that you have any day now," she laughs. "You won't have anything left but a name that doesn't even belong to you. You have nothing to offer me but dick," she looks down at my pants like a vulture. She is ready to pounce.

"We don't fail," I say calmly. I stare at her and she starts to look uncomfortable. "I don't fail," I add, "I'm not your son. Your son is a failure and you know this," I continue in a calm yet serious tone. She's not smiling anymore because she knows the truth. "I made the mistake of letting your son get away but I won't make that mistake again. He killed your daughter when he didn't get his way, what do you think he'd do to you?"

"My daughter died long before she got shot," she says like she's trying to fight off emotions. "He won't fail this time," she says, but I can tell she's not convinced.

"But if he does, you'll have nothing. I can offer you enough money to survive after I kill him. You know he's going to die."

She opens the door and shrugs at me. "You should have never let him go," she snarls and walks out the door. She doesn't slam it this time. That's how I know she's considering my offer.

She's right about me letting Ace go. The night Bobby and Billy came to me to tell me about Ace taking the women, I fucked up. I told them I would be right behind them, but I needed Ace alive because I knew he had the answers I needed. What they didn't know is that Vinchi did everything I asked him to do. Ace thought he had Vinchi but Vinchi had Ace. Vinchi put up cameras everywhere. I had eyes on the entire place. I saw the whole thing. Every room, every corner, every wife, every assault. It was hard to watch but a necessary evil.

Before Bobby and Billy came to me, I was on my way to get Ace and save our wives but they fucked up my plan. Especially Bobby. I thought he was dead. So I waited outside and watched. I told Vinchi that if things get out of hand to put Ace down but don't kill him. I trained my son three times a week for the past seven years on how to use weapons. Vinchi doesn't miss a shot. He aimed at his leg because that's what I asked him to do but somehow, he missed the shot. I saw Ace running for safety and I texted him to meet me somewhere. I told him I would help him. He was desperate and needed me, so he did it. He knew that I wouldn't kill him because he told me about the letters way before this attack. He knew I wanted them. He used me and I fucked up.

I took him to the second Ranch and integrated him. He wouldn't tell me shit. Then I left, and when I returned, they were waiting at my door thanks to Goldie. Some man without thumbs and two other men took me. Ace tried to get me to open the safe, but I refused. It wasn't about the money. I didn't keep much money in that safe. What I call emergency money. I didn't care about the money, but about the surveillance cameras I have of the Ranch. I figured, if the Ranch ever got taken from us, we could lay low at the second Ranch and watch what the fuck was going on while we planned our next move. I had to protect the surveillance with my life. It is more valuable than any money. He didn't press me about the safe as much because he wants the code to the main safe. But he'll never get it from me.

It's a matter of days before he takes it all. Whoever Ace's partner is, he knows more about us than Ace does. Ace is the mastermind and his partner is the muscle. Together, they make a perfect body. They're going to take the Ranch if I don't get out of here. They talk in front me now like I'm not even here. Like I'm dead already. But they haven't killed me yet.

I know their entire plan. They don't have the code to the safe on the main Ranch. That's why I'm still alive. They know I'll die before I give it to them. Dynamite couldn't blow that safe open. It's protected with the same metal that God has the gates of heaven coated in; it's unbreakable. They already have feet on the Ranch disguised as our security, waiting for the go ahead. Bobby is the only one with the code to the safe besides me and I trust him. He hasn't opened the Ranch back up for business yet, I don't think he will until he hears from me.

I was going to tell them everything that I knew during our phone conference. The letters. The affair. Everything. But they found me again. I can't warn them now. If they can keep the safe locked, that will buy us time.

But the moment they open it, it's all over.

# LERA BADD

"What do you see?" I ask Tony. We're meditating again. It's what we've been doing all day. Tony is sitting with his legs crossed. His eyes are closed, and his head is tilted up towards the mold stained ceiling of this shitty hotel. I've been working with him closely. I'm trying to get him to remember things his head injury makes him forget.

I think we're making progress. He keeps remembering things about his brother and Dalla. I think that he's remembering that Dalla is a snake and had something to do with his brother Keno's death.

"I see her again," he says excited. He's referring to Dalla. "I told Keno not to do it. I told him not to trust her."

"Why?" I ask, and he closes his eyes even tighter. He's so deep in concentration that sweat beads are popping up across his forehead before they burst and roll down the sides of his face. "Why?" I ask again and squeeze his hand. He's shaking his head and then he lets out a huge sigh like he's exhausted. He opens his eyes and stares back at me disappointed.

"I don't know..." he says defeated. "I don't. I don't know; I don't..." I grab his hand and squeeze it before giving him a reassuring nod, stopping his rant in the process.

"It's okay Tony. Let's take a break," I say before using his broad shoulders to pull myself up from the floor.

I get up and walk towards the bed. I flick on the T.V to distract him. I need to pull him back into reality. He doesn't get up. He's still sitting on the same spot on the floor talking to himself and beating himself against the head. He gets frustrated when he can't remember things. I hate seeing him go through this, but he needs to start working on his memory. Taffy says she loves her brother, but it doesn't look like she ever tried to get him help. After she married Brip, she forgot about him just as if he died like Keno.

"Let's watch TV," I say softly. I place my hand on top of his knee and he jumps. It's hard to get him back in the present after we meditate. We've been at this all day. I think it's time for us to call it quits for the night, but Tony doesn't move.

I care about Tony. He's been gentle and attentive towards my every need. Without him, who knows where I would be. That's why I'm helping him. But I have my selfish reasons too. I need him to remember Ace's house. I want to go back. After being on the streets these past few days, I realize that Ace is not going to come for me. That's why I need to go to him. It's the only way I'll be able to kill him.

Killing Ace is going to be easy. I know this for a fact because I put a bullet in a man's head the other night. It may have been the easiest thing I've ever done. Doing it again is going to be easy. Especially with Ace. Killing is going to bring me pure pleasure.

I killed a man. It wasn't hard to do. And although I strategically planned it, it was really self-defense. After I pulled the trigger, it frightened me how easy it was. I felt nothing. I was just as emotionless afterwards as I would be after spraying a roach with

Raid. Or squashing a spider with my flip flop. I felt nothing; that was the scary part. Feeling nothing after killing someone had me questioning if I really died that day Ace attacked me. If I died, I was instantly reincarnated back into my own body as someone else. A stranger. A strong stranger. A stranger who is fearless and brave. A stranger who has an insatiable appetite for revenge.

He was like Ace. He tried to kill me first. Killing him out of necessity didn't make me a murderer but a warrior. He helped me plot his own murder. All it took was me putting on my B-Necklace and walking into a nightclub alone. Everyone whispered amongst each other when they saw me. They snuck stares at me from the corner of their eyes. They recognized my B-Necklace but they didn't recognize me. I looked different than they remembered. I was different than they remembered. Unfortunately, the guy I had to kill didn't notice that. All he saw was the necklace. Not the fierce warrior wearing it. That's why he's dead.

The worst part about that night was putting the necklace around my neck. I felt like I was hanging myself. It felt like a noose. I couldn't breathe. It felt heavier than I remembered too. So heavy that it was hard to hold my head up; I instantly felt burdened. But it was all a necessary evil.

Once I got Tony onboard, I had to act fast. No changing my mind. Because if I didn't, Tony would forget. He was my back up.. I needed him just in case things got too crazy. I told him I would walk into a club wearing the necklace and when I walk out, someone would be following me. I would lead them where I wanted them to go and he should be right behind us. Hiding in plain sight. Tony does that better than anybody I know.

The man grabbed me and tried to rip the necklace from around my neck. I didn't fight him. I just let it happen. "Where did you get this from?" he asked. He didn't believe I was a Badd. "You coming with me, bitch," he said. That was my cue to make a move. I used the self-defense tactics Tony taught me and freed myself from his grip. I kicked my supposed assailant in the dick and when he was hunched over in pain, cursing and threatening to do horrible things to me. I blocked out his words and I pulled out the gun. I pulled the trigger before he even had a chance to beg for his life.

After I shot him, I felt disappointed. I thought killing him would make me feel more powerful, but I felt nothing. It was messier than I expected. Blood and brain bits splattered all over my clothes like someone had thrown a plate of spaghetti at me. I didn't run afterwards either. I stayed and stared down at his mutilated body and waited for my moment to come. I waited for the power that Ace stole from me to return but it never happened. That's when Tony grabbed me and we ran off.

I was disappointed because I didn't feel satisfied. I needed to feel satisfied. Too much has been taken from me. Satisfaction would bring balance back to my life. But it never happened. That's when I decided that killing Ace may be the one thing to satisfy me.

I look back at Tony. He's finally pulling himself off the floor. When he stands to his feet, he looks at me like he's waiting on me to tell him to do something. He's wearing a pair of light grey sweat pants and clean white t-shirt that's a size too small for him. It works though. His entire outfit shows off just how strong his body is. His biceps bulge out the sleeves of his shirt. Every time he raises his arms, it looks as if the shirt is going to rip. The sweat pants shows off his tight ass and it gives me a hint to how thick his dick is. I can see the print through his pants and he's not even hard. I lust after his body using all three of my senses.

Lusting after Tony is the healthiest emotion I've felt since Ace violated me. My lust for Tony makes me feel healed. After Ace and Bobby, I didn't expect certain feelings to return. But looking at Tony right now makes me wonder if they ever left at all. I'm going to help all I can with healing his mind, but I need him to heal my body with his touch.

Tony and I have only kissed but honestly, I don't think he even remembers it. Would he remember if I pull his sweats off and sit on his dick? Is it wrong for me to want Tony? Aside from being sexy, he's also brilliant in his own way. He's loyal and he's a warrior. The kind of warrior that will die protecting those he cares about. I feel safer with him than I ever felt with Bobby.

I want Tony. I'm not sure how long this feeling will last so I take advantage of it. I have to act fast before the feeling goes away. I let Tony know that I want him without telling him. A language I know he'll understand. I pull off my shirt and quickly take off my bra. My breast spring out at him and pull him into a deep trance-like stare. I wait for him to decide if he wants me too.

Tony's eyes bulge. He stares at me like he's stuck in time. His chest swells with air that he doesn't dispel. It's like he fears that exhaling will cause this moment to go back into the figment of his imagination. He blinks at me to see if it's real. I place my hand on his chest and allow my fingers to effortless flow down his waist. He's watching my hands as they move down his body. Now he's sure it's real.

I pull off the jeans and he looks down at my pink panties I bought at Walmart. All courtesy of this shitty ass necklace. I tug on my panties and stick my hands inside them and start to play with myself. Tony can't take his eyes off of me. I know he's alert and aware of what's about to happen when I see that hefty bulge swell from a sausage to an eggplant in size.

"Come here," I beckon.

He moves closer to me. I put my arms around his neck and he stares down at my breast. I kiss him on the lips. Tony is so shocked by what's going on, his tongue lays idle in my mouth. I initiate a kiss by rolling my tongue around his mouth, but he still doesn't kiss me back. Maybe he doesn't remember how. He's still breathing hard. Feeling the warmth of his breath against my neck gets me wet.

I step back and place his hand on top of my breast. For a second, he just holds them without caressing or squeezing. Then I grab the eggplant he has suffocating in his pants. I pull it out. My touch, a long stroke of passion. The power of it folds his entire body in half. Tony not afraid to act on his feelings anymore. He lifts me off the floor and squeezes my ass. He pulls me into a kiss using my entire body. Oh, this kiss. I'm sure it can cure cancer. Maybe I didn't need to kill anybody to feel satisfied. I just needed Tony's touch.

Tony carries me to the bed and manages to pull off his shirt and remove his sweat pants at the same time. He pulls off my underwear and buries his face in between my legs like my pussy is the place that stores all his missing memories. He is so good at moving his tongue in the right places that I wonder if he was even better before Brip shot him. I guess some things you just can't forget. He knows how to multitask. He rubs my breast while he licks. My body feels warm all over because of his touch. I can't wait anymore. I want him inside of me, so I pull him up and allow him to slide inside of me with ease. His eyes roll back into his head from the ecstasy of my warm insides. He moans and grunts over my body like he is going to explode, but he controls himself. I squeeze my legs around his waist and when he goes to flip me over, I have a flash of Ace and that night. I try to fight the flashback, but it wouldn't go away.

"Get off, "I yell.. "Get off!" Tony jumps off of me and grabs his pants. He looks afraid like he has done something wrong and couldn't remember. "No, Tony. I'm sorry." I try to calm him down, but instead he throws on his pants and runs out the room.

Fuck! What the hell did I just do? This was a mistake.

* * *

Tony is gone for exactly an hour before he walks back in the room and asks me if I am hungry like nothing had happened. I am excited to see that he came back but conflicted about him not remembering what happened. Should I tell him?

"Where did you go, Tony?"

I am curious.

"For a walk. I needed to take a walk," Tony says like he knows there is a good reason he needed air.

"Do you remember what happened?"

"Did I hurt you?" he asks and gives me a desperate look.

"No," I say and walk towards him. I plant a kiss on his lips and he jumps back like I had bit him.

"I don't want to hurt you Lera," he says to me in the most normal tone I've heard him speak in.

"You didn't hurt me," I say and stroke the side of his face. When my hand touches his skin, he leans into my touch and closes his eyes like he is trying to have a peaceful thought. Maybe he did remember having sex. For the little while it lasted.

"Ace is the one that hurt me," He nods like he agrees with me. "He hurt Taffy too," I add, and he pops open his eyes looking like he'd seen a ghost.

"Scrappy," he says through a silent yell.

"It's ok, Tony. We just have to find Ace. I need you to help me find Ace."

"Ok," he says.

Tony walks past me and sits at the edge of the bed. He picks up the remote and starts to flip through the channels like he'd forgotten everything again. I blame Ace for all this. For shooting Tony and taking away the best parts of his manhood. And for taking away my ability to connect with someone I care for. I feel an insatiable rage burning inside me again. I can't wait anymore. I need Ace dead.

I turn towards the bathroom to shower when I hear Tony start screaming Taffy's nickname. "Scrappy!! Scrappy!" I run back to calm him down. I feel responsible for triggering one of his episodes.

"Tony, it's ok. Taffy is ok." I kneel down in front of him and try to calm him down.

"No! Scrappy!" he jumps up and knocks me back. That's when I notice his eyes are glued to the TV. I turn to look at the screen and see the fake heist that Dalla and Mona planned playing on the local news. So, I guess they moved forward with the plan after all. I don't know why but seeing this pisses me off. I look up at Tony and back at the screen. Maybe I can use this.

"Tony, Ace has Taffy," I lie. "You have to remember the house. You have to remember so that we can go there and save her."

"Ok," he says, panting and out of breath. He sits back down and closes his eyes, forcing himself into mediation.

I just cross my fingers and hope that when he opens his eyes, he will be able to drive me back to Ace's mansion.

* * *

We've been driving in circles. Tony found an old Jeep Commander in a shed behind this random farmhouse. He popped the hood and did something to get the engine started. It's been hours now. My head is starting to spin, and Tony is getting agitated. I'm trying my best to be patient with him because I know that I'm pushing him to the max, but I can't wait any longer.

I have to find Ace.

Tony kicked in three doors as I ran into homes armed with my pistol. Everything inside of me knows that this is pointless and Tony who can't even remember last Tuesday will never be able to remember where Ace lives. But it gives me hope and hope takes away my urge to senselessly kill. So, I'm going along with it.

I know it's a horrible thing to say but bursting through the doors of innocent people reminds me of just how powerful I can be. They look at me, men and women alike, and know that I'm in charge. I can get them to do anything I want while I'm holding a gun. They beg me to leave. They beg for their lives too. That only makes me anxious for Ace. I wonder if he is going to beg for his life once I ambush him too.

"Here. It's here." Tony pulls up in front of another house and points. It's so dark I can barely see the house behind the gate and I know that Tony can't either, but I pretend with him. I need to feel more powerful before I call it a night.

"Ok, let's go," I say and cock my gun.

"But the gate! There's a guard at the gate." Tony points through the darkness and I squint and see a figure. His eyes are way better than his memory.

"I'll kill him," I say and place my hand on the door to leave. but Tony grabs me, pulling me back.

"No," he says firmly. "We're saving the rest of those bullets for Ace and the men that have Scrappy."

I look back at Tony. He answers orders, he never gives them. He has a serious look in his eyes, so I nod at him. Maybe Tony is right.

"How are we going to get inside?" I ask.

"I'll get us in. Stay right here. Right here," he says twice like he needs to be sure I understand him. "This is it. This is the house. This is it. I know it. I know it is," he says and starts to breathe heavily just like he did at the last three houses.

I begin to feel sorry for him, so I agree. "Ok," I say and wait for Tony.

Tony walks slowly towards the gate and I watch him until the darkness swallows him up and I can no longer see him. I allow my ears to pick up the slack and listen extra hard. I listen so hard it's almost like I can see what's going on. I hear a stern "excuse me sir," followed by a gag and a thud. Then I hear a creaking sound like metal scrapping against concrete. The gate is opening.

Tony rushes back to the car and says, "Let's go. Quick before it closes."

I rush out the car and stick my gun in the waist of my pants and follow behind Tony. I hear him chanting "this is the place" under his breath. "I found the place." It feels like we are jogging a mile before I finally can see the actual door to the house. The house is huge. It has a large cobblestone courtyard that's lit up like Disney world. Tony pulls me out the light and behind some bushes.

"We got to be careful," he whispers to me, staring at the house like it is made of glass, "he will see us."

"How do we get in?" I whisper back. I don't care if the owners of the house see us. When they see my gun, they will have to sit down and shut the fuck up. But I follow Tony's orders because I don't want to trigger one of his episodes.

Tony points at the bushes that surrounds the courtyard of the home and gestures for me to follow behind him. When we get to the side of the house, Tony pulls my body against his so that my back is against his chest. He slowly pulls his finger up to his lips and gestures for me to keep quiet.

Now, we're moving again.

I'm not sure who owns this house but it's huge. I follow Tony around the back. We get to a fenced in pool and Tony starts climbing like he's Rambo. I look up at him and wonder why he thinks I will be able to jump the fence. I hear him when he jumps down to the other side. He whispers in-between cracks in the fence for me to wait for him. I don't like this idea, but I have no choice.

A few seconds later, I hear a gate open and Tony is whispering my name loudly. I follow the sound of his voice and he snatches me inside.

"We're here," Tony says amazed. "We made it," he says. "Taffy's inside. I remember. She was inside."

"Let's go, Tony." I ignore him, and he runs to the sliding door like he's trying to disable a bomb. He pulls a card out of his pocket and unlocks the door. Seconds later, we are inside the house but before we can step one foot in the door, we are stopped by a man.

I don't hesitate and draw my gun, pointing right at his head.

"I'm not armed," the man says and raises his hands in the air.

"Don't do anything to get your head blown off," I say and cock my gun. I don't know why, but I want to pull the trigger. This person is no threat to me. But I still want them dead. Tony looks at me like he remembers what he told me in the car. He remembers telling me not to kill anybody.

"I know why you're here," the man says.

I'm confused. This doesn't feel so random anymore. Something's up. I take a quick look around trying to notice something. Anything. Could Tony be right? Did he find Ace's house? I take a deep breath and shake off the fantasy.

"Where is she? Where's Scrappy!" Tony grabs the man by the collar and pulls him to his chest with one yank.

The man doesn't try to fight back. I point my gun.

"Wait, I can help you. I promise, I can help you."

The tiny man is no match for a towering, muscular Tony. Tony looks like he can break him in half with his bare hands. The small man knows this too. It's not my gun that he's afraid of anymore, but the power of Tony's body.

"How can you help us?" I ask him. "We haven't even told you what we wanted, yet?"

I'm staring hard at this odd little man. Maybe it's a tactic to stall us before the police come, but I got a feeling something else is going on. I'm getting back to my original theory. This could be

Ace's house. My heart is bouncing off my chest in subtle thuds just like a basketball bouncing against a brick wall.

I look past the man. I take a quick glance and grab as many images as I can with my eyes. The couch. The color of the rug. The painting on the walls. I sniff the air and really try to feel the room. Shortly after, an eerie feeling falls over me. It feels like déjà vu.

It's all too familiar.

"You came for him," he says to me. "I can take you to him, but you have to promise that my wife and I will be ok."

The man is giving Tony and me a desperate look. His entire face is sunken with fear. His hands are in the air. They tremble more with every second of my delayed response.

"Angelo," I hear a voice say from behind us. Someone is walking into the room. I point my gun in the direction of the door.

"Baby, don't come in here," the man says quickly and Tony punches him in the face. The footsteps stop. Whoever was calling his name is still standing at the door.

"If you move, I'll kill," I yell to the person and they scream.

"It's ok, baby," the man called Angelo says. "Please, I can take you to him now. Just don't hurt us. I can help."

My heart starts to race. The longer I'm here, the more familiar this place is. Then a light bulb goes off and suddenly my memory kicks in. When my mind makes the connection to where I am, my entire body jolts upward and I let out a gasp of relief so heavy it feels like part of my soul ejected from my body. We made it.

We're at Ace's house and Angelo is going to lead me to him.

"Let's go," I say and nudge him with my gun. Tony has his hand on the back of the man's neck.

Being here makes me feel weaker than I expected. Even with the gun. A part of me died here and it feels like my ghost is haunting this house. Maybe she wants her body back. She wants back into my world. But there is no place here for her anymore. I take a deep breath and focus. I'm here to kill Ace. Not to mourn the ghost of my past.

I'm going to ensure Ace dies slow.

When we get to the hallway, the man's wife, who looks more like a man dressed as a woman, was about to scream but he silences her yells by covering her mouth. Tony yanks his hand away.

"Be easy man. She ain't gon hurt you," Angelo says. "He's just right down the hall."

My heart feels like it's going to burst through my chest like a rocket. The closer we get to the door the more I realize I don't have a solid plan to kill him. I know that I can't act erratically and just shoot him everywhere. I don't want him to die right away.

Angelo gestures for us to be silent and points at a gold-plated double door. I look at Tony and he nods. I place my hand on the trigger and slowly push the door open. What I see leaves me so stunned that my natural reaction is to lower the gun. I gape at Tony, but he doesn't notice. Tony doesn't see what I see. Who I see. He's just looking for Scrappy. But my sight is as clear as day.

Brock is sitting in a chair with his face buried in his hands. He isn't the target I want, but he still deserves a bullet. I raise the gun and keep a steady aim.

# BROCK BADD

Lera was the last person I expected to see bursting through the door armed and ready to blaze. At first, I didn't recognize her. I still got to look at her real close to notice. She's changed and it ain't just because she cut all her hair off either. She ain't got the same soul no more.

She's had the barrel of her gun against the back of my head for almost twenty minutes now. She wants to shoot me. I can see it in her eyes. It's almost like she struggling not to and, honestly, I don't know why she hasn't shot me already. She has no reason to keep me alive, but here I am. Her saving me is saving everyone on the Ranch and she don't even know it. She can't see it. She can't see nothing but red, but I understand why. I know what Ace did to her. And, if I know my brother Bobby good enough, he deserted her for Tara, but what Lera don't know is that if things were on the other foot, Bobby would be by her side just like he is for Tara. Bobby goes where he feels needed the most. That's just how he operates. It don't mean he don't love her.

"You know they all in trouble, right?" I say to Lera. She has me in the front seat. Some black Rambo looking dude is driving. "Bobby too," I say but she doesn't budge.

"Fuck them. Fuck you and fuck Bobby," she curses. Her voice is void of emotion. That's how I know she's dangerous and will use that gun she's holding against my head whenever she feels like it.

"Where you taking us?" I ask, and she doesn't respond. I don't think she knows yet.

Her driver has Ace's mother and the sister I thought was dead tied up in the back seat. This could be the break I need if I can get Lera on my side.

"Where is he? Where's Ace?" She asks and nudges the back of my head with the gun.

"The last time I saw him, I had him held hostage at the second Ranch," I admit.

"What second Ranch?" she says like she doesn't believe. "Why didn't you kill him?"

"I was going to, but I needed more information for him," I answer. "I made a mistake," I admit out loud for the first time.

"You're fucking dumb!" she says. "I should blow your brains all over this fucking car." She yells. She's getting angry.

"We got to save those bullets," her driver says like he's reminding her of something. Lera ignores him.

"He might still be there. He ain't got nowhere else to hide. He knows we looking for him," I say.

"We?" Lera chuckles. "You ain't doing shit. You're the one chilling at his house with his mother and sister. You must be working with him. You knew he was going to take us, didn't' you?"

"No," I lied. It didn't make sense telling her the truth. She wouldn't understand. No one will.

"Take me to this second Ranch to find him. If he ain't there... you're dead," she says and leans back.

\* \* \*

We're about twenty minutes from the second Ranch. I know Ace ain't there anymore. It would be too risky. I don't know how I'm gon talk Lera out of killing me, but I got to think fast. I need to take control of this situation. Otherwise I won't get back to the main Ranch to warn them. If it ain't too late.

I got my phone on me, but I need more minutes. If I can switch it on, then I can call Vinchi and tell him to change the code to the safe just in case Bobby cracks under the pressure. Bobby ain't the cracking type but with everything that's happened, I can't be too sure.

Vinchi is my back up plan. My first son. My pride and joy. And my only way out this shit. I told my brothers to take Vinchi to the prison in Zone 6 on purpose. I gave him the same holding cell I gave Billy on purpose too. Before Billy took up residency, Vinchi and I spent a lot of time at Zone 6. I was grooming him for situations just like this.

Vinchi knew just where to find the cell phone I stashed for him underneath the same table Billy used to draw. He also knew the way out. I called him when he first got there. It made me proud when he answered on the first ring. That meant Vinchi was listening. He did just as I instructed him to do the moment he got there. He went straight for the phone and waited for me to call. I was the only one with the number. All the drills we did paid off just like I hoped they would.

I haven't really talked to Vinchi since I sent him to Zone 6. I hope he don't think I'm mad at him. He did everything I wanted him to do. It's my fault shit got fucked up. If I give Vinchi the code to the safe, he'll know that I trust him. I also had him locked in the prison to protect him from my brothers and to keep him away from Mona. I don't need her fucking with his head, softening him.

"We getting close. We need to cover they eyes," I say referring to Ace's mother and sister.

196

Lera's guy got them tied tight. He got their mouths covered too. He had to put Ace's mother to sleep just to keep her under control. I don't know what the fuck he did, but he hooked his arm around her neck and held her until she fainted in his arms. It's only a matter of time before she wakes up wreaking havoc again.

"You don't call the shots around here," Lera says, "In this car, you have no power. I do," she says and nudges my head with the gun again.

"I know," I say and hold up my hands, "we just can't trust them."

"And I can't trust you," Lera says and leans back.

"Lera," her driver says, "I think we should listen to him. They took Scrappy. They can't be trusted," he says and gives her a serious look through the rear-view mirror.

They stare at each other for a while and then Lera finally gives him the okay with a head nod.

"Pull over right here," I tell the driver and point.

"I ain't got nothing to use," he replies anxiously.

"You can use your shirt," I suggest and he pulls off his shirt right away. Lera gives me an evil look like she doesn't want me talking to her guy.

"Tony, be careful," Lera says, "We don't want them to get away like Jayson did. Remember?" Tony looks at her like he's confused and Lera smiles at him like everything is ok. "Go ahead," Lera gives the final order and Tony rips his shirt in half and goes to the back of the Jeep to cover their eyes.

"He doesn't remember you but I can remind him if I need to" Lera says to me in a loud whisper. "If I tell him that, you're done but don't worry, I won't say anything. If anybody gets to kill you, it's going to be me."

"Who is he?" I say confused. I had a lot people killed, but they were all considered criminals. I was no murderer.

"Taffy's brother," she says and then it makes sense to me.

I remember Brip coming to tell me he remembers shooting him. He was so upset that he was going to tell Taffy, but I told him not to. It didn't make sense. Some things are better left unsaid. If only my mother would have followed that philosophy, none of us would be in this situation now.

"Killing doesn't always make you a murderer, Lera."

She giggles sarcastically at me.

"If you don't think you're a mass murderer, then your ego is even bigger than I imagined."

Is that what she thinks of me? A mass murderer?

"I only murdered one person in my life and I regret every second of it."

"Who? Your mother," she says and lets out another sarcastic laugh.

"Yes," I say sorrowful. "I can tell by the way you holding that gun that you done got blood on it. You dropped bodies. I can see it in your eyes. Us murderers got stains on us that no amount of good can ever clean up. After a while, that stain is gon eat its way inside of you and you ain't gon be able to rest. Trust me, I know..." Lera is looking off into dead space like she's battling unwanted emotions. "I know what that nigga did to you is foul and if anybody deserve to kill him, it's you but killing everyone who gets in your way in the process is just gon fuck you up and that's gon feel like him fucking you all over again."

At that, Lera leans up and busts the back of my head with her gun. She doesn't do much damage, but I shut up anyway. When I look back at her, she is wiping tears.

* * *

As soon as I walk in the door and see the bullet holes, I know Brip's been here. The place is shot up like the wild-wild west. I told that boy before that it don't take all those bullets to make a scene, but his ass is an emotional shooter. I told him time and time again that the worst thing he can do is use his gun while he's under the influence of his emotions. If Brip was here, that means so was Mona. That means she knows about Goldie. This is not how I wanted her to find out but what the fuck can I do now. If Lera don't kill me first, I'm sure Mona got first dibs on me.

I know Goldie ain't here, so I don't bother going upstairs to look. This house is empty. They took my Hummer too, but I knew that from the conversations I over-heard. They took out the tracking device and deactivated my panic button. My Hummer is how they plan on getting on the Ranch. When the guards see my signature Hummer, they gon open the gate without hesitation. I got to get back to them. I got to stop this shit.

"No one's here!" Lera yells and points the gun at my back.

"Calm down. Let's look around first. We need to move like mice," I say like it's an order.

I don't have time for Lera's emotional mini drama. I got a legacy to protect. Besides, if she was going to shoot me, I would be dead already. I ignore her gun and walk ahead of her. She follows behind me.

"We need to go down to the basement," I say and lead the way.

All I can do is pray as I'm walking down the steps that lead to the basement. I pray that Goldie didn't have the code and that the Ranch hasn't been compromised. But when I get to the bottom of the stairs and step into the basement I know things are fucked up. The next thing I notice aside from the safe door being open is six large muddy footprints leading from the patio door to the safe. When I see that size sixteen-foot print, I know right away who it belongs to. Mona's so called connect, Kong.

So, he's Ace's partner. All this time, he's been aiding Ace in his failed plots against us.

Fuck!

"I don't see anyone," Lera whines. "Where is Ace? Where the fuck is he!"

I take a deep breath and try to respond to Lera calmly, but I'm frustrated and anxious. If Kong is in on this, it's only a matter of time before they ambush the Ranch. I told Mona I never trusted that super-sized nigga. He always wanted the Ranch. And he wanted her. Mona will never admit it, but I know they had some kind of thing going on in the past. But that nigga ain't never respected that it was over between them. He has disrespected me and betrayed my family. For that, he will die.

Kong only has his power in size and fear. But I have no fear. And, even if Kong tripled in size overnight, I still would be bigger than him.

"I don't know where he is," I snap.

"Well find him!" She says and points that fucking gun at me again.

Without thinking, I charge at her and grab the gun from her hand. When I take it from her, she looks at me as if I snatched her heart out of her chest. She's lost without this gun. Now, she's looking like the timid girl I remember Bobby bringing home.

"I'm sorry," I say immediately. "But shit is real fucked up right now. I know you don't love my brother anymore and you want him dead, but you don't have to worry cause if we don't get to the Ranch soon, they all gon be dead."

I put the safety on the gun and toss it back to her before I walk inside the safe. Lera is stunned that I returned her weapon. It is a risky move, but it buys her trust. Lera reeks of vulnerability. The gun covers smell of her weakness and makes her less of a prey. And, after what happened to her, she deserves to have it.

A few seconds later, Lera follows me into the safe.

"What happened here?" she asks and unlocks the gun before stuffing it into her waist band. At least she isn't aiming it at me no more.

"I had him, Lera," I reply and she looks at me like she understands, "he was right there. I had him restrained and then that bitch!" I punch the wall and Lera jumps and grabs the handle of her gun.

"What bitch?"

I shake my head. "I trusted someone that I shouldn't have. She's the reason he got away," I look at Lera, expecting her to ask me to explain but she doesn't. "Ace is going to get what he wants. He's gon win this thing," I say and sigh.

"No!" Lera says. "We can't let him win. We can't!"

"We need to get back to the Ranch. If you want a chance to kill him, you will get it there because that's where he is heading to finish the job."

"How do you know?" Lera asks. Her hand is still on the gun handle.

"Whatever plan Mona had going to get into the safe is going to lead them there. That's all they waiting on. Once Mona opens the safe, she's going to be ambushed by the guards she thinks are under her command."

"Fuck!" Lera says and kicks at the ground. "Mona probably opened the safe already. I saw they already aired the news story of Taffy's faux abduction. She was going to use that as leverage to get Bobby to open the safe." When she said Bobby's name, her face dropped. "How do you know all of this?"

"I heard them discussing it. They said everything in front me because to them, I was good as dead. They confident they're going to get on the Ranch. I am too," I say and look at the surveillance equipment. Everything has been cut. Mona probably did that, but she probably was too late.

"What about Taffy?" Lera asks under her breath.

"You know what he's capable of," I tell her and her spirit drops. I walk away.

I'm no murderer but if I get a chance, I have to make Goldie pay for this. My father used to always say that the wrong woman could tear down an empire. He was right. I was foolish for thinking that she would be loyal to me just based off who I was alone. Of course, a woman's whose greatest contribution to the world is her ability to fuck and suck would betray me. She betrays her own self just by having nothing more to offer. That's why I married Mona. I knew she would never betray. Even now, I'm sure in some way, she's protecting me. I don't know how she explained all of this to them. This Ranch. Ace being here. The surveillance tapes. All of this makes me look like I'm the enemy, but she still is protecting me. I can feel it. She doesn't deserve what I did to her but if I can get us out of this situation, I can make it up to her. I promise I will.

I lean against the wall but before I know it, my body is sliding down in a slump. I'm getting weak. The last time I felt this weak, I smothered my mother to death with her own satin pillow. Now, I'm taking that same pillow and holding it over the Ranch and everybody I love. I'm suffocating them. I'm killing them.

Lera walks out the safe and towards me. She looks at me like she's shocked to see me so weak. Like she's seeing me as a human with emotions.

"How can I help?" she says. She's still holding that gun.

I jump up and force the weakness out of my body and refuel myself with the strength of protecting my family. I pull my phone out of my pocket and hold it up. "I need to get more minutes on this phone. I have to warn them and then we got to get to the Ranch as quick as we can, but we got to make a stop first. I need to get to my brother Billy's place and get a map. And I need to get you some more bullets." Her face lights up. "I'm going to need an extra shooter but..." I pause and she looks at me, waiting for me to speak, "you have to learn to think for the gun when you shoot not think with the gun. Otherwise, you gon get us all killed."

Lera nods like she understands what I'm saying. "Follow me upstairs. I got a few guns that I think you might like," I say to her and she nods.

*   *   *

"My father used to say that picking a gun is just like picking a spouse. You got to pick one that can be just as loyal to you as you are to it. You know what I'm saying?" Lera nods.

"This one is a little heavy. Maybe I should go for one that I can manage a little better." Lera looks up at my display. Her eyes lands on an assault rifle. "But when I kill Ace, I want something big like that," she says and points to the most lethal weapon I have. I smile. I can admire her ambition. Even if it is full of revenge.

I smile at her. I know where she's coming from. I pull the rifle down and hand it to her. She struggles with holding it.

"I can see what my brother saw in you. It's only now but I can see it," I tell her truthfully.

"He didn't see shit!" Lera spits back at me, still struggling with the gun.

"That's not true. He loves you."

"He loves her," she retorts, referring to Tara.

"Naw, he just got history with Tara. That's all. Bobby watched <u>our</u> father burn and mutilate her *father's* body. After that, he felt responsible for her. You know how I know he really loves you?" I pause to study her reaction. Lera reins in the emotions in her eyes and shrugs her shoulders like she don't care but I know she does. She replied too quickly.

"How?" There is an eager look in her eyes.

"He attacked me for having you in my dungeon that day. In all the years I've known my brother, I've never seen anybody make him lose his cool. Not even Tara," I say and Lera's entire face softens up. She struggling with her tears now.

"How did you know what Ace did to me?"

I hesitate at first. I have to lie to her. I can't let her know about the surveillance cameras I had Vinchi put up. It would make me look like an awful person and she wouldn't understand.

"Bobby told me," I say and she looks confused. "Before they ambushed me, I was in contact with all of them. Except Mona," I continue and drop my face. "Bobby called me upset. He wanted to kill Ace more than you. He felt responsible. I ain't never heard him sound so stressed."

"Why did he put me off the Ranch then?"

"He was confused. His son was there. Tara is dying. It was a lot going on Lera, but he regrets it. He wanted me to send someone to find you, but I was too distracted with trying to clean up this mess," I answer.

I lie to her so effortlessly that I believe it myself. Just like father used to always say, a white lie is just as clean as the truth.

"I didn't know," is all Lera can say. She hands me back the assault rifle.

"Whether you decide to be with my brother or not, you deserve to know the truth."

"I'm not the same anymore. I can't be with him," Lera says in a low voice.

"We all change Lera. I done changed fifteen times this week already, but I know that Mona will accept every part of me that's different cause she loves me. It ain't gon be easy, but she'll accept me. Bobby will do the same for you but first things, first," I say and pick up a 12 gauge shot gun to hand to her. "I need to train you on how to shoot, but we got to be quick."

Lera grabs the gun and looks at it like it's her newborn baby. And in many ways, it is.

"I think this is the one," she says.

"Good," I smile at her, "now let's go make that nigga pay!"

Lera returns my smile and nods. She tosses the other gun aside. She has a new toy now. She points the shot gun, holding it at her side.

"No not like that," I say to her and run behind her.

My chest is against her back. My fingers touch her skin as I ease up her arm and put her in the right position. "Use your shoulder to stabilize the gun. Otherwise you'll fall back. There is a lot of power behind that pull."

Lera does what I say with perfect posture then lowers the gun. She turns and smiles at me. She thanks me with her eyes. I think I have her trust. She leans the shot gun against the wall and turns to hug me like its second nature. On the way into the hug, we kiss. Once our lips touch, we jump back like we'd just burned each other. I don't know who kissed who, but it happened.

"It's ok," I say right away.

I dismiss the moment before it becomes something else. Something we won't be able to turn back from or ever understand. Lera rushes to get the gun. She quickly turns away like she's embarrassed. I just ignore it.

"Remember, keep it here," I say crouching down on my hips and patting my shoulder. Lera nods. I still have her trust. That's all that matters to me right now. The kiss is nothing. It doesn't matter. Now, I have to get in contact with Vinchi before it's too late.

I hope I still have his trust too.

# BRIP BADD

I don't know where the fuck Mona got the new guards from but if they keep watching me like I'm crazy, I'm gon put them all out. Out of work. Out of this fucking universe.

"You got a problem?" I say to one of them who staring at me like I stole something from him. When he doesn't respond I start walking towards him. I pull Bo out the waist of my pants and hold her in the air. Any reason he gives me to finger fuck Bo, I'm ready to pull the trigger.

He looks at me and half smiles then shakes his head no like he ain't got nothing to say. But why the fuck is this nigga smiling at me? I aim Bo at him and get ready to shoot his ass in the knee when Mona calls out from behind me. Shit!

"Brip, what the fuck are you doing? Put that fucking gun away! You ain't out of bullets yet?"

I lower my gun still staring at this cocky ass dude. "I don't allow myself to have those type of problems Mona. Me and Bo stay ready," I say still staring at him. What pisses me off is that the dude don't even flinch. This mutha-fucker is actually challenging me. Who the fuck does he think he is?

"Come here," Mona says to me. "I'll meet you guys at the next post. We got to have a conference," she says to a group of the guards.

What the fuck are they having private meetings about? Something is up with this group. I don't trust them. They follow Mona's orders and all hop in an Escalade and drive off. I got a right mind to light that whole truck up. My finger is itching to pull on this trigger. Bo ain't had her pussy wet in about two days and she don't like being dry.

"Where the fuck you get these new guards from?"

"Why?" Mona answers defensively. She trying to hide a look on her face, but I see it. Something is up with her. She ain't been right since we left Ace's spot.

I can't stop thinking about my wife. If that nigga is out there, then Taffy is in trouble. I was a fool for not trying to find her. The thought of what he did to my woman makes me sick to my stomach. I thought playing wild- wild west and shooting everything walking would make me feel better, but it doesn't. It only makes things worse. I ain't shooting the right target. I need that nigga's head. I'm gon chop off his dick first. I'm gon make his ass suck it and then it's going to be off with his mutha fucking head. Maybe Taffy can be there to see it. I think it's about time I start looking for her. I ain't saying we getting back together or anything like that but at least I can bring her home. I know for sure she'll be safe once she gets back to the Ranch. After that, we can take it one day at a time. Or maybe not.

Mona staring at me like she trying her best to keep a secret. I keep my eyes locked on her.

"I don't trust them niggas that's why!" I say and put Bo back in my pants.

"Maybe they don't trust you. They came from the East Meadows projects. I just got word back about the damage you done out there. Some of them niggas you put bullets in could be they family, Brip. We sent you out to send a firm message, not go on a massacre."

"Fuck them!" I say and turn to walk away.

"Wait," Mona yells at me and I stop.

"Do you know if anybody else heard from Brock? I know he's been in contact with you and your brothers," she says, desperate.

I look at her and shake my head. The way she worrying about Brock is the same way I'm worrying about Taffy. But, she ain't got to worry about Brock. My brother is invincible. I don't know what he out there doing, but whatever it is, I know it's right.

"Don't worry about, Brock. He'll make it back to the Ranch when he's figured things out. You know how he is."

"How if he's in trouble? It's time we started considering that," Mona says. "We need to have a family meeting..."

"If Brock was in trouble we would know, ok. Just be cool, Mona. Leave him to handle whatever it is he handling. Knowing Brock, he probably already got a lead on Ace."

"Well, why wouldn't he tell you all that?"

"You know better than me how Brock operates. He only speaks when necessary."

Mona takes a deep breath and exhales slowly. I never seen her this emotional before. She sniffs real hard and sweeps her hand over her face like she is wiping away emotions. When she's done, she's back to being rock hard again.

"You right," she says to me.

"I'm worried about Taffy though," I admit to her before she walks away. Mona turns and faces me. She gives me a sympathetic look but doesn't say anything. "I want to start looking for her. I need her on this Ranch."

"You ready to try and work things out with her?" Mona asks.

"No," I answer quickly, "I'm ready to keep her safe. I owe her that much. That fucking crazy mutha-fucker out there like he ain't got a care in the world. Who's to say he don't already got eyes on my wife? I heard about what that nigga did to Lera. I'm gon cut his fucking dick off, Mona."

I swallow a mouthful of air and take a deep breath. There is a time to recover and then there is a time to get your ass back on the battlefield and finish fighting the war. My brothers been slipping. I step back and look up at Mona. She looks at me like she is expecting me to explode. If my brothers don't do something, I just might. We been idling long enough.

"Bobby and Billy acting like they don't give a fuck but I want the mutha-fucka dead for putting his hands on my wife. End of story," I slice through the air with my hands.

Mona is looking at me like she don't want me to worry. "We gon find her," is all she says. "I'm gon meet with the guards. I got some things I want to go over with them, then we can talk." She turns to get back in her golf cart.

"You don't want me to go with you?" I yell, just to see her reaction. Mona shouldn't be meeting with the guards alone. The Ranch security is all of our concern. Not just hers.

"No," she responds too quickly. I give her a strange look and she starts to talk real fast. Like she's explaining herself. The Mona I know never explains. She just does. "You'll just intimidate them, Brip. I need they full attention. I will call you when I get done."

"Ok," I say to Mona and she cranks up the engine to the cart ready to speed off. "Where y'all meeting at anyway? I just want to know where you are just in case I need you."

Mona gives me a strange look. She knows I'm suspicious now. She hesitates at first and then quickly blurts out, "the conference room at the Casino." She drives off before I have a chance to ask her anymore questions.

I am feeling restless, so I decide to walk to the cemetery to talk to mama. I need to let her know what's going on. She's the only person that can make me feel like everything is going to be ok. I need to feel that right now. I decide to walk instead of drive because I need to clear my head. The cemetery is not too far from the big house. Hopefully, when I leave there, I know where to start looking for my wife. I need to let mama know what happened between us too. She gon be upset when she find out how me and Taffy been getting on. Acting like we enemies.

I got to give her an update on the baby too. She thinks she got a grandchild coming and she needs to know that the baby may not be mine. Maybe if the baby is still in heaven, she can walk right over to him and ask him who his daddy is. Then I won't have to wonder no more. Maybe the baby's a her and not a him. Mona and Brock are obsessed with boys but if this child is mine, I want it to be a girl just like mama and Taffy.

The sun is starting to set. The Ranch has been so quiet since we shut down shop. I'm used to the energy of it feeling alive. Cars zooming by. Music blasting from the Casino. People laughing. People screaming and begging for they lives and the people that are crying and rushing towards the clinic. All those things make up this Ranch and I feed its energy. Now, I feel low. Maybe that will change if I can find Taffy. Coming home to her after a long day of bathing in someone else's blood, felt like Christmas morning. Taffy made all the dirty shit I had to do clean. She was my angel. If only mama could have met her. She and mama had the same energy and big heart. They both loved me without fault and I'm beginning to think that anyone who can love me without judging may just be the most special person in the world to me. One of them is dead though and the other may be near death. I can't let that happen. I got to find my wife.

I'm about half a mile from the cemetery. There ain't no lights out here. It's getting darker and darker as the sun fades. That's perfect for me. I only come and see mama when it's dark cause I don't want her to see me. Or at least see what I've become. I start to feel anxious so I lean up, pick up a rock, and toss it off somewhere into the distance. I don't feel like I threw the rock far enough, so I lean down to pick up another one when headlights beam from behind me. What the fuck? I turn around so quick I almost fall. I drop the rock and pull Bo out of my pants. This area is restricted to family only. Everyone knows that. Even the guards.

Whoever is driving has on their bright lights. I try to block the light with my free hand so I can see who to aim at but I can't see shit. The car stops. It looks like one of the Escalades Mona's new guards been driving. I wonder if that nigga from earlier coming back to start some shit. Well he done came to the wrong place. I'm blowing his head off as soon as he steps out the fucking car. He got a lot of nerve stepping on sacred ground.

They turn out the lights. I blink hard to readjust vision. I feel blind but my aim is steady.

"Name yourself," I yell. "This is a restricted area."

"I'm guard 13," he says to me. By the sound of his voice, I already know he don't mean no harm.

"What the fuck are you doing here?"

"I know it's against the rules, but I had to find you sir. I got some information that I think you may want to know about. I can't let the others know I'm here."

"What the fuck are you talking about man?" I walk closer towards the car, squinting. "Step out the fucking car," I demand. I can tell by the sound of his voice that he ain't the same nigga trying to front from earlier but what the fuck does he have to tell me?

He steps out the truck with his hands up in the air.

"Come closer," I tell him, and he does just as I say. I take his gun from him and throw it to the side.

"What the fuck you got to tell me?"

"I got something you might want to see. Somebody sent it to me today."

I watch him as hard as I can. The sun buries itself behind a dark cloud and it's completely dark now. I don't trust this dude. I don't trust none of them.

"We don't know each other," I snarl.

"It's about your wife, sir," he says hesitantly.

I immediately lunge towards him, grabbing him by the collar. I pull out my gun and stuff it down his throat.

"What the fuck you say about my wife?" I throw him to the ground and he hops back up and throws his hands in the air.

"Sir, I'm only trying to help."

"Why! Why you trying to be so fucking helpful?"

"Because I know if it gets back that we knew and didn't say anything you will kill us all. I got a daughter. I need to live for her."

"Fuck your daughter!" I say. "You know where my wife is?"

"No," he says. His voice trembles. "But I know she's in trouble."

"Speak," I say and press the barrel of my gun against his jaw.

"My phone, sir. Get my phone. It's in my pocket."

I'm confused by his request, but I grab his phone out of his pocket anyway.

"What the fuck you want me to do with this?"

"This came in today. It's a ransom. Everyone on the street is talking about it. I don't know how it didn't get back to you. Somebody got your wife and is auctioning her off to the highest bidder. Look at the photo. They know she's a Badd wife. If you don't do something soon,"

I punch him in the mouth with the back of my gun and he gags and spits out blood. I think I bust a tooth out of his mouth, but I don't give a fuck. I look down at his cell and see a pic of Taffy all tied up and stuffed in a corner. He is right. Somebody has her.

"WHAT THE FUCK" I scream so loud that when I'm finished, I feel like I have strep throat. I pull the guy back towards me. "How did you get this? Is it you?"

"No! I ain't crazy, man. Somebody grabbed her from a store. It made the news...look it up."

"Find it," I hand him back his phone.

He wipes the blood that's dripping from his mouth and quickly starts searching for the video. His hands are trembling, and my heart is racing. I knew this would happen. I knew it. I waited too long to try and find her. This shit is on me.

"Who the fuck would do this?" I say to myself but the guard answers for me.

"It could be one of the family's members of the men you killed at the East Meadows."

When he says that, I punch him in the gut and he hunches over, spitting blood. He drops the phone.

"Find the fucking video!" I say, yanking him up from the back of his neck.

He does what I says, coughing and gagging.

"Here," he says and hands me the phone. I press play and see the whole thing play out. The video ain't that clear, but I know its Taffy just by the way she's walking. They grab her and run out the store just like they taking cash from the register. She's trying to fight. No one will help her. I watch it until the video ends and then replay it. The guard is rubbing his stomach and coughing. It's dark out here but I start to see red. Blood red. Before I know it, I'm howling at the moon like a fucking werewolf thirsty for blood. Not again. No one is taking my wife. She been through enough.

When I look up, I notice the guard 13 is running. I stop him with a bullet in both legs. He falls to the ground and I walk slowly towards him. His body is squirming on the gravels like a fish out of water. He's trying to crawl away. I aim Boo at him. He flips over to his back and holds out his hand. I don't even know what the fuck he saying. I can't hear nothing, but the gun shots that come next. His blood splatters onto my body, but it ain't enough. I need more. I jump in his escalade and put in reverse. When it feels like I'm running over a speed bump, I know it's guard 13. Fuck him. Fuck them all.

* * *

I speed the all the way to Casino and hope to find Mona meeting with the rest of the guards but to my surprise, they ain't there like she said. They all gon pay for this. I try to call her, but she ain't picking up. I try to call Bobby and Billy too, but they ain't answering either. I'm getting angrier by the second. I pull out Guard 13's phone and look at the pictures again. Taffy looks terrified. She has duct tape around her mouth and a blindfold tied around her head. My poor wife. Being married to me ain't worth all the stress I put her through. I got to make this right.

When I can't find Mona at the Casino I rush to the big house and press the panic alarm. The sirens sound and I continue to stare down at Taffy's helpless body. Did I cause this? Did I shoot the wrong nigga? We weak now. We have to be if they out there retaliating against us like this. Mona was right. I should have taken it easy. I should have been out looking for my wife instead of blowing off heads.

A few minutes after the sirens are going, Mona comes bursting through the front doors like the big house is on fire. There ain't no fire except for the one that is in my eyes. She screams when she sees me all wet with Guard 13's blood. I can't take my eyes off the phone.

"Brip!" she yells and runs towards me. "What's wrong?" she says like she's choking back tears.

A few seconds later, Bobby and Billy come running in the door. They all stop when they see me holding the gun in one hand and the phone in the other.

"What's going on man?" Bobby says in a calm voice. For some reason, the calmness in his voice calms me down.

Billy rushes up to me and carefully takes the phone out of my hand then Mona places her hand on my shoulders. "Breathe," she says. "Take a deep breath." I do like she says. The more I breathe in deep and then exhale, the less manic I feel. "Is it Brock? Is he ok? Is he still alive?" she says all in one breathe. I don't answer her and she starts to panic. "Brip, where's Brock? Billy you got to get him to talk. It's about Brock?"

"It's not Brock, Mona," Billy says. "It's Taffy," he says and Mona instantly stops raging.

"What are you talking about?" Bobby asks and takes the phone from Billy. "Mona, have them turn that siren off. I can't think with all that noise," he says and looks down at the phone.

"Somebody's got her," I say under my breath. "They got her hostage. They want money. Five million dollars wired to them by tomorrow or they gon kill her."

The sirens stop way before Mona returns.

"What the fuck!" Billy says. "What we gon do?" he asks Bobby.

"What the fuck you mean what we gon do? We gon pay the money!" I yell. "I ain't gambling with my wife's life. I ain't like you two bitch ass niggas. Somebody fucks with my wife, they gon get dealt with but first things first...We got to pay that money."

"How?" Billy says and looks at Bobby.

Mona returns. She's quiet. She doesn't even ask to look at the phone. Bobby is staring down at the phone and then back at us like he's trying to find the best way to handle this situation. Billy and Mona are giving each other weird looks.

"I agree," Billy says. "We need to pay the money."

"We got to be sure that..." Bobby starts his bullshit and I don't even let him finish before I cut him off.

"Fuck that Bobby. Open the safe!" I snatch the phone out of his hand and pull up the video. "Look," I show him, "there is a video too. The shit made it to the news. That's my fucking wife man! They got my fucking wife!" I say and before I know it, I'm pulling out my gun. They all jump away from me, holding out their hands like they don't know what I'm going to do.

"Calm down, Brip. I understand why you upset but you know how this shit works. We can't just meet their demands just cause they asking," Bobby says to me.

"Open the fucking safe, Bobby," I say and point the gun at him. "Now!"

"You gon shoot me little brother?" Bobby says like he's trying to get me to see that I'm making a mistake but this ain't no mistake and I will shoot his ass over my wife.

"I'm gon ask you one more time nicely, OPEN. THE. FUCKING. SAFE." I'm getting more pissed every second Bobby doesn't budge. If this was Tara, the safe would've been open already.

"Brip calm down man," Billy says. "Put the gun away. We gon do the right thing. Right Bobby?"

Bobby is looking at me like he don't know me anymore and Mona is just standing there like she's at a loss for words.

"Maybe Bobby's right," Mona says. "We need to think this thing out first."

"What would you do if it was Brock, Mona?" Billy says and they share a fierce stare.

"What would you do if it was Tara?" I direct Billy's question to Bobby and he gets uneasy. "How if there was a ransom on her life? Would you open it then? That can be arranged right now you know."

"You going too fucking far now man," Bobby says with a heavy voice. I'm pissing him off.

"You have no idea just how far I can go," I say back. "If you don't open that fucking safe, I'm going to kill her man. I'm gon put a fucking bullet in her head."

"Fuck you man," Bobby says and charges towards me and my gun. "You gon have to put me down first."

Billy tries to restrain Bobby. I'm still pointing the gun at him. He knows I'm serious. He knows that I will kill Tara if I don't get what the fuck I want. The bitch is already dead anyway. It won't be hard to put a bullet in a corpse.

Somewhere in the midst of the controversy, Jayson rushes through the door. When Bobby sees him, he backs down, but I don't take the gun off of him. He walks away from me like he knows I won't shoot him but my brother is really underestimating me tonight.

"Jayson?" Bobby says like he seeing a ghost.

"They setting you up, man" Jayson blurts out then exhales like he ran all the way here.

"What?" Bobby looks back at all of us in confusion before Mona's guards come and grab Jayson. "Let him go," Bobby orders but they don't budge. They look at Mona and wait for her to respond. She remains silent. Bobby looks back at Mona and then looks at the guards like he's putting two and two together. "I gave you an order," Bobby says in a grave voice. They still don't listen.

"Mona is involved. Taffy too. There was no kidnapping. They want you to open the safe so Mona can take the Ranch," Jayson blurts out all in one breath. "Brip," Jayson says and gives me a serious look, "Taffy is ok. No one has her... Bobby, don't open that safe. If you do.."

Before he can finish, I shoot him. I don't even know where the bullet lands or wait to see his body fall. Mona screams when

Jayson falls to the floor and Billy gasps. I point the gun back at Bobby who is looking at me like I'm the reaper. He knows I'm serious now.

"His sister is next if you don't open that fucking safe!"

# BOBBY BADD

Brip just shot Jayson. Now, he's pointing that fucking gun right at me and threatening to shoot Tara next. At this moment, I know I did the right thing sending BJ off the Ranch. This place ain't safe for none of us.

"Calm down," I say to Brip sternly. He doesn't loosen his grip on the gun and he's still aiming it at me.

"Let's take a walk to the safe." He starts walking towards me, but I still don't move.

I'm looking back at Jayson every chance I get. He lying on the ground like he dead, but Brip didn't kill him. He tried though. Brip shot him in the chest, but as long as I been knowing Jayson, he has to be wearing a vest. His bullet proof vest is just as much a part of him as his own skin.

I look up and Mona and Billy are staring at me with their mouths open like they don't know what the fuck to say. I don't know why Mona is so fucking quiet either. Her guards are looking at me like they will shoot me if Brip don't. Jayson is right. Mona is on this shit. Ain't no niggas grab Taffy on the street. It all seems too fucking strategic. By the silence of Billy, something is telling me that he in on this shit too. Now, I got to open this fucking safe, so I can get the fuck off this Ranch. If the money means so much to them that it's worth me and my family's blood, then they can have it. Shit, they can have this whole Ranch cause after tonight, I'm done with it all.

"Brip, just be cool," Billy finally breaks his silence then looks up at me and says the same thing with his eyes. "Bobby, just open the safe, we gon have to sort all this shit out later." He shoots Mona a quick glance that he don't think I noticed.

"Fuck it," I say, "I'll open the safe, but then I'm gone," I look at Brip and his face drops from the guilt, but he ain't putting down that gun. I start walking to the safe and they all follow me. Mona's five guards included.

Jayson has never lied to me. Not once. I trust him more than my family right now and that's fucked up. He mentioned Dalla and Taffy being in on the setup, but he didn't say anything about Lera. I walk towards the safe. I can't stop thinking about her. Repressed thoughts of Lera flood my mind. Before I leave, I have to make sure she's ok. I need to be a man and face her. It's the right thing to do. Lera is the most innocent one of us all. I sucked her into all this shit and I know saying I'm sorry ain't gon be enough, but an "I'm sorry" is all I have for her right now and it's real.

I'm walking down the hall now. Everybody is quiet. The only thing you can hear is our footsteps echoing off the marble floors that lead to the basement of the house where the safe is. When we walk past the house staff, one of the women screams when she seen Brip holding the gun on my back. This shit is fucked up. It's all so fucked up.

I got to think strategic. Once I open this safe, I'm gon grab a few stacks for myself, find Lera and then get BJ and get the fuck on. This ain't my life no more. But before I leave this Ranch, I need to make sure I do the right thing by Tara. I'm gon pull the plug on her. This shit ain't what I want her to wake up to anyway.

Watching how BJ reacted to seeing her body made me realize that me trying to keep her alive is just arrogant and selfish as me being pissed at Lera. I ain't been handling this shit like a man. How I did my wife, ain't me. This Ranch is making me weak. I got to go somewhere and get strong. I need a fresh start but first things first.

I open the double doors that lead to the wide basement stairway. Before I start to walk down I turn to them and say, "You know at this point there ain't no turning back." I make sure to make eye contact with each of them individually. Even Mona's guards. Each look I give them means something different. They all know just what my eyes are saying. Two tears run down Brip's cheeks like they are escaping from his eyes. Dilly stares back at me like it's the last time he'll see me again and Mona is giving me a blank look. Almost like she's having an outer body experience and is witnessing this whole thing take place in another dimension. When the guards look at me like this is the moment they've been waiting for, it only confirms that once I open this safe, the shit is going to hit the fan. One of them is whispering something in his two way. Mona ain't even watching her own men. She's too out of it.

I turn to walk down the stairs, but I don't like having my back to any of these people right now. About seven steps down into the basement, I hear them all coming down behind me. I can tell by the aggressive sound of their footsteps that they are all anxious. Greed can be more evil than murder. Brock gave me this code because he felt like he could trust me. Shit, that may be the only thing Brock did right in months. Had he given it to his wife or Billy, Brip wouldn't be forced to put a gun in their back because they both would have unlocked this safe weeks ago.

I ain't like Brock. I can't die for this shit. I gave up my life for it, but I can't die for it too. I got a son to look after. If I die, Blake will have no one. I've done fucked around and let Tara get killed then screwed Lera over. I can't let that happen to my son. I spent too long protecting him from all this to let it all blow up in my face. If Brock was here, he would take a bullet before he let someone take the Ranch. I only allowed myself the option of taking three bullets and no more. One was for Tara but she don't need that bullet no more. The other was for Lera but all that changed once I bailed on her. And the last bullet belongs to Blake. He deserves it more than any of us. I'll take the bullet for him but not this Ranch. That's why I'm doing what I'm doing now.

I step into the basement and pause. I look back at everyone who is now crowding behind me. Some with money stares in their eyes and the other blood. I give them one last look to be sure this is what they want, and no one budges. That's my cue to say fuck it all.

Brip sniffs up his tears and straightens his posture. He's struggling with his emotions but at the end of the day, I know my little brother is only doing what he feels is right.

"Let's go man! Get that shit open. Time is money," Brip yells and points at the safe with his gun.

I hunch over the metal keypad and take a deep breath. I remembered the code the moment Brock gave it to me. It is simple. Simple enough for us all to guess if we really sat down and thought about it, but I guess us Badds have gotten used to taking the easy way out. I type in the four-digit number: the month of mama's death and the day she was born. Numbers we all know. Everybody except Mona's guards.

When I press the last number, I try and prepare myself for the beginning of the end, but it doesn't open. There is a loud beep, a bright flash of a red light and warning sound that tells us all that the code I have is wrong.

"What the fuck?" Brip yells. I turn and face them, waiting for them to give me direction. "Try that shit again!" Brip demands and I do what he says only to get the same results. I do it a third time and the sirens of the Ranch go off and we all jump back, scared shitless.

"He must have changed the code before he left," I defend myself. Brip is looking like he just ran out of his last options. Mona seems relieved and Billy looks disappointed. The guards looking at me like they don't believe shit I say. That's because they don't know me like the others do. My family knows that I mean what I say more than anybody.

"How long you had the code?" Billy yells over the sirens. He leans in closer to hear my response. The red lights are flashing all over the Ranch. I'm so distracted by the chaos I can't think straight.

"Only since he's been gone," I say and look at Mona and wonders if she knows something, we don't.

"What we gon do about my wife? They gon kill her!" Brip pleads to Mona and Mona turns around to walk up the steps. Brip grabs her like he's desperate for a solution and all the guards draw on him. They draw on us all, Mona included.

"Put them mutha-fucking guns down!" Mona orders her men, but they don't listen. She stunned but she tries to keep her composure. She looks back at us like she's admitting she fucked up. "Stand down," Mona yells to them again but they only get more aggressive in their stance. They got us all right where they want us, and we lead them here.

Brip's got a firm stance. He steps in front of us and aims his gun at the guards. Brip's only got one gun but he's holding it with the same confidence as if he three.

"Y'all know this just worse than suicide, right?" Brip tries to warn the guards, but they don't give a fuck.

One of the guard's steps forward out of the crowd. "This ain't suicide," he says to Brip and then looks up at us, "this is the end," he says with confidence.

Then, all of a sudden, the sirens shut off and we all jump the same as we did when they unexpectedly came on. We look at each other. Only a Badd can give an order to turn off the siren. Is Brock back? It's the question our eyes are asking each other but the guards aren't asking the same question because they already know who it is. Then we hear the door at the top of the basement stairs open. Footsteps from a single person make their way down slowly.

The silence in the room is so loud, I can't hear myself think. The main guard is staring at us and smiling with his eyes. He knows more than who is going to appear at the bottom of the steps. He knows what's going to happen too. Brip is still standing his ground for all of us. He won't give up. The guards don't force him to either. They know that it doesn't matter how good Brip done got fucking Bo, his one gun is no match to their five.

The footsteps stop. Now it's time for us all to learn what's up. To deal with the punishment we knew we was giving ourselves when we allowed ourselves to be consumed by greed and selfishness and pride. I think about Blake and instantly a thought of Billy's son flashes in my head. Blake is safe, but BJ is out there on his own. BJ is my flesh and blood just like Blake. Although I only allowed myself to see him out of the corner of my eyes. I was so caught up in my shit that he became invisible to me. I look up at my brother and our eyes lock for a moment. He knows I'm thinking about BJ too.

Mona is looking like she has her fingers crossed. She needs the person at the other end of that door to be Brock more than she needs air right now. Even if Brock comes down and shoots us all, she still needs it to be him. A bullet from a Badd would be the only bullet Mona is willing to take right now because she knows Vinchi and BJ are somewhere on the Ranch.

The door opens and in steps the mystery person. Brip debates who to point the gun at. He turns from the guards to the basement doorway. But when Mona see who's standing at the end of the steps, facing us like this very moment was a fantasy come true, she screams for Brip to drop his gun.

"Brip, put it up," she yells, "drop the fucking gun," she charges toward him and snatches the gun out of his hand. Like most of us, Brip is so stunned by the visitor that he doesn't try to fight anymore. His mouth is hanging open. He looks back at me and Billy to see if we are sharing his reaction. And we are. This has all caught us off guard, Mona inclusive.

# VINCHI BADD

"Stand down," I say, and the guards lower their weapons. Mama is looking at me like she don't know if she want to punch me or hug me. She'll probably end up settling for both. My uncles look relieved to see me but confused. They ain't saying nothing now because they too busy answering the questions they asking themselves in their heads, "Is Vinchi for us or is Vinchi against us?"

Well, I'm only making moves for one person now and that's my grandmother. Beverly Badd. I'm doing this for her. Because I know what my dad did to her. I may be the only person that knows. I saw him. I was there that day. Even though I love my father, I can't seem to get over what he took from me. So, I decided that I was going to take something from him the first chance I got. And it's this Ranch.

"Vinchi? What's going on?" Mama asks me carefully. She's walking towards me. The guards aim their guns at her again. She stops dead in her tracks like somebody stabbed her in the back. She looks at them and then back at me like I let her down.

I don't blame my mother for any of this. She doesn't understand why I'm doing this and I don't bother explaining anything to her because I know she will never understand. She hated my grandmother but that only made me love her more. I was her first grandchild. Grandma Badd showered me with love. Not the tough love I got from my father. My mother. My uncles. But tender love. Her loved saved me. As a young child growing up around all this chaos on the Ranch, I needed that love more than anything. Grandma Badd's light lit up every dark place on this Ranch and when she was around, I was never afraid. She was like my nightlight; she comforted and helped me sleep through the night without fear of nightmares. I felt so lost after her murder. I felt like she'd abandoned me. I felt so alone.

Then, I felt angry.

I'm so happy that I didn't have to see her body. It was a part of her last wishes. Closed casket. I couldn't see her like that.

After she died, mama didn't even ask me if I was ok. She was too busy tending to the man that killed her. My father. I haven't been the same since and neither of my parents has taken time to notice. They treat me more like an asset, just someone to hand the cloth to when it's all said and done, not like a son. I've always been treated like I was just a tool for them. My parents' sole purpose for bringing me into this world was to make themselves immortal. Once they died, they would live on through me. Their little prodigy.

Then they decided to create a breeding house just to give me competition. They never asked me what I thought about it. I never liked dad being with other women. It was fucked up and embarrassing. Mama tried to act like it didn't bother her, but it did. I saw it in her face. I see a lot that they don't notice but I never said anything. Grandma Badd used to always tell me that sometimes it's better to be seen and not heard. I know what she means by that now. And it's perfect because that's just how everyone treats me. They only see me. They don't hear me, and they haven't been trying to hear me since infancy; even when I was screaming. But now, it's time for me to be heard loud and clear and I'm not going to have to scream this time.

"It's ok," I say to the guards and they lower their guns again. "Don't worry, Mama. Nobody's going to hurt you?"

"What about your uncles? Did your dad put you up to this?" She says in one breath.

She's trying not to cry. I can tell by the way she's struggling to keep the emotions from defying the gravity around her face. She looks like she's about to fall apart. I hate when my mother acts like showing emotions is like having cancer. You would think her tears were made of acid. She keeps them all trapped in the prison of her emotions. Grandma Badd used to tell me, never to be afraid to cry. She said tears were the gateway to the emotions you hold hostage in yourself. Maybe that's why she cried so much.

"Everybody is going to be fine as long as we don't do anything stupid," I give my uncles a warning look. I can tell that they don't want trouble. At least Uncle Bobby and Uncle Billy don't. Uncle Brip doesn't look very happy with me right now.

"Your Aunt Taffy is in trouble," he informs me and shoots Mama a sharp glance. "You gon handle that?" he says to me desperate but serious.

I look at Mama. I let her know with my eyes that I know all about her fake little heist. I'll give her the chance of breaking the news to Brip that Taffy is okay and will be here soon.

"Taffy isn't in any trouble Brip," Mama says, hesitant.

Uncle Bobby turns to face Uncle Billy and yells, "So this shit was a setup. You in on this shit with Mona."

"What the fuck!" Uncle Brip yells and reaches for the gun that he no longer has.

"I don't know what you talking about, man," is all Uncle Billy says to Uncle Bobby. "Vinchi, where is BJ?"

"With the nurse," I relieve him of his anxiety.

"What about Tara?" Uncle Bobby asks.

"Fuck Tara!" Uncle Brip yells. "Where is my wife?!" he asks me.

I give the room time to settle down before I speak. I don't want anyone here to feel threatened by me, but I do want them to know who's in charge. No one here has to get killed unless they want to. After a few moments of silence, the room settles down and I have the floor again.

"Taffy will be here soon. So, will Dalla," I say and look at both my Uncle Brip and Billy. "I let Jayson take Tara," I say to Uncle Bobby. "They left the Ranch with a nurse. They safe," I look at my uncle and he nods at me like he's thanking me.

I'm being very compromising right now, but I learned from my father that it is the best way to keep control. But if any of them get out of hand, I will shoot them down just like I did Brip. The plan wasn't for me to shoot my uncle. At least not my dad's plan but I knew Uncle Brip would put up more of a fight than I was willing to take. So, I did what I had to do. I probably know how to shoot a gun better than him. For one, we were trained by the same person, my father... And two, I'm not as emotional as my Uncle Brip so that alone gives me better aim. I knew exactly where to shoot my uncle. I wasn't trying to kill him. Only put him down. It was the only way.

I played my dad and Ace against each other. They both think they have my trust but they're wrong. Dad is going to pay for what he did to Grandma Badd and Ace Lucky is going to pay for what he did to my Aunts and my Uncles. I'm going to put myself right in the middle of right and wrong just to keep the balance. But first, I have to put my uncles on lock down.

"Be cool Uncle Badds," I say then order the guards to take them to their houses. "Make sure you got enough men to cover all areas. I want two inside the houses and two outside. No one touches them. No one speaks to them. You understand..." I say and notice that I sound just like my father when I'm giving orders.

My main guy nods and three guards step out the crowd and escort my uncles back into their homes. My uncles don't fight. They all look too weak to throw a punch anyway. Mama is looking at me like she's waiting for her sentence.

"You ok, Mama?" I say and turn to walk away. I decide not to put her on lock down. It doesn't make sense to. As long as she doesn't leave the Ranch, my mother is no threat to me.

"Why are you doing this?" she asks me.

I turn to face her. I stare at her before I respond. I want her to know that although this is personal, it has nothing to do with her.

"I love you, Mama, but somebody's got to make him pay."

"Who are you talking about, son?" Mama asks, but I think she knows who I'm talking about. She just don't want to accept it yet.

"The person that started all this," I say to her and she closes her eyes for a split second like she is willing herself to be somewhere else. "Did you know he did it?" I ask her.

"I just found out," she says to me quickly. "Your father has been under a lot of..."

I stop her from finishing her sentence. "Don't do that. Don't make an excuse for him." I try not to get angry with my mother. She can't help it if she's been mind-controlled into thinking my father is God. "He has to pay for what he did to her. It's the right thing to do."

"Pay how?" she asks.

I look at her and read her mind instantly. She is wondering if I mean that he has to die. I am not planning to kill my father, but I'm aware that what I do may lead to his death. But he brought all of this on himself. And if he is that man that he raised me to be, he would understand the choice I have to make.

"He's going to suffer a lot just like I did," I pause to give my words time to sink in. My mother is still confused. She can't phantom anything being taken from Mister Badd. So, I decide that

I would only let her in on my little secret, after everything has been said and done. "Try to stay out of trouble, Mother. Everything will go smoother that way," I say and walk back up the stairs.

# DALLA BADD

I'm in this kitchen, raiding the fridge and stress-eating. I'm putting everything in mouth that I can get my hands on. I'm so anxious plus Brock keeps calling me, but I won't answer. It was on the tip of my tongue to tell Billy that he called me that day at Walmart, but I didn't do it. I haven't heard from Brock since, but, today, he's already called me five times and sent multiple texts for me to call him back. I don't think he's interested in talking to Billy anymore. It's me he wants to speak to, but that's not happening. With Billy's help, I just pulled the plug on Mona's plan. Now, I'm just waiting on Billy to call me back to tell me where to meet him. We're out of here. I can't let anything get in the way of that.

After all of this, Mona decides to back out of the plan at the last minute. Taffy is pissed at me and then Lera's gone. I can't let all the shit I did to get this plan off the ground go in vain. And, I don't appreciate her misleading me. Hell, I don't appreciate her misleading any of us. The day of Taffy's fake abduction, I sent her everything she needed to help her get that safe open, but she never called back. I knew we only had a few days to get things going so Mona ignoring my calls was a red flag. All that shit she was talking about taking the Ranch and doing right by us wives was bullshit. At the end of the day, Mona Badd only cares about Brock Badd, the Ranch, and her kids. And that's the exact order of her priorities. I wasn't letting her fuck me over easily, so I took matters into my own hands. I got in contact with Billy and he helped me set my plan in motion. He texted me right before it happened. So, he should be calling me back any minute with a place to meet and the money. After all these years, we're finally going to be free from all this shit. Tonight, I feel like I hit the lottery. I finally feel like I got a much needed win.

The phone rings again and it's Brock. I send the call straight to voicemail and place the phone on the countertop, so I won't be distracted as I reopen the fridge. I'm hunched over the refrigerator all of thirty second when Brock calls right back. I sigh and try to block out the sound of the phone ringing. If I wasn't waiting on Billy to call me back, I would have turn the phone off or put it on silent, but I have the ring tone set to loud so that I won't miss his call.

The phone stops ringing, and I pull out a container with cubed cheese and chopped carrots. I don't know who the fuck is in charge of stocking this fridge but a few bags of potatoes chips and a couple sodas surely wouldn't hurt. Especially in stressful times like these. I settle for what I have and lean up but when I do, Taffy is standing behind me, holding the phone.

I instantly drop what I have on my hands and reach to snatch the phone away from her, but she dodges me, and I miss.

"Give me the fucking phone," I warn her.

"No," is all she says. She's giving me the evil stare that I've gotten accustomed too.

"Taffy, please," I say genuinely begging her. I can't miss that call from Billy and I don't want Brock to call while she's holding it. I know she will answer. Taffy smirks at me. Hearing the desperation in my voice she knows she now has the upper hand. I calm down and change my approach. "Look, I know you're pissed off at me, but Mona is going to call us any second about the money. After tonight, you will never see me again. So please, let's try to get through the rest of this day as peacefully as possible. I'll stay out your way," I say and hold out my hand, waiting for her to return the phone. She doesn't do it.

I told Billy that we would have to break Taffy off a portion of the money. At least enough for her get back on her feet. I just don't want to leave her stranded. I know she doesn't trust me or believe that I care about her, but I do. I know she has no reason to trust me.

"Who the fuck keeps calling you?" she asks.

"Mona," I lie but Taffy knows that I'm not telling the truth.

"Why not answer? You guys got in the safe right? Brip got you in?" she asks in a sarcastic tone. She waits a few seconds for me to respond and then rolls her eyes. "I'm not fucking stupid. This ain't Mona calling you. Tell me who it is right now or I will break this fucking phone in half," she says and holds the phone in the air.

"No," I say and jump towards her. Taffy twists her body and ducks right out of my way. I chase her around the kitchen for a few seconds like a school girl trying to get her lunch back from bully but it's not working. "I know you don't trust me," I say to her.

"I more than don't trust you," Taffy says holding the phone even higher in the air, "I fucking hate you, bitch!" she says so harshly I have no reason but to believe. My heart breaks a little, but my need to have the phone back suppresses how she makes me feel.

"You don't want to fuck with me, Taffy," I stop chasing her and stand my ground.

"I don't give a fuck about you, Dalla. All of this shit we going through is because of you and you really expect me to be grateful for you. Fuck you and Mona!"

"I'll let her know you said that when she calls," I try to threaten her, but it doesn't work. She laughs at me instead.

"I'll let her know it myself," she says and puts the phone in her bra.

I don't know how Taffy got out of her room. We have two guards in the house. I instructed them both to make sure she doesn't leave. But here she is with my fucking phone.

"Help!" I start to scream up the stairs. "Get your asses down here!" I yell for the guards for backup.

Taffy chuckles at me. "You so fucking dumb," she shakes her head at me. "Putting your trust in guards that only take orders from their dicks," she said through a laugh. "Both of them thought that I was going to let them fuck me. They're both tied to my bed posts," she flashes me a quick smile, "taking naps," she adds like she's warning me of what she's capable of doing. "Now, tell me what the fuck is going on? I'm going back to the Ranch tonight. What am I walking into? What does Brip know?"

I pull out a chair from the bar of the island and sit down. I sigh and wait for Taffy to join me, but she keeps standing.

"Mona's pissed at me," I say, and Taffy looks confused. "She's calling me because she was getting cold feet like you. After I sent her your ransom pics, she didn't push the button like I thought she would. So, I got the pictures to Brip anyway. He got the safe open," I add my lie and Taffy's face lights up like that is confirmation that Brip still loves her. "Mona is going to wire me the money for you but cut me out the deal cause she pissed at me for overstepping her. That's why I'm not answering right now."

"Brip got the safe open?" Taffy repeats like she needs to be sure she is hearing me right.

"Of course, he did," I say trying to wheel her back into me, "he's the only person who could have pulled this off for us. I knew he would do anything to make sure you're ok." Taffy is beaming right now.

"I got to get back to the Ranch. I have to let him know that I'm ok," Taffy says more to herself than me.

"I would wait if I were you. Wait until we get the money. That way Brip won't be so pissed when he sees you."

"Fuck you," Taffy screams. "All you see is blood and money. I don't give a fuck about that money right now. I care about my husband. Fuck your money, Dalla. If you love money that much, then ransom your own self. I'm sure there are a lot of niggas out there that would pay hundreds and thousands for the opportunity to kill you," Taffy says harshly. Her words cut through me like a knife because I know she's right.

Taffy stares at me. She wants her words to sink in and they do. She's right. Most people would rather see me dead but not the person that matters; Billy loves me and right now, he's going through extreme measures to make sure me and BJ stay safe. So, I have to do my part to make sure we come out on top.

"I lied," I say to her and Taffy looks at me like she already knows what I'm talking about before I even tell her. "I tried to protect you in more than one way. I even tried to spare your feelings, but since you give a fuck, I don't give a fuck!" I say to her and she stares at me with her arms defensively folded across her chest. "Brip didn't open the safe when he heard about you."

"You're lying," Taffy says immediately, but I give her a serious stare and then shrug at her like I don't care what she believes. I get up and act like I'm going back to the refrigerator. "Tell me the fucking truth?" Taffy demands.

"I've done enough to try and help you. When you show up on the Ranch, you can find out for yourself," I say. "I'm done trying, Taffy. Do what you want," I say.

Taffy is staring at me like she's a human lie detector test. She's trying to figure out what to believe. But her conscience is putting up a fight. She doesn't know what to believe. I pull out some Hennessy from the freezer and hold it in the air like it's a peace offering. She doesn't respond but slowly walks toward the bottle like it holds the truth in it. I carefully lean up and pull out two glasses and place them on the table and pour us both a shot.

Taffy is standing on the other end of the island. I slide her shot across the island and drink mine down quickly. Then I pour myself a second shot. "That doesn't mean he don't love you," I say and take another shot. Taffy stares at me hard and then picks up her glass. I'm close enough to jump over the island and tackle her. I place both hands on the granite countertop and discreetly prepare myself to leap over the bar. "He's just mad right now," I tell her, "so don't go taking it personal." On that note, she closes her eyes to take the shot and I jump over the bar like an acrobat, catching her off guard. I grab her, but she gets out of my grip in a matter of seconds. Now, we are fighting like teenage girls.

"You gon learn about fucking with me you devious, scandalous ass bitch!" Taffy yells and swings me into headlock. She's punching the top of my head and squeezing my neck at the same time. I wrap my arms around her tiny waist and squeeze her tight before trying my best to lift her off the ground and slam her on the floor. It's difficult but after a while, I succeed and land right on top of her. She's swinging and clawing at me like a wild alley cat, but I manage to pull the phone out of her bra and throw it across the room. Taffy digs her nails deep into the side of my face and pulls away a thin layer of flesh with her nails. While I'm leaning back in pain, Taffy kicks me and my body flies back and crashes against one of the wood base cabinets on the island. Then the phone rings and we both stop moving and share a brief stare before rushing towards it.

Taffy grabs it first, but I jump on her back and when she struggles to push me off, the phone slips out of her hand. I'm able to snatch the phone away from her but she grabs my arms. She's digging her nails deep into my forearm, breaking the flesh and trying to twist my arm back so that I drop the phone. My grip is too tight. The phone rings one last time. I don't know if it is Brock calling or Billy. I crouch down on all fours and position myself in a tight ball so that Taffy can't move around me. After a few punches and kicks, she gives up.

Panting, she steps back and pulls herself up. "You pathetic," she said through an exasperated voice. "Fuck that phone!" she yells and tries to catch her breath. "I'm leaving tonight. You can do what the fuck you want."

"You can't leave yet!" I scream to her back, but she shoots me a bird and keeps walking, then she stops and jumps like she just saw a ghost when she tries to turn the corner.

"What the fuck!" she screams and that's when I see a man grab her. I don't stay to watch what happens; I crawl into the dining room and escape through the back door. When I get outside, I run barefoot all the way down the street until I feel safe.

* * *

I'm in a random back yard. I sit on their patio furniture and try and catch my breath. Somebody grabbed Taffy. Who the fuck sent them? Did Mona give that order? Maybe she's pissed at me for cutting across her. I pray it's Mona, that way I will know Taffy is safe. I can't go back. I can't save her. I just can't.

I take a deep breath to keep from panicking. Then, I check my phone and see that the missed call was from Billy. Shit!! I call back right away but he doesn't answer. So, I call again but still no answer. Then I notice I have an unopened text message. It's from Billy. It reads, get out the house now. There on the Ranch and coming for you and Taffy next. Run now! He tried to warn us, but I was too busy fighting off Taffy. I try to call him back, but his phone keeps going to voicemail.

Has the Ranch been taken? Is BJ okay? Does this mean that Billy and I are back to square one again? I can't do this anymore.

I got to get to the Ranch to help Billy and BJ but I'm going to need help. Without Tony, I don't think I can survive. The phone rings again and I jump and answer, hoping it's Billy telling me that he's coming for me, but it's Brock.

# TAFFY BADD

"Where are you taking me?" I say and kick the seat of the driver.

He doesn't respond to me. Neither does his partner sitting beside me.

I can't believe this shit is happening again. Two real kidnappings and one fake in less than six months. All these years being married to Brip Badd, I would have never thought it would come to this. I've already decided that I will choose death before I let one of these niggas do me like they did Lera. I won't do it, so I just may be dying tonight. Me and my baby.

"I asked a question?" I say again.

I kick the seat with both feet. This gets his attention. He turns and gives me a stern look like he's warning me not to do it again. He's annoyed.

"Don't make us have to gag you," the driver says and grimaces at me through the rearview mirror. "We should be arriving shortly," he adds.

They talking to me like I'm a Badd wife. I don't feel threatened. If I wasn't so distracted by Dalla and all her nonsense, I would have been able to escape like she did. That bitch wasted no time running and leaving me behind. Dalla can't do anything at this point to surprise me but die. The bitch has nine lives.

"You like jazz?" the man in the front passenger seat ask me. I am not sure if that is a trick question or code for his partner to kill me, so I say nothing. He turns on the radio and saxophone tunes trail out the speakers. "Maybe this will keep you calm until we get you home," he says casually.

"Home?" I dart up and lean in closer to him. "Are you taking me back to the Ranch?"

"Yes, mam. We have strict orders from Mr. Badd," he says and leans back in his seat comfortably.

"Mr. Badd? Brip or Brock?"

He shrugs his shoulders like he doesn't know, and it doesn't matter. "They all the same to us," he says and turns the music up before leaning back to make himself comfortable again.

We just got cleared to go through the security gate. I'm back on the Ranch. My heart is racing because I have no idea what's waiting for me up the hill. How if Brip refuses to see me? If he knows about the fake heist, he may not want to see me at all. How if they put me in the prison? Or Mona is pissed at me because I didn't cooperate. I don't know what to expect, so I just expect the worse.

It hasn't been that long since I've been gone but everything looks different to me. I don't remember the road leading up the main house being so bumpy, and the place looks so dark and eerie even with all the lights on. Watching the guards march around with assault rifles and radio phones gives me anxiety. This place starting to feel more like a concentration camp with every Badd male taking the place of Nazis. I lean back and close my eyes and pray that when I reopen them, this place will feel like home again. But when my eyes see Vinchi standing in front of the big house, I know it's not home. Not anymore.

"I'll get your door, Mrs. Badd," the driver says before getting out the car. He opens my door and carefully escorts me out the car. Vinchi is walking my way now. I can barely look at him. I won't forget how he shot Brip and left him there to die then dragged me off and locked me in a room for Ace to grab. Seeing him isn't a good thing. Vinchi is dangerous and I don't trust him. Now I'm wondering, if I'm really going to die after all. Maybe Vinchi just called me here to kill me.

"Welcome home, Aunt Taffy," Vinchi says and then looks over my shoulder and back towards the car like he's looking for Dalla. He doesn't try to hug or shake my hand. He keeps his distance. "Don't worry, no one is going to hurt you here. I promise," he assures me. I don't say anything. "We're missing a Badd wife," he says and gives the guard a stern look. "Dalla. Where is she?"

"She wasn't in the house when we got there," the driver replies.

"Well find her," Vinchi says like he's warning him.

"Why am I here Vinchi?" I ask and then swallow hard.

"You're a part of the plan," he says and smiles at me. "Take her home," he instructs the guards and then turns to walk back into the big house.

I'm looking around the Ranch for a familiar face. Mona or maybe Brip but the place is like a ghost town. Aside from the guards, the Ranch is empty and eerily quiet. The guards escort me back to the car and drive me to the mansion I share with Brip. I knew what Vinchi's plan was a few months ago but it got destroyed when Bobby and Billy came to our rescue. Is he trying reactivate that plan again? Does he want us all dead? I'm so over this shit. As the guards are pulling into my driveway, I see someone peeking out the window from blinds in my foyer.

I know it's Brip by the aggressive way he's holding the blinds. Does he even want to see me? I don't know what to say to him.

The driver opens my door and helps me out again. He unties my hands and lets me go. I look back at him confused and then back at the house debating if I should enter it or not.

"We've been instructed to see you safely inside. Go ahead Mrs. Badd," he says and gives me a nudge.

Walking up the long driveway that leads to the entrance of our house feels more like walking the plank. I don't know what waits for me at the other end of the door and I'm not sure I'm ready to find out. Whoever was watching us through the blinds, stopped once I started walking towards the house. I'm standing in front of my door now. I don't know if I should knock or just walk in. I turn to look at the driver and he nods at me like he's giving me permission to open my own door. So, I do. At least I try to, but before I can turn the knob all the way, someone on the other end is already pulling the door open for me. It's Brip.

As soon as our eyes meet, we pull each other into a long emotional kiss. There just as much passion and intensity in our kiss as there is hesitation and resentment. That's when I knew Brip still loved me. But nothing is the same.

Brip looks at me all over like he's analyzing me for damages. He doesn't know that my bruises only show on the inside. I don't know if he's happy to see me or not because he's not smiling. After he's done looking at me, he steps back so I can walk in. He staring at me so hard I feel uncomfortable. I can tell by the look in his eyes that he's stressed. This tells me word must have gotten to him and he knows about my fake abduction. I open my mouth to apologize but nothing comes out.

I close the door behind me and notice two guards standing behind Brip.

"Give us some space," he turns and says. They scatter off somewhere in the house. Brip looks back at me like he's waiting on me to say something.

"What do you want me to say?" I shrug. He doesn't respond. He just shakes his head at me like he's ashamed. Like I went too far for the last time. "You have a lot of nerve judging me right now."

"I ain't judging you, Taffy. I'm judging your choices."

"Well it wasn't my choice. None of this was. I haven't had a choice since I married you, Brip," I say and take a deep breath. I start to look around the house. Right away I notice that I'm not connected to anything here. Not even the custom-made Italian couch I had imported here the day after our wedding. I look back at Brip. He's still staring at me like I'm a stranger. It feels like he's not connected to anything here either. Especially me.

"Even after I found you with that nigga you was fucking, I wasn't gon let nobody hurt you, Taffy," he says to me like he's shocked that I think he deserted me. "All these years together, I thought you understood me, but you don't. That makes me wonder what the fuck you've been doing here all this time."

"I know you, Brip. I know you better than any of them. You didn't try to find me. Yeah, the kidnapping was fake, but it could have been real! You guys left us on the streets to die! No money. No protection. No fucks given!"

Brip walks towards me. "Don't put me in the category of my bitch ass brothers cause they ain't built like me," he says and pounds against his chest. "They told me you don't want to come back." Brip looks back at me. He's hurting. I can see it in his eyes and by the way he's using his eyebrows to hold up his face. One wrong movement and all the emotions he's trying to control will cause his entire face to fall.

"Why am I here now?"

"I don't know what the fuck is going on," Brip turns to me and yells, "I guess we all gon die. I really don't give a fuck anymore," Brip turns to walk away.

"Brip wait," I rush towards him and hug him from behind. Feeling his body and the scent from his skin reminds me of how much I miss him. The more I hold him, the more connections I'm making. I don't want to let him go but he pries my hand from around his back and pulls away from my grip.

"Be cool, Taffy," Brip says without looking at me, like he's exhausted from life.

"Do you still love me?" I ask him.

He turns and looks at me like that is the craziest question he's ever heard.

"Yes, I still love you. Love don't just go away if it's real," he stares at me like he wants to ask me the same question, but he doesn't. "You can have our old bedroom while you're here. I'll take the couch," he says and continues down the hall.

I watch him until he turns the corner just to see if he is going to turn back and look at me. But, he doesn't.

I'm trying to get reacquainted with my couch, but the cushions don't feel as soft as I remember them feeling. Neither does Brip. I feel like a stranger in this house. But on the flipside, I'm sure this house feels like it has a stranger in it as well. I'm not the same. Neither is Brip.

I look around at the décor and all the positions that I once prized and I see nothing of real value. Everything in this room from the expensive couch I'm sitting on is so overpriced and pretentious that it all is starting to look cheap to me. Everything my eyes meet, from the rugs to the pillow, is something I picked out from a magazine catalogue. Nothing is original here. I wasn't original here. I look up above the fireplace mantel and notice the picture of me and Brip hanging above it. I used to think that picture was the bomb. It was so hard getting a photographer to agree to take a picture of us because of Brip's brutishness and my temper. It took them 90 shots and 95 threats from Brip whenever he would grow impatient. But finally I settled for the pretentiousness that's hanging above my head, making mockery of me for the fool I once was.

Brip and I are both dressed in all white. The diamonds we are showcasing stand out from the white. If I was a product, that picture would definitely be my sales tag. I can't stand the sight of it but I still love the man in it. That hasn't changed. If I thought Brip would agree to it, I would ask him to let me sleep on the couch tonight as opposed to our old bedroom. Me lying in that bed with all those memoires of us and all the shiny things that distracted us from our reality would be like cheating on the new me with the old me. A few miles from this house is a crematory where people come and burn bodies. Bodies that were once called brother, father, or husband. I was so blinded by the light from this all white home and the bright diamonds that gave us false sunshine; I never considered how the way I chose to live for comfort made me an accomplice... and a victim.

But there ain't no turning back for me now. This is my home. Brip is my husband and I'll be a part of this crime family until I die or until it kills me. That's the harsh fact of my faith. But in order to make accepting my faith ok, I have to get my marriage back on track with Brip. He just going to get to know the new me. And I'm going to have to get to know the new him too. Plus, I have to tell him about the baby. He won't believe me and when it happens, he's going to place his love for our son on standby until he learns the truth. If the baby ends up not being his, he'll take his love off standby and throw it in the trash. He won't accept this child and he won't accept me. But he'll force himself to live with it and we both will be miserable and outwardly bitter towards each other until the end.

What a life I chose for myself.

# BROCK BADD

I'm making my fourth call to Vinchi today. He's still not answering. I'm starting to get worried. Maybe he didn't change the code to the safe in time and now, the Ranch is under seizure. There ain't no other reason for him not to be answering my calls.

"You sure you trust your son?" Dalla says and frowns. I know she doesn't trust Vinchi but who the fuck is she to be concerned about trust? She's got to be the most untrustworthy woman in this world and yet, I need her ass. I guess we need each other.

I was shocked when she finally called me back. At first, I thought it was Billy. I was disappointed to hear her conniving voice but when the pickings are slim, you use what you have to make a feast. Dalla is going to be our way back on the Ranch. The day she came for Mona and Billy, she used his maps to guide her way to Zone 5. Now, I need her to help us into Zone 6; the only way for us to get on the Ranch undetected. Billy had to tell her where he keeps his maps. That's the only reason why she's here.

We saved her ass too. Right in the nick of time. Just as we was pulling off, the cops were pulling in. Whoever house she decided to camp out in, called the cops on her. She ought to be more grateful than she is. She standing over me with her arms folded, looking down at me like she's some fucking King. Like the choices she made up until this point are better than mine. In this situation, right and wrong don't exist. I don't give a fuck what Dalla thinks about me and I'm pretty sure she don't give a fuck what I think about her. She wants to get on the Ranch to save Billy and her son and I need to get on the Ranch to save our legacy which includes Mona and my children. So, we got to put being enemies aside for the time being, so we can think like partners. This is the first day that I haven't regretted not killing her the day she lied about Billy killing our father. I know it is her and she still has to be held accountable for her crime. Just like I have to pay for mine...but not today. Not tomorrow either.

"My son is me," I look at her and say. I stand up and she steps away from me like she's afraid that I'm going to grab her and strangle her to death. "And I trust myself more than I trust God."

Dalla rolls her eyes at me. She's a very emotional woman. That means she's more dangerous than what she assumes. I got to watch her close.

I look around the room. Everything about this house screams Billy, from the saw dust in between the floor boards to the masterpiece art works that are scribbled on notebook paper and napkins, lying around in various corners of the house, begging to be seen. It's only now I'm realizing just how complex my brother is. Being in this house is helping me understand the man he is. Only Billy would have his house out in the middle of nowhere; it's like he built it in a different realm of the earth. You couldn't find this place if you looked for it with a microscope. So, this is where Dalla avoided me all these years. Now I'm here, trying my best not to avoid anything. Isn't that fucking ironic?

"Well, why hasn't he answered?" Dalla says to me all sassy with her hands on her hip.

"I don't know," is all I say to her. I don't like assuming out loud.

Dalla sucks her teeth and laughs condescendingly at me. "You don't know shit," she says and gives me a look like she wants to spit on me. "I'm not hiding out here," she starts to grab a few things like she's going to leave, "I'm going to the Ranch to see what the fuck is going on," she yells. She's being emotional again. She storms towards the door like she's about to walk out, but Lera jumps in front of it and blocks her. She looks at me like she's waiting on me to give her an order.

Dalla looks at Lera and then back at me and smirks again.

"Get the fuck out of my way," she says to Lera but Lera isn't bothered by her tone or her language. Lera has her emotions in check. Lera looks at me again and I nod my head and she moves away from the door. "You're even dumber than I thought," she says to Lera.

I look at Lera and tell her with my eyes not to respond to Dalla's emotions and Lera listens. Dalla calls Lera dumb but Lera is smarter than her. She'll survive a lot longer.

"No need to start a fight, Dalla," I say to her calmly. "We need to save our fighting energy for the plan. Don't you think?" I look at her and she rolls her eyes.

"What fucking plan?" she yells out. "You're banking on your son as a plan when he betrayed us all. I was there. I seen how Ace had him wrapped around his finger. The things he stood back and watched happen. Plus, he shot Brip. Did you tell him to do that?"

"My son carried out my orders to the best of his ability. I don't need you to trust him in order for this to work. I just need you to help me find those maps," I say to her.

"He's not answering your calls," Dalla replies like she's informing me of something.

She doesn't know what the fuck she's talking about. Vinchi isn't answering my calls because he's betraying me. He's doing it because something else has went down. My son can never betray me. No more than I could betray my own father.

"Do you know why I wasn't answering your calls?" she asks me then rolls her eyes.

I smile at her like she's amusing me, and she is. "Why is that Dalla?"

"Because I didn't want to fucking talk to you," she says to me like she purposely formed her words into the shape of a knife to hurt me; well, it is a dull knife. Nothing she says or does can cut me. At least not the way it did when she killed my father. Dalla walks out the front door but she doesn't go far. She walks up the boat dock and sits down. Hopefully, she's getting her emotions under control.

Lera looks out the window at Dalla like she's going to personally make sure she doesn't escape.

"It's ok, Lera," I say and pick up one of the guns I use to train her, "she doesn't have anywhere else to go. She'll do just as we ask," I hand her the gun. "Take Tony out back with you and go calm your mind."

"Ok," she looks at me and smiles. She trusts me.

I made a mistake overlooking Lera. With the right tone and intention, Lera has proven herself to be loyal to me and to my cause. She's starting to feel like family. She listens when I talk. Not just thinks about what she's going to say next. And, she slow to speak and quick to hear. A great trait for a woman to have. I don't know much about Tara, but I now understand why Bobby married Lera. She's easy. Reasoning with her is effortless. She considers everything I say without pushback. She respects me for what I represent and not by what she assumes I've done like Dalla. If only I could go back and make things different. But in my world, you can't turn and go back. You push forward, without looking back. If I can get everything straight, I'm going to make sure Lera has everything she needs. Dalla's dead though.

Tony follows behind Dalla like a bee to honey and when they step outside and close the door behind them, I'm finally alone with Ace's mother and sister. I look at them thoughtfully. I'm trying to figure out just how I can use them. Ace's mother, who demands to be called Lady L, is squirming in her seat. She's been resistant the entire time. I have her hands tied and her mouth clasped shut. Even with her mouth taped, this woman is yelling at me with her eyes and the energy of her discontent covers the room. Her daughter is different though. She's quiet. Very still. To reward her for her good behavior, I took the tape off her mouth. I have to say she impressed me. She hasn't spoken a single word to me since I did that. She only speaks when spoken too. This shows me how disciplined she is. It also tells me that maybe she could work for me. The hate she has for her brother seeps from her pores and saturates the room. We all can smell it. We can feel it.

As I take slow calculated steps in their direction, I make sure to make eye contact with each of them. They understand that they are not in the best situation and that I now have the upper hand. Lady L starts struggling in her seat again in an attempt to free herself. She's bobbing her head, jerking her neck and cursing at me underneath the duct tape. Angelo is poised. She's sitting straight up, very militant-like she has a rod in her back. When she returns my eye contact, I know that I have her respect. I get on one knee in front of her.

"Do you think you can get in contact with your brother?" I ask her. I need to see what's going with Ace. Has he taken the Ranch or is something else going on with Vinchi?

"I can try," she says to me. "My brother is very smart," she warns me, "my call may tip him off that you have me."

I stand up and consider what she's saying. Calling Ace Lucky smart would not be my exact words, but I will give him clever. My eyes dart to Lady L. Her eyes are shifting. She's looking at me and all over the room like she can't focus. She's trying to say something to me, but I don't care to know. I look back at Angelo.

"Do you know why I brought both of you with us?"

"Leverage," she responds immediately.

Angelo's smart or maybe she's just being clever like her brother. "Yes but mostly because you have access to something I need."

"The letters," Angelo says.

"Yes," I say and get up. I look back at Lady L. At the mention of the letters, she squirming in her seat even more now. "I need those letters," I tell her and give her a somber look. Angelo looks up at me and nods her head.

"I understand that, but my mother and brother are the only ones that have access to them. I didn't know they existed until a few months ago."

"You have no idea where she could be hiding them?" I ask and we both turn and look at Lady L.

"No, but I do know how we can entice her to give them up."

"Money?" I make the obvious assumption.

"No," Angelo responds back and gives her mother an evil stare. "Believe it or not, the one thing she values more than money is her pathetic, useless existence."

Lady L tries to jump up but ends up toppling over in the chair. Now, she's kicking those little toothpicks she calls legs, twisting around on the floor like a fish out of water.

I look at her and then back at her mother. She looks like she wants her mother dead. I don't like the way this feels. I know this family operates off hate and greed but I'm not sure I want all their bad blood affecting my greater plan. I'm seeing the truth and hate is poison for the truth.

"I need the truth. Not blood," I say.

"I know that. I can help you get that and hopefully earn your respect." she gives me a sincere look. "Trust me. I can get you what you need. All you have to do is strip her down until nothing's left but her bare ugliness. Take off that wig. The lashes, the makeup, all of it. Expose her ass. She can't bear to look at her true self. That's why she buries all her evilness with makeup and weave. It makes it easier for her to face herself."

I take a deep breath. This sounds like a bunch of bullshit that I don't have time for. I pull out my cell phone.

"I'm going to call your brother again" I say to her and she sniffs hard like she's nervous and then nods.

She gives me the number and the phone rings exactly four times before he answers like he planned it that way.

"Ace," she says but he doesn't respond. She looks at me like she knew he would react that way. "I know you know we're in trouble. He wants to talk with you. Maybe you can come to a truce and.." the phone clicks. Ace ends the call.

"It's ok," I say to her.

I lean over her small body and untie her hands. "Do what you got to do to get those letters," I say to her. She stands up and rubs the red welts on her wrist. She nods at me and I close the door behind me. I need those letters and maybe she can get them for me.

Ace isn't on the Ranch. If he is, he would be boasting and threatening. Him ending the call the way he did tells me that he's feeling defeated by my escape. He probably ain't too happy about me having his mom and sister either. This buys me a little more time. But, if Ace hasn't taken over the Ranch that only leaves me with one question:

What the fuck is going on with Vinchi?

# MONA BADD

I'm going to visit every house today and assure them all that Vinchi ain't what they think he is. He protecting them. He doing what he can to keep them all safe until his father returns. My son is stepping up, not taking over.

I don't know how Vinchi managed to do it, but he got my guards. They ain't taking orders from me no more but they move out my way when they see me coming. I'm the only one that got free rein on this Ranch. Besides, Vinchi. That gives me a little power, but not enough to get things back on track. I told Vinchi that I wanted to visit each of his uncles today to assure them that everything is under control. He didn't oppose. I'm not sure what Vinchi is up to but he deserves his chance like everyone else. I trust my son. I have to trust him because I raised him. And, because I love him. I'm not sure what he meant by saying he taking something from his father. I just think he's frustrated. Vinchi loves Brock more than Brock loved Papa Badd. Betraying his father would be like cutting off his right hand. He's confused right now. He talking about him and his grandmother and none of it makes sense. He can't know for sure that Brock killed Mama

Badd although Brock admitted it to me. I know he ain't tell Vinchi that though. It had to be Ace.

Ace would do anything to poison Vinchi mind against Brock but I'm not going to let him do that. I'm gon respect what Vinchi doing, but I'm going to get his head back on straight too. Vinchi did love Mama Badd but I never did like her around my son. She always tried to make me look bad and she spoiled Vinchi rotten. Vinchi didn't need spoiling. Had she spoiled him, he wouldn't be taking a stance like he doing now. Vinchi know what's important. The Ranch. I just got to trust what he doing.

The first person I'm going to see is Brip. I'm walking up his driveway right now and I'm nervous. Brip always has been loyal to me. He'd give his life to me without even giving it a second thought, but I hurt him by setting up the fake heist with Taffy. I can tell him I'm sorry and try and explain myself but that ain't gon change nothing. I got word from one of the guards that Taffy is back on the Ranch. I'm not sure if she happy to see me or not but really, I don't give a fuck. I'm here for Brip.

I don't bother knocking on the door. I turn the knob to walk right in like I've been doing for weeks. To my surprise, the door is locked. We never lock doors on the Ranch and I never had to knock to get inside Brip's house. I knock on the door a few times and ring the doorbell about a dozen times. Shortly after that, I hear small footsteps walk to the front door and stop. I know it's Taffy. I can feel her staring at me from the peep hole, so I start to ring the bell continuously and a few seconds later, I hear the door unlock. She doesn't open it though. I guess that means she's not welcoming me inside. I have no problem letting myself in though. I turn the knob and walk in but instead of seeing Taffy, I see Brip walking away from the door.

"Brip," I say, and he doesn't stop walking. At least not right away. "Please, Brip," I say, desperate.

"I never expected this from you, Mona," Brip says as soon as he turns to face me. The look he gives me is indescribable.

My heart breaks but I take a deep breath and suck up all the excuses I had for doing what I did and just say, "I'm sorry."

"I'm glad you're fucking sorry, now," Brip says derisively. "You're not who I thought you were," he continues and shakes his head.

I suck up the tears that I feel flooding my eyes and take another deep breath.

"I was doing this for Taffy. I was afraid for her and you still weren't..." I started with my excuses but stopped. I knew they won't get me anywhere. "I love you, Brip. You know I would never try to intentionally hurt you."

"You hurt me, Mona, but you hurt yourself more. I would move the moon for you if it was in your fucking way, now...fuck that. You on your own."

His words hit me in places words never touched before. I was so taken back, I gasped and had to shift my weight on my right leg to keep from falling over.

"I'm gon prove to you that I got your back, Brip. Watch," I tell him, but he doesn't give a fuck about what I'm saying.

Brip chuckles and shrugs his shoulders like he don't give a fuck either way. "Don't nobody got my fucking back but this metal," Brip lifts his shirt and flashes his gun, "and the eyes I grew in the back of my head to help me see better. Not you..not Brock..Not Billy..Bobby or your fucking son!" He points his finger at me like it a gun.

"Vinchi is making this right for us," I say to him. I don't want him to be upset with Vinchi.

"Your son has taken over this Ranch, he worked with the enemy and he tried to kill me," Brip shakes his head at me. "I think it's safe to say he failed you...shit he failed us all."

In any other circumstance, I would knock the shit out of anyone talking about my son the way he is, but I have to let it slide. Everything he said is seemingly right but it's more to the story. I just don't know it yet.

"He wasn't trying to kill you Brip," I try to clear Vinchi's name just in case Brip gets angry and tries to retaliate against Vinchi.

"Believe what you have to believe to keep your head up Mona. If this Ranch means so much to you and your son, then take the shit. Pay me off. I'll fucking leave. Because to me, the Ranch means family first. Fuck the money and power. I'm in this shit for family but I'm learning real quick that family don't mean shit to no one else here."

"That's not true Brip," is all I can say without crying.

"Hm," is all Brip says and turns to walk away.

"Wait, where is your wife?"

"Taffy?" he says like he doesn't have a wife. "She's making herself at home I guess." He waves his hands in the air.

I look around and notice that the house isn't the same. Every picture on the wall has been removed. Rugs are rolled up and vases and lamps are in the trash. What the fuck is she doing? When I look up, Brip is gone.

I take a deep breath and wipe away the tears that almost fell from my eyes. "Taffy," I scream and start to search the house for her. It doesn't take me long to find her. She's in the kitchen, packing dishes in a box like she's moving out.

"Taffy," I say genuinely glad to see her, but she doesn't look up at me. She does nothing to acknowledge my presence. She leans over the cabinet and pulls out all the dishes she can and places them on the counter top. "You don't see me standing here," she says nothing.

This bitch is selfish as fuck. I sacrificed my relationship with Brip, who I love just like my own flesh and blood son, just to help her simple ass. This is the thanks I get from her?

"You got a lot of nerve!"

Taffy darts her eyes at me like she's ready to fight but instead of swinging at me, she pulls a wine glass from the cabinet and shatters it against her marble floor. I jump and look at her like she's crazy. I guess she don't give a fuck about my reaction because she keeps pulling out glasses and breaking them against the floor.

"Get the fuck out!" she yells at me.

Brip must have heard the commotion because he comes running in the kitchen. He stops in his tracks when he sees Taffy throwing dishes like a mad woman.

"Get the fuck out!" she continues to yell at me.

"It's time for you to leave, Mona," Brip says to me sternly.

My heart stops. Taffy is Brip's wife, but he's never undermined me in front of her before or ever for that matter. I swallow my pride and a few tears and turn to walk away. As I'm leaving, I hear one more glass break before Taffy burst into tears. When I turn around to check on her, Brip has his arms wrapped around her.

* * *

"I hope everything is going just the way you planned it," Bobby says to me. He's staring at me with this blank look on his face. You can never tell what Bobby is thinking or feeling unless he says it. "You been planning to take the Ranch this whole time," Bobby shakes his head.

I don't know if that's a question or statement.

"My only plan was to make sure the wives were taken care of. Lera included," I say to him and his face drops. "I understand you wasn't thinking straight because of what you had going on with Tara but Lera needed just as much help, just in a different way. Me getting into the safe was the only way I could see that through."

Bobby looks up at me and stares at me like he's considering what I'm saying and it's making sense.

"You knew Vinchi had the code?"

"No," I reply.

"You think Brock is the one that called this move?"

I shrug. "It sounds like Brock, but Vinchi ain't saying." I don't tell him what Vinchi told me about trying to take the Ranch. I know Brock wouldn't be in on that with him. "Vinchi don't mean no harm. He just trying to protect this place. He deserves his say in all of this too, but I know he ain't going about it right," I add quickly.

"Hm," is all Bobby says. "What is his plan?" He gets up and looks out the window. He's staring at the two guards standing outside his driveway.

"All I know right now is that he is trying to keep us safe," I answer and pray that I'm right.

"I heard he found Taffy, but Dalla got away."

"Yeah, but he'll find her. He wants all the wives back," I say to Bobby's back. He's still facing the window. I know he's trying to get around to asking about Lera, but he got too much fucking pride to just come out and ask. "He's looking for Lera too." I let him know to relieve the pressure.

"You think he good enough to find her?" He turns and faces me.

Bobby's face is covered in desperation. I never seen him look so vulnerable.

"I think he's determined to make sure that every Badd stays on the Ranch," I say.

Bobby walks back to his leather chair and takes a seat. He leans back and spreads his legs before sweeping the exhaustion from his face with one swoop of his hand.

"He got Tara and Jayson safely to a doctor we know on the outside," I let him know. I need Bobby to understand that Vinchi is not out to hurt us. Bobby leans up from his chair and scoots to the edge of his seat at the mention of Tara's name.

"You sure?"

"Yeah. He told me when I see him today."

"Tara should be here," Bobby says and darts up from the chair. Now he's walking in circles like he's trying to process his thoughts.

"At least he's trying to keep her safe," I say.

Bobby looks at me like I'm delusional. "So, he took your guards huh?"

I don't say anything. I still don't know how Vinchi got them on his side. I guess he learned a thing or two from me and his dad after all. When I leave here, I'm going to try and call Kong again. I 've been calling him all morning. He still ignoring me which is weird. I need to know if he still got eyes out on the street for Brock and Ace. Both of them are the solution to this problem.

"We all working together," I say in Vinchi's defense, but Bobby just laughs mockingly at me.

"This whole thing is fucked up, you know?" Bobby turns and says to me. He goes back to his chair like he's going to sit down but decides against it. "We really fucked up everything," Bobby says more to himself than me, "all of us got a part in fucking this thing up." He finally sits down and hunches over, resting his elbows on top of his knees. "When Lera gets here, I don't know what the fuck I'm gon say to her or how I'm gon say it. What can I say?" Bobby pops his head up at me, giving me another desperate look.

"Sorry is a good start. If nothing else comes after that, then it's going to have to be enough."

"I let that nigga fuck her," Bobby says like reality is just now setting in.

"No, you didn't," I tell him. "You still got time to make it right."

"I still got time to kill that mutha-fucka, but I don't know if I can ever make this right," Bobby says and leans back.

"You'll make it right, Bobby," I console him.

Bobby ain't never been my favorite person. He reminds of his mama the way he walk around the Ranch with his nose in the air like he better and smarter than everybody else, but I can't help but feel sorry for the asshole. It was fucked up what he did to Lera, but I ain't got to rub that in his face. It's already all over his face. The guilt is starting to weigh him down and it took Vinchi getting Tara on the Ranch for him to start feeling it.

"I just came by to tell you to be easy. Vinchi don't mean harm. We all gon get through this," I say to Bobby, but he doesn't look up at me. He's too trapped in his feelings.

I leave Bobby with his thoughts. He needs to feel every bit of the fucked that he's feeling. Probably a little more.

\* \* \*

On my way to see Billy, I notice the trail of smoke forming in the sky near the crematory. That's weird? We ain't burned no bodies since Bobby's fake death a few months ago. And, the only person that got rights to that place is Kong. I hope that Vinchi ain't do nothing to fuck that up. Him trying to keep order on the Ranch is one thing, but him cutting across Kong is another thing. That can only make things worse.

"What's going on over there?" I ask one of the guards and point to the smoke.

"Mr. Badd has re-opened the crematory," he tells me like it's something I should already know and he's right.

I decide to take a detour. I need to visit the crematory to see what the fuck is going on.

When I get to the crematory, an entirely new staff is pulling bodies out of the truck. They got about three gurneys out. When they look up and see me, they just keep on working like it's business as usual.

"Whose orders are you under?" I ask. The first time I didn't get a response. So I clear my throat and ask louder and then everyone pops they neck just to turn and face me.

"Mr. Badd, mam," they say to me and then roll the stretchers inside the crematory.

I don't have to ask them which Mr. Badd they talking about. I know it's Vinchi. What does Vinchi know about the crematory and does this mean that he cut Kong off? I got to get Vinchi to talk to me.

I turn to one of the guards for more answers. They know what's going on but ain't saying. I pick the weakest looking one and confront him. When I walk towards him, he shifts his eyes in the other direction, avoiding eye contact with me. If he could run, I'm sure he would but he's on duty at the Badd Ranch. He knows he can't run.

"Has Mr. Badd been in contact with Kong?" I ask straight out.

The guard doesn't even look at me. He just shrugs his shoulders and tries to walk off but I grab him and pull him back. "Does Kong know about this? Are these his bodies?" I say and point to the stretchers.

"Mr. Badd ordered us to direct all your questions to him. I will let him know that you are concerned, Mrs. Badd," he says and walks away. He used Vinchi name like it is his "get out of jail free" card.

I watch him walk into the crematory and join the other guard. They whisper something to each other, then both turn to stare at me. I got to find out what the fuck Vinchi is up to.

\* \* \*

Billy is putting BJ down for bed. The way BJ's body is slumped over Billy's shoulder, it looks like he cried himself to sleep in Billy's arms. He put BJ on top of a soft blanket on his couch and then turns and faces me.

"What the fuck is Vinchi doing?" Billy whispers loudly and then immediately turns to check on BJ.

I walk towards the kitchen and motion with my head for Billy to follow me. He stares back at BJ and then back at me before deciding it is safe to leave him on the couch alone for a few minutes. Billy seems paranoid. I hope he don't think Vinchi could ever hurt BJ. He would never do that.

"Vinchi is only doing what he thinks is right. All this shit is your fuckin fault! You and that bitch, Dalla!" I yell at Billy and he turns and peeks at BJ. BJ is squirming around a little, but he doesn't wake up.

"I don't know what you talking about," Billy whispers angrily at me.

"I don't know how you did it, but you made contact with Dalla. She told you all about our plan, and you went and fucked it up. Had you not given Brip those pictures, none of us would be in this situation," I say to him. "I knew what the fuck I was doing!"

"You paranoid, Mona" Billy says and immediately looks away from me, using BJ as his visual scapegoat. "I haven't seen Dalla since that night at Ace's and you know it. How would I have gotten in contact with her?"

"How the fuck I don't know you and Dalla ain't get in Vinchi's head. Are you in on his plan to take the Ranch?" I say and immediately want to take back my words.

"So Vinchi is trying to take this place?" Billy says and shakes his head like it's all over. "I got to get my son and get the fuck out of here, Mona," Billy says to me.

"No one is going anywhere!" I tell him. "We got to give Vinchi a chance to fix this shit. He's just as much a Badd as you are," I defend my son although I don't trust his motives. I look at Billy and he's looking back at me like he's waiting on me to leave. "Taffy's back," I say to him and look at him suspiciously. He and Dalla think I'm fucking dumb. I don't know how he did it, but Billy's been in contact with Dalla. They planning something.

"I heard," Billy says and turns around, avoiding eye contact with me. He peeks his head down the hall and looks at BJ who is sound asleep on the couch.

"I guess you warned Dalla right in time," I reply and he turns around and gives me a weird look.

"I don't know what you talking about, Mona," he says and looks away.

"Both y'all know one thing I'm not is no damn fool." I fold my arms against my chest and shift my weight to one leg. "So y'all had your own plan for the safe? Dalla was gon take it all, wasn't she?" Billy just ignored me like I was talking crazy. "I take that back, I was a fool," I admit. "I was a fool for trusting your wife and trying to help her. I actually thought that Dalla showed me a different side of herself. One that gave a fuck. The way she was treating Lera really had me fooled...she don't give a fuck about nobody. Not even you." I point my finger aggressively at Billy.

Billy instantly snaps at me.

"You don't know what the fuck you talking about Mona!" he yells and then looks over his shoulder at BJ. "I can say the same thing about your fucking husband but I'm minding my own business. I brought Dalla into all of this. All she wanted from me was love and our family. That's it." Billy slices through the air with hands. "And, no, Dalla wasn't planning to fuck over you or nobody else for that matter, but obviously you was planning to fuck them over. When it came time to make the move, you didn't do it," Billy said and walked into the living room.

BJ was squirming around on the couch.

"I got to get my son to sleep," Billy says to me and then his eyes lead to the front door.

I get the message and leave.

* * *

Before I can get out of Billy's door good enough, one of the guards from the crematory comes jogging my way, waving his hands in the air like he's trying to stop me. He's holding a small box in his hand. I jog towards him. What the fuck does he want?

"Mrs. Badd," he says and leans over to catch his breath, "this came for you today, ma'am," he says and hands me the package.

"What is it? Who's it from?" I asked two questions in once sentence and look over the box. There is no label on it.

"It's from Kong," the guard answers and straightens his posture. He's not smiling at me or trying to be polite. "He wanted me to make sure you got it," he says and walks away.

Kong? So many thoughts rush through my head. Why would Kong be sending me a package but not answering my calls? How did Kong get back in the crematory? Vinchi doesn't know Kong. Hell, he don't know shit about any of our business affiliates. I look at the box and don't waste any more time carefully tearing it open. Inside the box, is a small Ziploc. When I pull it out and see what's inside of it, I drop the bag like it's on fire. It's a tongue and two thumbs and I know exactly who they belong to. Vinchi is using Kong to get back at Brock. But, he don't know that he playing with fire.

I fucked up.

# DALLA BADD

"I hope you're not planning to fuck up our plan," Lera says to me and then pulls out her gun only to place it back in her bag.

She thinks she's intimidating me but she's not. She's been acting like a completely different person the short time she's been around Brock. That only makes me feel sorry for her. She's changed three times since Ace. Lera doesn't know who the fuck she is anymore and I'm not sure she'll ever find out.

We both are on our way back to the Ranch. Brock had a connection drop us off. Initially, we planned to go back to Billy place and find the maps that detailed the secret entrance to zone 6 but when we got there, we couldn't find anything. Surprisingly enough, Brock told me that he wasn't the person that ransacked Billy's place before I got there. I could tell by the look in his eyes that he knew exactly who had but he never said anything. So, he thought delivering Lera and I back to the Ranch would be the next best thing. This way I can get in contact with Billy who can then help me get Brock back on the Ranch. I'm not sure it's the best plan but the idea of reuniting with Billy and my son sounds like a winning plan.

I try not to let Lera bother me. I haven't said as much as two words to her during our drive. She's been badly staring me down and laughing under her breath every time she makes a random move that causes me to flinch. She thinks that having the ability to take a life makes her powerful, but it only makes her a murderer.

I turn to her and shake my head.

"You actually have the nerve to talk about fucking up a plan, bitch bye," I say and wave my hand in her face. "If it wasn't for you, none of us would be in this situation. I only tried to help you. I could have left your crazy ass on the street, but I didn't do that!" I look at her and she rolls her eyes like what I'm saying isn't fazing her. "This is a fucked-up way for you to thank me." I point my finger at her like it's a gun.

"You're right, Dalla," Lera says through a chuckle. She shifts her weight in the back seat so that she is facing me. "I'm the reason we are here. I'm the reason we found Brock and I'm going to be the reason the Ranch survives so you need to be fucking thanking me! I don't owe you shit. You put me in this situation. You're the cause of all of this. Tara's death. Ace's attack! All of it! I just pray that Brock makes you pay," Lera answers coldly.

"You really think that you are saving the Ranch? You're dumber than you look, girl," I say through a sigh. "Just because you got a crush on Bobby's older brother you think that that's going to get you back in the inner circle. Well you're wrong, bitch!"

"Fuck you!" Lera snaps and jumps towards me like she's going to hit me, but she stops herself and starts whispering something under her breath. Whatever she's saying, she's calming herself down. "First off, I don't give a fuck about Bobby," she says in a huff, holding her index finger in the air to signify how she feels about Bobby, "secondly, you don't know shit about Brock. He's the only one that has been genuinely kind to me without asking for a damn thing in return."

"Really, Lera?" I shake my head. I can't believe what she's saying. "You really think Brock gives a fuck about you?" I sigh and Lera pushes her back against the seat and rolls down the window like I no longer exist. "I know you don't give a shit about me, but I've been at this shit way longer than you and if you want to survive as long as I have, you got to learn who to fucking trust and right now, the only person that is, is Tony and he doesn't have the sense of a turnip so what the fuck does that tell you?"

Lera doesn't reply. She just stares out the window, looking like she's deep in thought. I wonder if she's thinking about what she's going to say when she sees Bobby again. I'm sure Bobby won't even recognize her. I don't know what the future holds for Lera and honestly, I don't give a fuck. I only care about my family. I can't give two fucks about Brock and the Ranch as well. As soon as I meet up with Billy. We're gone. The Ranch and everybody on it can burn to the ground and I wouldn't feel a flitter of emotion. I guess that's why these bitches think I'm so devious, but I don't consider myself to be devious, just resourceful.

* * *

It is hard to pull away from Billy's kisses, but I need to see my son. I've waited too long.

"Where's BJ?" I say looking around the living room.

"He's upstairs asleep," Billy says and looks towards our double spiral staircase.

"How can you hear him all the way up there?" I start to panic. "How if he's afraid?" I say and start to run towards the stairs, but Billy pulls me back.

"Calm down," Billy says and pulls me into his chest. He kisses the top of my head. "BJ is safe. You're safe," he says and strokes the side of my face.

He pulls out a toy-looking radio which is actually a baby monitor. I grab it from him as if it's BJ and place it close to my ear. I hear my son breathing and start to cry. Everything hits me all at once. My time away from him. Being on the run from Ace and Brock, and the attack. Suppressed emotions rise to the surface like a floaty in shallow water and I feel like my knees can't take my weight anymore. I fall onto Billy and he holds me up. He rubs my back and kisses me.

"It's ok. It's over. It's all over now," he whispers calmly in my ear.

For a second, I am caught in his trance, thinking that we are all safe now, but then I remember why I am here in the first place. It's not ok. None of us are safe. My son included.

"It's not over," I say and pull away from Billy. "Any moment now, Ace and his men are coming for this Ranch. We have to get out of here now. We need to leave here today," I yell and run towards the steps.

I don't stop running until I get to the door where BJ is sleeping.

"Be cool," Billy says from behind and startles me. I don't know he followed me up the stairs. "I don't want to upset him," he says and opens the door slowly for me to walk in.

I rush in the room and straight towards the oak crib that looks like it's made of wicker and wood chips. It's beautiful and by the look of it, I know Billy made it from scratch. I peek inside the crib and BJ is lying on his back with his hands above his head. His tiny hands are balled into fist and his eyes are closed in the gentlest way, like he's dreaming about angels. He looks so peaceful and healthy.

Tears fall from my eyes and I catch them quickly. I don't want my tears to fall into the crib. My tears are full of fear, anxiety, and desperation, and I don't want them tarnishing BJ's peaceful environment. I lean down and try to pick him up without waking him. He squirms a little but eventually allows his tiny head to fall onto my shoulder and continue his slumber. I sniff his soft skin and it smells like fresh linen, sunlight, and hope. His tiny body feels so warm and natural in my arms it's almost like he's an extension of my skin. Billy puts his arm around me and hugs us both.

"I promise we going to be ok," he says to me and kisses BJ softly on the head. "Let him get some rest. We got a few things to sort out," Billy says and steps back.

I don't want to put BJ down. I never want to put him down.

"Ok," I agree and gently lower BJ back in his crib. I'm looking down at him and it's like I'm in a love trance. I can't stop looking at my son.

Billy gently places his hand on my shoulder and leads me out the room. When he tries to close the door behind him, I stop him.

"No, leave it open" I say. I need access to BJ at all times. I don't even want a door in-between us. Billy leaves the door open and grabs my hand to lead me back down the steps.

When we get downstairs, I follow him to the kitchen.

"You want some coffee?" he asks and pulls out two coffee mugs.

I don't have a taste for anything but freedom and safety, but I tell Billy yes anyway.

"We have to leave tonight, Billy. I know it's not our perfect plan and we have no money, but we don't need all of that." Billy doesn't respond. He continues to pour the coffee beans in the grinder. "Brock said it could be any day now," I went on.

"How did you get back in contact with Brock again?" Billy asks me calmly, but his question feels more like an interrogation than curiosity.

"He called your phone. I thought I told you that," I answer.

"Was that the first time he called?" Billy turns to me and I can't lie. So, I take the easy way out and shake my head no.

"The day you gave me the phone back at Walmart, he called then but I was too afraid to tell you." Billy's eyes moves away from mine and down to the floor like he is disappointed. "I'm sorry. I just didn't want anything to mess up our plan and I don't trust him."

Billy places the coffee mug in front of me and sighs.

"We gon have to trust each other if we gon survive this. No more secrets. No more lies. No more assumptions. We need to put it all out on the table."

I nod in agreement. "I'm sorry," I say again, and Billy leans over and kisses my quivering lips.

"I know," he says like he understands. "I understand that everything you did was for us but I'm probably the only person on this planet that can understand that, Dalla," Billy says, and his voice drops like he's warning me about something. "There are a lot of folks pissed at you. Bobby wants you dead. Brock wants you dead. Ace and now you say Lera too?" Billy picks up his coffee mug and puts it back down. He leans over and pulls out a small bottle of Jack Daniels and dumps it in the coffee then takes a long therapeutic sip.

"I haven't always made the best choices, but I did what I had to do to survive for us. They won't forgive me Billy and they're not going to stop wanting me dead. So what do we do?"

"I can't just leave them to be slaughtered by the same mutha-fucka that tried to kill you and BJ," Billy says in a loud whisper. He grabs his empty coffee mug and walks to the sink.

Billy's heart is much bigger than mine. He talked a good game before about leaving the Ranch, but I know that it isn't going to be an easy decision for him. I get up and walk towards Billy. I can tell by the way he's scrubbing the mug that he's conflicted. When I wrap my arms around his back, he stops scrubbing the dish and allows himself to get caught in the moment of my embrace. Billy grabs my hands and kisses them before turning around.

"What do you suggest we do?" I ask him softly.

"I don't know yet, but Dalla is as fucked up as this place is and as fucked up as my family is, it's all I've ever known."

My heart drops. It sounding like Billy is reneging on the plan. "So, we're staying?"

"No," he answers quickly. "I'm getting you and BJ out of here, but I got to stay back and help my brother. I owe it to him. If not for him, then for my mother."

"Well, I'm not going anywhere without you," I say and defensively fold my arms around my chest. Us separating again is not an option. "If you stay, then I'm going to stay to help see you through it."

"No," Billy says sternly. "It's not safe for you here."

"You didn't force me to come here and you're not forcing me to leave. I fought too hard for this family just for us to split up again. Besides, I know Ace better than any of you. If you gon save this Ranch and take him down, I'm the best person to help you."

Billy is looking at me like he's considering what I'm saying. He knows that I'm right and that I'm capable, but he can't bring himself to admit it.

"Brock needs us to get him on the Ranch. Zone 6," I say to him and he looks at me like I just revealed his best kept secrets. "He thinks it's the only way he can get in undetected."

"He's right," Billy says. "It is the only way, but once I get him in, I want you and BJ to stay at Zone 6 until I send for you. Understand?"

"Yes," I say right away.

Billy looks at me one last time like he's having second thoughts that he can't afford, then turns around and continues to scrub the mug. He needs to take his mind off things and washing dishes isn't going to help him. So, I step in.

I press my breast into his back and stick my hands into his grey sweat pants. Instantly, Billy melts in my hand. He turns around and lifts me up and on to the sink. He wastes no time pulling down his sweats and moving my underwear aside. He shoves himself inside of me hard enough for me to cum but gently enough so that he doesn't hurt me. I wrap my legs around his waist and move with his pumps. His touch brings so much ecstasy that it feels like tiny shocks of electricity is rippling through my body.

"I'll never let anyone hurt you," he whispers in my ear in between kisses, "never" he repeats, and I squeeze my legs around his back even tighter.

I'm going to get my family to safety. It's just going to take a little longer than I thought.

* * *

A few minutes into our kitchen lovemaking, Billy and I make our way to the living room where I ride him on his favorite chair like it is the end of the world. We come at the same time, falling into each other's arms and into an instant deep sleep when Mona bursts through the front door, startling us both. The rude bitch.

"We got to talk," she says to Billy and then gives me the evil eye. She looks distressed. "Vinchi don't got good intentions and I got reason to believe that him and Kong are taking this Ranch. I need help," she says desperately.

Billy and I look at each other and when I nod at him, he knows that it's time we let Mona in on our little secret with Zone 6 and Brock.

We fill Mona in about the plan.

# BOBBY BADD

I didn't believe in ghosts until Lera walked through the front door just as casually as if she's always been here. Almost like nothing ever happened. For a second, I thought she wasn't real. She moves around the house so quietly. I'm sure her experience on the streets taught her that. She barely looks at me and hasn't said as much as two words to me since she's been here. It's only been a few hours now and I hope that she warms up in time for me to apologize even though my apology ain't worth shit to her. I really fucked her over and there ain't no coming back from that. But I'm a man and I got to deal with this shit the right way.

She is sitting on the couch she picked when we were planning our wedding. It's weird. I never noticed how nice the couch is until now. The sleek shape and custom leather is chic. Nothing I would have picked on my own. This definitely wasn't Tara's style either. Lera's uniqueness is what first attracted me to her. This couch looks like the Lera I remember. The Lera that I allowed to redecorate my entire condo when we were dating. She really has a special way of making a place feel like home but now, it's like I don't know her.

Maybe I never did.

She cut her hair off. Oddly enough, I like it. It brings out her sharp facial features. Her beautiful high cheek bones and sexy bedroom eyes. She looks like a super model, but I'm sure her decision to cut her hair is beyond beauty. Either Lera is showing me a side of her that I never knew existed or she's showing me a new part of herself that I helped create. I don't know which is worst. I allowed another man to dig a grave for her and then I pushed her inside of it and buried her alive. I don't know who did worse. Me or Ace? I guess that doesn't matter now because the damage has been done. I got to make things right with her some kind of way.

Except, I don't know this new Lera. I don't know how to approach the beautiful stranger in front of me.

"You hungry?" I ask her, and she shrugs at me without making eye contact. "What about a drink? I can fix you water or wine or…"

"All I need right now is privacy," Lera dismisses me quickly and then jumps up and looks at the window.

She ain't speaking to me, but she's talking. She wants me to feel irrelevant. She wants me to know that she doesn't give a fuck about me. I stare at Lera, although she ain't looking at me. I know she can feel my eyes on her. I ain't speaking, but I'm talking and she's listening.

"There is no privacy here," I let her know. "Why did you come back?"

It is obvious that she don't want to be here.

"I was forced," she says casually like it is a line somebody told her to say.

"By who?"

"I don't know," she says and looks at me for the first time since she got here.

When I see the sadness and anger in her eyes, it breaks me instantly. Long gone is the sweet humble woman that hung on to my every word. The woman that's looking back at me is no longer my wife; she's not Lera anymore. The aftermath of my betrayal gives her face a different shape. I never seen her look this way. If she was Medusa, I would be stone. Her voice even sounds different.

"We got to talk, Lera," I say and sit down in front of her. She's still staring out the window with her back facing me. She doesn't respond to me. "I don't know what to say," I start to feel uncomfortable. The silence in the air is eerie. I lean up from the couch and face Lera's back. I know she can still feel me looking at her. I feel her avoiding me. I turn around and take deep controlled breath. This is too much. It's all too much but I'm in this shit. The last thing you wanna do when you fall in a fucking trench is cry. When you in the trenches, you climb. You don't cry. You climb your way out. That's how I have to handle Lera. I got to climb my way back up to her heart somehow. Some kind of way. I pace around and try to collect my thoughts so my mouth can form the right words to say, but there are no right words to say to her. Not even "I'm sorry."

Lera turns around and looks at me, and then laughs derisively before turning back around. "Give your conscience a break, Bobby Badd," she says coldly, still staring out the window, "I don't need your apology, your protection, your money, or your blood. I'm good." She turns to me. "I know why you did what you did, Bobby."

She don't know why. She can't know because I don't even know.

"Why did I do it?" I ask her, but I don't expect her to respond. To my surprise, she does.

"Because you were taught something that I wasn't taught... how to not give a fuck."

"I do give a fuck, Lera" I say to her and she laughs again. "I do love you,"

Lera sucks her teeth at hearing the words love come out my mouth.

"It's over," she says like it's her final answer. "You have your son. Your wife."

"Tara and I never got married," I immediately reply. "We have a history that I planned on telling you about before all this shit went down. I was going to tell you about my son Blake too the day I came to get you from the Ranch but all that changed when you told me that shit about my mother."

"Sure," Lera says mockingly then shrugs.

Isn't she trying to hear what I am saying?

"I'm not sure of anything anymore, Lera but my love for you and my son."

"And Tara," she cuts in and locks eyes with me for the first time since she's gotten here.

I was going to add Tara to the equation, but she didn't give me a chance. I love Tara. That's something I can't explain or apologize for, but I love her too.

"Yes, Tara too," I admit to her, and she looks at me like she wants to kill me. "I was going to tell you everything," I continue, "it's just that too much shit went down."

"And when you decided to leave me at the place where I was brutally attacked and violated, was that loving me?" She looks at me and chuckles. She keeps laughing, but I know it's just her defense. "And when you put me off this Ranch," she smirks and shakes her head at me like I am slow, "the safe place I had at the time, was that loving me?" She raises her voice a few octaves. She is getting upset. "You don't love me, Bobby. You never did and it's ok to admit that now. You just needed me to get your inheritance money so you, Tara, and your secret son can have the life you promised me."

"I love you," I say and start to walk towards her.

"No," she says with her back facing me.

She still won't face me.

"You know I mean what I say…"

"No, you don't!" Finally, Lera turns around faces me. But she's angry. "All that shit that happened to me because of you and your family really woke me up. I spent all these years fucking sleeping but that's over now. I'm never falling asleep again. And I mean what I say..." she says and walks away from me.

I gently reach out to pull her back and she jumps and pulls a gun out of her pants.

"Lera, what the fuck?" I say with my hands in the air.

"Don't you put your fucking hands on me!" Lera yells. Tears are coming from her eyes and her hands are shaking.

"Baby, put the gun up," I say to her calmly. I try to act like I'm not shocked, but this is the last thing I expected. "It's ok, Lera," I say. Every step she takes away from me, I take one towards her. If she shoots me, that would be the one bullet I earned. The look in her eyes tells me that she wants me dead, but also tells me she still has love for me. The love is there. I can see it, but the hate has it buried so deep that now she has a gun in my face. If I didn't have Blake to live for, I would let her put a bullet in me just so she can feel better, but I can't let that happen.

"Nobody touches me, Bobby. Nobody! I don't need your fucking protection. I don't need shit from you and you need to understand that. Do you understand?" she asks me. The gun isn't shaking in her hands anymore. She has her aim on me steady. If I move the wrong way, she'll shoot me down. So, I back up.

"Ok," I say. "You right. You don't need me. You got this, Lera. You got it," I say to her and tears roll down her cheeks.

"I didn't kill Tara," she blurts out like it's something she needs to believe.

"No," I say to her carefully. "You didn't. She's not dead, Lera. You didn't kill her," I say and she looks back at me like she's shocked but relieved. "None of this is your fault. This shit is all on me. I know how it feels not to have a mother, Lera. I reacted the way I did because I felt like I failed to give Blake something I no longer have." Lera lowers the gun. I have her attention. "I vowed to protect them at all cost. And you know I keep my word, Lera. The day Tara saw you, things changed and I got confused. I didn't know who to trust and I been knowing T for over 30 years. That type of connection don't just dissolve with time plus my mother loved her like her own daughter. Tara is a part of our family.

"Tara used to live on this Ranch too. For a little while at least. She just understood that part of me which is no excuse for how I treated you, but it is what it is, Lera." Now Lera is no longer pointing the gun at me but holding it at her side. "I know you don't need me or want me anymore, but know that my love for you is real. My plan wasn't to marry you to get money or use you in anyway. I just fucked up, is all. I fucked up, but I'm gon give you your space. Ok?" Lera nods her head. I know she hears what I just said. "I won't let nobody hurt you, Lera. You need to understand that. Not even Brock."

"Brock wouldn't hurt me," she replies quickly. Her reaction confuses me. "You don't even know your own brother," she snidely says to me.

"You been with Brock?" I ask, but Lera just ignores me. That tells me something is up.

"I need the space you promised," Lera says and turns her back to me.

She stares vindictively out the corner of her eyes. She's acting like she's got one up on me. Like she knows something I don't.

I turn to go up the steps to do just like I promise her and give her space, but two of the guards come bursting through the front door. When they see Lera holding a gun, they draw at her. I immediately step in between Lera and their guns.

"Drop the gun!" one of them yells.

"Chill out, man. It ain't what you think," I say and move closer towards Lera so that my body is completely covering hers. Lera has her gun aimed at the men. "Lera, it's cool. Give me the gun," I say and hold out my hand. She doesn't even look at me. Her eyes are fixed on the guards. I can see it in her eyes that she is willing and ready to shoot, even if the bullet has to go through me to get to them.

"Lower your weapons," Lera says to them and they don't move. "You got seven seconds..." Lera says and starts to count.

"Lera, please," I turn to face her. Now, the gun is pointing directly at my chest. "Don't do this. It's only going to make shit worse," I say to her, soft and calm. "Them niggas behind me ain't what you think. They ain't taking orders from me and they'll shoot us both."

"Not if you move out the way," Lera says and finally makes eye contact with me.

"Naw," I shake my head slowly. "I'm ready to catch any bullet that got your name on it. It's gon go through me first and I ain't ready to die yet. I got Blake and somehow I got to make things right with you," I say, and to my surprise, Lera looks shocked that I will be willing to die for her. Now, it ain't a question; I know I fucked up bad. She don't trust me at all. To Lera, all this is fake and that ain't true. She needs more than hearing me saying it is real. She needs me to show her.

"Get her to drop that gun, man," the guard demands.

I turn back to face him. "No, you drop your shit first," I command, but they don't budge. "Y'all niggas feeling real powerful right now but know that this shit is only temporary. There will be consequences and you smart to know that you just don't shoot a nigga like me...you just don't." I give them a stern look and they look at each other.

One of them breaks and lowers his gun. It takes the second guard a little longer, but eventually he falls in line too.

"I'm glad you smarter than you act," I say and turn to Lera. I hold my hand for the gun, and at first, she hesitates but then lowers it and puts it back in her pants like it's a part of her body.

"We need that gun, Mr. Badd," one of the guards say like he's ready to draw again.

I look back at Lera and she stares at me. I hold out my hand without saying anything.

"Just for now," I say to her. "I promise I'll get it back to you," I add.

After several minutes of hesitation and evil stares at me and the guards, Lera finally hands over her gun and I give it to the guards.

"I want my gun back tonight!" she whispers loudly to me, and I nod at her, although I know she won't be getting it back at all.

I turn back to face the guards. "What the fuck y'all want?"

"Mr. Badd has called a meeting," they say. "But he wants to meet with your wife first."

"If she goes, I go," I demand.

"I'll go alone!" Lera says to the guards, ignoring my request. She walks right past me like I'm a ghost and bravely towards the guards. She's definitely not the same Lera I remember.

I watch them try and grab her arm to escort her out the house, but she pushes them off of her.

"We will be back for you later," one of the guards says.

"If you hurt her, you're dead," I say to them and Lera shoots me a quick look like she's shocked again. "And I mean what I say." I look Lera directly in the eyes and she shies away from my gaze like she's refusing to allow herself to hear what I'm saying.

I watch them walk out the door and once it shuts, I rush to the window and continue to watch. Lera doesn't look afraid. That scares me and breaks my heart.

\* \* \*

While the house is empty, I use that time to call Jayson on the track phone I had stashed in my office. I got to check on Tara and Blake. Jayson picks up on the first ring. He knows it's me.

"Yeah," Jayson says.

"How she doing?" I ask about Tara.

"She's still alive. One of the doctors here says she may pull through. She's responding to things like my voice and the doctor's touch."

I sigh, relieved. Then I start to wonder why Tara didn't respond to my touch and voice. I spent days by her side. Was she pissed at me too?

"But we got a long way to go. Her recovery is going to be extensive. I need to make sure she can be safe while she recovers."

"I'm gon take care of her. I promise," I say to Jayson.

"If Lera finds her...she gon kill her," Jayson says.

"Lera wouldn't do that."

"Don't be a fool, Bobby. I done already told you that you can't trust that girl no more. Something snapped in her head. I know. I've been with her. I wouldn't trust her around Tara or Blake. Ever!"

"Well, it ain't your call!"

"With all due respect, Bobby," Jayson clears his throat and speaks to me in a tone that I never heard him use before, "Tara is my sister. My flesh and blood. It is my call and my call only."

"Watch yourself. We ain't talking about your little sister no more. We talking about the mother of my child."

"I'm gon do what I have to do to protect my sister and her son. My nephew. Just like I always have," Jayson tells me resentfully. "You off the clock, Bobby. If you want me dead because of this, then come find me. Come find us," Jayson says.

My chest swells with anger and before I have a chance to expel it through my words, Jayson hangs up.

# VINCHI BADD

Everything is working out as planned. It won't be long before my partner gets here, and we can officially take this Ranch. But, first, I got to talk to Uncle Bobby's wife, Lera. I need to get something clear with her before I make my final move. Then, I can have the meeting with the others.

I'm sitting in my father's chair staring at Lera. She's looking back at me like she already knows what I'm about to ask her. Her arms are folded defensively around her chest. She wants me to know that she's not afraid of me, but I don't need her to be. I'm not my father and plan to operate this Ranch a lot differently.

"Aunt Lera," I say to her, but she cuts me off real quick.

"It's just Lera," she says and shifts her weight from one side of the chair to the next.

"Ok, Lera," I say to her. She looks like she gets pissed off easy. Aside from my father and mother not trusting her, I don't know anything about this woman. Before today, I don't even think I've ever said more than two words to her at once. "Do you know why I asked you here?"

"I can't read minds Vinchi." She rolls her eyes. They start shifting around the room like she's looking for something.

"I have a few questions about Ace Lucky," I say to her. At the sound of his name, she straightens her posture and looks me directly in the eyes. "I need to know what happened that night." I say to her and I don't have to explain what I mean by that night. She already knows.

"Why?" Lera asked quickly.

"Because if they say what happened to you is true, you may get your chance for revenge. But I have to make sure it's true. Murder ain't my style."

Lera smirks at me and leans back in the chair. She folds her arms against her chest again and crosses her legs. She's staring at me like she trying to hide what she's thinking.

"You already know what happened," Lera says to me calmly.

"No, I don't," I respond.

What Lera doesn't know is that I saw the tape. I watched it from beginning to end and from what I could see, the sex started off consensual. Lera initiated it. Then, something happened and towards the end, it either got too rough or Lera realized what she was doing and tried to push Ace but it was too late.

"Ace Lucky attacked me, your Aunt Taffy, your mother, and killed your Uncle Bobby's wife, Tara," she says to me and pauses, waiting for me to respond. I know nothing about my Uncle Bobby being married to Tara and I'm not here to entertain useless gossip so I ignore her.

"What happened between the two of you when you were alone?"

"He fucked me, Vinchi! That's what happened to me," Lera blurts out and then leans up like she's about to leave.

"Sit back down. The guards won't let you leave until I allow them. Let's not make a fuss of this." Lera is standing over me now and looking like she doesn't a give a fuck about my orders. "I was there, Lera. I'm glad you remember that, but I also saw the tape. I saw everything that happened," I say and look her directly in the eyes. She immediately looks away from me. That's when I start to think that maybe Ace isn't lying. Maybe he didn't rape Lera like she says.

Lera sits back down.

"He raped me," is all she says. "I told him to stop. I tried to push him off, but he wouldn't...he wouldn't get off." e wou

Lera is trying to keep herself from crying. She keeps blinking her eyes and sniffing in air.

"If he raped you...he deserves to die and you deserve to be the one to give him the first bullet," I say to her. "I can arrange all of that, but if he didn't...I'm not killing him," I say to her sternly.

"Even after what he did to your mom and Tara?"

"My mother is alive and well, and Tara isn't a Badd," I respond.

Lera jumps up again and wipes the one tear that fell from her eye. "I told you what happened, and I don't need your fucking permission or help to kill a murdering rapist!" she says and charges towards the door. She places her hand on the knob but doesn't open the door. She stands there a while shaking her head and then turns around to face me again.

"What you're doing to your father is sick! All he does for you and you return that love with hate. You're despicable, Vinchi. Betraying him like this is worse than putting a bullet in him."

I find it very odd that she mentions my father and even more odd that she seems so passionate about what she is saying.

"You don't know a thing about Brock," I tell her.

"Your father is more than you think he is and it's a shame you don't see it," Lera says and turns the knob to walk out the door.

Security grabs her right away and she fights them off.

"Take her to the dining room. Let her wait there until the meeting starts," I tell them. "Gather the others," I order and they scatter, and then Mama walks in.

"Vinchi, we need to talk!" she says and attempts to step through the door, but my guard stops her.

I look at the guard and nod and he steps aside. Mama gives him a mean look before pushing past him and walking in. She continues to stare evilly at him before closing the door behind her.

"How can I help you, Mona?" I say to her and she jumps like I pinched her. I never call her by her first name, but things around here are changing. She needs to start taking me more serious. Whether she likes it or not, this happening and a lot of things are going to change.

"I just came to go over your plan. If you gon do this, I want you to know you have my full support. I know this Ranch like the back of my hand and I can help you."

"The only plan I have is to reorganize our business model and you will learn all about that when I tell the others. Aren't you tired? You've done so much already." I look up at her.

"I'm not too tired to work, but I want to make sure that everything your father and I worked so hard for doesn't fall apart."

"Everything your husband has done will fall apart," I say quickly and she jumps again. "I'll make sure of it."

"Vinchi, I know you're upset with your dad, but you need to talk to him. All these years and no one knew how you felt."

I laugh at my mother before returning to my paperwork.

"You guys only listen to what pleases your ears. Nothing else. My time to talk has passed. Now, it's time for me to act."

"Are you sure you can trust your new partner?" she asks, and from the look in her eyes, I can tell that she already knows who my new partner is.

"I trust him as much as I need to," I look up at her and say.

"You don't know him like I do." She gives me a weary look.

"And you don't know me..." I say and call for the guard.

I don't look at Mama. I know what I said hurt her feelings, but it's the truth. She has no idea who she raised me to be or what I'm capable of. Kong doesn't scare me. Neither does Ace Lucky. The guard tries to grab mama's arm like he did Lera, but she gives him that deadly scare and he backs down.

"I'll meet you in the dining room, Mona." I dismiss her with a wave of my hand.

* * *

"They're ready for you, Mr. Badd," one of my guards peeks his head in the door and says to me. I look at him and nod. I stand up and take a deep breath before grabbing my note pad. I know my uncles aren't going to like what I have to say and neither will my mother, but I don't give a fuck. This is happening, whether they like it or not.

My father spent years protecting this place from outside threats, but truth is, the biggest threat to the Ranch has always been on the inside. I've watched him make one mistake after another. And all the things he thought he was teaching me, I was secretly learning how to use them against him.

I walk slowly down the hall towards the dining room. I can hear them all chattering and complaining before I see them.

"Has our guest arrived, yet?" I ask the guard.

"Yes, sir. They are here. I have them waiting at the Casino."

"Perfect. Keep them there until I'm ready for them, but don't allow them to roam."

"Yes, sir," the guard says and leaves.

I walk into the dining room and notice right away how burdened everyone looks. They look up at me like I'm about to give them a death sentence, but I don't plan to kill any of them. Not unless I have to.

288

"Good evening, everyone," I say and walk around to take my seat at the head of the table.

As soon as I sit down, Uncle Billy jumps up.

"Vinchi, what the fuck are you doing?" he says to me and waves his hands in the air.

"Have a seat," I say to him and get comfortable in my chair.

Hesitantly, Billy looks around the room at everyone before he takes his seat and then moves closer to his wife like he's her bullet proof vest. As soon as he sits down, Uncle Brip jumps up.

"My wife needs to see a fucking doctor now!" He stabs the table with his index finger. "I ain't playing the part of prisoner in my home any fucking more. The game is over, Vinchi!"

Aunt Taffy tries to pull Brip back to his seat. She's afraid. She was there the day I shot him. I wasn't trying to kill him then and I don't plan on killing him now but the only thing that can keep Uncle Brip under control when he starts his rampages is a bullet. Hopefully, I won't have to control him that way today but if he gets too out of hand, he's going to get a bullet.

"Is everything ok, Taffy?" I ignore Brip and speak directly to Taffy. She can speak for herself.

I watched my father, my uncles, and even my grandfather treat women like their accessories. Under my rule, that's not going to happen. This is a modern age and on this Ranch the women will have just as much power as the men. Taffy looks at Brip before she speaks and then looks back at me. She doesn't say anything.

"She's pregnant," Lera blurts out and everyone in the room besides Brip and Taffy seems surprised.

Taffy shoots Lera an evil look. Lera is purposely sitting away from everyone else. Especially Uncle Bobby. She's slouched down in the chair with her head tilted back like she's only here to kill time.

"Mind your fucking business," Taffy yells at her and she shrugs.

"Is this true, Taffy?" I ask again.

Taffy looks at Brip and he jumps up again.

"Get her a fucking doctor! Now!" he demands.

One of the guards walks towards Brip. Brip bucks at the guard. I send the guard away. I don't want any conflict. Not now. Now is the time for me to tell them all about their new roles on the Ranch.

"Taffy, I'm going to get you all the help you need, but first we need to get through this meeting. Do you think you can handle that?" I say in a calm and gentle voice and she nods her head and scoots closer to Brip.

Brip defensively drapes his arms around her shoulders and whispers something in Taffy's ear before kissing her forehead. Now, he's giving me the evil eye. I just ignore him. I pull out my notepad and look at everyone. They are all staring at me, sitting at the edge of their seats, waiting to learn their fate.

"Before I start, I need you all to know that I want no interruptions. If I'm interrupted, then there will be consequences," Brip clears his throat and shifts his weight around in his seat like he's anxious to cause a scene. When Taffy places her hand on his shoulder, he calms down a little. Uncle Bobby nods at me, he respects my position and Uncle Billy is just tolerating me. Mama is looking at me like she's trying to fight back tears. I've disappointed her. Now, she knows what it feels like to be disappointed by the one you love.

"Brock isn't returning to the Ranch," I say, and they all look at each other stunned. Mama shakes her head sorrowfully. "At least not in the way you think. I'm going to allow him one day to collect a few items and to confess and then, he's exiled."

"Confess?" Brip says aloud.

Brip and I have a brief stare down. We are challenging each other with our eyes. Neither of us backs down.

"Yes, confess," I repeat slow. "This Ranch was founded off loyalty to family and order. He's breached his contract. He exiled himself when he lied to us."

"Lied about what?" Billy asks me, but I can see in his eyes that he knows exactly what I'm talking about.

"Uncle Billy, you have my full respect. You always will," I say to him. Billy is the only one that fought against what my father did. He spoke out. "And you know just like I do, what he did."

"Billy, what's this little fuck talking about?" Brip says then looks at me like he wants me dead.

Billy clears his throat, and with eyes fixed on me, he slowly says, "Mama."

"What?" Brip yells.

He's getting amped. He's confused.

"My father killed Mama Badd to protect his position in the family. The day she died, she also confessed to him that he was not a full Badd. My father is the son of Carlo Lucky," I say and everyone gasps. Mama shakes her head at me. "He killed my grandmother in cold blood to protect his position and now, he has to pay for his crime."

"What the fuck!" Brip jumps up and a guard charges at him. "Not this shit again," he yells and looks at Mona. "This is fucked up. We should have never let this little nigga out the prison. If him shooting me doesn't prove how fucked up he is in the head, then this bullshit he talking should be enough. I'm not sitting here and listing to this shit and I'm not being held hostage anymore," he says and tries to pull Taffy up from her chair.

My guard grabs him, and he starts to fight him off but two more join him and they are able to restrain him and put tape around his mouth. It is the best idea I could come up with to tame him without killing him.

Taffy screams and Bobby and Billy jump up ready to defend Brip, but I stop them. Lera is still sitting in her corner but now she is laughing like all of this commotion is amusing her.

"Everyone needs to calm down now or there will be more consequences," I say and look at my mother. Tears are falling from her eyes.

"Just be cool," she says, and they all settle down.

"Vinchi, Ace got in your head," Billy says to me calmly. "I know because he did the same shit to me. That shit ain't true though, Vinchi," Billy swallows hard, "she killed herself," he says to me like he's forcing himself to believe the lie. "And Brock ain't no kin to Carlo or Ace Lucky. When he had me at Zone 6, he did blood test. We full blooded brothers, Vinchi. I had to come to the realization that Ace Lucky was just playing me. He wants what we have. He always has, and this is his way to get it."

"He's right," Dalla says. "I used to be married to him," she admits, but by now everyone knows all of her secrets. "All he talked about was taking down the Badds. He's a master manipulator."

"So why did you kill my grandfather?" I say to her and the room starts to stir. Dalla is speechless.

Billy jumps to her defense.

"That's another lie," he says. "My wife didn't kill anybody," he says and looks at Bobby.

Bobby jumps up. "She needs to pay for what she did to Tara, Billy. She caused all of this," Bobby says.

Lera is staring at Bobby like she's remembering a nightmare. He tries to move closer to her, but she stops him by throwing her hands up, gesturing for him to stay back.

"I didn't need Ace to tell me the truth. I always knew it."

"What, you talking about man?" Billy says.

Now, he's all ears. He leans in closer to the table and Dalla places her hand on his back.

"I was there the day it happened," I say and everyone in the room gasped.

Billy jumps up like he's been thrown back into a time capsule. His brow lowers. Brip is trying to say something under his breath but his voice is muffled from the duct tape plastered on his lips.

"Boy, don't you lie to us. What the fuck do you mean?" Billy says. He's pointing his finger at me and talking to me like he's my father.

"The day grandma was found dead, I saw my father running out her room. He didn't see me. He was too distracted by his guilt. Not that he needed any other reason not to see me," I add.

"I knew something was wrong because of the look he had on his face. I never will forget that look," I say and almost get lost in thought from the dreadful memory that I forget where I'm at. "I immediately thought to run into her room to try and protect her, but I knew it was too late. I was scared. I finally got the courage to peek my head inside the room and all I saw was her arm dangling down the side of the bed. A sheet covered her body, but I knew she was dead. When her body was discovered, dad never mentioned he was there. He said he hadn't seen her in days. That's when I knew what he done." I struggle with my words. I take a deep breath, and when I look up, Billy is frozen, Bobby's looking at the floor and Brip has tears in his eyes. They believe me. They know I'm not lying. "For that, he has to pay."

Mama burst into tears and Billy sits back down like he's conceding. Dalla wraps her arms round him and he sweeps his hands over his face like he's fighting back tears.

"What are you going to do to him?" Mama says to me through tears. "He's your father, Vinchi."

"He's a murderer," I reply. "But, I'll show him mercy if he agrees to my demands. After he confesses in detail how he killed grandma, he has two options. Leave the Ranch and this city for good or die."

Mama starts to cry even harder.

"No one is killing Brock!" Lera jumps up and yells defensively, catching Mama's attention. "I won't let that happen!" she warns.

"I hope it doesn't come to that, Lera. I know you've grown fond of my father, but you don't know him."

"No, you all don't know him!" she says and looks at everyone in the room. "Whatever he did that day, I trust him and his judgment."

"What the fuck are you talking about?" Billy yells at her.

"Watch your fucking mouth," Bobby yells back.

"No," Mama says. "We all want to know what the fuck she means."

Mama stands up and Lera gets up too. She stands her ground. Lera gives Mama a "try me" look and Mama is staring back at her confused.

"What the fuck do you know about my husband?" Mama says, and Lera smirks and sits back down.

"Probably more than you," she adds and Bobby shoots Lera a strange look.

This is not the time or place for this. It's not why I have them here.

"Enough," I say and stand up. "Mona, sit down."

"Boy, that's enough," Bobby is pointing his finger at me. "I don't give a fuck what chair you sitting in right now. I ain't gon have you disrespecting your mama like this. Call her by her name again…" He balls up his fist and stares me down.

My uncle isn't intimidating me, but I will respect his request just to keep the peace. Uncle Bobby never gets mad, but I think he's wondering what everyone else is wondering. What went down between Lera and my dad? He shoots Lera a weird look and she just stares back at him like he means nothing to her.

"I'm sorry, Uncle Billy," I say genuinely. "All those years you spent trying to investigate her murder and I never said anything. I was too afraid then, but not anymore. You were my hero because you were the only one that was bold enough to stand up."

Dalla shakes her head at me and turns to face Uncle Billy.

"Billy, he's lying. Don't believe him. This is Ace...he really got to him."

Billy turns to face Dalla like he's debating whether or not to listen to her.

"Believe what you want. All of you. But that doesn't change my decision or my position. Brock is out," I say and look at Bobby to let him know that I will never call that man father again.

"So, what's next?" Billy asks.

I pull out my notepad and flip the page.

"Things are going to change a lot around this Ranch. I'm taking new clientele and a completely different business model. I want to attract more of a younger group. We've been doing business the same way for years...it's time for a new generation of people to partake in the benefits our name offers."

"That's a bad move," Bobby says.

"I don't think so," I say. "I want to redevelop this Ranch to attract a new crowd. We have the casino and that's great but I want to entertain more."

"We can't do that! We got to stay discreet," Bobby says.

"That's not how I see things and what you all are forgetting is that it's not up to you anymore," I remind them.

"So what role do we play in all of this?" Bobby asks.

"I'm not sure yet, but until I decide, you're off the payroll."

Brip starts grunting and trying to bite through the tape and Billy almost looks relieved.

"But your wives stay on."

"What?" Bobby and Billy say in unison.

"At one point, you guys didn't give a fuck if they lived or died, but I did. They made a poor decision when they decided to marry into this family because there really is no way out, but it doesn't have to be a death sentence," I say and look at the women. "I want all of you to take a more active role in running this Ranch. I believe you have more to offer our business than sex appeal and submission."

They are all looking at each other now, considering what I'm saying.

"So, I have jobs for each of you. Even you, Mama," I say and look at my mother and then at Uncle Bobby. "Taffy, I want you to head up entertainment. I figure we need to open a few clubs on the outside and one main club on the Ranch. I think you will be great with hosting and promoting events."

Taffy looks stunned. She perks up and leans in closer to the table.

"What will I do?" she asks.

"Promote parties and run the clubs both on and off the Ranch. You'll get a generous percentage of everything we make," I say to her. "You don't have to live on the Ranch either or wear that necklace if you don't want. It's completely up to you."

Taffy is looking at me thoughtfully. I know the idea of having a purpose other than being a wife excites her, but she is so brainwashed, she still worried about what Brip thinks. She tries to hide how excited she is.

"Lera," I say and turn towards her. Bobby looks at me hard. "I can help you get the papers to divorce Bobby, but you always gon be a Badd wife. I'm sure you know that now. With everything you've been through, I think you've proven that you can handle a lot. I just don't know what that is yet, but I know there's something here for you."

Lera shrugs at me, but I know she's in. She likes the idea of being a part of something greater than her necklace.

"Mama," I turn to her. Her tears are dried up on her cheeks now. When I call her name, she perks up, but I know she's not going to like what I have to say to her. "You've done so much work here. I think it's time you conquered new territory. I want to make you the director of outreach for the Ranch. That means, you will leave the Ranch permanently and manage all of our connections on a face to face basis off the Ranch. Starting with your former home. The East Meadows projects."

"What! Vinchi, please don't do this, please stop breaking my heart."

It's sad that I have to put my mother off this Ranch, but she conspired and covered up my father's dirt for years. She doesn't belong here. Besides, I can't trust her, and she will never respect my authority on this Ranch. She won't see me as the leader but as her son and I need respect.

"It's settled, Mama."

She sniffs real hard and leans back in her chair like I just sentenced her to death by stoning. All she knows is this Ranch. I hope that when she leaves, she'll find the part of herself that she lost. I really think this will be good for her.

"What about my wife?" Billy asks.

"Dalla has proven herself to be more resourceful than all of us and I personally owe her for killing my grandfather. So I'll let her choose how she wants to work with us or I'll let both of you go. I'll pay you off and you can live happily ever after."

"We'll take the money," Dalla says quickly and jumps up. Billy pulls her back down.

"I'll give you time to think about it," I say.

"What about me and Brip?" Bobby asks.

"I'm going to have to put y'all on a furlough. You gon spend the first few months in Zone 6. I need you there until I can trust you. That's if you want to stay on. If not, you can leave, but you wont get paid out like Billy. You gon have to find your own way."

Brip is so amped he almost falls out of his chair.

"Hm," is all Bobby says.

Bobby leans back in his seat and keeps a straight face, but I know his blood is boiling. He's thinking his way out of this situation, but there is no way out. I'm giving them the option to stay, but I really want them gone.

"Now that we settled that," I say and close my notepad. I stand up and they are all looking at me like it's not a question anymore but a fact that I'm in charge, "I want you all to meet our new partner. He and his wife are moving to the Ranch and setting up their own headquarters. I know all these changes are tough, but I expect all of you to be welcoming to them. After that, I got a little surprise for you. I think you may like it," I say and look at Lera. She's going to like this surprise more than anybody.

"I need everyone to meet me at the Casino so that we can greet our new guest."

# MONA BADD

I thought what Brock did surprised me, but this shit with Vinchi takes the cake. I can't believe he's trying to destroy everything that his father and I sacrificed for him. All our hard work was in vain. What Vinchi is forgetting is that every move we made so far was for him and his brothers. I never thought that I would be a mother. Then I met Brock and had six kids.

I prided myself in motherhood. I thought that I was teaching Vinchi all the right things. How to be loyal. How to be strong. How to be respectful, but either I fucked up or he wasn't listening. Vinchi got five younger brothers that look up to him. What example will he be setting when he throws us off the Ranch?

I already decided that I don't give a fuck. I ain't going nowhere. This Ranch is the only home I know and I be damn if I get under cut by my own fucking flesh and blood.

I'm in the car with Billy and Dalla. We on our way to the Casino. Vinchi is in the car ahead of us. He got Brip and Taffy with him. He still got Brip all tied up. Bobby and Lera are in the truck behind us.

"So that big gorilla motherfucker taking the Ranch?" Billy asks. He's talking about Kong.

I don't respond. I'm trying to tell myself that this shit ain't my fault, but it is. I made it easier for Kong when I came to him for help. Him giving me the guards was his way in. All the years I known him, I never thought he would do some shit like this. Brock warned me about him. He would always say Kong was in love with me. I always knew something was still there, but I thought it was innocent.

"He said guests," Dalla added. "There is more than one person. You think its Ace?"

I don't know why they keep asking me questions. I don't know shit.

"Mona," Dalla screams my name like I can't damn hear. "You need to snap out of this shit."

I ain't never felt so numb and helpless in my life, but Dalla is right. I need to snap out of this shit cause I ain't got the luxury to go crazy like Lera and Taffy. I can't sit back and let nobody take shit from me, even if it is my own son, but at the same time, I feel like I got to protect him. He don't know what the fuck he doing and he ain't hard like his daddy; Vinchi is fucking soft. I don't know for sure that Kong won't put a bullet in his head the first chance he gets. I got to figure out how to protect him, this Ranch, and myself.

"Look, y'all asking me shit like I got all the answers. We all gon find out who the fuck is at the Casino soon enough," I say, then take a deep breath.

"This could work out for us," Billy says to Dalla.

"How?" Dalla says through a sigh.

I know Dalla wants to take Vinchi up on his offer and take the money and leave. She don't care about this Ranch. All she ever cared about is herself and Billy, but she knows better than I do that Billy ain't walking away that easy.

"I talked to Brock. He should be making his way to Zone 6 any moment know. Vinchi don't know the Ranch like I do. He'll never see his father coming. If Kong and Ace is here, then they just were we need them to be. Mona, you gon have to meet him when he gets here." Billy turns and looks at me to see if I'm listening.

I hear him, but I'm not listening. I'm tired and Brock is the last person I want to see right now. What the fuck is he going to do? And what the fuck is going on between him and Lera. Did he fuck her? I know I should have more important things running through my mind right now, but I can't help but to wonder.

"Meet him for what?" I ask.

"What you mean for what?" Billy says like he's getting annoyed. "He gon need your help. Vinchi don't know what the fuck he's doing and that y'all fucking son. Y'all need to handle this shit before we all end up dead."

"What the fuck do you care?" I turn to say to Billy. "You been granted clemency. You and Dalla can finally get what y'all wanted all along. The money you didn't work for and privacy you don't deserve."

"I ain't leaving until I know shit is right," Billy says and Dalla shoots him a strange look. "Dalla is though," Billy adds.

"What?" Dalla seems shocked. "When did we decide that? I'm not going anywhere without you, Billy and you know that. Let Mona fix this shit. She can handle Vinchi. They don't need us."

"They do," Billy replies.

"Billy, listen to your wife. Get the fuck out while you can," I say to him.

"Get your head back in the game, Mona," Billy says and pulls into the Casino. "I know you hurting, but you and Brock got the power to fix this shit. I ain't going nowhere until you do." He looks at Dalla. "After we leave here, I'll get you to Zone 6. Brock is expecting you," Billy says before jumping out the car and running over to the passenger side door to let Dalla out.

Before Dalla can get her foot on the ground, Billy grabs her and pulls her close to him like he's willing to protect her with his life. I can't help but to wonder if Brock would protect me with his life. The way shit is looking, probably not.

* * *

When we get to the Casino, the guard leads us to the conference room. Before I even walk in the door, I know my sister Nicchi is here. I can smell her cheap ass perfume and burnt weave smell. Vinchi is standing in front of the conference room door like a concierge. He is looking at us and wearing a smile I never seen on him before. I don't know if the smile is to reassure us that everything is ok or if he just feeling vindicated right now. I look at him and when he makes eye contact, I look away. I can't stand the sight of him right now.

"I expect that everyone here will treat our new guest with respect. Their permanent residence on this Ranch starts tonight," Vinchi says and opens the door.

I'm the first person to walk in room. As soon as I get my foot in the door, my eyes meet Kong's. He is smiling at me, exposing those yellow ass shark-like teeth and my sister is looking at me like she just been crowned a Badd. I look away from Nichii because she's a non-factor and set my sights on Kong. He looks directly at me. I can see the sarcasm in his grin. He knows he got one over on me, but I know that Kong can read what my eyes are saying. He knows he's going to pay for this. I keep my eyes fixed on him.

The guards lead us to the table and we all take a seat. Kong and Nichii are standing over us like dictators about to give a death sentence. As soon as I sit down, Nichii starts with her shit.

"No love for your sister," she says and opens her arms, but she knows better than to walk towards me. "I fixed our apartment building up real nice for you. You gon be real comfortable there," she says to me and smiles condescendingly.

I ignore the bitch. I don't even look at her. Her so-called claim to fame is going to be short-lived. When this is all over and we back on top, I'm cutting her off. She will regret this shit. I took such good care of her all these years. She didn't even need Kong, but what I gave her wasn't enough. It wasn't my money she wanted; it was my life and she think she has it now.

Once we are all seated, Vinchi goes and stands beside Kong.

"He needs no introductions. You all should know him very well. He's been an ally to this Ranch for many years. His partnership is going to be essential for our new business model," Vinchi says then looks at Kong and nods. "You got anything you want to say?" he asks him.

All Kong does is laugh and look at each of the men in turn. He holds his glare when he gets to Brip.

"Remove the tape from his mouth," Kong orders the guards and they eagerly snatch the tape from Brip's mouth with more aggression than necessary.

Brip doesn't flinch. He looks up and stares at Kong fearlessly. He and Kong stare each other down for a few seconds, only talking with their eyes.

"You gon give me trouble?" he asks Brip.

"You giving yourself trouble, but I ain't delivering it to you," Brip grimaces at him, "hand to hand," he adds.

Kong snaps his fingers and two guards rush towards Brip and start to attack him. I look at Vinchi. Praying that he does or says something to stop this, but he doesn't.

"Vinchi, stop this shit," I say and jump up.

Taffy starts screaming. She tries to intervene, but they push her back and she falls over a chair. Billy rushes to help Taffy up and then he and Bobby take two steps towards Brip to help. Before they can get their hands dirty, Kong snaps his fingers and the men fall back. Brip looks up and laughs before spitting blood out his mouth. His hands are still tied behind his back.

Then he looks over at Taffy to make sure she's ok. She's crying, but when he gives her that reassuring nod, she sniffs up her tears and returns to her seat. She tries to wrap her arms around him but Brip pulls away.

"This is how we doing things?" Billy says to Vinchi.

"There will be no violence or threats of violence between us. Uncle Brip has to learn to respect this new ownership. If not, there will be consequences. The same goes for everybody else," Vinchi says and looks at me. "Kong needs to be treated with the same respect as Brock. If anyone defies that, then they suffer."

Kong looks at Vinchi and nods, then he looks back at me and smiles.

"Mona, don't worry. Everything is going to be ok," he says and smiles again.

Kong gives me a strange look. It's like he winked at me without ever closing his eye. He's trying to let me in on a little secret. Does this mean everything is going to be ok? Is Kong trying to tell me not to worry? Nichii sucks her teeth and rolls her eyes my way. She knows that Kong still loves me. He just got a fucked-up way of showing it.

"Why the fuck are we here?" Bobby asks. "You all seem to have everything planned already. What do you need us for?"

"Some of your clients may be a little hesitant continuing business the way we plan to. We need you to continue to be the face of this Ranch until things get normal again," Kong says. "I'm sure Vinchi has already discussed our plans."

"He has," Bobby agrees. Bobby is keeping his cool. He's using his head and not his heart. That's one of his best qualities. "But what about after that?"

"We will cross that bridge when we get there," Vinchi replies. "Until then, as discussed earlier...you furloughed."

"Don't look at this like a death sentence," Kong says. "I think this new partnership will work out for the best of all of us,"

Kong says and looks at me. "And to prove that I respect this new partnership, I brought you all a gift," he says and raises his hand in the air. "Consider it a peace offering. I think you might like it," he says before snapping his thick, sausage-like fingers.

Three guards rush out the door and Kong rests his hands over his large stomach and chuckles under his breath. He has this anxious look in his eyes. When I make eye contact with him, he nods and winks at me. Nichii defensively folds her arms around her chest. I look away from him and set my sights towards the door. There is a lot of commotion going on outside the conference room. Finally, one of the guards uses his foot to kick the door open. It slams into the wall and the knob gets stuck in the drywall. Vinchi jumps up and opens the other door to make for a wider entry, and to our surprise, in walks the guards with Ace Lucky. They have him handcuffed and his mouth taped shut with the same tape they used on Brip. Bobby, Billy, and Brip jump up. Dalla, looking like monster, just stepped in the room. She jumps and scoots back in her seat. Lera gets up slowly and Bobby watches her. She's staring back at Ace like a thirsty bloodhound. She clutches her fist.

"Calm down," Kong says through a chuckle. "I knew this would excite."

Kong laughs and it sounds like he's having an asthma attack.

"He's all ours," Vinchi says proudly. "I told you I would look out for us. Tonight, we gon seal this deal with his blood," Vinchi says and Ace squirms.

I look up at Kong and no one is looking, he blows me a kiss and gives me that look again.

# BROCK BADD

"He played you, Brock," Mona coldly says to me. Almost like it excites her to see the disappointment that floods my entire body. "Just like you played me," she adds and folds her arms against her chest. "It's over." Her voice depicts defeat.. An emotion I never seen her express before.

She just told me about Vinchi and Kong. Out of all the people I thought would be a threat to this Ranch, Vinchi was never one of them. I raised him to be a clone of me. Just like I was a clone of my father, but somewhere along the way, I fucked up. It's not even about him taking the Ranch. It's about the fact that he hates me. He wants me dead. My own flesh and blood wants me dead. Ain't karma a bitch? I would say I couldn't relate to that, but I killed my own mother. I more than wanted her dead. I needed her dead. Just like my son needs me dead, although he ain't saying it. Vinchi doesn't have plans to let me live. It's not how I raised him.

"If anybody got played, Mona." I point my finger at her. We are standing nose to nose now. She flinches when I raise my hand and unfolds her arms ready to strike if she has to. Now, that's the Mona I know. "It was you," I tell her.

Now, she's pissed. She slaps my finger out of her face and takes a step toward me. Close enough for me to grab her, so I do. I grab and wrap my arms around her and she hold me because that's what she needs right now. To be held. To be loved. To be told everything is going to be ok.

She almost breaks down in my arms. I can feel the tears trickling in her eyes, but she sniffs real hard and pushes me off of her.

"Don't fucking touch me! You fucked up our entire lives and got the nerve to try and touch me. Fuck you!"

Now, she's pointing her finger at me. Mona might be right, but I'm not ready to accept that yet. I'm still fighting this. I know I can get things back under control, but I can't do this shit without her. I need her to know that.

"I need you, Mona," I say softly and drop my head.

I'm not trying to play her. I can't look at her right now because of the shame.

"Use that bitch to help you. She's here," she says to me.

"Lera?" I asked the question a little too fast.

Mona's eyes widen with suspicion and then she stares at me like I reminded her about something she forgot about.

"I was talking about Goldie," Mona says through an exasperated breath. "Did you fuck her?" she asks me like she's scared to know the truth.

I hesitate, but only because I don't know if she asking me about Lera or Goldie. I'm sure she already knows by now that I fucked Goldie.

"No," I respond, and then look away.

Mona gasps just as if I said yes. She turns to walk away and I grab her.

"Listen to me. Everything we worked for is about to go up in flames and all for a lie. I need you to get your emotions together."

"What lie?" Mona asks me. "More lies, Brock?"

Mona looks at me like she's had enough. I can see in her eyes that she's doing something that I never thought she could do. She's giving up on me.

"I got Ace's mother to talk," I say to her. Mona looks at me like she confused. I don't tell her that I have Ace's mother and her sister at the other Ranch, locked in the basement with Tony keeping guard.

"What are you talking about?" Mona rolls her eyes like she refuses to believe anything that comes out of my mouth.

"That night it happened," I look at her and she instantly looks away. She knows I'm talking about the night I killed my mother, "I don't think I heard her right. When she told me, I ran off before she could finish. I was scared. Upset. I didn't hear what she was saying to me," I say and my anxiety starts to kick in. I start retracing that moment out loud and mumbling under my breath. Truthfully, I don't remember much about that night. I push it down somewhere so far, only bits and pieces come back to me once I start to dig it up again. "When I returned later that day, I should have just woken her up and asked her, but…"

Mona looks at me like she's looking at a demon. I may have acted too fast in killing my mother. When I went back to my mother's room, I went back for a solution rather than answers. I did what I did.

"Brock, what are you talking about?"

"We can't kill him," I blurt out. "He knows too much about our family. About who we really are," I start on my rant.

Mona is looking at me like I'm having a mental breakdown and maybe I am. For a second, I almost see the compassion that I've been missing in her eyes. The compassion that I can rely on to make everything better for me. Then it goes away with the flick of her wrist. She's had enough of my shit.

"Brock, I don't know what you talking about, but…"

"No, Mona," I yell desperately and grab her. She doesn't try to pull away this time. She's giving me a weird look. Like I'm going to slit her throat and forget I did it. "Mona, don't let them kill Ace. If he dies, then the truth behind our legacy dies too."

"You actually trust that lying psychopath?"

Mona places both her hands on my face like she's trying to get me to see something I'm refusing to see. She doesn't understand. She can't. I put her through too much and after tonight, her life will never go back to being the same again. Mona can't hear me right now. She can only hear her own fear and anxiety. Mona will rather die than not be a Badd, and right now, she's planning her funeral.

"Mama was writing letters. I don't know how Ace had them, but he does. I read a few. I don't know who they were from, but I bet my life and this Ranch they were to Carlo Lucky. The rumors were true, and not only because I'm standing here, but because the rest of my brothers are too. Mona...none of us is Badd; we are Lucky. Just like...Ace."

"What?" Mona says like she doesn't believe a word of what I'm saying. "That's all bullshit."

"I didn't tell you this before, but I did a blood test on Billy. We brothers. Full blooded. I got a feeling that Bobby and Brip are too."

"I can't...I can't deal with this right now."

"So, don't, but you need to do what I say. We can deal with it later, but this is something we have to know...all of us. But first we got to take the Ranch back and we have to keep Ace breathing."

Mona looks at me and sighs heavily. She lowers her head to the ground and it looks like it's about to roll off her neck.

"There are more letters. The letters reveal the truth and we need to learn the truth."

Mona sighs again and drops her head like she's finally had too much. I slowly walk up to her and place my hand on her shoulder.

"I'm gon make all of this right, baby. I'm gon prove to you that I'm the man you married."

Mona looks up at me and I see that she believes me, even though she don't want to.

"They want him dead. How am I going to convince him not to kill him? Brip, Lera, Billy...everybody got dibs on him. Vinchi is doing this shit tonight."

"I don't know how you gon do it, but I know you gon be able to pull it off. In the meanwhile, do what Vinchi asks of you. If he wants you off the Ranch, then leave. I'll find you and put you up somewhere safe, but before you go...I'm gon give you the code to the safe to override Vinchi's new code.

"You can change the code to the safe?"

How?" Mona asks incredulously.

She is shocked and relieved. Mona knows that whoever has the code to the safe has the real power.

"I guess I'm smarter than what you think," I say to her and smile. Mona almost gives me a half smile back. She's getting her faith back.

"You trust me with the code?" she asks like she's shocked.

"I trust you with the blood in my veins," I say to her. "Of course, I trust you with the code. You the only one I trust right now."

Mona's whole mood changed like I just said the magic words. She perks up and straightens the slump in her back.

"Change that shit before you leave the Ranch," I tell her again and she nods, agreeing with me. "Tell everybody that I got a plan to fall in line with Vinchi for now. I'm gon have to find my way back here to free Bobby and Brip from the prison. I need them on my side. I think Billy should stay on the Ranch though. I need someone on the inside to help me move around."

"How long will all this take?"

"I don't know, but I got about 70 niggas that are ready to be a part of this war. Taffy's brother, Tony, is helping me. He a real soldier, Mona. I know we can pull this shit off. But, I don't want you on the Ranch when all this shit go down, so play the game and leave like Vinchi wants you to."

"And what about Vinchi?"

Mona looks at me. I know what she's asking me. I will try my best to ensure my son doesn't get caught in the crossfire, but I can't make any promises. I know that's a fucked-up thing to say but it's a real thing. This war may have more than one causality and, unfortunately, it may be my first born.

"I'll make sure no one hurts him." It is the second lie I've told Mona today.

I'll have to deal with the consequences of the other lie later. But, first things first. It's time for us to find out who we really are. I got to get those letters.

# BILLY BADD

"Billy, this shit is fucking ridiculous. We have to kill him," Dalla says to me. "This is our only chance. Don't let him weasel his way out of this. If we don't kill him, you know that he'll hunt us for the rest of our lives. It's our only chance to be free, Billy. Please," Dalla says and grabs my hand.

We all sitting in my living room waiting on one of Vinchi and Kong's guards to lead us to the cemetery where we plan to kill Ace Lucky once and for all. Mona looks at me like she needs me to listen to her more than she needs air right now. I look at both of them.

Dalla is afraid. She's been living in fear for years now. I have to free her of that, but I have to consider everything Mona just told me too. Besides, it ain't up to me. I lean over and kiss my wife on the forehead and whisper "I got you" in her ear. She sits back in her chair relieved because she knows that means Ace is going to die. My family comes first. All this shit from the past that Brock is trying to pull up doesn't matter to me anymore. I'm done with all that.

"Mona, you know that nigga got to go," I say and sit down beside Dalla.

Dalla is giving Mona that "fuck you" look that she gives so well. Mona doesn't even respond to Dalla's look. She's too desperate.

"You don't care about the letters?" Mona asks me.

"No, he doesn't," Dalla answers for me.

I turn to Dalla and give her a "calm down" look. She's anxious to get off this Ranch and away from this life. She has been for years. I plan to give her and my son everything they deserve and more. But, first, I got to make sure that nigga Ace dies an awful death.

"That's in the past," I say to Mona. "I feel for my brother. I was just where he was two years ago. Ace got his mind, Mona. You don't need to support him in that. It ain't healthy."

"I know how much you hated Papa Badd. You hated him so much you let her," she points to Dalla who immediately looks away, "kill him and not suffer any consequences. Brock is willing to forgive that because he is sure that..." she pauses and takes a deep breath. She looks me deep in the eyes. "He's sure that all of you aren't really Badds but Luckys."

I immediately jump up.

"That's a fucked-up thing to say, Mona!"

"Get out!" Dalla jumps up and yells and storms towards her.

I grab Dalla back to my side and squeeze her shoulders, trying to calm her down. She's been acting like she's suffering from PTSD all day and I can't blame her. Even with Ace on lockdown, she still hates that he's on the Ranch. She more than wants him dead. She needs him dead. We all do. But this shit Mona is talking about is fucked up and I want no part of it.

"What about Brock's plan? Are you gon stay on the Ranch? He needs you here."

I look at Dalla who is watching me like a hawk. Vinchi offered Dalla and I money and safe exit from this Ranch and life. We discussed that before Mona got here, and I decided that Dalla is right. It is time for us to leave and finally start our new lives. I can't stay.

"No, Mona. After tonight, my wife and I," I grab Dalla's hand and squeeze it, "are gone for good. So, really, this is goodbye for us," I say and hold out my free hand for Mona to grab. She doesn't take it.

"You a punk and your wife is a scandalous ass bitch," she hisses at us. "I can't believe you gon leave your bother and your entire legacy to turn to ashes."

Before I can reply, Dalla is speaking for me again.

"Bitch, you and your husband are the scandalous ones. You all started this shit with your fucked-up greedy ways. I hope you both burn in the flames you started and you need not worry about me and my husband and concern yourself with why Lera is fucking your husband, bitch."

Dalla's words pierce through Mona like a bullet, but instead of falling, she leans forward and snatches Dalla by the hair, ripping her from my hand and pushing her to the ground. Dalla leaps up from the floor like she levitated and charge towards Mona who is ready for her, but before they can get to each other, I put myself in between both of them. I take two jabs in the face and scratch on the neck, but they eventually back down.

"Fuck both of y'all," Mona says out of breath. "Billy, you know what you doing is beyond fucked up. It's...it's..." Mona is struggling for the right word to describe how disloyal I am, but it never comes to her. So, she runs out the front door instead.

Vinchi is facing all of us. We standing outside the gate of the cemetery. I don't know why he chooses this place for us to kill Ace. It don't feel right. Vinchi knows that we consider the cemetery to be sacred ground. The only people allowed on this part of the Ranch are Badd family members. Now, he got the big ass fuck nigga Kong and his entire crew, hurdled around the gates with their guns waiting to open it and Ace tied to a chair with a black sack covering his face. I just pray that my mother's spirit ain't lingering around here. Even in death, I don't want her to be a part of the violence that's about to take place tonight. As for my father, or whoever the fuck the man that raised me is...fuck him. With all the shit that he put my mother through that led to her death, he deserves a seat right next to Ace and I wouldn't be afraid to throw the first stone.

For a nigga that's about to die a brutal death, he seems real calm. I can't see his face, but he ain't squirming or nothing. He almost looks like he's meditating under the bag. Maybe he's praying to God to forgive him for all his evil so that he don't spend a lifetime in hell. Hopefully, Vinchi will let us kill his ass before God gets a chance to answer his prayer.

Everybody got an anxious look on their face. We all ready for this nigga to bleed. All of us except Mona. She staring hard at Vinchi. Vinchi hasn't looked at his mother yet, but I know he feels her stares. Hell, we all do. I guess she ran to him after she left my house and begged him to spare Ace's life, but, obviously, Vinchi ain't listening to none of it, because we all here.

Vinchi installed these big ass fluorescent lights all around the cemetery. So, although it's almost midnight, the place is lit up like Disneyland. We can see everything clear as day. I look into the eyes of my brothers. They all are sharing an equal amount of hate in their eyes. Before we got here, I talked to both Brip and Bobby and told them everything Mona told me. They wasn't trying to hear it either. Bobby says that Brock is believing in fairy tales and Brip said he don't care if it's true or not, he wants Ace dead. I'm with my brothers, but I can't help but wonder myself. Could it be true? I guess I'll never know. But I pray that later in life, this shit don't fuck with me because tonight is the last night to ever get the truth. When we kill Ace, everything dies with him, including the bitter parts of our identity.

Dalla is holding on to my arm like Ace is going to leap out that chair and kill us both. That ain't happening, but I don't tell her that. I just squeeze and give her reassuring kisses on the face. Brip has his arm draped around Taffy. He's whispering something in her ear that I guess is comforting her. She keeps turning and looking back at the trucks that we came here in like she just wants to leave. Lera is standing as far away from Bobby as she possibly can. He's looking at her with that face he gives when he don't want nobody to know what he's thinking, but I know my brother well enough to know exactly what he's thinking. He's thinking that he fucked up and don't know if he can fix it.

Lera is avoiding Bobby's stares the best she can. It don't really seem hard for her though. She's looking at Ace's body like she's thirsty for his blood. I think she wants him dead more than any of us. I make eye contact with Mona and she gives me one last pleading look. She gets her answer when I look away from her. This is happening. I don't know what this will mean for Brock's plan or the Ranch, but it's over for me. All of it.

"I know everybody is anxious to get on with the night, but, first, we have to pay our respects to the one responsible for bringing us this gift," Vinchi says.

Kong walks beside him and blocks a few of the lights. His shadow looks even bigger in the night. He almost doesn't look human standing in front of the gate. All we can see is the white of his eyes and those tiny bite-sized teeth grinning evil at us.

"Fuck him," Brip yells out. "We ain't here to kiss that nigga's ass. We here to make sure his ex-partner bleeds to death slowly," Brip says, reminding us that Ace and Kong were partners at one point.

"I appreciate all of this, Vinchi," Bobby says, "but your uncle made valid point. I hope you see how your new partner treats his partners when he's done with them."

Vinchi looks uncomfortable for a few seconds. Almost like he's starting to second-guess this whole thing, but he shakes it off with a half-smile and a nod. He turns to Kong and respectfully places his hand on his forearm. Vinchi's hand looks extra small on top of Kong's massive arm.

"Don't mind my uncles," he reassures Kong who is no longer smiling. "This is a bitter-sweet moment for them. But Uncle Brip you're, right," he walks towards us, "we aren't here for all of that."

"So let's get on with it," Brip demands.

"We'll do just that," Vinchi says and snatches the bag off of Ace's head.

Ace looks right at Dalla like he's been looking at her all along and sneers, like he's not fazed that he's about to die.

"There are a few ways we can do this," Vinchi says to us, "but I'll leave it up to you all to decide how this maggot dies."

"Let's cut off that nigga's eyes," I say and look directly at Ace who is still looking at my wife.

I step in front of Dalla so all Ace sees is me.

"I say we cut off his dick," Lera yells and walks up to Ace and spits in his face.

"I agree," Bobby says and stands beside Lera.

Then all of a sudden, Ace bursts into laughter like all of this shit going on is a joke. Like he ain't got a fucking care in the world.

"We can do all those things, but let's ask Mr. Lucky how he prefers to die," Vinchi says and turns to Ace.

"Fuck that," Brip yells. "He don't get a say."

He's about to go off. Taffy is trying her best to calm him down. Vinchi ignores Brip and looks at Ace, waiting for him to speak.

"How do I prefer to die?" he says condescendingly like he's invisible. "I prefer not to die at all," he says in a matter-of-fact tone and then starts to taunt us with laughter. "Trust me, you think you want me dead, but you don't want me dead just yet."

"Why is that?" I blurt out.

Mona looks at me like maybe she still got a chance and Dalla tugs on my arm like she's trying to stop me from doing whatever it is that I'm doing. I don't even know. I'm being curious, I guess. I can't help but to be and what would it hurt? Maybe Ace will tell us everything we want to know before we kill him in hopes that we keep him alive. That way, all of us can get our peace.

"Because I have all the answers to the questions you don't know how to ask." He chuckles. "All the rumors about your mother and grandmother," he says and turns his neck slowly to look up at Vinchi.

"What answers?" Vinchi ask.

"Vinchi, don't let him fuck with your head," Dalla pushes me aside and yells. "Fuck all of this barbaric shit. Let's kill him now!"

"If you want to kill me, fine. But you will never know what really happened to your grandmother," he said.

Everyone is quiet. That means we are all thinking the same thing: *What the fuck really happened. What is he talking about? What does Ace know that we don't?*

"I read every letter between your mother and my father and the last letter...the last letter will shock you. If you want to kill me, then cool, but don't expect me to beg all of you for my life. A life that you didn't give me. All of us got to go sometime and I ain't afraid to die. But you'll be sorry if you kill me before learning the truth."

"And what's the truth?" I ask.

No one objects this time.

"I'm not going to tell you the truth. But, I'll let you know where to find it. Then, you'll know," Ace says through a smile.

"Fuck this bullshit!" Dalla yells.

"I agree," Lera says. "Let's get this shit over with."

"You really want me dead?" Ace winks at Lera and Bobby and Lera both charge toward him, but are stopped by the guards.

Ace laughs. "You still got your husband believing that I raped you?" Ace says to Lera and shakes his head. "I done told some lies in my life, but I ain't never lied on my dick. You wanted to fuck me. You liked it. You don't remember? Ask your nephew, he got the whole thing on tape."

Bobby looks at Lera who instantly looks away and then back at Vinchi who also avoids eye contact with him. He steps away from Lera for a few seconds and then reaches to embrace her, but she backs away like she's ashamed.

"The truth don't affect your women like it does you all, does it? They don't give a fuck. Look, just do this one thing and then y'all can kill me. If you want the truth, open that gate and dig up your mother's grave. The truth is in her casket."

"What the fuck!" Brip yells and charges towards Ace.

Before anyone can stop him, he leaps in the air and flies like superman, tackling Ace and his chair to the ground. Then he starts to punch him in the face like he's trying to break a walk in half. Kong's men pull Brip off and prop Ace and his chair back up. Ace spits out blood and a tooth and smiles.

"What do I have to lose? You gon kill me anyway." Ace gurgles and then spits more blood.

I don't know how this psychopath does it, but he's making sense. One by one, he's reeling us all in. What does he have to lose? He's right. We gon kill him anyway. Vinchi leans over and whispers something to Kong. Kong looks frustrated. He's shaking his head, but Vinchi convinces him. Kong whispers to his main guard and they all scurry off. Then Vinchi turns to face us again. One of Kong's guards is covering Ace's face with the bag again.

"I'm putting this thing on hold. We digging up that grave tonight," Vinchi says and rushes off before any of us has time to object.

The guards escort us back to our truck and we all head back to the casino to wait.

*   *   *

"I can't believe you all are falling for this shit! It's insane," Dalla yells.

We are all sitting at the conference room table at the Casino. Brip is taking shots of Vodka back to back. He can't handle the stress of seeing Mama's skeleton in her casket. Mona seems temporarily relieved that Ace is still breathing a few more seconds than she expected.

"Let's just wait this thing out. Ace ain't going anywhere," Mona says and looks at me.

"He's going to hell," Lera says under her breath but loud enough for us all to hear.

"What was he talking about, Lera?" Bobby reluctantly asks Lera calmly.

Bobby asked the question we all were wondering about.

"I don't know," Lera says defensively.

"I can't believe you would have the nerve to ask her that?" Dalla defends Lera, but really she's fueling her cause to kill Ace quick and not slow. "He's fucking with all of you!" She wipes tears from her eyes. I immediately place my hand on her shoulder to calm her. "How do you know he doesn't have a bomb planted in that casket? He's just that sick! He could be trying to kill us all. This is wrong!" Dalla starts to panic.

I wrap my arms around Dalla, but she pushes me off.

"Baby, that's not possible," I say to her calmly.

"So what happens if Ace is lying?" Taffy asks.

"Then we sticking dynamite deep in that nigga's asshole and lighting a match and that shit is final!" Brip says to us all before taking another shot.

No one disagrees with Brip. A few minutes go by and we are all silent. We all thinking about the same thing, but in a different way. I remember when Ace had my mind and I asked Brock to dig up the grave so we could do another autopsy, but everyone looked at me like I was crazy. Now, it's happening. This shit is surreal.

"Brock said it was a letter. Her last letter," Mona said. "Brock was right. He read all the letters but the last one."

"I guess we gon learn the truth soon enough," Bobby says to us all while looking at Lera.

Lera looks away again. What's that about? Could Ace be telling the truth? Did he rape Lera? Why would she lie?

We all go silent again. This time, the silence is longer and louder. A few minutes in and it feels like we've been in this room for hours, then one of the guards walk in.

"Mr. Badd is waiting for you all at the cemetery," he says.

We all jump up too fast. All of us except Brip. He's trying to milk the last few drops of Vodka out of his glass. Taffy pulls on his shirt collar and, reluctantly, Brip gets up and joins the rest of us. They herd us to the trucks and we head back to the cemetery in silence.

We get out the car and the first thing we see is Mama's custom-made pink casket. Dad had it made for her. I always hated it because he and everyone else knew that Mama hated the color pink. That didn't matter to him though. Even Mama's funeral was about him.

"I can't do this shit man," Brip starts to sob.

Bobby puts his arm around Brip and I grab his shoulder.

"We got you, man," Bobby says. "We all here with you."

"Let's get this shit over with, man," I yell to Vinchi.

This shit is breaking us quicker than what I thought.

"I agree," Vinchi says.

Once again, Vinchi snatches the bag off of Ace's face. His left eye is swollen shut from Brip's punch and his nose is still pouring out blood like a water fountain. It must be broken. But through all that, Ace is sitting comfortably and smiling like this is the moment he's been waiting for. Vinchi motions to one of Kong's men and they point the light directly on the casket. The chrome casket with red dirt patches is now shining brighter than the moon. We all stare at it mesmerized. Even Kong is staring. All of us except Ace.

Vinchi walks up closer to it and leans down like he's about to open it, but he can't.

"Uncle Billy," he calls my name with a cracked voice sounding just like he did when he was ten years old.

"I got you, man," I say.

I try to step forward, but Dalla pulls me back.

"I'll do it," she says.

"No," I say right away, suddenly considering her bomb theory.

"It's ok. I won't let you do this," she says and kisses me softly on the lips.

I watch her walk away and it looks like she is moving in slow motion. Everything looks like it's moving in slow motion. My heart is racing. I turn to face my brothers. Bobby's eyes are glued to the casket and Brip's eyes are closed tight. Dalla leans down and puts her hand on the casket, but turns to look at us first. She takes a deep breath and swings it open. Then, she gasps and falls back, hitting the ground. I can't move. None of us can.

"What the fuck!" Brip yells. His eyes are open now.

"Oh my God! I don't understand," Mona screams and runs towards the casket, almost falling inside to take a closer look. "This isn't possible. It isn't possible," she says before fainting.

Vinchi leans down to aid his mother, but hops back up and looks at the casket a second time like he has to be sure. Bobby is frozen in time and Brip is crying silently. Lera puts her guard down and wraps her arms around Bobby, but he still doesn't move. He's like a statue. Taffy is crying and I'm stuck in time. I no longer know where I am or why I'm here for a minute. I tell myself I'm dreaming. I have to be dreaming.

I walk closer to the casket. I don't even know that Dalla is at my side until I mistakenly knock her back to the ground. I step over her body, lean over, look inside, and squint my eyes to be sure I'm seeing correctly. When I hear Ace's laughter, I know I'm not dreaming anymore.

The casket really is empty. Mama's alive? The day she died, everybody think I found her body, but I just seen her stiff lifeless arm hanging off the side of the bed. I saw her wedding ring too. Seeing that and the smell, I knew she was dead. I didn't bother going in. I couldn't see her that way. She left a note too. She said that she wanted her funeral to be closed casket and her last wishes was for us to remember her the way she was. No one seen her body, except the first doctor that did her autopsy, but he wouldn't know Mama from Beyonce. If she's still alive, then she had help and I got a feeling that Ace knows just who helped her.

I look over at Ace and he has this Grinch-like smile on his face. He looks up at me and winks his good eye.

"I told you, you don't want to kill me." Ace snickers.

Brock is right. We can't kill Ace. At least not yet. And Dalla is going to be pissed at me, but I can't leave with her. Not until I find out what the fuck is going on. I got to help Brock take back control of the Ranch and then we got to find our mama.

This changes everything.

To Be Continued in Badd Endings...

# Badd Endings Coming Soon

## PLEASE LEAVE A REVIEW

If you enjoyed this book, please leave a
review and/or share this story.

# LET'S KEEP IN TOUCH

## FOLLOW ME:

FACEBOOK @THISWRITERSLIFE

INSTAGRAM @AUTHORZEE.W

www.ingramcontent.com/pod-product-compliance
Lightning Source LLC
Chambersburg PA
CBHW070211260626
47160CB00002B/524